Alone in the moonless midnight, high atop a cliff overlooking Qualinost, Gilthanas continued to sing the ancient song that had been a part of the elven coming of age ceremony since Kith-Kanan had formed the elven kingdom more than two thousand years before.

Yet somewhere, out in the darkness, a murderer lurked. Tanis waited alone in the shadows, the only one who could save Gilthanas. Flint was gone, swallowed by the earth as though he had never existed.

At that moment, Gilthanas's song broke off with a cry. "You should not be here!" the elf proclaimed. "The ceremony forbids. . ."

Tanis watched as a hooded figure advanced on his cousin.

"Who are you?" demanded Gilthanas, edging backward. The cliff, with its six-hundred-foot drop, loomed dangerously near his heels.

Tanis, drawing his sword and moving as quickly as he could, slipped from boulder to boulder.

The figure, wordless, drew nearer. Gilthanas looked desperately about, but the stranger blocked the only escape. Then Tanis saw the figure move as if to gather its forces for a lunge. The half-elf dashed from behind a granite block, shouting, "Gilthanas!"

His cousin turned. In that same heartbeat, the robed figure feinted at Gilthanas. With a scream, the youth pitched off the cliff. Another scream broke off abruptly.

The murderer sprang away toward the forest, and Tanis followed.

The DRAGONLANCE® Saga

Chronicles Trilogy
Dragons of Autumn Twilight
Dragons of Winter Night
Dragons of Spring Dawning

Legends Trilogy
Time of the Twins
War of the Twins
Test of the Twins

Tales Trilogy
The Magic of Krynn
Kender, Gully Dwarves, and Gnomes
Love and War

Tales II Trilogy
The Reign of Istar
The Cataclysm (July 1992)
The War of the Lance (Nov. 1992)

Heroes Trilogy
The Legend of Huma
Stormblade
Weasel's Luck

Heroes II Trilogy
Kaz, the Minotaur
The Gates of Thorbardin
Galen Beknighted

Preludes Trilogy
Darkness and Light
Kendermore
Brothers Majere

Preludes II Trilogy
Riverwind, the Plainsman
Flint, the King
Tanis, the Shadow Years

Meetings Sextet
Kindred Spirits
Wanderlust
Dark Heart
The Oath and the Measure
Steel and Stone
The Companions (January 1993)

Elven Nations Trilogy
Firstborn
The Kinslayer Wars
The Qualinesti

The Art of the DRAGONLANCE Saga
The Atlas of the DRAGONLANCE World

DragonLance Saga®

MEETINGS SEXTET

VOLUME ONE

Kindred Spirits

**Mark Anthony and
Ellen Porath**

Cover Art
CLYDE CALDWELL

Interior Illustrations
VALERIE VALUSEK

DRAGONLANCE® Saga Meetings
Volume One

Kindred Spirits

Random House and its affiliate companies have worldwide distribution rights in the book trade for English language products of TSR, Inc.

Distributed to the book and hobby trade in the United Kingdom by TSR Ltd.

Distributed to the toy and hobby trade by regional distributors.

All DRAGONLANCE characters and the distinctive likenesses thereof are trademarks of TSR, Inc.

DRAGONLANCE is a registered trademark owned by TSR, Inc. The TSR logo is a trademark owned by TSR, Inc.

First Printing:April 1991
Printed in the United States of America.
Library of Congress Catalog Card Number: 90-71494

9 8

ISBN: 1-56076-069-9
All characters in this book are fictitious. Any resemblance to actual persons, living or dead, is purely coincidental.

TSR, Inc.
201 Sheridan Springs Road
Lake Geneva, WI 53147
U.S.A.

TSR Ltd.
120 Church End, Cherry Hinton
Cambridge CB1 3LB
United Kingdom

Thanks to Sharon S., for a mysterious conversation; Sharon B., for asking how I was doing; Carl and Carla, for being such wonderful primates; and my family, for all of their love, and for believing I could do it.

This is for Beth, and all the stories she read me.
—MRLA

_____

For Eric and Jo,
who taught me the meaning of "carpe diem."
—EP

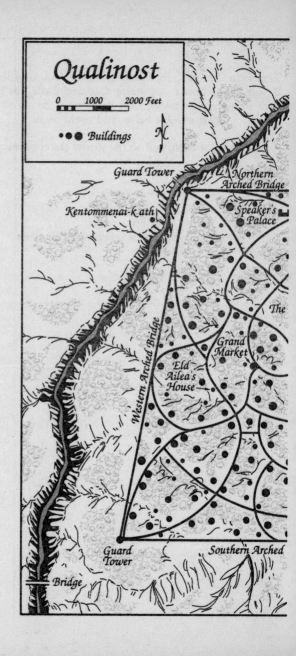

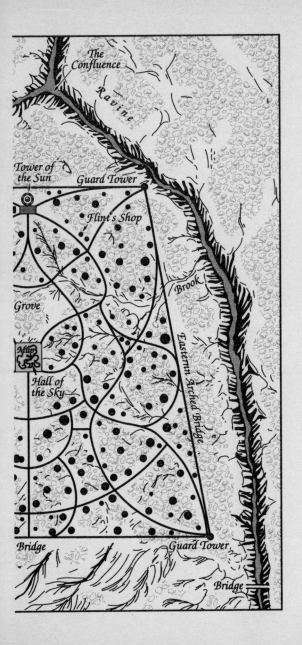

PROLOGUE

A.C. (After the Cataclysm) 258

The infant's cry was not the cry of an elven child.
Eld Ailea, ancient even in the eyes of the long-lived elves,
cast a sympathetic eye on the infant as she wrapped him in
swaddling clothes of silvery linen. The firelight reflected off
the rose quartz walls of the midwife's Qualinost home, bath-
ing the angry newborn in a peach-colored glow as he
wailed, small chest shuddering as he drew in gulps of air. A
breeze entered from a window overlooking a Qualinost
lane, freshening air redolent with sweat, blood, and sorrow.

"Such passion," Eld Ailea whispered. "Even with your
first breaths, you reveal your parentage." As if to give lie to
her murmuring, the baby, arms swaddled against his chest,

ceased his cries, yawned, and fell asleep. His ruddy face eased into repose.

The midwife gathered the tiny bundle to her and stepped to a rocking chair placed before the fire. The chair, nearly as old as Eld Ailea herself, contrasted with the living rock walls much as a well-worn pair of slippers offset a new-sewn robe. The chair, its wood burnished with centuries of use, creaked comfortably as Eld Ailea settled into it, lay the infant on her green skirt, and traced a finger around one baby ear.

"Not so pointy as a full elf's ear, yet clearly no round human ear, either," Eld Ailea told the infant, who opened one eye, squinted in the firelight, and shut it again. Her words were like music, the song of a wooden flute that had been polished a thousand thousand times. She bent toward the infant and, like a ritual, breathed in the smell of a newly bathed infant; she never tired of this moment.

The human blood in his veins warmed his sluggish elven heart with its fire, she thought. "Oh, yes, small one," she whispered fiercely, eyes glowing like hazel agates. "You will need that passion. The life of a half-elf is not easy in these times, in Qualinost."

Beyond her pleasure that the boy waxed robust, the moment held little joy for the elderly midwife. Slowing her rocking, she glanced at the bed nested in an alcove, out of the firelight. She'd extinguished the lamp that had burned for seemingly countless hours at the foot of that pallet; upon the bed lay a figure shrouded in dimness, the face peaceful after hours of exhausting fight.

Eld Ailea was tiny for an elf and displayed the round hazel eyes so rare in Qualinesti, the eyes that showed that she herself carried human blood from generations back. Nonetheless, she also displayed the pointed ears, slender build, and long fingers of her own elven mother.

She'd lived so long among the Qualinesti elves that they could not remember a time when Eld Ailea had not dwelt among them, delivering their few, precious children. She was a familiar sight, striding among the treelike, rose-hued dwellings of the city of Qualinost with her midwife's satchel swinging at her side; most of the city's inhabitants—

certainly every elven woman who'd had a difficult pregnancy—overlooked the old nurse's mixed elven-human blood. She was experienced in herbal lore that had soothed the way of many a laboring mother, and, while no mage, she knew enough of magic to ease all but the deepest pains.

Nevertheless, she had lacked the skill to save Elansa.

Unconsciously, Eld Ailea's arms tightened around the orphaned baby until he awakened and squawked. She quickened the pace of the rocker and stroked his tiny forehead, his cheeks, the bridge of his nose until his eyelids drooped and he slept again.

Suddenly, faint music reached her ears—the sound of bells tied to the harness of a horse, or several horses, by the sound of it. Soon, she heard the alto tones of her servant in the anteroom below, followed by footsteps on the stone stairs that wound to the second level of her towerlike home. She nestled the infant against her shoulder as the wooden door, detailed with etchings of aspen leaves, swung open.

The Speaker of the Sun, Lord of Qualinesti, stood in the doorway, his face lined with concern. Firelight glittered off one side of his golden-threaded robe; the other side was bathed in the light of the silver moon, Solinari, which streamed through a window to one side of the door. Red tinged the beams where they struck the floor, like a few drops of blood; Lunitari, Krynn's crimson moon, was on the rise as well.

Eld Ailea's gaze shifted to the figure on the bed. The Speaker's eyes followed. "She sleeps?" he asked softly. Another breeze wafted through the open window, and the sound of laughter drifted up from the street below. Eld Ailea shook her head once and swung her wrinkled face toward the sleeping baby, watching out of the corner of her eye as the Speaker walked slowly to the woman's body. His hand trembled as he reached out to touch Elansa, the widow of his dead brother, but then his arm halted and the hand fell limply to his side.

He swallowed. "You, Ailea, with all your skill . . . If you could not save her, no one could."

The midwife shook her head gently. "She was too weak,

3

Solostaran. She stayed until the babe was born, and she nursed him once, but then she let herself go."

The Speaker of the Sun stared at her. He seemed unaware that she had used his true name and not the title he had taken when he ascended the rostrum in the Tower of the Sun to rule the elves of Qualinesti more than a century ago. A flicker of pain shuddered across his hawklike face. "She let herself go . . . ," he repeated softly. To elves, life was sacred, and the willful ending of it, blasphemy.

"The child . . .?" he asked.

The midwife's lips parted in an odd smile, neither joyful nor sorrowful; briefly, she remembered the night Solostaran himself was born, so long ago. How different the surroundings then, how opulent the chambers, blazing bright with torchlight. How reverent the retainers who crouched in the shadows beyond the birthing suite. It was all a far cry from the quarters of a mixed-blood midwife, even the best midwife in Qualinesti. Elansa could have borne her baby at the court, but she had chosen to come to Eld Ailea's rooms instead.

Eld Ailea held the baby so the Speaker could see him. Solostaran knelt and examined the child for barely a moment and then dipped his head. "So," he said coolly. "It is as we feared."

No, Eld Ailea almost said, it is as *you* feared. But she held her tongue. Kethrenan, the Speaker's younger brother, had been slain when ambushed by a band of rogue humans upon the road to the fortress of Pax Tharkas, to the south of Qualinesti. Although the elven and human races had once—thousands of years ago—been close, such human raiding bands had become all too common since the destruction of the Cataclysm. The band had raped Kethrenan's wife, Elansa, and left her for dead, lying in the mud of the road. For the last months, she had lived much as one who was dead, her eyes empty. She had eaten only enough to sustain the life growing within her; *quith-pa*, nutritious elven bread, and clear wine formed the basis of her diet. The infant could have been Kethrenan's or the human rapist's, and Elansa had waited to confirm the answer she had already suspected.

"The child is half-man," Solostaran said, still kneeling, his hand on the arm of the rocker.

"He is half-elf as well."

Solostaran said nothing for a time, but then Eld Ailea saw the proud mask crumble, and the Speaker shook his head. The baby still slept. Gently the Speaker touched one of the tiny hands; reflexively, like a sensitive blossom, the hand opened and closed, clasping the Speaker's finger. Eld Ailea heard Solostaran catch his breath, saw kindness grow in his eyes. "What sort of life can there be for one who is half of two things and all of nothing?" the Speaker asked. But Eld Ailea had no answer for him, and the silence that followed stretched long. The gaze of the midwife stayed steady.

For a moment, an expression of anguish showed in the Speaker's aspen-leaf-green eyes. Then the proud visage returned. "He is the son of my brother's wife, and he will come with me. He will be raised in the manner of a true Qualinesti elf." Eld Ailea sighed, touching the newborn's cheeks and kissing his forehead, and handed the bundle wordlessly to the Speaker. "Does the little one have a name yet?" Solostaran asked, seeming to avoid looking at the still form in the corner bed. "Did Elansa name him?"

"Yes," the midwife whispered after a pause. She faltered over the lie. "She named him 'Tanthalas.' " Eld Ailea smoothed the wool of her skirt, not daring to meet the Speaker's eyes lest he guess the truth. But her gift to the child would be something lasting—a name. "Ever strong," the name meant in the human dialect Eld Ailea had learned as a child.

Solostaran merely nodded. He stepped to the doorway, holding the baby with the ease of an experienced father; his firstborn son, Porthios, was only fifty years old, only a youth. Eld Ailea pushed her suddenly weary body out of the chair and followed him. They paused in the night air at the window; it carried the freshness of spring, catching his golden hair and blowing it back from his brow. A gold circlet rested there, glimmering silver and scarlet in the light from the moons above.

"I fear I do him no favor, taking him to the court," the Speaker said. "I doubt he will find much peace there in his life. But he is my kin, and so I must."

Solostaran pulled the linen up around the infant's face, protecting him from the damp, and midwife and Speaker tarried before the window. Just then, a streak of silver flashed across the sky. A falling star, the light of the heavens come to Krynn, sped northward as it flung its fiery tail out behind. The Speaker appeared mindless of the omen, but Eld Ailea pressed hopeful fingers against the amulet that the dying Elansa had forced into her hand; to the midwife's people, a shooting star portended good fellowship. She hoped the star soared for the child sleeping against the Speaker's shoulder; a half-elf would need good friends.

"I will send others to see to Elansa," Solostaran said, his voice brittle for a moment. Then he left, taking the baby with him. Eld Ailea stayed at the window until the jingling of bells and the muffled beat of hooves on the tiled streets receded into the distance.

* * * * *

Far to the north, a small town slept in the darkness. It was a town of wooden houses, most tucked high among the embracing branches of ancient, towering trees, joined by footbridges high above the ground. In one of the few houses that stood upon the ground—and the only one with a dim light still glowing between the open shutters of its windows—a figure sat alone. He was short, a human child's height, but thick-limbed and broad-shouldered, and coarse whiskers curled down his chest. He sat at a table, turning a piece of wood over and over in his hands. He worked at it with a small knife, removing flakes of wood with precision despite his stubby fingers. Soon a smooth and delicate shape emerged from the soft wood: the image of a single aspen leaf. Only once had he seen an aspen, and that had been far away to the south, near the homeland he had left not so very long ago to seek his fortune in the wide world. The tree had stood, pale and slender, at the summit of a high pass, leading—or so his father had told him—toward the land of the elves beyond. Perhaps the Qualinesti elves had planted it there as a reminder of their forest home should they have occasion to travel that way. He had thought the tree one of the loveliest sights he had seen, the leaves as green and shiny as emeralds on one side, all frosted with silver on the other. Maybe one day he might have the fortune to see an aspen tree again. But for now, the wooden leaf would have to do.

Finally, the dwarf grew weary and, standing, blew out the candle on the table. As he passed the window on his way to his bed, a flash to the south caught his eye. It burned for a long second as it streaked across the darkened sky, and then it was gone.

"Reorx! I've never seen such a shooting star!" he muttered, shivering though the spring night was not chilly at all. And then, unsure why he stood gaping out the window like some whelp who'd never seen such a sight, he shook his head, closed the shutters, and trudged off to dream of aspen trees.

Chapter 1

The Summons

A.C. 288, Early Spring

"*Flint Fireforge of Solace, dwarf and mastersmith,*
by summons of the Speaker of the Sun!" a voice rang.

Flint peered warily through the gilded doors that swung
open before him, and then his steel-blue eyes went wide
with wonder as his gaze traveled up, up, and up—following
walls of white marble, unaided by column or buttress or
brace—nearly six hundred feet to the domed ceiling. To
Flint's eyes, the dome seemed almost as distant as the sky itself, and indeed, the illusion was completed by a tiled mosaic that glittered on the dome's surface, portraying night on
one side and day on the other. The two realms were divided
by a translucent rainbow. The vastness of the Tower made

him giddy just to look at it. Flint's jaw dropped and his eyes watered as he squinted to examine the tiled pattern far above, until a polite cough on the part of the servant who'd announced him brought him back to his senses. "Fireforge, don't act like a tourist," the dwarf chided himself softly. "Anybody'd think you've never been out of Hillhome." His tiny native village lay far to the south of the elven lands. He stood as tall as he could, straightened his blue-green tunic and stepped farther into the chamber. A dozen courtiers, dressed in silver-belted, knee-length tunics in tones of brown, green, and russet, turned to follow his progress as his iron-heeled boots, so practical for battle, thundered on the marble floors. The padded shoes of his escort, in contrast, whispered on the marble. Flint tried to tiptoe, a difficult prospect in boots. He caught a slight smile, quickly stifled, on the face of his companion, whose brown, almond-shaped eyes nonetheless showed kindness. A few courtiers smiled, but most of the elven faces remained as if carved out of the ice of the polar cap to the south.

The western—Qualinesti—elves were descendants of the Silvanesti elves, who lived many weeks travel to the east. Nearly twenty-five hundred years before, the western elves had split with their eastern kin and, led by the hero Kith-Kanan, traveled to a forested refuge along the borders of the dwarven kingdom of Thorbardin. The Qualinesti elves had joined with the Thorbardin dwarves to build the Tower of the Sun. They also had cooperated to build Pax Tharkas, a massive fortress between the two kingdoms, and had manned the fort together for more than fifteen hundred years, until the elves withdrew to Qualinost at the time of the Cataclysm, three centuries before, in the time of Flint's grandfather.

Since then, no nonelves had entered the Qualinesti capital.

A hiss dragged Flint's thoughts back to the present. "The surroundings are a bit grand for a *dwarf*." The words that startled Flint came from a tall elf who stood near a pillar to the dwarf's left. The elf's silver-gray robe complemented the white hair that framed an icy face; elderly lips puckered in disdain.

Flint stopped, considered, and spoke to the elf, whose face showed the arrogance sometimes seen in those who believed a long life had given them reason to speak their minds regardless of the consequences. "Have we met, sir?" Flint queried, his voice low. "If not, it seems to me that you've formed an opinion with little information." His hand strayed to the battle-axe at his belt.

Blue eyes met brown for a moment, grappled, then elf and dwarf grew aware of the courtiers who gaped around them. The elf turned on one leather heel and noiselessly left the Tower.

"Who was that?" Flint asked his escort in a too-loud whisper.

The servant's voice was barely audible. "Lord Xenoth, adviser to the Speaker of the Sun since longer than you or I have lived. Some say he was here when Kith-Kanan and his dwarven allies fashioned the Tower," came the answer. The escort was remarkably agile at speaking out of the corner of his mouth, Flint decided, yet the elf seemed to be struggling to mask some emotion—his lips twitched almost uncontrollably.

Flint was the first dwarf to lay eyes upon the central chamber since the Tower had been constructed long ago, in an age more than two thousand years past. Not bad, he thought; his mother would be proud.

Only short weeks ago, he'd been back in Solace, sipping ale in the Inn of the Last Home. He turned to his escort to ask if Qualinesti elves drank ale, but his companion was gazing elsewhere.

The dwarf knew he cut an odd figure amid the grace of the Tower and the elves. Just over half their height, he boasted a barrel-shaped chest and forge-hardened arms twice the thickness of those of the strongest among his hosts. Besides his blue-green tunic, he wore rust-colored breeches belted with a thick strap of leather, and he had tossed a gray, travel-stained cloak over it all. He had tucked the end of his thick beard in his belt and had bound his black hair with a leather thong at the back of his neck in an effort to make himself presentable. Unfortunately, Flint hadn't had much of an inkling of how one was supposed to dress when presented to the ruler of an elven kingdom, and though he had tried his best, he had the sinking feeling that it hadn't been nearly enough. But the dwarf's wardrobe was a bit short of tunics spun of golden thread. His travel gear, he thought with a sigh, would have to do.

They were queer folk, these elves, he thought as he walked through their midst, their chatter continuing before and behind him but stilling as he passed. All height and no substance they were, thin and shimmering as aspen saplings, but beautiful, too, cloaked in golden light—or so each of them seemed to the dwarf's eyes. Perhaps that was only a trick of the light. Long ago, when the Tower had been constructed, the dwarven craftsmen had arranged a thousand mirrors so that the Tower might always know the light of the sun, no matter what its position in the daytime sky.

The elves, their voices stilled, watched the bearded dwarf with expressions of polite curiosity, and finally, after what seemed an age, Flint found himself standing before the low rostrum in the center of the chamber.

"Welcome, Master Fireforge," said the elf who stood there. His clear voice held a tone of warmth. The Speaker of the Sun of Qualinesti was tall, even among his people, and his stance on the rostrum gave him still more of an edge. Flint felt physically overwhelmed. The Speaker, a descendant of the hero Kith-Kanan himself, overawed him.

The Speaker smiled, and some of the nervousness fled Flint's stomach. Solostaran's smile was genuine, and it touched his wise eyes—eyes as green as the deepest forest. Flint sighed, feeling more at ease. The chilled glances of the elven courtiers seemed less important. "I trust your journey was uneventful," the Speaker said.

"Uneventful! Reorx!" the dwarf expostulated.

He'd been summoned peremptorily from his favorite chair at the Inn of the Last Home by a pair of elven guards and asked to accompany them to the mysterious elven capital, the city that so few nonelves had seen over the last centuries. They had traveled up staircases hidden behind waterfalls, along precipices, and in damp tunnels.

To say the city was well protected was putting it mildly. The peaks to the south of Qualinost loomed so daunting in their height and ruggedness as to give the most determined foe pause. Two converging streams in deep, five-hundred-foot-wide ravines sheltered Qualinost to the west, north, and east. Two narrow bridges—easily cut down in case enemies managed to find their way through the woodlands and forests to the city proper—formed the only passages across the ravines.

The Speaker was waiting for an answer, the dwarf realized. "Oh. I—uh—fine, thank you. Sir. Sire," he stammered, trying to recall what Solostaran had asked him. His face blazed even as those of the courtiers gathered around him tightened. His escort bowed and padded away. Flint felt suddenly bereft.

"Have you found our beloved city to your liking?" the Speaker asked politely.

Flint, more comfortable at his forge than in what his mother would have called "polite company," found himself once again at a loss for a reply. How to describe his first view of what might well be the most beautiful city on Krynn? The Qualinesti elves celebrated their forest home with buildings that called to mind the aspens, the oaks, of the surrounding forest. Eschewing the ninety-degree angle as a vestige of the too-analytical human mind, the elves created dwellings as varied as nature. Conical, tree-shaped homes and small shops dotted the blue-tiled streets. But the dwellings themselves were built, not of wood, but of rose quartz. In the light of midafternoon, the city had glittered, light refracting from the faceted quartz. Pear, peach, and apple trees bloomed in profusion. Even in the Tower of the Sun, the thick scent of blossoms penetrated.

"The city is beautiful, Sire," Flint finally said.

His heart sank as several courtiers gasped. What had he done wrong? The Speaker descended from the rostrum and bent toward the dwarf; Flint stood firm but quailed within.

"Call me Speaker," Solostaran said softly, his voice too quiet to catch the ears of the nearby elves. Flint nodded, and

Solostaran straightened again. But one pair of sharp ears had caught the Speaker's words. A giggle, quickly stifled, made the dwarf look behind the Speaker and raised a tremor of annoyance on the Speaker's face. Three young elves—no, one, a resentful-looking lad with auburn-brown hair, was a half-elf, Flint realized— clustered at the back of the rostrum. The Speaker gestured toward the two full elves. "My children. Gilthanas. And Lauralanthalasa, who needs a lesson in court decorum." The girl giggled again.

The boy was clearly a young version of his elegant, slender father. And the girl . . . ! Flint had never seen the likes of the elf girl. To say she was lovely would be like calling the sun a candle, Flint reckoned, although he was no poet. She was willow-thin, with eyes the color of new leaves and hair as gold as the morning sunlight. The Speaker narrowed his eyes at her, and the radiant girl pouted. The only creature in the room shorter than Flint, she had the ways of a human child of five or six years of age, but he would bet she was at least ten.

"And this?" Flint asked, nodding to the half-elf, who reddened and looked away. The dwarf felt suddenly as though he'd embarrassed the lad terribly by calling attention to him. He was older than the other two, and Flint didn't think he was related to them. There was a certain huskiness to his frame where the others were thin as switches, a bit less of a slant to his eyes, and less smoothness to his features. All of it put Flint in more of a mind of some of the human folk back in the village of Solace.

The Speaker spoke smoothly. "This is my ward, Tanthalas, or Tanis."

Once again, Flint found himself without words. The boy was obviously uneasy with the attention. At that moment, the adviser that Flint's escort had identified as Lord Xenoth emerged from an anteroom behind the rostrum and slipped in front of the young half-elf. Tanis edged aside. Resentment radiated from the boy like heat from a campfire, but at whom the emotion was aimed, Flint couldn't tell.

The Speaker gestured toward another elf, standing off to the right under one of the carved marble balconies. The elf lord had dark blond hair and square, regular features and might, Flint thought, be considered handsome save for the set of his eyes; they were close together and deep beneath his brow. His face probably glowered even when he was happy, the dwarf conjectured. The elf lord stood with three other equally proud elves, two men and a woman.

"My elder son, Porthios," Solostaran said proudly. The elf lord inclined his head slightly. Oh ho! Flint thought, that's a prideful one; and probably not too happy having anyone other than a full elf—one with bloodlines pure all the way back to the Kinslayer Wars—in his precious Tower, either.

The Speaker, once again, seemed to be waiting for something. Flint decided that honesty was the best idea.

"I'm afraid I know little enough of noble houses, and of elves even less, though I hope that last will be changing soon," he said, allowing his shoulders to relax somewhat.

"Why did you accept my summons?" Solostaran asked. His green eyes were so deep that Flint felt momentarily as though no one else were in the rotunda with him. Briefly, the dwarf spied the authority that must have been every Speaker's since Kith-Kanan. I would not want to cross him, he thought.

"I've had time to ponder that, on these last few weeks' journey," Flint said. "I must say my chief reason is curiosity." Lord Xenoth curled a puckered lip and turned aside again, silver robe swishing against the rostrum. "Curiosity killed the kender," the elderly adviser said in a stage whisper to the boy and girl the Speaker had called Gilthanas and Lauralanthalasa. Gilthanas snickered. The girl looked askance at the old elf, glanced pointedly away, and sidestepped toward the half-elf, Tanis. Tanis stood unmoving, seemingly unaware of the nearness of the exquisite young girl.

Solostaran gave Xenoth a look that caused the old elf to blanch, drawing a tight smile from the half-elf. When the Speaker turned back to Flint, however, his eyes were kind. "Curiosity," he prompted.

"Like most, I had not seen Qualinesti," Flint explained. "It's common knowledge that the forests of Qualinesti are nearly impossible for common folk to penetrate. To have escorts offered to me—by the Speaker of the Sun, no less—is a rare honor indeed." Not a bad speech, the dwarf thought, and the Speaker's slow nod gave him the nerve to push on. "The craftsmanship of the Qualinesti elves is known throughout Ansalon. Your crafts are prized in Haven, Thorbardin, Solace, and other cities of the region. Truth, I hoped to pick up a few pointers for my own metalwork."

And besides, the dwarf added to himself, the Speaker's envoys had bought so many rounds of ale for Flint's friends at the Inn of the Last Home that the dwarf's head had swum. He had awakened the next morning, his traveling gear packed and slung across the back of a mule. And he had been slung, head and feet drooping, right along with the baggage.

"Do you mean what you've said, Master Fireforge?" the Speaker asked him evenly, and Flint blinked.

"I—I'm not sure what you mean," he managed to stutter.

"You said you knew little of elves, and that you wished to change that. Is that truly so?"

Flint looked around himself, at the airy Tower, at the golden-haired elves, and at the regal figure of the Speaker, resplendent in his robes of green stitched with gold. The odor of spring blossoms was growing a bit thick, but even that carried a note of the unique. Strange as it all was, especially for a hill dwarf more accustomed to battlefields and taverns than gilded towers, Flint found he could only nod "yes."

"I must confess that, of late, our knowledge of dwarvenkind has become poor as well," the Speaker said. "Our people were friends once. Together they built the great fortress of Pax Tharkas—and this city. I do not propose such a dramatic undertaking for ourselves, Master Fireforge. I would be content if, together, you and I could simply build a friendship."

Some of the elven courtiers murmured their approval. Several, including Lord Xenoth and the conclave surrounding Porthios, remained silent. Flint found he could only grin sheepishly as he stuck his hands in his pockets. "Reorx!" he swore suddenly, and then his eyes went wide. "Er, begging your pardon, uh . . . Speaker."

Solostaran no longer made any attempt to temper his smile. "I imagine you are wondering why I summoned you, my dwarven friend," he said. He raised a gold-ringed hand, and a silver and moss-agate bracelet slid from his wrist to his forearm; Flint gasped, recognizing his own metalwork. Then a servant stepped forward with a silver tray decorated with the likeness of a silver dragon. Atop the tray were two goblets made of silver hammered thin and polished to a brilliance. Three aspen leaves "grew" out of the stem of the goblet, cradling the bowl that held the wine.

"That's. . ." Flint blurted, and stopped. The servant waited until the Speaker and the dwarf each had selected a glass from the tray, then Solostaran lifted one goblet.

"I drink to the artisan who fashioned this bracelet and these goblets, and I hope he will do us the honor of staying at court here awhile to fashion some items especially for us." He took one sip, watching Flint from almond-shaped green eyes.

"But that's. . ." Flint started again.

"You," the Speaker finished. "I have commissions for you if you accept our hospitality. But we can speak more of that tomorrow. For now, please drink."

Mind reeling with the idea that the lord of all the elves of Qualinesti, a people noted for their own craftsmanship in silver and gold, would laud the efforts of a dwarf, Flint bolted the entire contents of the goblet he'd fashioned a year earlier. On the bottom of the drinking container, he knew, was his mark, the word "Solace," and the year. He wondered at . . .

He lost the thought as the taste of the elven wine slammed into his brain; his eyes misted and his throat went into paroxysms. "Reorx's hammer!" Flint squawked.

He'd heard of elvenblossom wine. It was known for its stultifying bouquet of fruit blossoms and the battle-axe power of its alcohol content. Only those of elven blood could stomach the sweet stuff, he'd heard, and it was the alcoholic equivalent of being kicked in the head by a centaur. The odor of apple and peach blossoms seemed to permeate his body, inside and out; Flint felt as though he'd been embalmed alive in perfume. Two or three Speakers wavered in front of him; the cadre of three elves around Porthios turned into a convention of fifteen or sixteen. Lauralanthalasa's giggle rose above the chorus of Abanasinian nightingales that soared suddenly in his brain. Flint gasped and tried to sit on the Speaker's rostrum—protocol be damned—but the rostrum seemed to have grown wheels; he couldn't quite catch up with it.

Suddenly another elf was at his side. Flint found himself looking through tears into eyes so pale that they were nearly clear. The new face was framed by equally colorless hair and the hood of a dark crimson robe. "Breathe in through your nose, out through your mouth," the figure said hoarsely.

"Ark," Flint croaked. "Uff!"

"In through your nose . . ." the elf repeated, and demonstrated. The dwarf, deciding he would die anyway, attempted what the elf commanded. "Wufff!" he wheezed.

". . . Out through your mouth."

"Hoooofff!" the dwarf responded. The elf scattered some herbs and uttered words that were either an old elven tongue or magic—or both. Flint immediately felt better. He lay sprawled on the rostrum steps, the empty goblet in his hand. The hall had been emptied of all but the Speaker, Lauralanthalasa, the young half-elf, and the magic-user who'd saved the dwarf.

"With all respect, Speaker, I would posit that our guest will not desire a refill," the elf rasped, helping Flint to his feet. "Elvenblossom wine *is* an acquired taste." The dwarf swayed, and the half-elf leaped forward to support him. Flint nodded his thanks.

"Perhaps Master Fireforge would prefer to conclude this interview at another time, Speaker," the robed one said smoothly.

Solostaran raised his brows and looked at the dwarf. "Perhaps you are right, Miral," the Speaker replied.

"Ark," Flint hacked. "I'm fine." He coughed and felt his face grow pale. The magic-user snapped his fingers, and thinly sliced *quith-pa* appeared in his outstretched hand. Flint chewed a slice of the bread while the Speaker, more casual now that court was over, waved his daughter forward.

The elf girl, pointed ear tips barely showing through her spun-gold hair, drew a slender chain from her neck. At one end dangled a single, perfect aspen leaf, glimmering green and silver in the golden light. Although it looked natural, as if it had just been plucked from a living tree, this leaf was fashioned of silver and emerald, so skillfully wrought it could not be discerned from a real leaf save for the sparkles of light it sent dancing across the little girl's rapt face.

The dwarf gasped in surprise; the movement brought up a peachy belch, prompting another chuckle from Lauralanthalasa. "I made that leaf six months ago," Flint exclaimed, swallowing the last morsel of *quith-pa*. "Sold it to an elf passing through Solace."

"My envoy," the Speaker said. Flint started to speak, but the Speaker held up one hand. "The leaf is perfect in every way. No tree is closer to the heart of an elf than the aspen. I determined to find the artist who could translate such feeling into his work. And I discovered that this artisan is no elf, but a dwarf."

The Speaker turned away for a heartbeat, then paused. "You must be weary from your long journey," he said. "Miral will show you to your chambers."

Solostaran watched as the dwarf and the magic-user walked from the chamber. It had been a long time since a sight such as that had been seen in Qualinost. Too long. Times had been dark of late. It still seemed only a moment—instead of thirty years—since his brother Kethrenan had been slain, and such raids had not yet ended.

"Friendship . . . ," Solostaran echoed his earlier words. The world could do with a bit more friendship.

* * * * *

The streets of the elven city spread out beneath Flint's feet. Before being shown to his chambers, Flint had asked Miral to take him someplace where he might see more of the city. The elf had led him along the tiled avenues, past buildings fashioned of marble and rose quartz, the crystals splintering the light only to spin it again in dazzling new colors.

Aspen, oak, and spruce surrounded the buildings so that the houses of Qualinost seemed living things themselves, their roots sunk deep into the earth. Fountains bubbled in courtyards where elven folk, the women in dresses of cobweb silver, the men in jerkins of moss green, spoke softly or listened to the music of dulcimer and flute. The air was warm and clear, its touch as gentle as midsummer, although Flint knew that winter had barely loosened its grip on the land.

As he watched, the sun drew low in the west, the crimson sunset combining with the rosy hues of the living stone to bathe the town in pink light. The azure and white tiles of the streets deepened to purple. The scent of baking *quith-pa* and roasting venison filled the air, and few elves were too busy to come to the portals of their homes and businesses to enjoy the closing of the day.

The odor of blossoms still discomfited the dwarf, but he resolved to ignore it.

Miral led him to a lane that wound in arcs up a rise in the center of the city. The lane ended in a great square, the Hall of the Sky, walled only by the pale trunks of aspens and roofed only by the blue dome of the heavens. "This is a hall?" Flint asked after the magic-user identified its name. "There's no roof."

Miral grinned. "The sky is its ceiling, we say, although some believe that at one time there was a hall here, guarding something beyond value. Myth has it that Kith-Kanan caused the structure to rise into the sky to protect that which was within." He looked wistful and drew in a great breath of pear-blossom-scented air. "It's said that whoever finds the structure will enjoy great success."

"That's nothing to sneeze at," Flint agreed.

Miral darted a look at him and, after a pause, laughed shortly. The two looked over Qualinost, details beginning to vanish in the deepening twilight. Pinpoints of lamplight appeared in the uncommon glass windows of elven dwellings.

From the Hall of the Sky, in the center of Qualinost, Flint could gaze upon much of the ancient city. Four towers rose above the treetops at each point of the compass, and between each stretched a single delicate span of metal, a bridge connecting each of the towers in a single archway high above the ground. The four arches seemed like gossamer, shimmering even in the absence of the sun, but Flint knew that each was strong enough to bear the weight of an army, and an ache touched his heart as he marveled at the skill of the ancient dwarves who had built them. He wondered if Krynn would ever know such greatness again. Directly north, on a hill higher than the knoll he stood on now, rose the Tower of the Sun, so tall Flint could not help but imagine that if one stood upon it, he had only to reach up to brush the surface of the sky. So high was the Tower that its gold surface continued to reflect the westering sun even after that orb had left lower buildings wreathed in shadow.

"Do you see the two rivers?" Miral asked him, gesturing to the deep ravines to the east and west of the city. Flint grunted. Did he *see* them? Reorx above, he had had to *cross* one of them on a swaying bridge that seemed hardly strong enough to hold a rock dove, let alone a stocky dwarf. The thought of that deep, rocky ravine yawning beneath him still made his skin shiver.

"The one to the east is called *Ithal-enatha*, the River of Tears," Miral continued in a soft voice. "And the other is *Ithal-inen*, the River of Hope. They join at the confluence beyond the Tower to flow northward, to the White-Rage River and then to the sea beyond."

"Peculiar names," Flint said with a grunt.

Miral nodded. "They are very old. They were given to the rivers in the days after Kith-Kanan and his people journeyed to the forests of Qualinesti. The names represent the tears wept during the Kinslayer Wars, and the hope for the future when the wars finally ended."

The dwarf's companion fell silent, and Flint was content to stay in this peaceful place for a while, gazing out over the city. Finally, however, it was time to go.

Miral escorted Flint to the Speaker's palace, just west of the Tower of the Sun, and Flint found himself shown to his temporary chambers, a suite of high-ceilinged, marble-floored rooms three times the size of his own house back in Solace. He was free to rest and refresh himself as he wished, the mage informed him, showing him the door that opened onto a small room with a wash basin filled with cinnamon-scented water. Then he was left alone, with promises of food and ale—but no elvenblossom wine—to come soon.

"A dwarf in Qualinost!" Flint said with a soft snort to himself one last time. Reflecting that elven taste in scents and wine scarcely matched his own, he shed his tunic and leggings and dipped into the spicy bath to wash away the grime and dust of the road.

When an elven servant arrived not long after, he found the dwarf ensconced in a russet robe and sprawled on the sheets of the bed, snoring raucously. Quietly, the servant set down the tray of red ale, sliced venison and diced potatoes, then blew out the few candles that lit the room, leaving the dwarf to sleep in the darkness, and dream.

Chapter 2

Beware of the Dark

When the adult dreamed, he dreamed as a child.

He dreamed he was a toddler stood poised in the opening of a tunnel. Around the opening, quartz and marble and tile, once burnished, were now dirty with age and disuse. A small tree—no aspen, no oak, nothing the youngster had seen in his short life—grew out of the stone at the side of the cave mouth. The child's nostrils twitched with the smell of damp rock and—blue eyes widened—the scent of cinnamon! Cinnamon and rock sugar on *quith-pa*—the child's favorite afternoon treat. And he was hungry, tired of this day's outing.

The mother's voice called from a nearby thicket in the Grove, the sacred forested area near the center of Qualinost. The child stood, irresolute, at the tunnel's open-

22

ing, clutching a stuffed animal, a kodragon, in one fat hand. The cave had not been there the day before, the child thought, but it was there now. Anything is possible in a child's world, and this child had never known fear.

A Presence beckoned from within. Perhaps the Presence would play with the toddler; his own big brothers were far too busy with big brother things. The mother called again, a note of fear creeping into her voice.

The toddler debated. Was it The Game, where baby hid and mother found him? What better place to hide than a pretty tunnel? Its quartz and marble and tile now shone as though some magical Presence had polished them between one moment and the next.

The mother demanded that the little boy come out of hiding. At once, young elf. Or else, she warned.

That decided the issue. The child darted into the cave. And in that instant, in that first uncertain pause in the darkening tunnel, the opening grew over. Vines shot up from the dank earth. Rocks tumbled and blocked the afternoon light. In seconds, the opening had disappeared.

The child stood, uncertain, at the pile of rubble that had been the cave's door. He wanted out, but there was no Out anymore. There was no light, no scent of cinnamon.

There was only the tunnel.

The man awakened, whimpering.

Chapter 3

Flint Settles In

A.C. 288, Late Summer

The weeks following his journey to Qualinost were busy ones for Flint. This day, as on almost every other, the smith headed for the Tower of the Sun, waiting only a few moments with the guard in the chilly corridor outside the Speaker's chamber before the elven lord bade him enter.

Even now, after months in Qualinesti, the spare grandeur of the Speaker's chambers spoke directly to Flint's soul. Hill dwarves, like elves, felt deeply their link with the natural world. Light flooded through the great clear walls—extravagant glass walls—that made the tree-dotted land outside the private chambers seem like an extension of the room. In recent weeks, pears and peaches had hung ever heavier on the branches; apples blushed red. Solostaran's quarters were nearly bare of decoration. White marble walls with veins of gray showed stark against window ledges of pinkish purple quartz. Torches, rendered unnecessary in the light that flooded the room during the day, lay cold and black in iron wall sconces. A marble-topped desk stood along one side of the room; behind it, in a heavy oaken chair placed to give the occupant a clear view of door and outdoors, waited the Speaker. Solostaran's forest-green cloak formed the brightest spot of color in the chamber, and his innate sense of authority commanded the viewer's attention.

"Master Fireforge!" the Speaker greeted, rising to his feet, green eyes twinkling over hawklike features. "Come in. As usual, you are a welcome diversion from affairs of state." He gestured toward a silver bowl filled with candied nuts, dried apricots, apple slices, cherries, and other fruit, no doubt grown on the very trees outside the chamber. "Help yourself, my friend." Flint declined the treat and fumbled with sheaves of parchment, trying to avoid sending any tumbling to the white and black marble-tiled floor. Finally, he scrunched them together, disregarding the wrinkles in the paper, and tipped them onto the Speaker's desk. As usual, Solostaran exclaimed over the charcoal drawings, selecting a few designs from the many that pleased him.

The Speaker seemed distracted today, although his conversation was as sociable as ever. "As I have said often, you are a gifted artisan, Master Fireforge," he commented.

The two spent minutes discussing the design of new wall sconces for the Speaker's quarters, and whether Solostaran would prefer them with a standard black finish or polished to a metallic shine. The Speaker selected a combination of both. Suddenly, a knock resounded from the door to the chambers. It was Tanis. He moved to the table with little of the grace that elves were known for.

"You wished to see me, sir?" the half-elf asked Solostaran. Tanis's features had the look, his limbs the awkwardness, of a youth just shy of manhood. He appeared doubly poised between two worlds—elf and human, child and adult. He'll be shaving soon, the dwarf thought. Yet more evidence of Tanis's human blood. The dwarf winced at the hazing the half-elf could expect from some of the smooth-faced elves. Tanis stood before the Speaker's desk, sparing a nod for Flint, who, despite his earlier refusal of refreshments, was nibbling a slice of dried apple and did not speak.

"It's time for you to begin advanced training in the long-bow, Tanis," Solostaran said. "I have selected a teacher." Tanis looked in pleased surprise at Flint. "Master Fireforge?" the half-elf asked tentatively.

Flint swallowed the fruit and shook his head. "Not me, lad. The longbow's not my weapon, although I'd be glad to demonstrate the fine points of the battle-axe." And an excellent job the half-elf would make of it, too, with those growing human muscles, Flint said to himself.

"The battle-axe is not an elven weapon," Solostaran gently corrected Flint. "No, Tanis, Lord Tyresian has agreed to take up your training."

"But Tyresian . . ." The half-elf's voice trailed off, and the dissatisfied cast clamped down over his countenance again.

". . . is one of the most experienced bowmen in court," the Speaker concluded. "He's Porthios's closest friend and heir to one of the highest families in Qualinost. He could be a valuable ally for you, Tanthalas, if you impress him as a student."

Apparently forgotten in the exchange, Flint squinted at Tanis and plucked a sugared pear from the silver bowl. Tanis and Tyresian would never be allies, the dwarf thought, recalling the elf lord from Flint's first day at court. A member of the cadre of four or five well-born elves who stuck to Porthios, the Speaker's heir, like flies to honey, Tyresian had a knack for charming the aristocracy. But rare was the common elf who could meet Tyresian's high social standards. Considered handsome by courtiers, Tyresian had sharp blue eyes and—odd among elves— hair no more than an inch long, cut with precision. Not surprisingly, a hill dwarf, however skilled, did not quite measure up in Tyresian's eyes, and Flint guessed that a half-elf would fall even lower. The dwarf wondered how much of Porthios's ill-concealed condescension toward his father's ward was born of Tyresian's opinions.

Tanis dared one last protest. "But, Speaker, my studies with Master Miral take most of the day—"

An irritated Solostaran cut him off. "That's enough, Tanthalas. Miral has taught you much of science and mathematics and history, but he is a mage. He cannot demonstrate the arts of weaponry. Tyresian expects you to meet him in the courtyard north of the palace at midafternoon. If you wish to speak with him before then, you can find him in Porthios's quarters."

Tanis opened his mouth, then seemed to think better of it. With a curt "Yes, sir," he walked with stiff back across the marble tiles and out the door.

Solostaran continued gazing at the door a few seconds after it banged shut. It wasn't until Flint began rolling up the drawings that the Speaker's attention returned to his audience with the dwarf. "Can I offer you anything?" Solostaran said again, with a vague wave toward the now half-empty silver bowl. "Some wine? Dried fruit?"

Flint declined, commenting that he'd eaten before he arrived at the Speaker's chambers. Solostaran suddenly grinned—why, Flint couldn't see—but the smile soon faded. Flint tucked the rolled parchments under his burly arm and was preparing to leave when the Speaker's voice halted him.

"Do you ever have cause to wish you could rewrite history, Master Fireforge?" The words were wistful.

Flint paused, staring with alert blue-gray eyes into the Speaker's green ones, and thought, He has no elves he can call friends. Since taking up the Speaker's mantle in the tumultuous years after the Cataclysm had changed the face of Krynn, Solostaran had been the focus of one rumor of deposition after another. He held his post through the force of his personality, through the truth that few elves could trace their bloodlines back several millennia to Kith-Kanan, and through the innate elven horror of drawing the blood of their elven kin. Still, Solostaran had to be aware of the occasional murmurs of unhappiness among courtiers, Flint thought. Some believed Qualinesti should be opened to wider trade with the rest of Ansalon. Others felt that all but pure elves should be deported over the border into Abanasinia.

The hill dwarf cast about for an answer to the Speaker's query. He drew in a breath of air tinged with the scent of fruit, and said, "Certainly I would change history if I could. My grandfather's family lost many numbers because of the Cataclysm."

Three centuries before, the Cataclysm occurred because the old gods retaliated against the pride of the era's most influential religious leader, the Kingpriest of Istar. When the Cataclysm rained destruction upon Krynn, the mountain dwarves retreated into Thorbardin, the great underground kingdom, and sealed the gates; as a result, their hill dwarf cousins, trapped outside, suffered the brunt of the gods' punishment.

The Speaker's eyebrows rose, and, confoundedly, in the face of Solostaran's sympathy, Flint found himself unable to go on. "They died because the mountain dwarves locked the gates . . . ?" the Speaker asked, and Flint nodded, unwilling to say more.

Solostaran stood and walked slowly to the clear wall. The gold circlet on his forehead glittered. The room was silent except for the breathing of the two figures. "I would give almost anything," Solostaran said, "to have Tanis be my true nephew, to have my brother Kethrenan back among us with his wife, Elansa. To see my brother Arelas one more time."

Miral, the Speaker's mage, had told Flint the story of Kethrenan Kanan and Elansa and the birth of Tanis. But he had not mentioned the existence of another brother. The Speaker seemed to wish to speak, and Flint knew no one but himself that he would trust with the Speaker's secrets. Taking a handful of glazed almonds, the dwarf chewed one and prompted, "Arelas . . . ?"

The Speaker turned. "My youngest brother." At the rising of Flint's furry brows, he went on, "I barely knew him. He left Qualinost as a little boy. And he died before he could return."

"Why did he leave?" Flint asked.

"He was. . . ill. We could not cure him here."

The ensuing silence stretched into minutes, and Flint cast about for a response. "It is a sad thing when a child dies," he said.

Solostaran looked up suddenly, a look of surprise creasing his features. "Arelas was a man when he died. He was returning to Qualinost, but he never got here." The Speaker stepped back toward Flint, seemingly trying to control his emotions. "Had he lived another week, he would have found safety here. But the roads were dangerous, even more so than today." The Speaker sat heavily.

Flint found himself unsure what to say. After a short time, the Speaker asked the dwarf to leave him.

* * * * *

Almost mindless of the parchment drawings, Flint walked somberly back to the small shop the Speaker had given him, a squat building southeast of the Tower. Here, in the last few months, he had wrought many things: necklaces of jade woven with near-fluid chains of silver, rings of braided gold as fine as strands of hair, bracelets of burnished copper and emerald.

The workshop stood at the end of a small lane in a grove of pear trees. Climbing roses entwined about its wooden doorway. Flint, remembering his mother's fondness for morning glories, had planted the flower at the feet of the roses, and the pink, blue, and white blossoms now intertwined with the white, pink, and yellow roses.

The dwelling had been awarded to Flint for as long as he wished it, but how long that might be, the dwarf was unsure. Certainly he would stay until the end of spring, he had told himself at first; after all, what was the use of journeying so far if he only went dashing back home right off? Still, thoughts of his warm house far away in Solace—and of a foamy tankard of ale—often ran through his mind. Elven ale had proved to be a pathetic imitation of the real thing, as far as the dwarf was concerned, although it was head and foam above elvenblossom wine.

Busy as he was, what with near-daily appointments with the Speaker and more commissions for his work than he could shake his hammer at, it was hardly surprising that the last day of spring had slipped by quite unnoticed and the warm, golden days of summer stretched out before the dwarf.

Often the window of his shop could be seen glowing as red as Lunitari, late into the night, and it was not uncommon that the first elf to wake in Qualinost the next day did so to the ringing of hammer on anvil. Many marveled at the dwarf's diligence, and just as many hoped the Speaker would make them the lucky recipients of a gift of one of Master Fireforge's creations.

On this afternoon, he stomped back to the heat of the forge, hefted his iron hammer, and once again used blazing fire and the blows of his hammer to transform a lifeless lump of metal into a thing of beauty. He spent several hours at his task, losing all sense of time in his absorption with the metalwork.

At last Flint sighed, wiped the soot from his hands and brow with a handkerchief, and ladled a drink of water from the oaken barrel that stood by the door to his shop. As he stepped outside into the afternoon sunshine, a smile touched his face, easing the lines that crisscrossed his forehead. The path leading to his front door passed through a stand of aspen trees. Their pale, slender trunks swayed gently in the breeze, as if they were faintly bowing toward the dwarf, and their leaves rustled, flickering green and silver and then green again. His hand moved slowly to his chest, as if it might ease a heart aching with the beauty all around. And part of him still hurt with the Speaker's sadness.

But then Flint noticed a few traces of gold high in the trees, and he felt, deep inside, that same restlessness that had plagued him all his life. There was a coolness to the mornings now, sharper than the gentle coolness of the summer nights, and there was a heaviness to the gold of the late afternoon sun. And now the trees.

All of it spoke of autumn and carried his thoughts to Solace and the houses tucked high among the vallenwood trees. The leaves of the giant trees would just be showing the first touches of variegated colors about their fluted edges, he supposed, and he sighed again. Autumn was a time for traveling. He should be going home, where he belonged.

With a start, Flint found himself wondering if Solace really were where he belonged. He had settled there years ago more out of weariness at wandering than anything else, in those days after he had left his impoverished village to find his fortune in the world. And how was living among elves any different for a simple dwarf from Hillhome than living among humans? In either case, he was the odd one; he couldn't see that it made much difference. Besides, he thought, breathing the cool air deeply, there was a peace here he'd never felt anywhere else.

Flint shrugged and stepped back inside his shop, and soon the ring of his hammer drifted on the air.

* * * * *

Flint looked up from his work several hours later and saw that the clock—the one he'd made from oak, with counterweights fashioned from two pieces of granite—showed the time nearing the supper hour. His thoughts, however, were not on food or on the silver rose he was fashioning at the request of Lady Selena, a member of Porthios's crowd who'd overcome her distaste of dwarves shortly after she'd realized that "fashions by Flint" were the new style among courtiers.

"It's time!" he exclaimed, put his hammer down, and banked the coals on the forge's furnace. Every few weeks he followed the same ritual. He splashed his face and arms in a basin, washing away the sweat and smoke of the forge. He grabbed a sack and, opening a hutch built into the stone walls, began filling the bag with curious objects. Each was made of wood, and Flint lovingly smoothed an edge here, polished a curve there. Suddenly, a figure, a shadow in the window, crossed his peripheral vision, and he straightened and waited. Another commission? His heart sank. He knew the elven children had been watching for him for days, watching for the dwarf who appeared on the streets every other week or so, presenting hand-whittled toys to every youngster in sight. He hoped no one would delay him now.

Flint thought he heard a scuffling outside and stomped to the doorway to check. But he heard and saw no one.

"Fireforge, you're growing old. Now you're imagining things," he complained as he went back to loading the sack.

He felt a warmth deep inside as he touched each of the wooden toys. Metal was good to shape; it gave one a sense of power as the cold substance submitted to the hammer and took on shape by the force of the forger's will. But wood was different, he thought, stroking a wooden whistle. One did not force wood into a shape or design, the dwarf said to himself; one found the shape that lay within it. There was no time Flint knew greater peace than when he sat with a carving knife in one hand and a piece of wood in the other, wondering what treasure lay hidden within its heart.

"It's like folks are, my mother used to say," he explained to his shop at large, which was as familiar to him by now as a close friend. "Some folks are like this metal, she'd say," and he displayed a metal flower brooch to the deserted room. "They can be forced into line. They'll adapt. Other folks are like this wood," and he held up a tiny squirrel, carved from softwood. "If you force them, they'll break. You have to work slowly, carefully, to see what's within."

"The key, my mother said," he intoned gravely to a stone bench near the door, "is to know which is which."

Flint paused as though waiting. It occurred to him that a fellow who made speeches to his furniture probably had few friends. With the exception of the Speaker and Miral and the city's children, most elves were reservedly polite with him. But there was no one to slap on the back and treat to an ale at a tavern, no one to swap stories with, no one he'd particularly trust to protect his back on the open road.

"Perhaps it *is* time to go home to Solace," he said softly, a look of sadness crossing his face.

Just at that moment, a thump resounded from right outside the door, followed by a quickly stifled "Oh!" He paused only a heartbeat in his movements and tiptoed to the open portal. Suddenly, he leaped through the doorway, booming, "Reorx's thunder! To the battle!" and laying about him with the carved squirrel as though it were a battle-axe. With a flurry of dust and a shriek of "Tanis, help!" a wispy figure topped with ash-blond curls sped away between the pear trees and the aspens. Her turquoise playsuit mirrored the deepening sky of twilight.

"Lauralanthalasa!" Flint called, laughing. "Laurana!" But the Speaker's daughter had disappeared.

The elf girl had called to Tanis, but Flint saw no evidence of the half-elf. Presumably, from Laurana's call, Tanis's afternoon archery lesson with Tyresian had been concluded.

Smiling, Flint went back into his shop. He was grinning still when he emerged, tossed the bag over his shoulder and bounded out the door of the shop. In the center of Qualinost, at the foot of the rise crowned by the aspen groves of the Hall of the Sky, stood an open square. It was a sunny place, bounded on one side by a row of trees that seemed to have grown especially for climbing and, on the other side, by a small brook spilling into a series of moss-lined pools. Between the two was plenty of space for running, shouting, and playing all sorts of noisy games. The square was a perfect place for children.

The sun had begun to dip into the horizon when Flint's footsteps brought him to the square. Dozens of elven children, dressed in cotton outfits gathered at neck and wrist and ankle, halted their games as the stocky dwarf stepped across the footbridge and into the clearing. The children stared at him, none daring to break the silence. Flint glowered, his bushy eyebrows drawn down almost over his steely eyes, and then he snorted, as if they were hardly anything to bother with. He marched through the square, his back turned to all their wondering eyes.

Finally, an elf girl dressed in turquoise dashed forward to tug at the dwarf's sleeve. Flint whirled, his eyes flashing like flint on steel. Oh ho! Flint thought, keeping his expression dour, so it's Laurana, is it? "You!" he exclaimed. The other children turned pale, but Laurana held her ground. He continued, "Were you spying on me?"

Laurana tilted her head, and one pointed ear tip poked out of her profusion of curls. "Well, of course," she said.

"What do you want?" he snarled. "I haven't got all day. Some folks have to work, you know, instead of playing all the time. I've got to take a very important order to the Tower, and it's nearly sundown."

The elf girl chewed on a pink lower lip. "The Tower's the other way," she said at last, green eyes sparkling.

Tremendous self-possession, Flint thought, for a youngling; must be the royal blood. Or else it was the figure of Tanis lounging in the background that gave Laurana courage.

"Well?" he demanded again. "What do you want of me?"

"More toys!"

Flint looked amazed. "Toys? Who has toys?"

She started to giggle and pulled on his sleeve. "In the sack. You've got toys in the sack, Master Fireforge. Admit it. You do, now."

He growled, "Not possible." But the cries of the children— "Yes." "Toys!" "Last time, I got a carved minotaur." "I want a wooden sword."—drowned out his reply. They swirled around him like a multicolored maelstrom. "Oh, all right," he muttered loudly. "I'll take a look, but the sack's probably full of coal. Just what you deserve." He peered inside, hiding the contents from the children, who crept closer.

About twenty feet away, Tanis sighed loudly and selected a new pear tree to lean against. His face held the bored look of the adolescent—although he did remain at the scene.

"Bent nails," Flint said, rummaging in the sack. "That's what I've got in here. And rusted curry combs and worn-out horseshoes and a month-old loaf of *quith-pa*. That's all."

The children waited for Laurana to take the lead. "You always say that," she pointed out.

"All right," he sighed. "Here's an idea. You put your arm inside the sack and pull something out."

She nodded. "Fine." She placed one hand near the opening. "Just watch out for the baby sea dragon," the dwarf said. "It bites."

She snatched back her slender hand and glared at Flint. "Want me to do it?" Flint finally offered.

Laurana nodded again.

He pulled something from deep in the corner of his sack, a gleeful grin on his face. She gasped, clapping her hands, and suddenly she wasn't the Speaker's royal daughter, but an ordinary elven girl. Frowning still, he laid the object in her hand.

It was a flute, no longer than the span of the elf girl's hand, but perfect in every respect, carved of a bit of vallenwood that Flint had brought all the way from Solace. But he knew its tone would be sweeter than any other wood, and this was proved true as Laurana raised the flute to her lips. The tones that bubbled forth were as clear as the water in the brook.

"Oh, thank you!" Laurana exclaimed, and ran over to Tanis, who stooped to examine her treasure. Laurana's brother, the elf boy called Gilthanas, and the other elven children pressed about Flint, begging him to please look and see if there was anything in his sack for them, too.

"Now, stop shoving," Flint said testily, "or I'm liable to leave at any second, you know." But somehow, despite the dwarf's grumbling, when the bag was empty every child in the square held a new, perfect toy. There were tiny musical instruments, like Laurana's flute, and small puppets that could be made to dance on the palm of the hand, and miniature carts pulled by painted horses, and wooden disks that rolled up and down on the end of a string tied to a finger.

All of the toys were made of wood, each carved lovingly by the light of the fire. Flint would work for weeks in his spare moments, filling up the cabinet, and then, when he'd made enough, he would find some excuse to pass through the square. Not that he'd admit it was anything other than chance that sent him when he just happened to have toys in his sack. He would merely scowl.

As he folded up the empty bag, Flint searched the gathering of children with his eyes. The dwarf saw Tanis, now sitting on the edge of the square, apart from the others near one of the pools. He sat cross-legged, staring silently into the water, where Flint could see the faint shadows of fish drifting by. In the midst of all this elven loveliness, there was something about Tanis, with his human qualities, that seemed decidedly familiar to Flint. The elves were a good people, but once in a while he found his thoughts turning to the times he had spent with folk a bit less *distant*. At any rate, he had come to the square like this four or five times now, and always Tanis had hung back from the other children when the dwarf was giving out the wooden toys. Tanis was growing old for youngsters' fripperies, but still . . . He wasn't all grown up yet. Not that Tanis hadn't seemed interested. Nearly every time the dwarf had arrived at the area to pass out toys, Flint had looked up to see the youth's not-quite-elven eyes upon him, as if he were studying the dwarf. Flint would motion for the boy to come forward, but he never would. He would just keep watching with that thoughtful gaze of his, and then, when the dwarf would look for him again, he would be gone.

But this time would be different. Flint thrust a hand in his pocket, making sure the one last toy he'd been saving—a wooden pea-shooter—was still there.

The rest of the children had dissipated, gone home to suppers of venison with fruit sauce, basted fish, or *quith-pa* with roasted fowl. The only figure in sight was Tanis. The Speaker's ward sat by the pool, arms clasped about his knees, resting his chin on them, watching Flint with his hazel eyes. He wore a loose white shirt and tan deerskin breeches, clothing reminiscent of that of the Que-Shu plainsmen, quite unlike the flowing tunics and robes that full elves preferred. He stood, unfolding his husky frame without the sense of grace that the other elves carried. Tanis brushed back a wing of reddish brown hair.

"Tanthalas," Flint said, nodding.

The half-elf echoed Flint's nod. "Master Fireforge."

They stood, both seemingly waiting for the other to make the first move.

Finally, Flint gestured at the pond. "Watching the fish?" he asked. Brilliant start, he thought.

Tanis nodded.

"Why?"

The half-elf looked surprised, then thoughtful. His answer, when it finally came, was delivered in a nearly inaudible tone. "They remind me of someone." The half-elf didn't meet his gaze. Flint nodded. "Who?"

Tanis looked up sullenly. "Everybody here."

"The elves?"

The half-elf signaled assent.

"Why?" Flint pressed again.

Tanis kicked a clod of moss. "They're satisfied with what they've got. They never change. They never leave here except to die."

"And you're different?" Flint asked.

Tanis drew his lips into a straight line. "Someday I'm leaving here."

Flint waited for the half-elf to say something else, but Tanis seemed to consider his part of the conversation over. All right, Flint thought; I'll give it a try. At least he's not slipping away into the shadows, for once. "How was today's archery lesson?" the dwarf asked.

"All right." The boy's voice was a monotone, and his eyes were focused on the pool again. Children chattered and screamed delightedly in the distance. "Tyresian and Porthios and their friends were all there," he added.

It sounded appalling, given the way Porthios's friends felt about the half-elf. Flint wondered what he could say to cheer up the Speaker's ward. "It's suppertime," he said, thinking, Sparkling conversation, Master Fireforge. What was there about this lad that rendered him conversationally inept?

Tanis smiled thinly and nodded his agreement. Yes, indeed, it was suppertime. The half-elf moved three paces to lean against another pear tree.

Flint tried again. "Care to join me for"—What did one offer elven children? Although Tanis's thirty years would make him a young man in human years, a thirty-year-old elf was years away from being considered grown up—"some supper?"

"With elvenblossom wine, perhaps?" the half-elf asked.

Flint wondered if the Speaker's ward were laughing at him. The dwarf had become able to sip the perfumey drink without gagging—for state occasions, for example, when sharing the elven wine was part of court decorum. "Ah, Reorx's beard," Flint muttered, and he shuddered.

Tanis examined Flint, a half-smile still playing on his lips. "You dislike that wine," the half-elf finally said.

"No. I *loathe* it."

"Why do you drink it, then?" Tanis asked.

Flint surveyed the half-elf; he seemed sincerely curious. "As a stranger, I'm trying to fit in here."

Off in the distance, a child's shrill laugh accompanied the shriek of a wooden whistle. At least one parent was going to be less than thrilled with Flint this evening. Tanis sneered. "Are you trying to be 'one of the elves'?" he asked, almost contemptuously.

Flint debated. "Well . . ." he said, "when in Qualinost, do as the Qualinesti do. My mother used to say that, or something very similar." He caught a whiff of baking venison, and his stomach growled, but he maintained his stance. Oh, how he wanted his supper. Oh, how he wished he'd never started this conversation. The half-elf kept sneering, but his eyes seemed to beg for reassurance, and the dwarf suddenly thought that maybe the sneer was directed, not at him, but at Porthios and Tyresian and the others. "Don't try, Master Fireforge," Tanis said.

"What?" Flint asked.

Tanis pulled a half-ripe pear from the tree, dropped it to the moss, and ground it under the heel of his oiled leather moccasin. "Don't try. They'll never accept you. They don't accept anyone who's not just like them." He kicked the fruit off to one side and stalked off without another word. Soon his figure was lost in the trees.

Flint walked slowly back into his shop, closed the door, and put the empty sack in the hutch. Somehow he wasn't in the mood for supper anymore.

Chapter 4

A Lesson

A.C. 288, Early Fall

Tanis strode along the road from Flint's shop, his moccasins scuffing against the blue and white tile. He cursed himself for his stupidity. Why had he been so curt with the dwarf? Flint Fireforge seemed to have the best of intentions; why hadn't the half-elf responded in kind?

Without paying much attention to where he was going, Tanis found himself pacing across the Hall of the Sky in central Qualinost. Patterned into the tile of the open area, now shrouded in twilight, lay a mosaic showing the region of Ansalon centering on the elven city; the map detailed lands from Solace and Crystalmir Lake at the northwest to Que-Shu at the northeast and Pax Tharkas at the south.

The half-elf stared at only one point on the map, however: Solace, the dwarf's adopted home. What kind of place was it?

"Imagine, to live in a house in a tree," he said, his whisper swallowed by the silence hanging over the deserted square. He thought of the elves' stone buildings, which never quite lost their chill. Would a wooden house in a tree be so warm?

He kicked at a loose tile that marked the position of the village of Gateway, between Qualinost and Solace; the movement sent the shard spinning. Contrite, and hoping no one had seen him deface the sacred map, he bounded after the chip and returned to replace it, kneeling. Then he sank back on his haunches and surveyed the open area.

The chilly twilight air carried delicious scents of supper and warm echoes of dinnertime chatter. Tanis stood slowly and stared around the Hall of the Sky; around him, the purplish quartz spires of elven homes, rectangles of lamplight along their curved sides, poked like the beaks of baby birds above the rounded tops of trees. Girdered all around by the arched bridges, with the gold of the tall Tower of the Sun still reflecting the sun's rays in the evening sky, the city was a remarkable sight; understandably, the Qualinesti elves believed it was the most beautiful city in the world. But how could elves bear it, living and dying in the same place?

Did his dissatisfaction, Tanis wondered, come from his father? From his human side?

Tanis raised his gaze to the deepening sky; almost as he watched, the evening darkened and stars began to appear directly overhead. He wondered about the myth that the Hall of the Sky once had been a real structure, guarding some rare and precious object, and that Kith-Kanan had magically raised building and object into the sky to hide them, leaving only the map that had formed the building's floor. As a toddler, he'd been told by the other young elves that the exact center of the map was a "lucky spot"; stand there and wish very hard and you would get what you desired, they claimed.

"I'd like to go up there, to see that hidden place in the sky," he whispered fervently now. "I'd like to see all of Ansalon.

I'd like to travel, like Flint . . . to have adventures . . . and friends . . ."

Looking around embarrassedly, hoping no one had seen or heard him, Tanis nonetheless continued to wait—not really hoping, of course, that a magical being would appear to grant his wish. Naturally not, he told himself. That was a child's dream, not a young man's. Still, he waited a few minutes more, until a breeze through the pear trees raised goose flesh on his arms and reminded him that it was time to go home.

Wherever that was, he thought.

* * * * *

"History," Master Miral told Tanis the next morning, "is like a great river."

The half-elf looked up. He knew better than to ask the tutor what he meant. Miral would either explain his point or make Tanis figure it out himself. Either way, questions would gain the half-elf nothing but an irritated wave of the hand.

Today, however, in the dim light of Miral's rooms in the Speaker's palace, the mage was inclined to be garrulous.

"A great river," he repeated. "It begins with small, clear streams, single voices, rushing quickly past their banks until they join their waters with other streams, growing larger and larger as they mingle again and again, until the small voices of a thousand tiny streams have been collected into the roaring song of a great river." He gestured widely, caught up in his metaphor.

"Yes?" Tanis prompted. The half-elf widened his eyes in the shadowy room; for as long as he could remember, the mage had kept the windows in his quarters blocked off. Bright light, Miral explained, affected the potency of the herbs and spices that formed the basis of the little magic he did. Besides, strong light hurt the nearly colorless eyes that Miral kept shaded in the hooded recesses of his deep burgundy robe. Tanis had long wondered why the Speaker had hired a mage to tutor his children; at one time, Miral had taught Laurana, Gilthanas, and Tanis—Porthios had been too old for a tutor when Miral arrived at court—but Laurana now received lessons from an elf lady. Gilthanas and Miral, on the other hand, had clashed from the start; the speaker's youngest son now took lessons in weaponry only—from Ulthen, one of Porthios's friends, who was well-born but chronically without money.

Tanis, fond of the eccentric mage, had remained with Miral, who was one of the few people at court who did not treat the half-elf with polite iciness. Perhaps the difference in Miral's attitude toward him had to do with the mage's years outside Qualinesti, Tanis reasoned; although Miral was an elf, he had not grown up with elves. All the more reason to leave Qualinost someday, the half-elf thought.

Miral now pointed a bony finger at Tanis, and the hood fell partially back from his face. His eyelashes and brows, like the shoulder-length hair that puffed from the hood of his robe, were ash-blond, lighter even than Laurana's tresses. Miral, with his shelves upon shelves of books, his magical potions, his habit of taking exercise indoors by pacing the corridors of the Tower late at night—a habit that raised giggles and conjecture from the young elves—had the colorless look of one who spent too much time in the dark.

"The great river," Miral continued, and Tanis shook his head, trying to regain his train of thought, "in turn flows into the deep and endless sea. History is like that sea."

The mage smiled at Tanis's befuddlement, and the expression gave Miral's sharp features the look of a falcon. "And although it might be simplest to study the great oceans and rivers—the wars and mighty events of ages gone by—sometimes the past is best understood by listening to the music of a few of those tiny brooks instead, the stories of the single lives that, one by one and drop by drop, made the world what it was."

Awash in the mage's rhetoric, Tanis inhaled the potpourri of spicy scents that managed to escape from corked containers around the room, knowing Miral would get to the point eventually. While another young noble might have dreaded these lessons, Tanis looked forward to his hours with Miral.

There were other subjects to study, as well as history: the written word, the movements of the heavens, the workings and habits of living things. But all of it was interesting to the half-elf. "For example," Miral said, settling back onto a huge pillow covered with cured hides of woodland stags, and waving Tanis into a similar, smaller, but no less comfortable, chair off to one side, "have I told you about Joheric?"

When Tanis shook his head, the mage told this story:

"As you know, Tanis, elves are the embodiment of good; theirs was the first race on Krynn." Tanis opened his mouth to ask if the other races believed *they* too were the first, but the mage silenced him with a look.

"The elves were affected less by the passage of the Graystone than the other, weaker, races were, but—"

"Tell me about the Graystone," Tanis interrupted, hoping this storytelling session would last into his early afternoon archery lesson with Tyresian.

Miral glared, and the shadows seemed to draw in deeper around the pair, as though the light reflected the mage's ill-humor. "I've told you about the Graystone. Now . . ." The mage's voice resumed hoarsely. ". . . We were less affected by the Graystone than other races were, but still the passage of the stone—which, as you know, is the embodiment of chaos—gave rise to unsettlement wherever it went.

"In Silvanesti, where I hale from . . ." This was news to Tanis, who sat up, prepared to ask a question, but instead slumped back down with another glare from the mage. "In Silvanesti, near the main city of Silvanost, lived an elven lord and his two children, a son named Panthell and a slightly younger daughter named Joheric. As was custom there in the years before the Kinslayer Wars, the eldest son stood to inherit his father's title, his lands, and his wealth. The daughter, Joheric, would receive a large enough dowry that some young elf lord would be encouraged to marry her, but she would have no title to anything else that her father owned."

"That seems unfair, put that way," Tanis interjected.

Miral nodded and drew his robe tighter around him. "So it seemed to Joheric," the mage continued. "The situation tortured Joheric, especially as it seemed obvious to her that she was the worthier child. Elven women, then as now, were trained in weaponry, though then, as now, their use of weapons was more ceremonial than practical. The men still did most of the fighting, when it became necessary.

"Well, Joheric was so skilled with a sword that she could defeat her brother, Panthell, in the mock battles they held about the castle. She was stronger than her older sibling, and smarter. But because she was the younger child, she knew that eventually she would see everything she thought she deserved passing to the unworthy one. Everyone should be able to see, she reasoned, that Panthell was a poor fighter, with no moral judgment at all. She knew that he was not above thievery, that he was greedy and a coward, and that, moreover, he was none too bright."

Tanis's stomach growled and he glanced at the plate of toasted *quith-pa* that the mage had placed just out of reach on a low table near the two chairs. The half-elf had come in too late the previous evening to join the Speaker's family at the dinner table; misgivings about his conversation with Flint had kept him awake until the early morning hours, and then when he'd finally fallen asleep, he'd risen too late to break his fast before hurrying off to see Miral.

The mage, however, correctly interpreted the abdominal gurgle and the wistful glance, and uttered a command in another language, a command that, with no help from elven hands, sent the plate sliding across the table toward the half-elf. Tanis grunted his thanks, spread a slice of *quith-pa* with pear jelly, and stuffed it in his mouth.

Miral continued. "Joheric grew increasingly bitter over the knowledge that all her skills, all her talents, would gain her nothing. She yearned to go into battle and bring glory to her house. Soon the Dragon War gave her that opportunity. The war drew her father into fighting, and he, over his son's vehement protests, sent Panthell off to join the other elven soldiers. Joheric, however, remained at home, practicing her swordsmanship, her skill with the bow, until she was sure she could defend herself with honor. Long months went by, however, with no word of Panthell since he'd left with his regiment."

"He was killed?" Tanis asked.

"Joheric's father feared so. He feared his son and heir had been captured. Joheric went to her father and vowed to find her brother—a vow nobody at home took terribly seriously because, after all, she was a girl and she was only twenty-five or so, younger than you are now. In the cover of night, she left the castle and set off through the forests of Silvanesti, hunting for her brother's regiment."

"Did she find him?" Tanis asked around a mouthful of *quith-pa*. He picked a crumb off his sand-colored breeches.

Miral nodded. "She did, but not in the way she'd expected. She came upon Panthell just as the regiment of elves was engaged in battle with a troop of humans. She fought her way to his side, where she discovered, to her horror . . ." the mage's voice trailed off. "What do you think she learned, Tanis?" Miral prompted.

Tanis looked up and swallowed. "What?" he repeated.

Miral resumed. "Panthell was fighting on the side of the humans."

The half-elf felt a thrill go through his body. He sat up so swiftly that the room spun from gray to black before his eyes. He shook his head to clear it. What was Miral trying to tell him?

Relentless, the mage continued, no longer meeting the half-elf's eyes. "Joheric was so enraged that, without thinking, she shouted her brother's name and, when he turned toward her, ran him through with her sword. It turned out that the elves had been seeking the human troop that Panthell had joined and was leading. The elves decimated the humans and brought Joheric home a hero."

"A hero? For killing her brother?" Tanis gulped. He'd heard the Silvanesti elves were colder, more calculatingly rational than the Qualinesti, but . . .

"For killing a *traitor*," Miral corrected. "She inherited her father's estate and went on to great success as an elven general." He stopped and cast a glance at his student.

Tanis was horrified. "That's *it*?" he demanded, his tone rising despite himself. "She killed her brother and was rewarded for it?"

"For the rest of her life, she was troubled by sadness," Miral conceded. "For years afterward, she was pursued by dreams of her brother, nightmares in which she ran him through again and again and again, until she awoke screaming."

Tanis considered, looking around the shadowed room but seeing instead an armored elven woman impaling her own brother in battle. "Bad dreams seem a poor price to pay for slaying another elf," he said finally.

"It depends on the dreams," the mage said.

The two sat in silence for a short time, until Miral leaned forward. "Do you understand the moral of what I've told you?"

The half-elf took the last bit of *quith-pa* and thought some more. "That one person can change the course of history?" he offered.

The mage's face displayed approval. "Good. What else?"

Tanis thought hard, but no reasonable alternative came to him. The mage leaned close, his eyes suddenly shards of crystal. *"Decide which side you're on, Tanis."*

Startled, the half-elf felt his face go white. "What did you say?" he asked weakly.

"Decide which side you're on." Then the mage turned away.

* * * * *

At that point in the morning's lesson, Laurana arrived, and Miral called a break, prompted also, no doubt, by the shock that still showed on his young pupil's face. The lad had to learn the hard truth sooner or later, the mage thought; Tanis couldn't exist half-elf and half-human without choosing which race to align himself with. Still, it had pained Miral to hurt his young pupil, and he wished he could have found a gentler way of making the same point. If Tanis didn't develop a shell between himself and the court, he'd go through life bruised and battered.

Still, it was a shame, the mage thought.

* * * * *

Tanis returned several minutes later, having successfully fended off his youngest cousin's attempts to lure him into the sunshine for some childish fun.

"There might be few days like this left before winter," the Speaker's daughter had argued. "You'll blink your eyes, and winter will be here, Tanis."

She had laughed, but Tanis had shivered a little. He already could feel the winds of winter in his bones, and he knew, somehow, that the changing of the seasons meant more to him than it did to other elves. Maybe it was that he could feel himself changing with the season, growing older. Maybe it was that individual seasons meant more to races that expected fewer of them than the elves did; a half-elf lived a shorter life than the centuries that a full elf could expect, although a half-elf in turn could expect a longer life than humans could.

The mage and his pupil turned to a new subject—the workings of wings. Miral had found a dead sparrow and a brown bat in a walk through the woods this morning; he and Tanis examined the two creatures lying on a tray on the tutor's desk, illuminated by a lamp that lent the room a scent of spiced oil. Still, as the two stood head by head examining the dead bat and the bird, there was a strain between master and pupil. Tanis tried hard to turn his attention back toward Miral's lesson.

"Do you see the differences between the bat and the sparrow, then, Tanis?" Miral asked. His breath smelled of bay leaves.

"I think so," Tanis said. He traced the fragile lines of the bat's wing with a finger. "In the bat, the wing is made of skin stretched between the finger bones, which have grown very long, except for the thumb." He turned his attention to the sparrow lying still on the desk. "And in the bird, the fingers are lost, and the wing is fashioned of feathers springing from the arm."

"Good," Miral said gravely. "I suspect that's enough for today. I wouldn't want you to get ideas about flying, yourself."

Tanis smiled with Miral. "I'm afraid if I tried that, my fate would be the same as these poor fellows." He looked wistfully at the animals lying still on the desk.

"Life and death are both part of the cycle of nature," Miral said, catching his expression. "And if we can learn from death, then so much the better." He moved the tray aside, and poured a cup of wine for each of them to sip as they talked. "Now, I think there's time left for another story. What shall it be?"

"You," Tanis replied. "I want to hear your life story."

The shadows in the room deepened again as the mage's clear eyes took in the half-elf's serious expression. The stone floors seemed to radiate a chill, and the half-elf shivered. Miral appeared to come to some decision, took another sip of wine, and asked, "What tale of myself is there for me to tell?"

"What about all of your journeys?" the half-elf pressed.

Miral turned away from the table. "The aimless wanderings of a foolish young elf, that was all," the mage said with a shrug. "My life was of little importance until I finally had the sense to come to Qualinost."

Tanis took another swallow of wine, then another, gaining a weak form of courage. "How did you get here? You say you are Silvanesti. Why come to Qualinost, then?"

"It's early afternoon. Aren't you late for your archery lesson?"

"You said we have time for another story," Tanis said stubbornly.

Miral sighed. "I see you will not leave this until I satisfy you with some explanation of a middle-aged mage's life. Come, then. Let me walk with you to your session with Tyresian. We can talk along the way."

They drained their goblets, and Tanis followed Miral into the hallway, the mage careful to set the lock in the door. At Miral's request, the corridor outside his chambers was always dimly lit. A guard was never present, also at his request.

"What do you know of me, Tanis?" Miral asked as they stepped slowly along the corridor.

Tanis matched his gait to that of the mage. Both made little noise as they walked, the half-elf because he wore leather moccasins, the mage because he shod his feet with padded slippers. "I know that you were a friend of the Speaker's brother, Arelas. And that you came here when I was a child." Tanis flushed, hoping that the mage would not say the half-elf was a child still.

The mage, however, appeared engrossed in examining the gray veins in the marble floor as the pair progressed along the hallway. They'd gone far enough from the mage's quarters that the wall sconces again held torches for light; they stepped from one circle of light into darkness and then into the next illuminated circle. Finally, Miral spoke, his voice seeming to come from deep within his hood.

"We were longtime friends," the mage said hoarsely. "You know that Arelas grew up away from court?"

Tanis nodded, then realized that Miral could not see to the side as he walked, hooded, facing forward. "Yes, of course," he said.

"Arelas was the youngest of the three brothers. Solostaran was eldest, of course. Kethrenan was many years younger, and Arelas was only a few years younger than Kethrenan. Arelas was sent away from court as a very young child—some say because he was frail and could not thrive here," Miral said. "He was sent to a group of clerics near Caergoth, several weeks' travel north of here, through mountains and across the Straits of Schallsea. Shortly before that, I had come to the same area as an apprentice with a group of mages.

"You would think two elves living in a human city would become friends easily, purely out of loneliness," Miral continued. "But such wasn't the case. We lived near the same city for long years, passing each other in the marketplace, nodding but never speaking. He never went home to Qualinost. I never went home to Silvanost." He paused, and Tanis practically heard his friend groping for the correct words. As they passed one doorway, Lord Xenoth, the Speaker's elderly adviser, emerged with a swirl of his silvergray robe, but passed without acknowledging the pair.

"Xenoth disliked me from the start," Miral murmured. "Why, I don't know. I've never done anything against him. I certainly am no threat to his position at court, which is all he seems to care about."

As they passed by a window, a vertical slash in the quartz, Tanis sidestepped a freestanding planter overflowing with ferns. "Yet you and Arelas eventually met," he prompted.

Miral turned right and headed down wide stone steps to the courtyard. "We met through my magic. One day in the Caergoth marketplace, Arelas took ill. He was ever a frail elf. I was nearby and rushed to his aid. I know many spells for easing minor ills, although I am not an accomplished healer, as you well know." Tanis rushed to disagree, but Miral waved aside his polite assurances with one of his characteristic gestures, and the half-elf fell silent again. Miral, in fact, *was* only a minor mage, but his friendly personality and willingness to share his time had made him relatively popular.

"At any rate," Miral said, "I was able to ease Arelas's pain, and in the days afterward I visited him often. At last, we became friends."

They had arrived at the double doors that opened from the Speaker's palace into the courtyard. The doors were fashioned of polished steel—making them particularly valuable in an era when the constant threat of war made steel, used for weapons, worth more than gold or silver. Each door stood as high as two elves and as wide as one, although the precision of the elven craftsmen meant that any elf, regardless of strength, could set the doors swinging open. Tanis opened one, enough to see Tyresian lounging arrogantly against a pillar forty feet outside the door. Miral stepped back into the shadows, and the half-elf let the door swing shut again.

"How did you end up in Qualinost?" Tanis asked. "And what happened to Arelas?"

Miral pulled his hood back from his face. "Perhaps this should wait for another time. It is not the kind of tale to be tossed out as two friends part." But at Tanis's look, he continued. "Arelas decided to visit Qualinost, and he asked me to accompany him. I had always wanted to see the western elven lands, so I agreed. We could have sent to Qualinost, to court, for an escort, I suppose, but Arelas wanted to enter Qualinesti anonymously—why, I never did discover. In so many ways, he was a secretive sort.

"It was in the unsettled times in the early centuries after the Cataclysm. Bands of brigands were not uncommon on the highways. But Arelas assured me that we'd be safe in the small group that we traveled with."

Miral dipped his head and seemed to be struggling to breathe. Tanis was fascinated by the narrative, yet he wished he had not asked the mage to relive what was obviously a painful experience.

Finally, the mage sighed. "Arelas was wrong. We sailed safely from Caergoth to Abanasinia, and we traveled inland without incident for a week. Then, a day's ride out of Solace, near Gateway, our small group of fellow travelers was attacked by human brigands. We killed one of the highwaymen, but they slew the guards who traveled with us."

"Arelas?" Tanis asked. Through the door, he heard impatient footsteps; he could only guess it was Tyresian, come to get him for archery lessons.

"There was an . . . an explosion," Miral said softly, stepping back another pace as the door began to open. "Arelas was badly hurt. I did what I could. He told me to come here, that his brother would find a place for me in court. You see, even Arelas, fond friend that he was, knew that I wasn't a good enough mage to find a position on my own."

At that moment, Tyresian crashed through the door, shouting, "Tanthalas Half-Elven! I have waited . . ." He saw the two and stopped, then evidently dismissed the mage as beneath his notice. "You are late!" he snapped at the half-elf.

Tanis ignored the angry elf lord for the moment. "And so you came here," the half-elf said to Miral.

Miral nodded. "And I've been here ever since. I've been happy—happier than I would have been in Silvanesti, I suspect. I do miss Arelas. I still dream about him."

As Tyresian fumed silently behind him, Tanis watched in sympathy as the mage padded back up the steps.

* * * * *

"Keep your head up," Tyresian snapped. "Hold this arm straight. Plant your feet thus. Don't look away from the target while you're aimed at it. By the gods, do you want to kill someone?"

Off to one side, Lady Selena laughed. She was a regal-looking elf lady with violet eyes and dusky blond hair, but there was an unsettling hardness to her features. Still, the great wealth she would inherit upon her parents' death added a great deal to her attractiveness in many elf lords' eyes.

Tanis had spent two hours firing arrow after arrow into several bales of hay that Tyresian had ordered set up in a block against a blank wall of the huge courtyard. "That way, we'll be relatively sure you won't send an arrow into some passing courtier," Tyresian had said, prompting more laughter from Litanas, Ulthen and Selena. Porthios sat on a bench, watching his half-elf cousin with an intensity that almost guaranteed Tanis would miss the target nine out of ten times.

"Can't you ask your friends to leave?" Tanis had asked Tyresian, whose blue eyes narrowed.

"Do you think they'll clear a battlefield for you someday, half-elf, just so you'll feel at ease with no critical eyes upon you?" the elf lord retorted loudly. Litanas snorted, and Tanis felt his face go red. With the exception of Porthios, the group seemed to find Tanis's performance remarkably entertaining.

Tanis's arm ached, and his fingers were numb. Nerveless hands dropped an arrow on the ground, and he flushed as the crowd behind him found merriment in his efforts to pluck the arrow from the moss with fingers that refused to do what he wished. Actually, what his fingers wished to do was wrap themselves around Tyresian's corded neck and tighten, and Tanis fought to hold his temper in check. Lady Selena had a particularly irritating laugh, too—a giggle that trilled up the scale and gurgled back down to the starting note. It was enough to make his hair curl, but Litanas and

Ulthen seemed to find it enchanting.

"It does little good to be skilled in defending yourself against an enemy in the distance if you are vulnerable to an enemy standing before you," Tyresian said self-importantly.

No kidding, Tanis thought, but grimaced as the elf lord thrust a heavy steel sword into his hand. The half-elf was forced to lift it in a hasty parry against a fiercely grinning Tyresian. Deftly, Tyresian edged one foot behind Tanis's and shoved his adversary's chest with the flat of his sword; Tanis fell over backward in a flurry of arms and legs, narrowly missing his own sword as he landed.

He lay there, panting, stinging from the shrill laughter and the force of his fall but refusing to look at the elven nobles chortling on the stone bench.

Suddenly, Selena's screech rose above the clamor. "He's split his breeches!" she shrieked, and dissolved in giggles. Tanis looked down; his sword had, indeed, slit the right side of his breeches, and his fall had split it wider, leaving an expanse of unbecomingly hairy thigh exposed to the gaze of Porthios's friends. Finally, a new voice joined the others, and Tanis saw Porthios wipe tears from his eyes as he rose and, shaking his head, led his friends back into the palace through the steel doors. Tyresian leaned over and, with one easy movement, swept up Tanis's sword, saluted the fallen half-elf with it, and stepped after his friends. He paused at the door, however, holding it open with one strong hand.

"See you tomorrow, half-elf," he said, and grinned.

From inside, Selena's laughter trilled back at Tanis.

Chapter 5

A Battle of Arrows

Laurana was waiting in the courtyard the next morning when Tanis arrived with his bow and arrows, his mood matching the glower of the overcast skies. Miral had given him the morning off, and he resolved to practice his weaponry until Tyresian could find nothing to criticize.

But there was the Speaker's daughter, attired in a hunter-green gown with gold-embroidered slippers, her long hair loose except for a thick braid on each side of her face. She sat, legs swinging, on the edge of a stone wall, managing both to hint at the alluring woman she would become and to show the indulged child she was now. Tanis groaned inwardly.

"Tanis!" she cried, and hopped down from the wall. "I have a terrific idea."

The half-elf sighed. How to deal with her? She was only ten years old to his thirty, a mere baby compared with him; the age gap was similar to that between a five-year-old human child and a fifteen-year-old.

He was genuinely fond of the little elf girl, even though she was a touch too aware of how her cuteness affected people. "What do you want, Laurana?"

She stood, arms akimbo, in front of the half-elf, her chin pert and her green eyes sparkling with fun. "I think we should get married."

"What?" Tanis dropped his bow. As he stooped to pick it up, the child tackled him and, giggling, pulled him to the moss. Gravely, he kneeled, set her on her feet again, and then stood. "I don't think it would work, Lauralanthalasa Kanan."

"Oh, everybody uses my full name when I'm in trouble." She pouted. "I still think you should marry me."

Tanis prepared to aim for the mutilated target, which still leaned against the high stone wall, but Laurana danced before him, getting in his way. "Do you want to get hurt?" he demanded. "Sit there." And he pointed to a bench off to his left, the same bench that Lady Selena and the others had used yesterday. Laurana, amazingly, obeyed him.

"Why not, Tanis?" she chimed as he released an arrow that missed the target, clinking against the stone two feet above the padded hay and falling harmlessly to the ground.

"Because you're too young." He nocked another arrow and squinted at the target.

She sighed. "Everyone says that." This arrow hit the hay bales, at least, though it was about three feet to the right of the dragonseye. "How about when I'm older?"

"Then maybe *I'll* be too old."

"You won't be too old." She spoke with stubborn force, her lower lip puckered, tears threatening like the thunderclouds overhead. "I asked Porthios how long half-elves live, and he told me. We'll have plenty of time."

Tanis turned. "Did you tell Porthios you wanted to marry me?"

She brightened. "Of course."

55

No wonder the Speaker's heir had grown especially chilly of late. Didn't want the Speaker's daughter running around telling people she wanted to marry the palace's bastard half-elf, Tanis thought bitterly. He released the arrow without thinking, and it thunked into the canvas-covered bales mere inches from the dragonseye. Another arrow bit into the cloth between the first arrow and the dragonseye.

Laurana had been watching carefully. "Pretty good, Tanis. So, will you marry me? Someday?"

Tanis walked forward to gather his arrows. When he came back, he'd made up his mind. "Sure, Laurana," he said. "I'll marry you someday."

She clapped her hands. "Oh, hurray!" she chattered. "I'll go tell everybody." She scurried out of the courtyard.

The half-elf watched her go. That's right, Lauralantha-lasa, he thought; tell everybody. Especially Porthios.

* * * * *

Later that morning, as rain still threatened, Tanis encountered his "future bride" again as he neared the Hall of the Sky, seeking to clear his head after four hours of archery practice. "There you are!" the small, breathless voice said, interrupting his reverie. The half-elf turned with a start to see Laurana scurrying across the square, hiking up her green-gold dress about her knees so that she could run toward him. The shiny material contrasted with the grayness of the midday light.

Laurana had taken to dressing less like a child lately and more like an elven woman, abandoning the soft, gathered playsuits that elven children wore. Perhaps her new mode of dress reflected the strictures of court decorum, though Laurana, to be honest, seemed to be less concerned with the intricacies of etiquette and social protocol than were elves of lesser birth. She'd probably lose that naturalness as she grew up, he thought with a sigh, feeling terribly old all of a sudden.

"We've got to go," she chirped. "Gilthanas said he saw him heading for the square!"

"Saw who?" Tanis asked.

"Master Fireforge!" Laurana said, as if this should have been terribly plain.

Tanis groaned inwardly. Watching another session of the children and the toymaker was not what he wished to do right now, but Laurana's grip on his hand was firm, and he had no choice but to stumble along beside her.

Sure enough, the dwarven smith was there when they reached the square, surrounded by laughing children; Laurana promptly dove into the fray. Tanis sighed and hung back among the trees as usual. Soon the crowd began to break up as children ran off to experiment with their new toys. Laurana was caught up in the gift the dwarf had given her, a small, paper-winged bird that really glided. Tanis shoved his hands in his pockets and turned to leave.

"All right, lad, hold it right there!" a gruff voice said behind Tanis, and he jumped, startled, as a heavy hand fell on his shoulder. "You're not getting away this time."

Tanis spun around and found himself looking at the dwarf. Master Fireforge's eyes glimmered like brightly polished steel. Tanis didn't know what to say, so he remained silent, though he felt his heart jump.

"Now," the dwarf began carefully, "I know that—for a few folks, anyway—a simple toy isn't enough to make them forget their cares." He cast a wistful glance back at the merry children. "I wish it was that easy for everyone." His eyes met Tanis's again. "But be that as it may, I want you to have this all the same." He held a small parcel forth, and Tanis found himself taking it with uncertain hands.

Not knowing what else to do, he fumbled with the string, but finally the knot loosened and the parchment fell away. He gazed at the object in his hand, and his throat grew tight. It was a pair of wooden fish, carved in perfect detail. Each hung by a tiny golden thread from a small crossbar mounted over a wooden base that was carved to resemble the rocky bed of a brook.

"Here," the dwarf said softly, "let me show you." He touched the crossbar gently with a stubby fingertip and it began to spin. The fish traveled round and round the base, bobbing gently on their strings. It looked as though they were swimming, graceful and free, there on the palm of Tanis's hand.

"If you're embarrassed at receiving a toy, perhaps you can call it a 'wooden sculpture,' " the dwarf suggested, and winked.

"It's wonderful," Tanis whispered, and a smile crossed his face.

* * * * *

Tanis was waiting at the courtyard, the fish sculpture perched on a stone sidewall, when Tyresian arrived that afternoon, once again trailed by Selena, Ulthen, and Litanas. Porthios stepped through the double doors a few moments later. Just at that moment, a drop of rain splattered on one of the paths that crisscrossed the area, and Tyresian, wearing a knee-length tunic the color of storm clouds, glanced irritatedly at the leaden sky.

"I think we'd best cancel today's lesson," the elf lord said, and his companions—minus Porthios—groaned. The Speaker's heir merely looked somberly at the group, his light eyebrows drawn together, his face wearing its characteristic frown.

"Now what'll we do for entertainment?" Tanis heard Litanas mutter, and Selena covered her mouth with one gloved hand and trilled. Tanis cringed.

But he hadn't spent most of the morning slinging arrows into hay bales to be put off now. He nocked an arrow and drew aim on the target. His tone was intentionally mild. "I'm not too frail to stand a little dampness, Lord Tyresian. If you are, you're welcome to retreat inside. Perhaps one of the servants will light a fire for you. As for myself, I will remain."

The short-haired elf lord flushed from his square chin to his hairline. "We will continue," he said flatly.

The rain held off as Tanis sent arrow after arrow toward the target, blue feathers, then red, flashing as they sped across the courtyard. A few arrows clattered against the wall, but more and more consistently he hit the hay bale. He even struck the round target itself once in four or five tries—but never the dragonseye at the center. Tyresian offered his usual litany of criticism. "Hold that shoulder steady. Keep that elbow back! You shoot like a gully dwarf, half-elf. Keep both eyes open. You want to be able to tell how far away the target is, don't you?"

Finally, Tanis, his face damp with sweat in the heavy air, placed one arrow only two inches from the dragonseye. He turned triumphantly to Tyresian and the chattering crowd of commentators. Selena, dark smudges visible under her violet eyes, was draped like a cloak against Ulthen, giggling helplessly. Ulthen's medium-length, light brown hair swept against her shoulder as he attempted to stifle her laughter by placing one hand over her mouth. Litanas's brown eyes crinkled into slits as he snickered. By contrast, Lord Xenoth, the Speaker's adviser, stood by the door, his face impassive. Off to one side, Porthios looked unimpressed; he picked up Flint's toy and idly twirled the crossbar, sending the pair of fish whirling.

"There!" Tanis cried desperately. "What's wrong with that? It's almost a dragonseye!" He found himself fighting off tears, to his horror. If I cry now, I might as well move to Caergoth, he said to himself.

Porthios set the fish carving on a deserted bench and moved forward to take Tanis's smooth ash longbow. Pride battled with unease in his face, and for a short moment Tanis thought his cousin was embarrassed by the turn of events.

"Here." The elf lord's voice carried a ragged edge.

Seemingly effortlessly, Porthios swung the bow up and placed an arrow into the target, splitting Tanis's arrow with a thunk of steel arrowhead against wood and canvas. Wordless, he handed the bow back to the half-elf and began to turn toward the steel double doors. Again for a moment, Tanis saw discomfiture show in Porthios's deepest eyes.

"But you didn't get any closer than I did!" Tanis protested, and Porthios swung back. Several raindrops splashed on the two, and Tanis heard Selena order Litanas inside for her oiled-cloth cloak. Off to one side, Tyresian snorted.

With his back to the onlookers, an expression of sympathy crossing his features for the first time, Porthios reached toward Tanis and gripped his upper arm. "I aimed for your arrow, little cousin, not for the dragonseye," he said softly. His green eyes, so much like the Speaker's, flashed a warning.

"So you say now!" Tanis said loudly, despite himself. He felt his hands clench into fists at his side. A raindrop plopped on Porthios's head, flattening a lock of the dark blond hair. "I say you missed the dragonseye!"

He felt, rather than saw, Tyresian appear at his elbow, and heard the elf lord say smoothly, "That sounds like a challenge, my lord. Let's see how our hotheaded half-human friend can do against you, Porthios."

The sympathy flew from Porthios's face. "You challenge me?" he asked softly.

They were all looking at him. Tanis decided quickly. "I do!"

"It's hardly fair, Lord Porthios," Ulthen called from the bench. "The half-elf has barely begun his lessons. You do have a bit of an advantage."

"I can outshoot you, Porthios," Tanis cried recklessly.

Porthios watched Tanis carefully, then moved close. "Don't do this, Tanis," he murmured. "Don't force me to do this."

But the half-elf's temper had heated to boiling. "I can defeat you under any conditions, Porthios!" he said. A steady drizzle now began to mist the area. "You name them."

Porthios sighed and surveyed the moss at their feet. "Four arrows apiece," he finally said. "We will use your bow, Tanis."

Servants scurried to bring small pavilions that could shelter the silk-clad young nobles under their striped canvas. Lord Xenoth vanished, and returned with a hooded cape.

Tyresian appointed himself referee and, hair by now plastered against his angular skull, his pointed ears drooping slightly in the steady shower, took a stance between Porthios and Tanis. "Porthios Kanan names these conditions: Tanis Half-Elven will go first, shooting four times." His military voice boomed off the damp stone walls. "A dragonseye brings ten points. Hitting any other part of the circular target brings five points. Striking the hay bales outside the target carries two points. Missing the bales completely—" He smiled snidely—"loses the bowman ten points." He coughed. "Catching pneumonia in this godsforsaken weather costs both archers fifty points, but we all hope that won't happen." Litanas, who had returned by now with two extra cloaks, applauded the jest. "Scarlet arrows for Porthios, cobalt for Tanis. Let the contestants begin."

The rain grew harder. Occasional bunches of laurel leaves flopped to the ground, bounced, and lay still, like bits of forest flung by an angry, skybound god. Tanis took his position, and aimed through the slants of rain. The crowd behind him drew silent, to his surprise, though the weather may have had more to do with their quietude than courtesy had. Ulthen and Litanas looked like sea elves, their leggings damp to the knees. Selena, who had selected the favored spot in the yellow and white tent, had fared better.

Almost without thinking, Tanis released the arrow. It wobbled, caught in a fold of canvas to the right of the target, and stuck there, a bright splash of blue against a dun backing.

"Two points for the half-elf!" Tyresian called. "The next is Porthios."

The Speaker's heir, his face a mask of resignation, accepted the longbow from Tanis. "Remember, Tanis. I did not ask for this." Tanis met his stare impassively, as though they'd never met.

Porthios nocked an arrow, drew his arm back—and Tanis froze in humiliation.

Porthios was right-handed. Yet in this contest, he had reversed the bow, drawing the bow with his weaker arm. Tanis felt his face go white, then red. Shooting with the offarm was like saying Porthios could defeat the half-elf without trying. Porthios barely seemed to aim before the crimson-feathered arrow struck solidly in the dragonseye.

"Ten points for the full elf!" Tyresian cried.

The next turn brought the same result, and the score stood at twenty for Porthios and four for Tanis.

"It's not too late to back down," Porthios said softly as he handed the bow back to Tanis after his second dragonseye. For once, Porthios's friends had grown quiet. "We could call off this farce because of rain."

The words stung like the downpour that drilled into the moss around the two contestants. Even Tyresian had moved to one of the pavilions. Only the two combatants remained in the deluge. The half-elf stepped back to the line.

On the third round, Tanis's shot slashed through the rain toward the target—and past it, chipping a shard of stone from the wall behind.

"Minus ten!" Tyresian cried. "The score stands thus: Tanthalas Half-Elven, minus six in three. Porthios, twenty in two."

Porthios sighed and gestured in a way that suggested he'd like nothing better than to abandon the contest. "Go ahead," Tanis said. "Shoot."

Porthios, still shooting left-handed, took even less time on this round, and his arrow arced overhead, striking the target a hand's breadth from the center. He barely seemed to hear Tyresian call, "Five points. The score stands at minus six for the half-elf and twenty-five for Porthios."

"There's no way you can win," Porthios urged. "Let's stop this."

Tanis felt his jaw stiffen, and Porthios looked away as the half-elf took more care than ever lining up the shot, concentrating on what was to come, visualizing a successful hit in the dragonseye. Tanis closed his eyes, willing the gods to be with him on this one. He thought of the contemptuous stares of Xenoth, Selena, and the rest, and felt anger rise like a boil within him. He narrowed his eyes against the rain, lined up the target, and released the arrow.

The cobalt-feathered projectile arced slightly, and Tanis's heart sank.

Then it arced back to earth and neatly struck the dragonseye.

"Ten points! The score stands at plus four for Tanis,

twenty-five for Porthios."

Porthios refused the bow when Tanis handed it to him. "Let it rest, Half-Elven. You are new to the sport. Let it rest."

For a moment, Tanis almost succumbed to the sympathy that sprang up once more in Porthios's green eyes. Suddenly, Tanis was painfully aware of his surroundings—the damp green smell of wet moss, the perfume of battered apples lying beneath a nearby tree, the faint cheep of a sparrow hiding from the storm in the branches of a spruce.

Then Tyresian spoke up. "Perhaps you should have chosen a more 'human' form of competition than the bow, half-elf." Tanis felt rage mount in him again.

"Shoot, Porthios," he snapped. "Or forfeit."

Obviously tired of the charade, Porthios raised his arms and, sparing only a half-glance for the target, did as Tanis demanded. The arrow missed the target by more than ten paces.

"Final score: Porthios, at fifteen, is victor. A total of four for the half-human who seeks to show his expertise at an elven sport," Tyresian said flatly, and turned on a muddy heel to head into the palace.

Even Selena and Litanas gasped at the vitriol in Tyresian's words, but they followed Tyresian toward the steel doors, which shone dully through the gray downpour. Only Ulthen protested. "Unfair, Lord Tyresian," he complained. "He did the best he could."

Tyresian's reply was smooth. "And it wasn't enough, was it?"

As the courtyard emptied, Porthios stood uncertainly before Tanis, seemingly oblivious to the deluge that bent tree branches like reeds. Something like shame showed on the elf lord's hawklike face. "Tanis, I . . ." he said, and trailed off.

Tanis said nothing, merely bending deliberately to pick up the discarded bow; then he paced to the wall to retrieve the arrows, blue and red, their feathers sodden in the mud that welled up around the patches of moss.

"Tanis," Porthios repeated, and his face, for once, showed the strength of character that could be his as Speaker, if he only let it grow.

"I want a rematch," Tanis interjected.

Porthios's jaw dropped, and his upper lip drew up crookedly as though he couldn't believe what he'd heard. "Have you no sense, Tanthalas? You are thirty to my eighty years. I've embarrassed myself enough already with this travesty. Would you duel with Laurana, by the gods? That's what this comedy is to me."

Tanis intentionally misunderstood Porthios. "Perhaps this is humorous to you, Porthios. It is dead serious to me. I want a rematch."

Porthios's shoulders slumped in resignation. "It is raining, Tanis. I do not want to match bows with you again . . ."

"Not bows," the half-elf insisted. "Fists."

"What?" the elf lord snapped. Tanis could practically hear his cousin thinking, What a human method of settling a dispute.

All the spectators but Lord Xenoth had straggled inside for dry clothes and mulled wine. Xenoth hovered near the doorway however, possibly attracted by the cutting undertone in the pair's voices. With his puffy, white hair, puckered lips and silver robe, his hands folded before his chest, the old adviser resembled an aging long-haired cat, minus a few teeth but curious still.

Fine, Tanis thought. You want something to report back to the Speaker? This will do.

And he slugged Porthios in the face.

A second later, the Speaker's heir lay sprawled on his backside in the mud, a clod of dislodged moss still sailing through the air, a look of stunned shock on Porthios's face that might have been funny in another situation. The rain had caused the colors in his long, silken tunic to run, and rivulets of yellow, green, and blue ran down the elf lord's arms. He looked positively jaundiced with surprise, and Tanis burst into laughter.

. . . and found himself slung against a small peach tree. It was like being tossed headfirst into a huge Darkenwood porcupine. He felt twigs scratch his face, heard small branches crack around him, and felt wet, ripe fruit bump against him as he knocked them loose. A smell of squashed peaches rose in his nostrils.

The battle escalated quickly. Porthios fought to defend himself, but Tanis battled out of sheer rage. Porthios, older and quicker, could outmaneuver Tanis. But the human blood of the half-elf gave Tanis a strength that the lithe elf lord lacked. Thus, while Porthios drubbed the half-elf early on, Tanis soon felt the tide of the fight swing his way.

"Boys! Boys!" The new voice penetrated the miasma of anger clouding Tanis's brain. The blood stopped roaring in Tanis's ears long enough for him to focus on Lord Xenoth. The old adviser danced hysterically between Porthios and Tanis, all three of them mindless now of the rain that continued to pelt them. The dye of Porthios's tunic had been washed to sickly greenish yellow, and the front had been torn from collarbone to abdomen. A rivulet of blood dripped from the elf lord's mouth, and one eye was swelling shut. Xenoth's gown bore a splash of mud down the front. Tanis looked down at his own clothes; one mud-caked moccasin lay against a bench. The sand color of his breeches had disappeared under a coat of slimy mud. And the bow—the weapon that had started all this—was in pieces at his feet. Although spots of blood dotted his shirt, he didn't appear to be injured beyond minor bruises and cuts, however.

Then Tanis's breath caught in his throat. For on the granite path, cracked and broken, lay Flint's carving.

As the wheezing adviser helped Porthios into the palace—screeching, "You'll hear about this, half-elf!"—Tanis dropped to his knees and tenderly picked up the fragments of the carving. One fish survived unbroken, but the thin chain that had attached it to the crossbar had snapped. The crossbar itself was missing. And the base—the delightfully carved representation of the bottom of a rocky stream—had cracked right through the middle. He gathered the pieces together, finding the crossbar in a puddle about five paces away, and wrapped them in the front tail of his loose shirt.

Tanis looked up. The door had slammed behind Xenoth and Porthios, and he stood alone in the gray courtyard.

The rain continued to pour down.

* * * * *

The Speaker of the Sun strode swiftly down the corridor, his forest green cloak billowing out behind him like some fantastic storm cloud, its golden trim flashing like strange, metallic lightning. But it was the lightning in his eyes that caused startled servants and courtiers to step quickly from his path as he passed through the palace on his way toward the family chambers. All knew from experience it took much to anger the Speaker, but mercy to those unfortunate enough to be caught in his path when he was finally moved to ire.

"Tanis!" he called out sternly as he pushed through the door to the half-elf's bedchamber. "Tanthalas!"

The room was unlit by lamp, but a form, silhouetted in the red light of Lunitari, which streamed in through one window, shifted on the bed.

"Tanthalas," Solostaran repeated.

The figure sat up. "Yes." The voice was like lead—flat, heavy, immovable.

The Speaker moved to strike a flint and light a small lamp. He looked over at the slumped figure on the bed, and caught his breath.

Bruises and scabs stood out against the pale skin of Tanis's face and arms. He shifted his weight, inhaled sharply and grasped his side, then just as quickly sat up straighter.

Over the years Solostaran had learned to force his emotions into the cool mask that he presented at court. That training stood him in good stead now as he watched the adopted nephew he loved so well struggle to maintain a look of nonchalance—as though a wealth of welts and bruises were a normal part of everyday life.

The Speaker remained standing, voice devoid of warmth. "To be fair, I will tell you that Porthios refuses to explain what happened. And apparently he has cowed, coerced, or cajoled everyone else out there—even Lord Xenoth, to my surprise—into keeping silent as well. Will *you* tell me what occurred in the courtyard today?"

The figure on the bed remained silent. Then Tanis looked

down at his lap and shook his head.

The Speaker's voice continued implacably. "Somehow, I am not surprised at your reticence, Tanthalas. And I will not force you to speak—if, indeed, I could. This appears to be something that you and Porthios must work out on your own. But I will tell you one thing." He stopped speaking. "Are you listening?"

The figure nodded but didn't look up.

The Speaker went on. "Good. Then let me tell you this: This will not happen again. Ever. I will not have my son and my . . . nephew rolling in the dirt, acting like . . . like . . ."

"Like humans," Tanis finished softly. The phrase shivered in the evening air.

Solostaran sighed, searched for another way to phrase it, then decided that bluntness might work best. "Yes, if you will. Like humans."

The figure on the bed waited several heartbeats and nodded again. Solostaran stepped closer; Tanis held something in his hands. A carved wooden fish? A shock of suspicion went through the Speaker.

"Don't tell me that all of this was over a broken toy," he demanded.

When Tanis didn't answer, Solostaran sighed and prepared to go. "I will send Miral with salves. Get some sleep." His tone grew gentler. "Can I have anything or anyone sent to you, Tanthalas?"

The reply, when it came, was so soft that the Speaker barely heard the words.

"Flint Fireforge."

Chapter 6

A New Friend

"You can drop that over by the furnace, lad," Flint
said as he led the way into the clutter of his shop.

With a groan of relief, Tanis let go of the heavy sack. It
plummeted to the floor.

"I didn't mean that literally," Flint growled at the winded-
looking half-elf as he carefully set down the sack that had
rested on his own shoulder.

"Sorry," Tanis said wearily, rubbing his aching arm.

The two had just returned from an ore-gathering trip,
though Tanis wondered now how he had ever managed to
let the dwarf talk him into it. An hour or two ago, in the
early morning sunshine, Flint had led the way south out of
the city, empty sacks in hand. After a pleasant mile, the forest had given way to a rocky outcrop, littered with rusty-

looking chunks of stone that Flint said was iron ore. Ten minutes later, Tanis had found himself staggering under the weight of the load the dwarf had lifted onto his shoulders.

"Wouldn't it be easier to bring a horse to carry this back?" Tanis had asked through clenched teeth.

"A horse?" Flint said with a snort. "Are you daft? Reorx! No dwarf in his right mind would trust a crazy animal to carry his ore."

Tanis knew there was little point in arguing with the dwarf. Flint had lifted his sack—which must have held five times the ore Tanis's had—as if it were filled with feathers and started back toward the city. Tanis had followed, stumbling along as best he could, reminding himself to be wary next time Flint suggested they go for "a nice little walk."

Tanis had visited with Flint nearly every day, ever since the Speaker sent the dwarf a message late in the evening a week ago, asking him to go to the half-elf in his quarters in the palace. They'd spoken of precious little of importance in that visit—weather and Solace and metalworking and carving—but Tanis, looking a bit battered, seemed to draw some comfort from the meeting. Since then, the half-elf's scrapes and bruises had nearly faded, but the rift between him and the Speaker's heir would be much longer in healing.

"But how are you going to turn that rock into iron?" Tanis asked now as the dwarf lifted the heavy cover of the furnace out behind the shop.

"You'll only learn by doing," Flint told him. "At least, that was what my father's father, old Reghar Fireforge, used to say. Or so my mother says he said."

The furnace was round, as tall as the dwarf, made of thick, fire-scorched mudbricks. The bottom was funnel-shaped with a small hole, and below that rested a crucible the size of a helmet. Under Flint's direction, Tanis half-filled the furnace with layers of iron ore, hard coal, and a chalky kind of rock that Flint called limestone. Through a small door in the bottom of the furnace, Flint lit the coal, then Tanis helped him replace the lid.

"What now?" Tanis asked.

"We wait," Flint said, dusting his sooty hands off. "Once

that coal starts to burn hot, the iron will melt right out of the rock, leaving the slag behind, and drip down into the crucible. But that will take a good day, so we might as well turn our hands to another task."

Flint showed Tanis what the iron would look like after it had collected in the bowl: a heavy, black lump he called "pig iron," though Tanis didn't think it looked at all piglike.

"Is that what you forge into swords and daggers?" Tanis asked, and Flint guffawed.

"You need a few lessons in metalsmithing, lad," he commented.

"Me?" Tanis asked. He had watched the dwarf at work at the forge, and he knew how much strength and will Flint exerted to force the metal into the shape he desired. How could Tanis ever make something as hard as iron do what he wanted?

The sparks in Flint's eyes told Tanis there was no room for argument. The half-elf listened carefully as the dwarf explained that pig iron was too brittle to make a good blade; it had to be heated to melting again. Flint showed Tanis how, putting the pig iron in a crucible and setting it amidst the coals in the fire pit by the heavy iron anvil. He made Tanis work the bellows until the coals looked like liquid jewels. As the iron melted, it gave off curls of black smoke. When it cooled, it would be wrought iron, Flint explained, and not nearly so brittle as pig iron.

"But if it's too soft, it couldn't possibly make a good sword," Tanis complained.

Flint nodded. With a pair of heavy tongs, he heated a lump of wrought iron in the coals until it was glowing hot. He set it on the face of the anvil and sprinkled it with a fine black dust that looked almost like coal dust, except it was shinier. Flint called it Reorx's Breath.

"You see, long ago," Flint said, "a wicked thane ordered his smith to forge an iron sword that would not lose its edge. If the smith failed, he would be put to death. It seemed an impossible task, but the smith was a favorite of Reorx's, and the god breathed upon the smith's soft iron sword, making it strong and hard, so that its edge would long remain bright and true."

With his hammer, Flint folded the glowing lump of metal over on itself and then pounded it flat. He heated it in the coals again, sprinkled on more of the black dust, and then pounded it flat once more. He repeated this several times.

"What we have now," Flint said with satisfaction, holding the hot lump of metal with the tongs, "is a piece of metal that will be hard enough to be strong without being so brittle that it will easily break. This, Tanis, is steel."

Tanis gazed at the glowing metal in a new light. Gold was beautiful, and elves delighted in silver, but in these dark times, steel was the most precious substance on Krynn.

"What are you going to do with it now?" Tanis asked.

"I'm not going to do anything with it," Flint rejoined. "You are."

"I can't forge steel!"

"Neither could I until I tried," Flint said gruffly, and he thrust a heavy hammer into Tanis's hand.

Obviously, there was no way out of this. Tanis sighed. First he had to decide what to make, but that was easy enough. For a long time, he had wanted a hunting knife like Porthios had.

Guiding his hands, the dwarf showed Tanis how to heat the steel, how to hold it on the anvil with the tongs, and how to strike it with the hammer so that none of the hot, flying scale hit his hand.

"Don't just flail at it, lad," Flint said. "It's your will as much as your arm that shapes the steel. Picture what you want it to look like. Get the image good and clear. Then strike the steel and see what happens."

Tanis followed instructions, thinking how much easier it was to learn from Flint or Miral than from Tyresian. And the knife began to take shape.

Tanis felt a warmth creep up his arm and into his chest. It's only the heat of the forge, he told himself, but somehow he knew that wasn't so, and he thought that maybe he understood a little of what Flint felt when he stood here at the anvil, discovering a blade in a lifeless lump of metal and releasing it with fire and hammer, with heart and mind.

"Now quench it while it's still red-hot," Flint said, and

Tanis plunged the thin, pointed strip of steel into the half-barrel of water by the anvil. Steam hissed into the air, glowing red in the light of the furnace. "Quenching makes the metal harder," Flint explained.

Tanis pulled the blacked, rough strip of steel out of the water and looked at it critically. "It doesn't really look like a knife."

"Nonsense," Flint growled. "Your knife is in there, all right. It just needs to be polished and to have its edge sharpened on the grindstone. You do that, and bind a hilt to it, and you'll see."

Tanis grinned then. The strip seemed lopsided, and it wasn't exactly flat, but it would be *his* knife. "Thank you, Flint," he said, but the dwarf shook his head.

"You're the one who did it, not me," Flint answered.

*   *   *   *   *

Flint reflected. The autumn days were dwindling. The leaves of the aspen trees shone in the sun like burnished gold, the oaks like beaten copper. More than once, now, the dawn light had sparkled off a glazing of frost on the grass and trees. But as the morning wore on, the frost would melt, the sun would burn the damp mist from the streets, and by afternoon, although the clear air was cool, the warm light spilling through the city would be drowsy.

Behind Flint's shop stood a low wall of mossy stones, and beyond it stretched a small meadow, which ended in the ivy-tangled wall of a grove of aspen and pine. Unlike the countless gardens and courtyards of Qualinost, the meadow and the grove were not tended. Rather, they were simply remnants of the forest, left as they had been since before Kith-Kanan had led his people to Qualinesti. It was a reminder of the time when there had been no city, and no elves, but only the deep, shaded forest and the music of the wind.

Sometimes Flint would take a break from the smoky heat of the forge and come sit on the wall, pulling the clean air into his lungs as he dangled his stumpy legs over the edge. The grove of trees across the meadow tended to make him think of his journey from Solace, through the forest of Qualinesti, and once again he found himself wondering if he shouldn't be on the road soon. *These days are bright and warm, Flint,* he told himself, *but sure as steel is strong, winter's just around the corner. And while I wouldn't doubt its touch is a mild one here within these woods, in the rest of the world that won't be the case, and if you were fool enough to try, you'd be frozen clean through long before you ever reached Solace.*

But there always seemed to be one more thing he had to do before he could possibly consider leaving. He had promised the Lady Selena an entire set of goblets, crafted to look like the gilded blooms of tulips. Those alone had taken him a fortnight of work, but when they were finished, he found himself hurrying to fashion a pair of intricate wedding bands he had promised a young noble anxious to court an elf maiden. And then the captain of the Speaker's guard stepped through the door of the shop, despairing of the balance of his long sword, which he claimed the elven smiths had had no luck in correcting. The problem was so obvious to Flint's eye—the decorative handguard on the hilt had thrown the balance completely off—that he would've thought a good bit less of himself if he hadn't agreed to help. Sure as his beard kept growing, the tasks kept coming.

Other than a new set of clothes, compliments of the Speaker, Flint looked hardly different from the day he had first set foot in Qualinost, with his dark hair tied behind his neck and his bushy beard tucked neatly into his belt. However, he had traded his heavy, iron-soled boots for a pair made of soft gray leather, and although his feet were still twice as big as any elf's, at least his footsteps didn't sound quite as much like thunder now.

And his clothes . . . Green wasn't Flint's usual color, but the tailor the Speaker had sent to him four days ago had clucked his tongue and shaken his head at the rust-colored wool Flint had picked out for his new autumn outfit. The old elf insisted on emerald green, but Flint protested that it was too gaudy. However, when Flint finally tried it on, the old tailor clapped his hands.

"It's definitely you, Master Fireforge," he had declared.

"You think so?" Flint had asked, scowling at himself in the polished silver mirror.

"Indeed," the tailor responded firmly. "You look positively dashing."

"You do, Flint," Tanis had said from his seat in a corner.

Dashing? Flint had thought, looking at his reflection critically, and then he grinned at himself. "Well, maybe I do, at that," he said. Tanis laughed.

Now, the half-elf, brownish red hair bouncing, sprinted around the corner of Flint's beetle-browed shop—made more squatty-looking by the contrast with nearby elven homes.

"Lucky me. Company," Flint snorted, though he smiled all the same. "Where's that imp Laurana? I'm surprised she didn't drag you off to play some noisy game or some such."

"She tried," Tanis said. He plucked two apples off a laden tree, tossed the better one to Flint, found a comfortable spot on the wall, and leaned back and closed his eyes, letting the sunlight fall on his eyelids. With a start, Flint realized that despite the slightly pointed ears and the faint slant to his eyes, Tanis looked very much like a human child at the moment. It made the dwarf think of Solace again, and a twinge of homesickness gripped him.

"I didn't feel like a game, not today," Tanis resumed. "Besides, Gilthanas was with her, and I don't think he wanted me to join in." He opened his eyes.

"Bah," Flint said, tossing his apple core over his shoulder and wiping his hands on his beard. "I'm sure Laurana's brother doesn't feel that way."

Tanis said seriously, turning toward the dwarf, "He doesn't want to have anything to do with me anymore. I always thought he was like my own brother, but now all he seems to want to do is follow Porthios around like a puppy. And Porthios certainly never acted like my brother."

A shadow passed over the half-elf's rugged features. Flint sighed and laid one of his strong, calloused hands on Tanis's shoulder. "Now, lad," he said softly, if gruffly, "there's no telling why folk do what they do sometimes. But don't hold it against him. I'm sure it will all work out."

"I've got a pretty good idea why he's been acting that way," Tanis said, but didn't elaborate. And Flint, sensing that there were areas in the half-elf's life in which he needed his privacy, said nothing. Of course, Flint had wormed the tale of the Porthios-Tanis match out of Laurana—only the gods knew where she'd found it out—but the dwarf had forgone mentioning his knowledge to his new friend.

They basked in the sun for a time, and eventually Tanis asked Flint to tell him more about the outside world and of Solace. It was a common theme. The boy couldn't seem to get enough of such tales.

"But then what did you do after the four highwaymen had knocked out the guards?" Tanis asked him. Flint was relating the tale of the day a band of brigands had stirred up trouble in the Inn of the Last Home.

"Well, I'll tell you, lad, it was looking dark. So I hefted my hammer in my hand—" He grabbed a stray stick firmly for emphasis—"and then I . . . er . . . and then I . . ." Flint was suddenly conscious of Tanis's shining eyes gazing at him.

"And then you what, Flint?" Tanis asked excitedly. "You did battle with all four at once?"

"Well, er, not exactly," Flint said. Somehow this all sounded better when he told it after a few tankards of ale. "You see, there was this stray mug on the floor, and, well, it being dark, and, mind you, I wasn't watching my feet . . ."

"You tripped," Tanis said, a smile lighting his face.

"I most certainly did *not* trip!" Flint fairly roared. "I feinted, and my hammer caught the leader of the brigands square in the forehead, just like that." He smacked a half-rotted apple with the stick. The apple exploded in a juicy spray, and Tanis got the rather graphic point.

"That's wonderful!" Tanis said, and Flint snorted as if it were nothing.

"Sometimes I wish I had been born in Solace," Tanis said softly then, looking off into the distance, to the north, where he knew Solace lay. He tossed the apple core away, and bid Flint farewell for the day.

* * * * *

True to the hopeful words the Speaker had uttered when the dwarf had first arrived in Qualinost, Flint and the Speaker had become unlikely friends during the course of the past months. Half a year ago, had anyone told Flint he would find himself companion to the elven lord of Qualinesti, he would have bought the fellow a tankard for telling such an uproarious joke. Although there seemed a world of difference between the tall, regal elf lord and the short, uncomplicated dwarf, each had an openness in his point of view that made bridging the gap a simple step.

And so Flint had found himself walking through the palace gardens side by side with the Speaker, talking of distant lands and ages, or sitting at the Speaker's right at a courtly dinner. There were grumbles from some of the courtiers, of course, but Flint discovered from whom Porthios and Laurana had inherited their stubbornness.

In recent weeks, especially, Flint had grown as close to Solostaran as he had to Tanis. The Speaker's ceremonial guards, each wearing a breastplate decorated with the emblem of the Sun and the Tree wrought in silver filigree, didn't bother to stop him at the Speaker's anteroom at the Tower anymore. Rather, they greeted Flint with a grin and ushered him forward to knock on the door to the Speaker's glass-walled anteroom. And the Speaker's private servants had strict orders to keep the silver bowl on the Speaker's desk filled with the dried fruits and glazed nuts that the dwarf favored. Today, the autumn sun streamed through the glass onto the new green rushes that had been strewn upon the floor, and the light in the room had a soft, heavy quality, like the light in a forest clearing.

The Speaker said he hoped Tanis wasn't becoming a pest by following Flint so closely.

"Bah," Flint said with a snort. "I can't imagine hanging about a smoky forge with an ill-tempered dwarf like me can be all that much of a joy. But don't you worry over Tanis. He's a good lad."

The Speaker smiled and nodded. "Yes, I think he is." He

stood up then and moved back toward the window, gazing out into the distance as if pausing to consider something. Then he turned around and regarded the dwarf with his clear eyes. "Tanis means a great deal to me, Flint, and I think he is your friend as well.

"I know you've heard the circumstances of his birth, how my brother, Kethrenan, was slain by a band of rogue humans and how his wife, Elansa, was attacked." He sighed. "But I don't think you understand how dark a time that truly was. Those months Elansa carried the child within her, it seemed as if she had died already herself. She appeared lost. And when he was born, she passed on. But Tanis was son of my brother's wife. I could not turn my back on him."

It seemed almost as if the Speaker were arguing with someone who opposed him, rather than telling a tale to a friend. "And so I brought him with me here, to raise as my own child."

He sighed and then returned to sit facing the dwarf. Flint fidgeted with the end of his beard. It was a hard tale. "There were those who did not care for my decision," the Speaker said softly, and Flint looked up. "Not all seemed able to forgive the child the circumstances of his birth. A child, Flint—a tiny child! What fault of his was it that my brother was dead? What fault of his that Elansa had gone as well?" A trace of remembered anguish flickered across the Speaker's face.

"And those who didn't accept him . . . ?" Flint asked softly.

"They remain, and as is the way of my people, little have they changed. I am still unsure just how much of it Tanis has noticed—though I suspect there is much the lad does not tell me. I can only hope his will be a strong enough heart to bear it. I suppose it was little enough favor I did, bringing him here. But do you see why it had to be so, Flint?"

The Speaker regarded the dwarf intently, his dark blond hair glinting in the strong light. "Despite the peace we have wrought for ourselves here, these last centuries since the Cataclysm have been dark ones, times of sorrow and upheaval. Tanis is a child of that sorrow. And if I can't bring joy to *his* life, then how can the sorrow be healed for any of us? For the elves or for Qualinesti?" The Speaker shook his head, and then smiled faintly. "I'm afraid I am rambling." He stood, and Flint followed suit. "I'm sorry to have taken so much of your time. I simply wanted to tell you I am glad that you've been a friend for Tanis. I fear you are probably his first, aside from his cousins."

Flint nodded and clomped to the door, but before he left, he turned around and gazed at his elven friend, his blue eyes thoughtful. "Thank you," Flint said gruffly. "He's one of my two first as well." And the dwarf left, shutting the door behind him.

* * * * *

The dwarf's first stay in Qualinesti ended at last. He and Tanis and the others stood at the edge of the city, by the bridge that crossed the confluence of the two rivers, the one of Tears and the other of Hope. The morning was gray and cool, and there was a sharpness to the air that smelled like snow.

"So you really have to go," Tanis said softly, gazing across the ravine.

"Aye, I think it's time I did," Flint answered. "If I'm lucky, I'll beat the first snowfall home."

Tanis only nodded. "I'll miss you," he said finally.

"Humph!" Flint said gruffly. "You'll most likely forget me inside of ten minutes, I wouldn't wonder." But weathered skin crinkled around the dwarf's eyes, and Tanis smiled.

The dwarf bade farewell to the small group gathered by the bridge: his friend the Speaker and the hooded mage, who restrained Laurana from exploring the ravine's edge. Lord Xenoth was conspicuously absent, as were Porthios and his friends. After many promises to return, Flint followed his guide and clomped across the bridge, though not without booming an oath or two that echoed off the cold stone.

With a smile and a sigh, Tanis gathered his gray cloak more tightly around him and turned to walk back to the city.

Chapter 7

A Death in the Forest

A.C. 308, Early Spring

Flint loathed horses—claimed to be allergic to them—and wouldn't ride one to save his life—well, maybe then. At any rate, he patted the neck of his gray mule, Fleet-foot, and surveyed the silvery aspens and broad oaks of Qualinesti with fond regard.

After twenty years of coming and going between Solace and the Tower of the Sun, he was almost familiar with the trail to Qualinost—a claim even few elves could make beyond the specially trained guides the Speaker of the Sun hired to escort visitors there and back. Of course, he occasionally took a wrong turn or two, but the hill dwarf who couldn't find his way by forest signs was a poor excuse for a dwarf, he thought.

Truth to tell, however, he wasn't quite sure where he was at the moment. He sat back on Fleetfoot, noting the rich earthen scent of the forest. A squirrel chattered at him from a bur oak and flung a clump of green leaves down upon him. The dwarf reached with broad fingers, deftly caught the bunch, and tossed it back into the air at the creature. "Save it for your nest!" he cried. "For if I'm not mistaken, you have family duties on your mind these days." Another squirrel appeared on a nearby branch, and the first creature, tossing one last insult at the mounted dwarf, darted off after it.

Flint drew in a large breath. It was spring, and time to return to Qualinost. It had been a hard journey back to Solace, that autumn after his first stay in the elven city. The snow had begun to fly just as he'd reached the fringes of the grove of vallenwoods, the great trees that housed the village of Solace in their branches. His elven guide had quickly disappeared back down the road, and Flint had been left alone to trudge through the snow to his little house on the ground. He found his home cold and empty, save for a single mouse cowering in the corner.

It had been a lonely winter, twenty years ago, despite the warmth of the hearth and the companionship at the Inn of the Last Home; the following spring, he had found his thoughts turning toward the forests to the south, and Qualinost, wondering how Tanis was.

Not a week later, Flint had encountered a stranger in the Inn who turned out to be none other than a Qualinesti elf bearing a message from the Speaker: Flint was welcome to return, should he wish it. And he did. His next stay in Qualinost lasted more than a year before he grew lonely for human folk again. Eventually, with some variation, he'd worked into the pattern of visits that he found himself in now, living in Qualinost from the earliest spring to the latest autumn. Lately, he'd begun to wonder why he returned to his joyless little home in Solace at all.

The Speaker of the Sun had given up bothering to send for the dwarf each spring, knowing that Flint's love of the city would draw him back south, until one spring morning would find the dwarf clattering across the bridge west of Qualinost. Flint, queasy about heights, never crossed the structure without paragraphs of oaths that would make a Caergoth longshoreman's skin blister.

His entrance never ceased to amuse the elves.

Now, though, he still had several hours' ride ahead of him. He prodded the laden Fleetfoot in the flanks with his booted heels, hoping that for once she would pick up the pace without protest.

Naturally, she balked.

* * * * *

Han-Telio Teften had had a good trading expedition. He whistled tunelessly and, not for the first time, blessed the Speaker of the Sun, whose relaxed attitudes toward relations with nonelves had made it easier in recent years to make a living by trade.

The young elf's brown eyes glowed as, for the fiftieth time this trip, he slipped a slender hand into his canvas saddlebags, each time unwittingly tightening the knot in the thong that held the bag nearly shut. As he and his horse entered a widening of the trail, a small clearing, he drew out a small leather sack and shook the contents into his palm. Three white opals shone translucent against his weathered, tanned hand.

"Beautiful," he breathed. "And the key to my future."

A rustle off to his left brought his head up, a wary look on his face. Brigands had been virtually unknown on the inland trails of Qualinesti for years, but recent months had brought reports of lost travelers. After minutes without incident, however, Han-Telio returned to admiring the opals and fell to listing the wonderful things they would buy.

"A home, that's first," he mused. "And furnishings, of course. And a plot of land for my Ginevra to grow fragrant herbs on."

Then, of course, there was Ginevra herself, the sloe-eyed elf who had promised to marry him once he could handle his part of the wedding expenses. Her practical-minded vow had spurred him to spend months on the road, trading fine elven jewelry, silken cloth, quartz sculptings, and, of course, her popular herbal remedies. And now he had finally earned enough to meet his half of the arrangement.

He didn't see the creature right away. It was the smell that first caught his notice—a sweet smell of rotting garbage. The odor, and the sudden shiver of his horse, caught his attention.

Han-Telio looked up and felt his limbs go leaden. Waiting in the trail not twenty paces ahead stood a huge lizardlike creature. Its hide was dun-colored, the same hue as the worn dirt path behind it. Horns about the length of the elf's arm tilted back from the lizard's horny brow. It sported five toes with six-inch claws on both front feet. Its mouth was slightly open; each exhalation sent another cloud of fetid breath swirling toward the elven trader. The creature, resembling a wingless dragon, had a horned body as long as four elves, with a thin, whiplike tail only slightly shorter.

"A tylor!" the trader said. The beasts were rare even in the arid regions they preferred. None had ever inhabited the forests of Qualinesti. And even though the trader had ranged far from the elven homeland in his travels, he'd never seen a tylor.

But he knew they were strong, capable of great magic if brute force didn't succeed, . . . and deadly.

Beneath him, Han-Telio's horse stood stock-still in fright, eyes wide, nostrils flaring, forelegs locked. Han-Telio sawed at the reins, but the animal was heedless of his commands and kicks. The woods lay silent of all sounds except the creaking of the oak branches overhead.

"Your steed will not move, elf."

Han-Telio looked around wildly, hoping that a rescuer—preferably one armed more heavily than an elven trader—stood ready to pitch into battle with him. The voice had been deep but raspy, as though air flowed over scales of sandstone. Over scales. . . Han-Telio felt another flood of fear pitch through him. He looked at the lizard.

"That's right, elf. I speak."

The tylor spoke Common.

The sounds spurred Han-Telio into quavery action; he slipped the opals into a pocket of his split tunic, and, hands shaking as the creature advanced two paces, its dangerous, sharp-edged tail twitching, the elven trader attempted to draw his canvas saddlebags open wider, to draw forth the short sword that he kept there.

But the knot in the thong that bound the saddlebags resisted his efforts, tangled hopelessly. The tylor moved another step forward; the smell grew stronger. Han-Telio recognized the odor.

It was the stench of rotting meat.

The voice rumbled again. "Where are you going, elf? Your horse does not appear willing to carry you."

Han-Telio was not sure why he answered. Perhaps to win time. "To Ginevra," he replied, yanking with one hand at the reins and with the other at the saddlebags. He breathed raggedly. "I must get home to Ginevra."

Finally, the trader, with strength born of fear, snapped the thong and drew forth his short sword.

When Han-Telio looked up again, the tylor, head weaving as it sought to mesmerize its target, stood mere paces away. As the trader watched, fascinated despite himself, the creature passed before a spruce tree, then before a boulder of quartz, and its flesh turned first green, then rose-pink, then back to dun as the gray-brown path once again comprised the creature's background. Camouflage, the elf found himself thinking, irrelevantly. With a burst of bravado, he pointed his sword at the beast.

"A slender pig-sticker like that short sword will do you little against the likes of me, elf," the monster thundered, its plated face two arm lengths away. Then the tylor rent the clearing with a screech that shook Han-Telio to his spine.

The trader's horse, terrified finally into movement, reared and wheeled to flee. But the tylor lunged and caught the horse by the neck in its jagged jaws as Han-Telio screamed and leaped from the animal. The trader screamed again as the tail of the tylor lashed with cobralike speed.

The elven body that hit the rocklike floor of the path was split nearly in two.

Three opals rolled to a stop in a pool of blood.

*   *   *   *   *

The roar came from a distance as Flint tugged vainly on the reins of his mule, trying fruitlessly to browbeat the beast into resuming the trip to Qualinost. For a moment, Flint stood frozen, his alert blue eyes inches from Fleetfoot's dumb brown ones. Then a thin scream rocketed through the forest, and Flint's hand went to his battle-axe as he twisted on the trail, seeking to locate the direction of the sound. Behind him, Fleetfoot shuffled nervously.

The scream came again, louder, but ended abruptly. It came from directly in front.

"Reorx's thunder!" the dwarf exclaimed, throwing himself on Fleetfoot's back. "Move, you cursed mule, or I'll see you fed to a minotaur and enjoy the sight!"

Fleetfoot, for once, responded, and gallumphed down the trail as fast as her huge feet would carry her. Flint pulled out his short sword as he rode. Ten minutes later—an eternity for the anxious dwarf—Fleetfoot came to a wheezing halt in what was unmistakably the site of a battle.

The dwarf sat quietly at first, not dismounting, trying to gauge whether the creature that caused such mayhem still lurked in the area. Huge slash marks showed in the tough wood of the oaks. Dozens of slender aspens lay in splinters on both sides of the trail. The packed earth beneath his feet displayed a splash of what was undeniably blood, already fading from scarlet to brown. A rose-quartz boulder up ahead showed a wide smear of blood, drying against the backdrop of dense underbrush. Fleetfoot stirred as if to bolt. Flint calmed the mule and slipped quietly from the saddle.

The surrounding forest was silent of all but the most sylvan of noises, as though nothing on Krynn was amiss. Tiny blood-root flowers stood open in the damp earth off to Flint's right, but he couldn't see more than ten feet beyond them into the underbrush, fresh with new-sprung leaves. Battle-axe in his right hand, short sword in his left, he waited. A slight breeze, scented with old snow, raw soil, and a salty odor of blood, moved a few black and gray hairs in Flint's beard.

Nothing happened.

Relaxing only slightly, grasping the mule's reins in the same hand that held the short sword, the stocky dwarf moved warily around the clearing, pausing to note the claw marks, the slashes, that had ravaged the vegetation.

"Clearly a creature with a long tail," Flint mused, never loosening his grip on his battle-axe and constantly searching the undergrowth with sharp eyes. "Built like a lizard. But in woodlands?"

He felt his eyes drift out of focus as he moved slowly in a circle. The bur oak, the boulder, another oak, and a dozen aspens went by in a blur.

"A woodland lizard makes little sense," he reflected, gaze coming to rest on a knobby oak about twenty feet away. As he pondered, his vision eased back into focus.

Another smear of blood was daubed on a piece of wood jutting out halfway up the tree trunk. Above that, the trunk. . .

. . . was looking back at him.

And the eyes were intelligent.

Flint felt the tylor's razor-sharp jaws snap past his head as he hurtled across the clearing and into the underbrush. He dived to the wet earth and heard, rather than saw, Fleetfoot thunder by. He scrambled up again, beard clotted with clay, and looked frantically about for the monster. What in Reorx's forge was that thing? he thought.

The creature, temporarily caught between an oak tree and a spruce, lunged again, snapped the evergreen, and pounded across the clearing.

It came right at Flint, who took off running with a speed that would have stunned his slower-moving dwarven relatives. After fifty paces or so, he caught up with Fleetfoot, who, being larger, couldn't slip through the trees as quickly as Flint could. However, the mule was stronger than the dwarf, so the race appeared to be neck and neck. Behind them, the tylor pushed trees aside in its bloodlust, and roared. The dwarf and mule crashed through underbrush until Flint no longer had any idea where he was.

"Reorx!" he gasped as he dashed into another clearing, the mule a half-pace behind. In the center of the opening stood a huge dead oak—so large that it would have taken six or seven men to encircle it with their arms. One side showed a shadow—no, a depression in the trunk.

No, an opening. The tree was hollow.

As the tylor crashed out of the woods behind Flint, the dwarf bolted into the opening in the tree. The mule followed close on his heels.

"Fleetfoot!" the dwarf protested as the smelly mule, lathered with sweat, pressed against him in the dark interior of the oak. Flint turned toward the gap in the trunk, half-thinking to shove the mule back through it.

But the opening was gone. Outside, the tylor roared and screeched in protest, pounding against the tree again and again. Then it began to chant magic words.

Flint found himself standing in utter darkness, short arms flung around the neck of a trembling mule. At least he *thought* it was Fleetfoot who was trembling.

"God's thunder," he muttered. "Now what?"

He groped along Fleetfoot's back to the saddlepack and drew out flint and steel. Moments later, as the trunk continued to reverberate with the sound of magical chanting and the force of the tylor's blows, Flint, groping, found a stick on the pine needle-littered floor of the tree and lit it. Fleetfoot cuddled ever closer to the dwarf, who swatted her aside with an irritable hand.

"Move over, stupid," he hissed. Flint held up the glowing chunk of wood and examined the bottom of the trunk. There was a thin layer of soil, which he poked a stubby finger into—and felt wood.

That would not seem surprising in a hollow tree, except that his fingers also felt something carved into that wood.

Nudging Fleetfoot aside again, Flint brushed aside the rich soil until the carving stood exposed.

"Reorx's hammer!" he breathed. "A rune!" He leaned closer, heedless of the torch, which suddenly spat out a cinder, smack into the dry pine needles. The needles flared up in a blaze, which soon spread in a circle to the wooden floor of the trunk. The mule stood and trembled in a cylinder of flame, disregarding Flint's attempts to haul her out of the blaze.

Flint was never sure what happened next. One moment he was tugging at the halter of a stalled mule, and the next moment he was standing in a huge oaken chamber, seemingly *below* where he'd been just a second before.

There was no sound in the chamber but the harried breathing of a hysterical pack mule and an only slightly calmer dwarf. He held up his makeshift light. A regiment could have fit comfortably in the spherical chamber.

"By the gods, we're in the heart of the oak!" he told the mule, who appeared unimpressed. The dwarf stooped and poked at the floor with his short sword. "This tree is still alive." He stood erect again and gazed around the chamber.

Firelight flickered off coppery walls of living wood, leaving knots and burls in shadow but exposing the smoother, rounded portions of the tree's interior. Several passages appeared to open onto the chamber, much like enormous hollow roots.

Off to his left, Fleetfoot sighed and nickered, seeming finally to be emerging from the panic of the moments before. The mule looked around, an expression of torpid curiosity rising in her eyes. Then the creature spied what appeared to be an enormous water trough in the very center of the oaken room, and, mulelike, she acted immediately upon her impulse. She shuffled over to the wooden trough and snuffled the edge with quivering nostrils.

Clear liquid filled the basin, which was about five feet across. On the surface floated a lily—a golden lily, with the leaves of a normal water flower but a blossom of pure gold. Flint reached forward and touched the blossom with a reverent finger. Something so beautiful could not be evil, he thought.

As he touched it, the blossom opened and the pure voice of an elven woman chimed through the chamber:

"Well met, well met, the portal is set, the star is silver, the sun is gold, cast your coin where you're going, then take hold and touch the gold."

Flint drew back, casting a suspicious glare around the room, as though expecting a beautiful elf with a voice like a bell to step out from one of the rootlike caverns. "What should I do?" he whispered and turned, as if for an answer, toward Fleetfoot, who gazed back dimwittedly. "Oh, of all the creatures to get trapped in a magic tree with," the dwarf said disgustedly. "Well, it said to cast in a coin, that the portal is set. A portal's a door," he explained to Fleetfoot. "And it seems to me I see no real door hereabouts, so perhaps this flower will help us. As my mother would say, 'A bird in the hand makes light work.' "

Flint dug into a pocket and drew out the sum total of his winter's wages from Solace: one gold coin. "Well, if I starve here, it doesn't matter if I'm broke or not," he reasoned, and tossed the coin into the honeylike fluid.

The liquid lit up as though a lamp burned deep within it, within the woody flesh of the oak. "Reorx!" Flint muttered, and grabbed Fleetfoot's mane for support. The sweaty animal nuzzled him again, as if to encourage him. "Oh, all right," he snapped, then continued more thoughtfully. "Maybe I should've tossed the coin into the flower; the lily seemed to be doing the speaking." He touched one golden petal and . . .

. . . Warmth suddenly flooded the dwarf's body, and, turning to the mule—whom Flint now realized he had never appreciated for the dear, devoted creature that she was—he saw a similar warm glow glisten in Fleetfoot's limpid eyes. Flint would later swear that the music of a hundred lutes filled the cavern at that moment. The room faded around them. Flint saw the mule's heavy eyelids begin to close, and he let his own drift shut as well.

Suddenly the room grew noisy, and Flint felt stone, not wood, beneath his feet. His eyes flew open.

He stood, daubed in mud, pine needles, and mule sweat, embracing the odoriferous Fleetfoot. Around him, and slightly below, stood the open-mouthed figures of Tanis, Miral, and several elven courtiers. Flint gazed around him.

He was on the rostrum of the Tower of the Sun. With Solostaran, Speaker of the Sun. And a mule.

Fleetfoot opened her mouth and brayed. Flint took that as a suggestion to speak.

"Well," he said. "I'm back."

Chapter 8

Reunion

In a guest room at the palace, the dwarf lay floating in a huge bath mounded with blossom-scented bubbles, happily digesting the huge meal the Speaker had ordered prepared for him—wild turkey basted with apricot sauce, and robust Solace ale from Flint's own saddlepack. All but one of the flasks had leaked; the rough ride certainly had not improved the last container of ale, but the beverage was drinkable, at least by Flint's standards.

Off in the palace stable, the dwarf knew, Fleetfoot also was being treated to a fine feed. The animal, apparently still awash in warm feelings from being teleported with Flint, had initially refused to be separated from the dwarf. As Flint told his tale to Solostaran and the rest of the court—and heard Xenoth explain that other elves had spotted a rare, magic-wielding tylor west of the ravine during the past few weeks—the gray mule followed the dwarf around the Tower of the Sun, nuzzling him with a fond muzzle, resting her hairy chin on his shoulder, and aiming a deadly kick at anyone who came too close. She finally consented to leave the dwarf after he led her to the stable himself, fed her a carrot and half a peach, and introduced her to the stablehand who would wash her and give her a proper feeding.

Flint had paused in his tale only when the Speaker ordered a troop of Tower guardians out to hunt for the tylor. The search was made more difficult because the dwarf was uncertain exactly where he'd been attacked. He knew only that it was along a trail several miles from Qualinost, and the pell-mell pace through the underbrush had left him utterly confused as to where he'd encountered the oak tree.

The Speaker, worried about leaving Flint unattended so soon after such a potentially devastating attack, insisted that Flint rest for a few hours at the palace, attended by Miral, who, if need be, might be able to assist the dwarf. Flint protested, professing himself as hale as a dwarf half his years, but Solostaran proved astonishingly stubborn.

Now, as Miral lounged on a bench near the bath, Flint soaked in the bath water, holding his thick salt-and-pepper beard underwater and watching little bubbles escape through it to the surface. He wondered if he could equip his regular quarters at his shop with such a wondrous invention. Dwarves normally hated water—cold, running water, that is, inhabited with fish and frogs and worse, and deep and dangerous enough to gather the unwary dwarf to Reorx's smithy—but this was something else entirely.

"You encountered a *sla-mori*," Miral explained to Flint.

"Oh, no, I don't believe so," Flint rejoined distractedly. "Lord Xenoth said that lizard was a tylor. Unless tylors and *sla-mori* are related?" He raised his brows in question.

The mage wiped a patina of sweat from his face and pushed his carmine hood back. His pale face appeared gaunt; circles smudged the skin below his eyes. Yet he spoke patiently. "*Sla-mori*, in the old tongue, means 'secret way,' or 'secret passage,'" he explained. "Myth says there are many of them in Qualinesti, but they are nearly impossible to find. The oak tree was the entrance to one, apparently."

He had Flint's attention now. "Where do these . . . these 'sla-mori' . . . lead?" the dwarf asked.

"To important places, obviously," Miral said matter-of-factly. "After all, you ended up on the rostrum in the Tower of the Sun." He paused, seemingly gathering his thoughts, and his normally hoarse voice sounded raspier. "Some elves even say the Graystone could be found in a sla-mori somewhere in Qualinesti. But the most famous sla-mori is said to lead into Pax Tharkas," he said, naming the famous fortress in the mountains south of Qualinesti. "Some believe that the body of Kith-Kanan lies in the Pax Tharkas sla-mori."

"There's more than one sla-mori, then?" Flint asked, sinking back in the perfumed water until his hair floated and spread around his face like a corona. He gazed at the roseate ceiling high above him and sighed.

Miral waited for the dwarf to surface. "There have been tales from the oldest elves that the area around Qualinost is host to several sla-mori, their entrances well hidden and accessible only to the elf—or dwarf, I see now—graced with the proper power to open them." The mage broke off his account. "What's wrong?" Miral asked.

The dwarf had sat up and was gazing about the luxurious room with a worried expression.

"I'm looking for the bucket," Flint said.

"The bucket?" Miral asked. Suddenly, the mage laughed. "No, we don't empty the water with buckets." He stood and walked to the foot end of the tub.

"Magic, then? You know how I feel about magic," Flint said, worry creasing his face again. "Is this bath magical?" Such a creation would almost have to be aided by magic, he said, suddenly sad. Hill dwarves distrusted magic.

Miral just shook his head. "I forgot that you had not been here since we had these contrivances installed. They were designed by gnomes."

"Gnomes?" the dwarf demanded incredulously. "Reorx!" Nothing gnomes made *ever* worked right. In fact, he was probably lucky to be alive. Ignoring the mage's chortle,

Flint vaulted over the edge of the tub and burrowed into the thick yellow towel that a servant had left on a stone slab.

Shaking his head and smiling, the mage pushed the sleeve of his heavy woolen robe up to his elbows. He plunged his arm into the bath water, fished around a bit, and yanked. With a damp belch, the water level began falling. Miral held up a cork with a chain attached.

"The water drains into the floor," Miral explained.

Flint looked dubious. "With all respect, that doesn't seem very practical," he ventured. "Hard on the building foundation. It's not surprising, coming from gnomes, I guess. But I confess I'd expected a bit more from elves."

Miral rolled his sleeve down again and handed the dwarf a freshly laundered white shirt. "We redesigned it. The gnomes originally had the drain—the hole this cork fits into—at the upper edge," the robed elf said. "It took forever to drain. You had to wait for the water to evaporate."

"But still . . ." the dwarf protested as he drew on his russet leggings.

"The water goes into a circular, tubelike contraption under the floors." Miral's hands sketched in the air.

Flint dropped to his knees and peered under the tub. "How do you fill it?" he queried.

"Buckets."

* * * * *

Later, Flint retrieved Fleetfoot, now clean, curried, shiny, and—the final touch by a livery elf with a waggish sense of humor—with her mane braided and adorned with pink ribbons. Flint made her comfortable in a makeshift stall in an outbuilding near his shop and forge—a job that required two extra trips between shop and outbuilding because Fleetfoot deftly chewed through the stall's leather latch and arrived at Flint's shop moments after he did.

He finally barricaded the beast in the stall by wedging a log between the building door and a small apple tree. He had almost finished unpacking his ale-soaked saddlepack when a figure appeared at the doorway.

The figure was not immediately recognizable, outlined as it was in the setting sun, but the silhouette of the container the figure carried was obvious enough.

"Elvenblossom wine," Flint commented. "Only Tanis Half-Elven could get away with bringing me that."

Tanis smiled widely and placed the bottle on the wooden table. "I thought you could use it to start the fire in your forge," he said. "Quicker than kindling."

The two stood apart, Tanis with his arms folded before his muscular chest and Flint with a stubby hand draped with unpacked tunics in brown and emerald green. They smelled wonderfully of ale, from the dwarf's point of view, but Flint supposed he would have to wash them before he'd be accepted in court.

Flint finally spoke, his voice gruff.

"I suppose now that you're a full-grown lad, tall as an aspen and nearly strong enough to lift me with one arm, you're too good to hang around the forge with a middle-aged grouch of a dwarf."

The half-elf replied, "And I suppose that because you've traveled around the continent of Ansalon and fought off a raging tylor, you don't want me pestering you."

A few minutes passed in silence as the two studied each other. Then, as though each was satisfied with what he saw, they nodded greetings. Tanis settled onto a granite bench, slung one leg up on its surface, and rested a curved, muscular arm across a bent knee. His human forebear was evident in the huskiness of his frame, Flint thought.

The dwarf set to fixing up his forge after a full season of disuse and congratulated himself on the job he'd done of cleaning out the place when he'd left it five months before, at the end of autumn.

The forge, which resembled a raised fireplace, took up much of the back wall of the tiny home. A stone-and-mortar chimney rose up through the back wall like a thick tree trunk, with an opening at the back large enough to accommodate a kender—although Flint would let himself be damned to the Abyss before he'd allow one of those perpetually curious creatures near his beloved forge. The front ledge of the forge, designed for someone of elven proportions, was just above waist-height for the dwarf, an awkward height that often prompted grumbles from him.

"So," Flint said as he placed twigs and dry bark in the depression at the back of the forge, "what have I missed in the past five months?" He looked dubiously at the container of wine, then uncorked it and tossed a liberal splash on the kindling. "Hope this doesn't blast us to Xak Tsaroth," he muttered, patting his pocket for his steel and flint, then realizing he'd probably dropped both in the entrance to the *sla-mori*. "Got a flint and steel, lad?" he asked.

Tanis fished in his pocket, drew out the desired objects, and tossed them to Flint, one after the other. Mumbling "Thanks," the dwarf cracked the two together. With a whoosh, the kindling exploded into flame, sending the dwarf backpedaling hastily. When the conflagration dwindled to a glow, he warily placed a few pieces of coal on the kindling and waited for them to catch fire. He looked over at Tanis, ready to hear the local news.

"Lord Xenoth is still chief adviser, though Litanas has been added as Xenoth's assistant, at Porthios's request," Tanis explained, watching Flint reach to a nearby pile of coal and toss a shovelful onto the blaze. "The Speaker was unhappy at hurting Lord Xenoth's feelings—after all, Xenoth has been adviser to the Speaker of the Sun since Solostaran's father held that post, and the Speaker would not want Xenoth to feel that he could no longer handle the duties alone. Although *that* certainly seems to be true." The last words were uttered in a bitter tone.

"Grab the bellows, would you, lad, and give me a hand," Flint said. Tanis leaped over to that instrument and directed air on the fire. Flint, meanwhile, mounded coal on each side of the blaze. "So Xenoth took it ill?" Flint inquired.

"He wasn't happy." The curt reply spoke volumes about how vocal the adviser had been about the change.

Flint shook his head and spared a sympathetic thought for Litanas, even though Porthios's brown-eyed friend had never seemed particularly fond of dwarf or half-elf. Flint had long suspected that Porthios's friends made a career of making Tanis's life unhappy, though Porthios himself merely stayed aloof. But the dwarf rarely asked Tanis about that aspect of his life, and the half-elf never volunteered any but the most roundabout information on the subject.

Last autumn, before Flint had left for the winter, Litanas and Ulthen had appeared to be vying for wealthy Lady Selena's hand. The elven lady adored the attention, of course, but the situation chipped away at the friendship between Litanas and Ulthen.

As Tanis worked at the bellows, Flint fed chunk after chunk of coal into the fire and wondered how the latest development would affect either elf's suit for Lady Selena. Litanas had wealth, good bloodlines, and the position with Lord Xenoth. But Xenoth could easily destroy an assistant's standing at court if he felt moved to do so.

Ulthen, on the other hand, boasted a fine old Qualinost family, but he—and it—were perennially broke; years ago, tight finances had forced the elf to take on the job of teaching weaponry to Gilthanas, Porthios's younger brother.

At any rate, Flint wouldn't want to be on the bad side of the irascible old adviser—though it seemed that the dwarf perpetually was, anyway. Lord Xenoth, whose age and tenure gave him protection of sorts for his criticism of some of the Speaker's policies, was vocal in his condemnation of allowing any outsiders into the court.

But as Flint took his favorite wooden-handled hammer from a selection in his bench, he had another thought.

"Have you heard of the Graystone?"

From his position at the bellows, Tanis looked surprised at the turn of the conversation. "The Graystone of Gargath? Of course. Every elf child has to memorize the tale."

"Miral mentioned it to me just today." Flint's voice was distracted, most of his attention on the forge. "Tell me the story as the elves know it," Flint urged.

Tanis cast his friend a curious glance, but—careful to keep the bellows operating regularly—launched into the tale that Miral had made him learn by rote years earlier.

"Before the neutral god Reorx forged the world, the gods fought over the various races' spirits, which at that time were still dancing among the stars." He repositioned his hands on the wooden handles of the bellows.

Flint nodded, as if that checked out with the story the dwarves told. From a pile on a table next to the forge, he drew out a rod of iron about as long as a man's hand and as thick as a little finger, and heated the rod in the coals.

The half-elf continued to recite. "The gods of good wanted the races to have power over the physical world. The gods of evil wanted to make the races slaves. And the gods of neutrality wanted the races to have physical power over the world *plus* the freedom to choose between good and evil—which was the course eventually decided upon."

"Reorx thump you, lad, keep pumping that bellows!" the dwarf ordered. Tanis, stepping up the tempo, watched as Flint used iron tongs to retrieve the piece of metal from the coals and pound it into a rectangle with the hammer.

"Three races were born: elves, ogres, and humans—in that order, according to the elves," Tanis said with a wouldn't-you-know-it glance at the ceiling, his shoulder-length hair swinging as he kept pace with the bellows. "And so Reorx forged the world with the help of some human volunteers. But four thousand years before the Cataclysm, the humans angered Reorx by becoming proud of the skills Reorx had taught them and using them for their own ends. The god took back their skills but left their desire to tinker, and the gnomish race was born."

The half-elf drew in a breath almost as great as the one the bellows was forcing across the coals. "Eventually, Reorx forged a gem to anchor neutrality to the world of Krynn. It would hold and radiate the essence of Lunitari, the red—neutral—moon. Reorx placed the Graystone on Lunitari.

Tanis broke off. "Does that match what you know?" Flint nodded, concentrating on placing the rectangle against the edge of the anvil and using the hammer to draw out a small finger at one end of the metal. Deftly, he rapped against the metal finger to make it cylindrical again. Then he turned it over and fashioned the finger into a ring at the end of the rectangle. As usual, Flint felt himself get caught up in the rhythm of the process: four raps on the metal, one on the anvil, four on metal, one on anvil.

Tanis broke in. "Why do you do that?"

"What?"

"Pound the hammer on the anvil," the half-elf said, pausing the bellows to look more closely. "It seems intentional—not as though you've missed the metal."

"Keep pumping! Reorx above, lad, am I going to have to hire a gully dwarf to take your place?" Flint complained. "Of course I'm intentionally hitting the anvil. The metal of the hammer picks up heat as I tap it against this gate latch I'm making for Fleetfoot's stall. Banging the hammer against the anvil every so often cools the hammer. See?" He demonstrated. "Now, go on."

Tanis grinned at his friend. "The gnomes built a mechanical ladder that reached to the red moon, and they captured the Graystone, which some call the Graygem."

Flint quickly rapped the other end of the rod into a point, and forced it perpendicular to the rod.

"But the gem escaped and floated away." Tanis's voice lost its recitation note and took on more enthusiasm. "The stone caused havoc on Krynn. As it passed by, it caused new animals and plants to spring up; old ones changed form."

Flint reheated the rod, which was now recognizable as a gate latch with a loop at one end and a catch at the other.

"Finally," Tanis said, "the gnomes split into two armies to search for the gem. They found it in the high tower of a barbarian prince named Gargath."

Holding a pair of strong tongs at each end of the squared-off rod, the dwarf put his considerable strength into the operation and twisted the latch one full turn. The four edges of the rod swirled into a four-lined decoration at the middle of the latch. Flint thrust the latch into a half-barrel of cool water and then held it up for Tanis to see.

The half-elf raised his eyebrows, but kept pumping and talking. "The prince refused to hand over the stone, and the two groups declared war on him. When they finally penetrated the fortress, the stone's light exploded through the area. And when the gnomes could see again, the two factions had changed."

Flint was looking proudly at the latch. "I could sell this for a good price in Solace," he told the half-elf.

"The curious gnomes," Tanis said, "became kender. The ones who lusted for wealth became . . . uh . . . became . . ." Tanis stopped and blushed.

"Became . . .?" Flint prompted, still displaying the latch.

". . . dwarves," Tanis concluded, a bit shamefacedly.

"Ah," said the dwarf. "You can stop the bellows now."

Tanis bit his lower lip and studied the dwarf. "Is it the same story you knew?" he asked.

Flint smiled and nodded. "Same old story," he said.

*　*　*　*　*

That night, Miral tossed on his pallet and drifted in and out of the same dream that had plagued him almost nightly since reports of the tylor had come in from the countryside.

He was very small, the size of a child, cowering in a crevice of an enormous cave. He knew that he was far underground, yet light from somewhere provided dim illumination.

Enough light penetrated the murk of the chamber that the tiny Miral could see the beaklike, open maw of the tylor that ranged this way and that as though seeking his scent.

"Come out," the creature boomed. "I will not hurt you."

Miral shuddered and pulled still farther into the opening, knowing he was dreaming and knowing, also, that he could do nothing to stop what was coming in this nightmare.

The dragonlike beast thrust one clawed foreleg into the crevice. Miral the child cringed back as far as he could go and, to his embarrassment, cried for his mother. He moved sideways and pressed his right side farther back, against the converging walls of the crevice.

Once again, as always in this dream, he felt cool air against his right arm—where there should have been nothing but dead, unmoving air. Miral knew that the worst part of the nightmare was ahead, the part that shocked him into wakefulness and the realization that he'd sleep no more.

As Miral shoved still harder against the angle of the crevice, a hand clutched his right arm.

Chapter 9

An Adventure

The next day got off to a good start, dawning fine
and clear. Although frost sparkled on the green leaves in the
first light of the morning, within an hour it vanished, and
the day promised to be warm and gentle.

It had been Tanis's suggestion to go looking for the *sla-
mori*; the half-elf craved an adventure. Flint, after looking
at his forge and considering what duties he could put off, finally accepted. Other groups of armed elves were out
searching for the tylor, especially since the Speaker of the
Sun had offered a considerable award to the hunter who
downed the rare beast.

Tanis raided the larder of the palace kitchens, appearing
at Flint's door shortly after dawn, bearing a sack containing
a loaf of brown bread, a yellow cheese, a flask of wine for

himself, and a clay jug of ale for the dwarf.

Armed with battle-axe and short sword, Flint led Tanis, grumbling and carrying his longbow, across the five-hundred-foot bridge spanning the ravine that guarded the city to the west. The dwarf had heard that an ancient race of air elementals, creatures composed of air itself, guarded the regions above the rivers, prohibiting anything from crossing over it into Qualinost by any way except the bridge. Knowing that a peeved elemental was waiting for him to poke an arm or a leg over the bridge's side so that it could blow him into the ravine five hundred feet below didn't improve Flint's opinion of the situation at all.

Tanis pointed to the north. "I've never been to the *Kentommenai-kath*," Tanis said. "Let's go."

"I thought we were hunting for the tylor," Flint said.

"We're just as likely to find the lizard at the *Kentommenai-kath* as anywhere else. From what I hear, the lizard is more likely to find us than the other way around."

"That's reassuring," Flint groused, trudging along behind Tanis and staying well away from the edge of the ravine. "And what in Krynn is a *Kentommenai-kath*?"

"When an elf undergoes a *Kentommen*, a close relative, one who has not yet undergone the ceremony himself, goes to an open area overlooking the River of Hope to keep vigil alone all night."

"Don't make me work so hard, boy," Flint huffed. "What's a *Kentommen*?"

"It's a ceremony that elves undergo when they reach their ninety-ninth birthday—when they become adults. Porthios will have his *Kentommen* in a few months. Gilthanas, I imagine, will perform the *Kentommenai-kath*."

The trail wound through the dense forest of aspen and pine, occasionally following the edge so closely that Flint felt his palms grow sweaty, and sometimes swerving upward back into the forest, to his relief. Finally, after more than an hour, they arrived at the *Kentommenai-kath*. The path opened into a sun-bathed outcropping of purple granite, dotted with white, green, and black lichens and looking east over the ravine. Flint could see the Tower of the Sun shining in the distance; the homes of the elves looked like pink stumps of branchless trees. The Grove, the forest in the center of Qualinost, was visible just north of the open area that must have been the Hall of the Sky.

The cries of birds carried faintly through the air. In the center of the *Kentommenai-kath* was a huge outcropping of purple granite, nearly flat but dotted with hand-size depressions that cradled clear water. The outcropping inclined gently toward the ravine's edge.

"This is where the relative of the *Kentommen* elf kneels to pray to Habbakuk, to ask the god's blessing on the young man or woman, to keep them in harmony with nature throughout their centuries," Tanis said reverentially.

Flint wandered around the *Kentommenai-kath*, scuffing the rock with his traveling boots and admiring the purples, greens, and whites of the glade, surrounded by aspen, oak, and spruce. A sense of peace permeated the area. He looked over at Tanis and continued to stroll.

"Flint, no!" Tanis yelled, his face horrified.

Flint looked ahead . . . out . . . and down. The outcropping, which had a gentle grade on three sides, ended sharply at the edge on this side. The dwarf was a scant foot away from a drop of at least six hundred feet, maybe more.

He felt his blood freeze. Then a strong hand clamped down on his collar and jerked him back. Tanis and the dwarf lost their balance together on the uneven rocks and landed with a "hoof!" on the safe, solid granite. The half-elf was pale, and Flint patted the rock appreciatively with one clammy hand while his brain whirled.

"I . . ." Flint paused.

"You . . ." Tanis paused.

They stared at each other for a protracted moment, until Flint drew a shuddery breath. "The edge comes up a bit sudden there," he said.

A crooked smile stirred faintly on the half-elf's face. "A bit," he agreed.

Flint, recovering his grumpiness, sat up and recovered his money-pouch, which had fallen from his tunic in the tumble. "Not that I was ever in any real danger of falling, though," he reassured himself.

"Oh, no," Tanis said, a little too quickly. "Certainly not."

"Perhaps this would be a good time to stop to recov—ah, to stop for lunch," the dwarf added.

Tanis nodded and retrieved their lunch sack. By unspoken agreement, they moved back from the edge another ten feet or so.

"I'm not worried for myself, mind you," Flint said. "I just don't know how I'd tell the Speaker you'd gone and dropped yourself off a cliff." Tanis said nothing.

They broke bread in the bright sun of midmorning, with Flint pressing on Tanis the largest slices of cheese, the tastiest chunks of bread, and the finest pieces of fruit. Then they sat for a short time enjoying the view from a decent space back from the cliff, and decided to head back to Qualinost; Flint had work to do at the forge.

The problems began as the adventurers started the way back. The path must have forked as they came to the *Kentommenai-kath*, and neither had noticed. When they returned, they took the wrong path. Then the weather entered the picture. First a single dark cloud drifted past the sun.

"As my mother used to say, 'One cloud gets lonely,' " Flint pointed out to the half-elf. Within a short time, a gray phalanx of clouds had crossed the sky overhead. The cloudy sky seemed to lower at an alarming rate, so that Tanis half thought it would drop right onto their heads, but the only thing that did was the rain—big, cold drops. Before long, half-elf and dwarf were soaked and chilled, and Flint had taken to grumbling the words "No more adventures . . . no more adventures . . ." over and over again.

All this might not have been so bad had it not been for the shortcut. Tanis expressed reluctance, but Flint only glared challengingly at him as the dwarf pointed down a barely visible footpath that cut off from the main trail.

"I thought I was the one who had traveled the face of Krynn," Flint griped. "I suppose I was just mistaken."

Tanis spent the next ten minutes assuring the dwarf that, indeed, Flint was the one who had had the experience on the road, that Flint was the one who knew forests like the back of his hand, and, yes, that he was the one who had been paying enough attention to practical matters on the way up to have seen the shortcut. Furthermore, he had fought off a rampaging tylor the previous day, practically unarmed. And so they plunged through the undergrowth onto the faint footpath leading into the rain-soaked woods.

They plunged deeper into the woods, watching worriedly for the tylor and growing soggier with each moment.

Two hours later, as the rain continued unabated, they ran into a tylor-hunting party and accompanied the group of unsuccessful hunters home. But Flint was coughing by the time they reached the outskirts of Qualinost, and feverish by the time Tanis pulled off his friend's waterlogged tunic, breeches, and boots. Tanis wrapped him in a blanket, pushed him into a chair, and fired the forge for extra heat.

Now, in late afternoon, as Tanis stirred a pot of venison stew over the fire, the force of Flint's sneeze sent the chair tilting backward so precariously that Tanis leaped to grab it before it tumbled over.

"Oof!" Tanis grunted, his knees nearly buckling as he pushed against the big wooden chair. "I know you aren't terribly tall, Flint, but you are a bit on the dense side." With a good deal of effort, he righted the chair, but the dwarf seemed less than grateful.

"Ah, what does it matter if I fall, seeing as I'm dying anyway?" the dwarf said glumly. He blew his nose into his linen handkerchief, a gift from the Speaker of the Sun, with a sound like a badly tuned trumpet. "At least that way I'll be all laid out and ready for my coffin." Flint huddled deeper into his woolen blanket and stuck his big-toed feet back in a steaming pail of water. Close as he was to the glowing coals of the forge, the heat couldn't drive the chill from his dwarven bones, and his teeth chattered as he shivered.

"As it is, I'm practically frigid with cold anyway. Might as well be officially dead," Flint complained.

"I could mull you some elvenblossom wine."

Flint glared. "Why not take your sword and end my pain quickly? I'll not go to Reorx embalmed in elven perfume!"

"Flint," Tanis said gravely, "I know you'll be terribly disappointed. But you've only got a cold. You're not dying."

"Well, how would you know?" Flint growled. "Have you ever died?" Flint let out another monumental sneeze, his bulbous nose glowing red, a complement to the glow of the setting sun. Tanis could only shake his head. There was an odd sort of logic to the dwarf's statement.

"No more adventures," Flint roared. "No more tylors. Give me ogres any day. No more *sla-mori*. No more walks in the rain on the edge of the elven version of the Abyss." He paused to gather strength for another volley. "This is all because I took that bath. Dwarves were not meant to be immersed in water two days in a row!" That last sentence, Tanis noted, sounded more like "Dwarvz were dod bed du be ibbersed id wadder du days idda row."

It's hard to believe the two had been sitting comfortably here at the forge only a day earlier, the half-elf thought.

Flint sniffled and blew his nose again. He set a warm washcloth on the top of his head, and, draped as he was in his dark blanket, he looked almost like some cheap mystic at a petty fair. "That's the last time I'll make the mistake of listening to you," he grumbled for the umpteenth time.

Tanis did his best to hide his smile as he poured hot tea for the dwarf and set the mug in his stubby hands. "The rain has stopped. I should go practice with Tyresian."

"This late? Fine, leave me to die alone," Flint said. "But don't come back and expect me to say, 'Hullo, Tanis, how are you? Come inside and ruin an old dwarf's day, won't you?' After all, I'll be dead. You've got an hour or two left of daylight. See you later," he said, waving his hand at Tanis. "Or then, probably not," he added glumly.

Tanis shook his head. When Flint was like this, it was simply best to leave him to enjoy his misery. Tanis made sure the kettle was in the dwarf's reach and that the water in the bucket was hot enough. He spooned a healthy portion of stew into a wooden trencher for Flint, then gathered his longbow and arrows and prepared to abandon the dwarf.

But as the half-elf gained the doorway of the dwarf's shop, he came face to face with two visitors—the Speaker of the Sun and Lord Tyresian.

Tyresian ignored the dwarf and snapped, "Are you always late for your lessons?" to the half-elf, then resumed a heated discussion with the Speaker. It seemed to be a one-sided discussion; Solostaran appeared unflappable today, nodding gravely in response to the elf lord's vigorous comments but making no statements that could be interpreted as affirming them.

If possible, Tyresian had become more sure of himself in the twenty years that Flint had known him. Even with his short hair, so unusual among the elves, the elf lord was handsome, with sharp, even features and keen eyes the color of the autumn sky. Tyresian gestured with grace as he spoke with the Speaker, and even standing in the doorway of the dwarf's rude lodgings, clad in only a plain, dove-gray tunic, there was a commanding presence about him.

"People are saying that the appearance of a creature as rare and as dangerous as a tylor is evidence that your policies regarding outsiders"—and here the lord's gaze flicked to Flint, then, preposterously, to the half-elf—"are misplaced."

Solostaran halted and faced the elf lord, the Speaker's face finally showing a shadow of emotion. The emotion, however, was amusement. "That's an interesting leap, Lord Tyresian," he said. "Tell me how you made it."

"Understand, please, that I'm not stating my own views, Speaker, rather the views of others as I've heard them," the blue-eyed elf lord said smoothly.

"Indeed," Solostaran said drily.

"I simply know that you, as Speaker of the Sun, are interested in the views of your subjects," Tyresian added.

"Please get to the point." Solostaran's voice showed annoyance for the first time since the pair had appeared in Flint's doorway. As yet, however, neither newcomer had greeted the dwarf. Flint glanced at Tanis. The face of the dwarf's friend had reverted to the mulish expression that the half-elf always showed when anyone other than Flint, Miral, or Laurana were around. Tanis's expression would have done Fleetfoot proud, the dwarf thought.

Flint opened his mouth to interject, but Tyresian resumed, brushing one hand through his short blond hair.

Flint noticed that the elf's arms, exposed by the short-sleeved spring shirt he wore under his tunic, were marked with scars—the results, no doubt, of years of swordplay with his companion Ulthen.

"They say that tylors tend to prefer hidden lairs near well-used trails, so that the creatures can prey on travelers. They say that even though you have continued to bar *most* travelers from Qualinost"—and the elf lord speared Flint with a glance—"trade has increased the numbers of elves heading out of the city, and out of the kingdom, with goods."

"Lord Tyresian . . ." Solostaran's patience had been strained, but the elf lord was too wound up now to give way to court decorum.

"They say, Speaker, that it was wrong, was 'unelven,' to install those . . . those *gnomish bathtubs* in the palace."

Flint snorted—a fairly easy task with a cold; Tanis laughed. Tyresian flushed and looked daggers at the two.

Solostaran appeared to be caught between laughing and launching into a tirade. His gaze caught that of Flint, whose steel-gray eyes were twinkling. "Care for a cup of mulled elvenblossom wine, Speaker, Tyresian?" the dwarf said, and snuffled. "My friend here has offered to prepare some for a sick dwarf."

Solostaran, turning his back to Lord Tyresian, winked broadly at the dwarf and Tanis. "I'll pass up your kind offer, Master Fireforge, but thank you. And I believe Lord Tyresian was looking for Tanthalas."

Tyresian's anger was barely controlled. "Speaker, I must press for a commitment on that other matter."

Solostaran whirled. "You 'must press'?" he demanded.

"Your actions now could affect your children later, Speaker," Tyresian said coldly.

Solostaran drew himself up to his full height. His eyes flashed green fire. Suddenly he appeared half a hand taller than the young elf—and a good deal too strong a presence to be contained in Flint's bungalow. "You *dare* to press me on such a matter in a public setting?"

Tyresian paled. The elf lord hastened to apologize and withdrew hastily with the half-elf in tow. Even as the two disappeared out the door, Flint could hear Tyresian begin to transfer his ire to Tanis. "You had better hope you practiced that technique I showed you yesterday, half-elf." The threat hung in the air as the pair's footsteps faded.

The Speaker made a gesture as if to follow them; then his hand fell to his side and he turned back to Flint.

"I don't envy Tanis his archery lesson today," the dwarf said mildly, daubing his nose with his handkerchief. He gestured toward the forge. "The fare isn't of royal quality— Tanis is only a passable cook—but it's wholesome. If you care to join a dying dwarf, that is." He coughed weakly.

Flint put on such a pathetic look, bundled and clutching his nearly empty mug, that Solostaran burst into laughter.

"Dying, Flint? I don't think so. You're the healthiest one among us—physically and otherwise."

Confined alone with Flint, the Speaker let some of his formality fall away; he refilled Flint's tea, ignored the dwarf's wheezing request for "one last tankard of ale before I die," and decided, after all, to enjoy a mug of mulled elvenblossom wine. Waving aside Flint's movement as if to prepare the wine, Solostaran heated the beverage and dropped in a pinch of mulling spices he found in a tiny crock in Flint's hutch. Sipping the drink, the Speaker sat comfortably on the carved chest that held Flint's meager wardrobe. That's the leader of all the Qualinesti elves who just served me tea, Flint thought, wondering at his fortune.

"I have a metalsmithing project for you, Master Fireforge, if you're willing and healthy enough."

"I'm healthy enough. And when have I not been willing?" Flint rejoined, knowing full well that he could get away with reduced court decorum when he was alone with his friend. Still, Solostaran's recent display of authority reminded him not to strain the friendship too far. "Sir."

Solostaran looked quickly at Flint, then let his scrutiny wander over the dwarf's tidy cot, well-kept forge, and damp clothes—including the emerald-green tunic the Speaker had ordered made for the dwarf twenty years earlier—spread over two chairs. The boots, leather already growing crinkly as it dried, had been placed several feet from the forge, under Flint's table. The room smelled of wet wool.

The Speaker's voice, when he finally began to speak, was weary. He took a sip of wine. "You may wonder why I stand such insolence from someone in my court," he said.

"Actually, I figured it was none of my—"

"As you know, Tyresian comes from one of the highest families in Qualinost—the Third Family. Tyresian's father did me a great service years ago—so great, indeed, that had he not stood by me then, I might not be Speaker now."

Flint wondered what kind of good deed had been involved, but he decided that if Solostaran wanted him to know, he would tell him. Instead, the dwarf slurped his tea, poked his feet nearer the fire, and waited.

"Tyresian is one of the best archers at court," Solostaran mused, as if his thoughts were far away. Outside, the sun settled lower in the afternoon sky, casting a buttery glow over Qualinost that was matched by the orange light emanating from Flint's forge. It's more like autumn than spring, the dwarf thought, then forced his attention back to the Speaker as the lord of the elves continued. "He has been hard on Tanis, I am aware—Yes, I know more of what passes at court than I let on, my friend—but I cannot forget that Tyresian's teachings have made Tanis nearly as good with the longbow as Tyresian himself is.

"I only wish Lord Tyresian were not so . . . so . . ." Solostaran groped for the word.

". . . so traditionally elven?" Flint supplied.

". . . so unbending."

Flint gulped down the rest of his tea, not venturing to sneak a look at the Speaker until he'd drained the last drop. Still, he looked up to find Solostaran watching him intently, face pitched downward so that his pointed ears were visible through his golden hair.

"If we elves seem unbending to you, Master Fireforge," Solostaran said gently but evenly, "try to remember that our 'unbending' elven commitment to tradition and constancy has protected us when other, more changeable, races have foundered in turmoil. That is why I proceed with such caution in allowing increased trade with outside nations—

although any relaxation of tradition is anathema to some of the courtiers—and why I take reservations such as Tyresian's and Xenoth's very seriously."

The dwarf nodded, and the Speaker added briskly, "But I am here for a reason—in addition to investigating rumors that my dear friend was about to breathe his last. I am glad to see that the rumors appear unfounded."

Don't count on it, the dwarf started to say, but held his tongue. He merely contemplated the Speaker, who asked, "You have heard of the ceremony called the *Kentommen*?"

Flint nodded, and the golden-robed lord went on, "We have spent much of this past winter planning for Porthios's *Kentommen*, which will be held in the Tower of the Sun less than two months hence."

The two looked at each other across the bungalow's bare stone floor, then Solostaran cast a glance toward the forge.

"I would like you to fashion a special medal honoring the occasion. I would present such a cherished medal to Porthios during the *Kentommen*."

The Speaker of the Sun drew in a deep breath. "I would like this ceremony to draw the elven nobles back together, Master Fireforge. I fear that recent . . . changes . . . have fostered some division, and I want this ceremony to draw their attention to my commitment to certain—" He smiled— "unchanging elven traditions.

"I don't need to say, my friend, that the success of this ceremony could go a long way toward cementing Porthios's claim to the Speakership. And your medal, which I would give him, would be part of that."

"Do you have a design in mind?" Flint asked.

Solostaran rose and placed his empty mug on the table. "I have ideas, of course, but I would prefer to see what you devise. Of all those around me, Master Fireforge, you may well know me the best. And this knowledge could stand you in good stead now."

He fell silent, as though thinking of something far off the subject, and Flint quietly said, "I would be honored to fashion such a medal for the ceremony."

Solostaran looked up and smiled; rare warmth sprang into

his eyes. "Thank you, Flint." The dwarf suddenly saw how tired the Speaker appeared, as though he had spent long nights in restless—or no—sleep. The Speaker seemed to note the sympathy in Flint's perusal. "The way to the Speakership is full of hurdles, Flint. Look at my own family."

Flint, deciding that he wasn't going to die after all, shrugged back the blanket, reached over to his wooden chest, and pulled out a fresh shirt, white linen embroidered with aspen leaves along the collar, compliments of the Speaker's tailor. He pulled the garment over his head. "You mean the death of Tanis's fath—of your brother?"

"The deaths of Kethrenan and Elansa, certainly," Solostaran agreed, "but also the death of Arelas, my youngest brother. My parents had three children, but only one survives. Qualinost may well find the Speakership going, not to Porthios, but to Gilthanas or even Laurana, if the occasion warrants."

"Arelas?" Flint said, prompting the Speaker.

"Arelas was born only a few years after Kethrenan, and he died shortly after my middle brother did."

"What a painful time for you," the dwarf said softly.

Solostaran looked up. "For all of us, yes. Kethrenan died, and Elansa was like a living ghost, waiting for her child to be born. There was a pall over the court that we could not shake." He watched as the dwarf struggled into green breeches and socks of dark brown wool. "Then we got word through a visitor to Caergoth that Arelas had left that city and was coming back here."

He smiled. "You should have seen the difference in the court, my friend. My younger brother had left Qualinost as a young child, decades before, and had not returned. Then in the middle of all this . . . this pain, he was returning.

"I felt as though I had lost one brother and gained another, and although the pain was still great over Kethrenan's death, there was some solace in realizing that I would finally get to know this young brother. I hardly knew Arelas, you see. He left court at a very young age."

Flint pondered. Why would a noble family of Qualinost send its youngest child away? Although he said nothing, the question must have shown in his eyes.

"Arelas was quite ill as a child. Several times he almost died, and elven healers seemed powerless to help him. Finally, my father, the Speaker, ordered him sent to a group of clerics near Caergoth, across the Straits of Schallsea, where there was an elven cleric whom my father knew, who had had great success with illness that seemed beyond hope.

"Arelas thrived there, and the cleric sent him back here after a year. But he quickly sickened again. It almost seemed as though something in Qualinost itself was draining him, drawing off his strength. My father, fearing to lose his youngest son, sent him back to Caergoth for good. There were no visits. You know how it is here. The highest families leave Qualinost only rarely, sometimes never. But we received regular reports that Arelas was doing well."

Flint drew closer to the Speaker. The only light in Flint's shop, the fire in the forge, threw strange shadows on Solostaran's face. "Something happened when Arelas returned?"

Solostaran frowned. "He never arrived. Weeks went by, until I thought my mother would weaken and die from the suspense." He shrugged. "Then we received word in the form of Miral, who bore a letter from my brother and a sad tale of his death at the hands of brigands. The letter expressed Arelas's love, his indebtedness to Miral, and a request that I offer Miral a position at court." He smiled sadly. "It was obvious that Miral was a very low-level mage. He could do little magic, easing stomach-aches and headaches, casting minor illusion spells. But little else."

Flint remembered how the mage had been able to ease his choking fit after his first bout with elvenblossom wine. "Such skills are nothing to sneeze at," he said.

Solostaran moved into the doorway and laid a gentle hand on the climbing rose blooming around the portal. "Miral is an intelligent, kind elf, and if he is of little use as a mage, he was a gifted tutor for Tanis, Gilthanas, and Laurana. I've never regretted my decision to let him live here."

The Speaker glanced at the late afternoon bustle of elves winding up their day's business. "I am late," he said simply, and left the discussion at that.

Chapter 10

The Grand Market

After practice with Tyresian, Tanis found himself wandering the streets of the city. The clouds that had drenched him and Flint only hours before had dissipated. The heavy gold of afternoon slipped toward the deepening purple of twilight, and the air was sweet with the scent of spring blossoms.

To the north, the Tower of the Sun glittered. In the city's center, the Hall of the Sky opened its arms to the heavens.

On the west side of the city, however, was what might have been, at least to some, Qualinost's greatest wonder, and it was there that Tanis found his footsteps leading him.

Built into a natural hollow in the earth was a vast amphitheater. The only seats were the gentle, grassy slopes themselves, encircling a great platform in the amphitheater's center. The circular area was laid with the type of tiled mosaic that Qualinost was famous for; this mosaic depicted in sparkling hues the coming of Kith-Kanan and his people to the forest of Qualinesti. The mosaic spanned the surface of the circle, and Tanis had always believed it must contain as many glimmering tiles as there were stars in the night sky.

Here, after sundown, in the flickering light of a thousand torches, the ancient dramas would unfold, works written by the poets of Qualinesti long ago for Kith-Kanan's own eyes. Philosophers, too, would walk upon the circle's surface to speak their oratories, and here musicians would ply their art as the folk of Qualinost looked on.

By day, the amphitheater served in another incarnation— the Grand Market. There the finest craftsmen in Qualinost came to display their wares on cloths spread upon the ground while brightly colored silk banners snapped in the breeze. On market days, the mosaic of Kith-Kanan was obscured by a sprawl of green silken tents, wooden stalls, and woolen carpets spread out on its surface, laden with all manner of wares imaginable: pungent spices, lacquered boxes, bright daggers with jeweled hilts, and fresh-baked pastries still steaming faintly in the damp air. Common artisans also brought their goods to sell here. There were basket-makers, potters, weavers, and bakers, for not every elf in Qualinost was lucky—or wealthy—enough to take a place in the court of the Speaker. While no mouth ever went hungry and no back ever went unclad in Qualinost, as in any city those who possessed both wealth and power were few, and the simple folk far more numerous. However, most of these elves looked on the glittering court with only vaguely curious eyes, content to let the nobles work their petty intrigues and courtly amusements, as long as it didn't interfere too much with their own day-to-day lives.

Most of the elves at the market were the common folk of Qualinost. The nobles tended to avoid the Grand Market, except on the most important festival days, and instead sent their servants or squires to purchase anything they required. However, this tended to suit these same servants and squires quite well, for it gave them a chance to escape their noble masters or mistresses, at least for a time.

Although all of these folk were as fair of feature and spoken word as any courtier in the Tower—though their manner of dress tended more toward soft buckskins and bright woolen weaves than toward doublets and gowns and golden robes—a warmth seemed to radiate from them that always made Tanis feel more at ease in the market than he did in the expanses of the Tower or the corridors of the palace. And while Tanis received stares for his exotic looks here, just as he did at court, the gazes tended to be curious rather than disapproving. At any rate, in the market a stare was far less common than a cheerful smile or nod.

As Tanis entered today, the market was just beginning to break up in the low light of the sun. He descended the stone stairs leading down to the tile circle where the merchants were gathering up their wares. He tried on a copper bracelet and examined a quiver filled with arrows painted yellow and green, but he had left his small purse of coins at the palace, so he was forced to disappoint the merchants hoping to make one more sale before the day ended.

He was just leaving the market when a tall, familiar figure caught his eye, recognizable even at this distance and in this crowd because of her luxuriant blond hair and lithe figure. It was Laurana, and her brother Gilthanas was with her.

Tanis sucked in his breath and tried to edge behind a potter's booth, but an old elf gently pushed Tanis back.

"The shop is closed," he informed the half-elf.

"But . . ." Tanis said.

"The market is over," the elf said firmly. "Come back tomorrow."

Tanis stumbled backward, but before he could turn and dash away, he saw Laurana's green eyes gazing at him, and he swallowed hard. He couldn't run now, not when the young elf lady had seen him. Even now, her coral lips had parted in a radiant smile and she was hurrying across the tired marketplace with an astonishing mixture of determination and grace. Marketkeepers, both men and women, paused at their work and watched with respect and admiration as she moved by. Gilthanas trailed behind her, looking less pleased than she.

"Tanis!" Laurana called as she drew close to the half-elf. Her voice was resonant as a bell. She reached out slender arms and caught Tanis in a brief hug, then turned to Gilthanas and said, "I haven't seen Tanis in nearly a week. I think he's avoiding us."

Gilthanas, flicking his golden hair away from his eyes, looked as though that would be fine with him.

Tanis sighed and shifted uncomfortably, acutely aware that the Speaker's daughter continued to hold one of his hands—and just as aware that the people around the trio were noting the exchange and raising their eyebrows. He tried to back out of her grasp, and Laurana released him; a faint frown creased the skin between her eyes.

Surprisingly, it was Gilthanas who diverted Laurana by asking if Tanis were going to the Tower for the big announcement the next day.

"What is it?" Tanis asked. Laurana shifted back a step and pouted slightly, then appeared to change her mind and join in the conversation. At age thirty, she seemed to be half-woman, half-girl, and Tanis never knew which part of her personality would be in ascendancy when he spoke with her. As a result, he *had* been avoiding her.

"I don't know what the announcement is," she said. "Father won't tell anyone. All I know is that he looks worried and Lord Xenoth looks pleased, which always concerns me.

"You look wonderful today, Tanis," she said suddenly. Her green satin dress shimmered in the deepening sunset. All of a sudden, he was tremendously aware of his human blood. He felt huge and ungainly. Although she had years to go before she would be considered "grown up" in elven culture, she had attained her full adult height; still, she was so slight, bright, and quick that he felt like an ogre next to her.

Gilthanas, looking annoyed, put one hand on his sister's arm and said, "Laurana . . ." warningly. Tanis blushed and looked down at the outfit she'd praised: a sky-blue shirt under a leather vest fringed with feathers, and brown breeches woven of softest wool. He still preferred beaded moccasins to the more customary elven boots; it was a habit he'd found difficult to outgrow.

Laurana flounced, and Tanis suddenly saw the spoiled girl she'd been only a few years before. Her voice, however, was that of a woman. "Gilthanas, I will do as I please," she snapped. "We have discussed this. Now leave it."

Tanis felt awkward. The days he and Gilthanas had spent together, running about the city or trekking deep within the forest, seemed shadowy and far away now, as if they were a dream rather than something that had ever truly been. They had been friends. Now Tanis couldn't think of anything to say, and he shifted his weight from one foot to the other.

Gilthanas nodded shortly at the two of them. "I'll leave, then." He wheeled and stalked away, threading through the departing merchants and their carts.

"I am sorry," Tanis said, more to himself than to Laurana, but the elven woman didn't appear to have heard him. Instead, she took his hand and drew him along with her through the Grand Market.

"I don't know what father has planned for tomorrow," she complained. "All I know is that no one in government ever simply comes out and *says* anything. Even the most ordinary proclamation has to be accompanied by sheaves of parchments, yards of ribbon, and gallons of sealing wax."

Tanis found himself smiling. Adjusting for a certain amount of hyperbole, Laurana was right.

"Perhaps they are declaring tomorrow National Elvenblossom Wine Day," he suggested.

Tanis was so rarely whimsical that it took Laurana a moment to match her mood to his. She laughed. "Or passing a resolution urging every elf to eat *quith-pa* at every meal?"

She giggled again, and suddenly Tanis felt like a child— not the sullen youngster he had been, but the carefree child he could have been under different circumstances. The thought made him both happy and sad.

As always with the half-elf, it seemed, sadness won out. "Most likely, it has to do with the tylor," Tanis said.

Laurana shivered. "That's probably true. Palace guards were out all day, but none was able to find the creature."

She appeared to lapse into deep thought, and he wondered what conversational shift she was making now.

They had reached the edge of the Kith-Kanan mosaic, leaving the clamor of the Grand Market behind them. Laurana drew him up the stone steps and through a break in the blooming lilac bushes at the edge of the mosaic, into a small clearing. The bushes dulled the sound from the public area; suddenly, Tanis was aware of how alone they were.

Laurana pulled a small, tissue-wrapped package from the pocket of her dress. "I have something for you," she said. "I've been carrying it around all week, hoping to see you."

"What is it?" he asked, puzzled, but Laurana only smiled mysteriously. At that moment, she was not at all a child, and Tanis shifted uncomfortably.

"You'll see," she said, and then suddenly she stood on her toes and kissed his cheek, ignoring his incipient beard, her touch as cool and soft as the spring air. A scant moment later, she had slipped through the lilacs and out of sight, only the faint fragrance of mint lingering where she had been. Bemused, Tanis touched his cheek, unsure what she was up to. With a shrug, he unwrapped the small parcel.

A sudden coldness sank deep into Tanis's stomach despite the warmth of the spring air. On his palm, in the sunlight filtering between the new leaves of the trees, glimmered a ring. It was a simple thing, fashioned of seven tiny, interlocking ivy leaves, gleaming as bright and gold as the hair of the elven woman who had given it to him. It was lovely, delicate, a ring one might place on the hand of a lover. Tanis shook his head, clenching the ring in his fist.

Still shaking his head, Tanis emerged from the lilacs moments later, slipping the slender ring into the pocket of his vest until he could ponder its meaning.

"Interesting," said a cold voice.

Tanis whirled. Standing at the top of the steps, shaking in anger as several laden tradesmen watched and waited to get by, stood Lord Xenoth.

"Tanthalas Half-Elven," the elf lord said portentously. "You will come to regret this."

As Tanis, blinking, watched Lord Xenoth stomp away in indignation, he had no doubt that the elf lord was right.

Chapter 11

A Visitor From the Past

THE SOUND OF HAMMER BLOWS RANG LIKE CLEAR MUSIC on the spring morning air. Flint grinned fiercely as he worked the crimson-glowing slab of steel, periodically quenching the metal in an oaken half-barrel of water. Sweat trickled down his soot-stained brow.

He had begun late the previous day, shucking his blanket onto the bed, tossing down a mug of ale—for his frail health, he concluded—then firing the forge and hammering irregular chunks of iron into several small bars of metal. He beat the bars into strips and heated them to a high temperature in the charcoal fire, converting them to carbon steel. Then he sandwiched the strips into a slab, continually reheating the slab in the coal and thrusting it into cold water to harden the metal.

Now, finally satisfied with the thinness and evenness of the piece of steel, he lifted it from the heat of the forge with a pair of iron tongs and quenched it again. Clouds of steam hissed into the air like the breath of some fabled dragon, until finally the metal had cooled. Flint set it on his workbench and eyed it critically. It was still rough and crude—little more than a flat strip of steel, really—but soon enough, it would be something far different—a magnificent sword. Flint's blue eyes glimmered, for already he could see the finished weapon, smooth and shimmering, beneath the blackened surface of the steel bar.

Flint wiped away the sweat and grime from his forehead and gulped water from a tin ladle dipped in a bucket in the corner. He sat on a low wooden stool and closed his eyes for a moment. He'd arrived in Qualinost two days ago, and already it seemed as though he had never left it for the winter. How long had it been since that day he had first set foot in the city? Probably twenty years to the very day, he thought, opening his eyes to glance out the window.

Outside, the new leaves of the aspen trees flickered emerald and silver in the sunlight.

His heart felt right in Qualinost, and despite the occasional unfriendly stares from Lord Xenoth, Litanas, Ulthen and Tyresian—stares rarely converted to comments because of Flint's popularity with the Speaker of the Sun—the dwarf felt almost as if he belonged in the elven capital more than anywhere else on Krynn. Not for the first time, he wondered what his relatives back in the dwarven village of Hillhome would think of him now.

A small chime sounded on the smoky air, and Flint looked up to see the door of his small shop opening. Hastily he tossed a cloth over the bar of steel on the workbench. It wouldn't do to have the surprise spoiled.

"Flint! You're still alive?" Tanis Half-Elven said with a smile. "I thought I would need to arrange a funeral."

Flint reached hastily for his handkerchief, snuffled, and affected a frail expression. "As my mother would say, 'Don't count your chickens on the other side of the fence,' " he said.

A flutter of incomprehension flitted across the half-elf's

face; Flint's mother's sayings tended to affect him that way. Then he shrugged and forged ahead. "Are you in the mood for another adventure, Flint? I thought perhaps we could search again for the tylor."

Uppity snit, Flint thought, and his grin returned.

"You still haven't got it through that thick skull of yours, have you, lad?" the dwarf said gruffly. "I have work to do. I don't have all day to parade about the city all dandified, like some folk."

Tanis laughed, looking down at his outfit. He wore the same clothes that had drawn Laurana's eyes in the Grand Market yesterday: blue shirt, fringed vest, and woolen breeches.

"Flint," Tanis said, his hazel eyes dancing, "take a day off."

"'Day off'?" Flint sniffed, assuming a martyred air. "Never heard the term in my life."

At that, Tanis laughed aloud.

Flint glowered at him. "You young folk don't know the first thing about respect, do you?" he grumbled. Young folk. . . the words echoed in his mind, and then it struck him again as it had several times since he'd returned from Solace. Tanis was a far cry from the lad he had been when Flint had first come to the elven city. Even after just that first winter, Flint had been stunned by the changes, by how much more. . . well, how much more *human* the lad had looked. Especially compared to the other elves, particularly the younger ones, who seemed to have changed so little.

Flint himself looked hardly different than on the day he had first set foot in the Tower of the Sun, except perhaps for those few flecks of grey—well, maybe more than a few— that had found their way into his beard and the dark hair he still bound in a thong behind his neck. Aside from a deepening of some of the lines on his face and a slight expansion of his midline—a change Flint would flatly deny—he was still the same middle-aged dwarf, his steel-blue eyes just as bright and his grumbling just as common.

But Tanis was a different story. He had grown tall in these last years—not as tall as the Speaker, but enough that Flint was forced to crane his neck to speak to him. The differ-

ences between the half-elf and his full elf kindred were more
apparent now. He was stronger than any of them, and his
chest was deeper, though compared to a strong human man,
he would have appeared slender. His face, too, showed evidence of the changes. His features lacked much of that characteristic elven smoothness, looking more as if they had
been hewn from stone rather than polished from alabaster.
His jaw was square, the bridge of his nose straight and
strong, and his cheeks angular. And of course, his eyes were
less almond-shaped than the eyes of other elves.

Back in Solace, Flint knew, Tanis would be considered a
handsome young man, but here . . . well, most of the residents had seemed to have grown used to him by now, and
much of the staring had ended—or at least had given place
to occasional muttered comments, never uttered loudly
enough for Tanis or Flint to actually confront the speaker.
Still, it had been a hard time for Tanis. Humans matured so
much faster than elves and dwarves that Tanis seemed, to
his elven kindred, to have changed overnight.

"Shouldn't you be doing something now?" Flint said testily, making sure to keep himself between Tanis and the concealed sword.

"Like what?" Tanis asked. He seemed to sense that something was up with the dwarf.

"Like doing whatever it is that you do around here," Flint
finished grumpily. "I'm too . . . too ill to entertain you today, lad. I need my rest." He peeked out of the corner of one
blue eye to see if the half-elf was buying this.

Tanis shook his head. So Flint was in one of those moods.

"All right, Flint. I was going to suggest we go off on a bit
of an adventure"—Flint's eyes went wide, and a sudden
sneeze burst violently from him—"but I guess it can wait until another day." The half-elf scratched absently at his chin.

"Better take a razor to that thing again," Flint said, "or let
it grow. One or the other unless you want to look like a
highwayman."

Tanis looked startled, and he ran a hand across his cheek,
feeling the stubble of a few days' growth of beard. A gift
from his human father—or a curse, however you wanted to

look at it, Tanis supposed. It had become noticeable a year or so ago, and Tanis still hadn't gotten used to it. He'd have to take the razor, the one Flint had fashioned for him, to it again.

"Why you'd want to shave a perfectly good beard in the first place, I wouldn't know," Flint complained.

Tanis shook his head absently. Let it grow? He couldn't do that. Flint saw this, and so let it go.

"All right, Flint, I'll leave you to your grumbling," Tanis said. "I really came by to deliver you a message. There's going to be some sort of announcement at court tomorrow afternoon, and the Speaker asked me to invite you."

"Announcement?" Flint said, drawing his bushy eyebrows together. "About what?"

Tanis shrugged again. "I have no idea. The Speaker's been closeted with Lord Xenoth and Tyresian for a day. I suppose you'll find out when I do." With a smile, the half-elf left the shop. The small chime sounded on the air again. Flint waited a long moment, just to be sure Tanis wasn't coming back, and then he uncovered the sword, rubbing his hands together. Ah, yes! It would be a wonderful sword!

Soon, the rhythmic music of his hammer could be heard again on the warm spring air.

*　*　*　*　*

Flint's shop was destined to receive a few more guests that day. The sound of Tanis's footsteps on the tile streets had no sooner receded than the chime sounded again. Flint flung the cloth across the sword once more and hastily stood before the weapon.

But it wasn't Tanis. It was an old woman, aged even for an elf—but Flint thought he saw a hint of human blood there, too. She was short and wiry, dressed in an eccentric fashion for an elf; elves tended to prefer flowing garments, but the old one wore a loose green top of some open weave and a gathered wool skirt that reached nearly to the ground, making her appear even shorter than she was. In fact, she was nearly eye to eye with the dwarf, a situation he had never experienced with an adult elf. The eyes that peered from the triangular face, however, were round and hazel— another hint at some human forebear. Flint would warrant that the human blood had come into her family line centuries before the Cataclysm. The wideness of her face across her eyes, combined with the narrowness of her chin, gave the old woman a catlike appearance. Unlike other elves, she wore her silver hair in a braid and a bun, exposing the ears that reflected her elven heritage. Her fingers were so long and slender that they appeared out of proportion to the rest of her body. Like Tanis, she wore moccasins; these were embroidered in deep purple beading, matching her skirt. Over all, she wore a lightweight hooded cloak of mottled lilac and pale green.

Attached to her skirt was a toddler, who looked up at the wrinkle-faced woman with an expression akin to adoration. The little boy—who hadn't been walking for many months, judging from his death grip on the woolen skirt—smiled milkily at Flint.

"Flink!" the youngster said, and dared loosen one hand's grip enough to point at the dwarf and smile at the old woman. "Flink!"

"Flink?" the dwarf repeated, stooping to look the child full in the face. Flint's brows shot up near his hairline. "I don't remember you from the Hall of the Sky—Oh, yes I do! Last autumn. You weren't walking yet. You were with your big brother. I gave you—What was it?"

The youngster shoved a hand into a pocket in his loose, teal-green coverall, and brought out a thumb-size chip of rose quartz, a fuzzy piece of *quith-pa*, and a carving of a robin. The child put all three treasures in Flint's hand and smiled again. The dwarf examined all three, nodded gravely, and handed back the rock and the bread; then he stood and looked at the elven woman, the wooden bird upright on his palm.

"You made that?" she asked in an alto that sounded like the tone of an elf several centuries younger. She reached out one slim finger and poked the bird.

The robin was fatter on the bottom than on top, and was

rounded along its lower edge so that the toy, when bumped, rolled to the side, then bobbed back up again. Flint had fashioned the simple toy out of two pieces of wood, fastening a heavy chunk of iron near the bottom, between the two pieces, so that the bird could not be knocked over.

Flint nudged it a few more times, entranced as ever with its bobbing, until he realized that the hazel-eyed woman was waiting for an answer and the little boy was lunging for the toy. The dwarf handed the bird back to the youngster and nodded to the woman.

"You are Flint Fireforge," she stated. It wasn't a question.

Flint nodded again.

"I would like to buy some toys from you," she said abruptly.

"Well," Flint said, drawing it out, "that could be a problem."

"Why?" she demanded.

The dwarf turned and leaned one haunch against the oaken table. He rested one hand on his knee and looked past her toward the oaken hutch. "First of all, I don't *sell* toys. I give them away. Second, I never sell to strangers."

Her sharp features fell into an offended mein, and she turned so fast that the toddler practically swung off his feet. "Well, I guess that's that, then, Master Fireforge," she said, and reached to open the door.

Flint took a deep breath of the shop's metallic air, then spoke just as the woman's hand grasped the door handle. "Of course, if you would bother to introduce yourself, you wouldn't be a stranger," he said mildly, examining the nails on his left hand and using a sliver of iron to clean out the forge dirt he found encrusted there.

The woman stopped, her back to Flint; she appeared to be thinking. Then she swiveled, eyes snapping. "Ailea," she said brusquely. "Eld Ailea to those who know me well." "Eld" meant "aunt" in the elven tongue.

Flint inclined his head. "And I am Flint Fireforge."

"I know th—" she started to say, then sighed and waited.

"And," he continued as though she hadn't spoken, "while I wouldn't sell toys to a stranger, I might be inclined to *give* some to a *friend."*

She sighed again, but a faint smile found its way onto her thin lips. She resembled an Abanasinian cat, offered some prize it had long coveted. But her words showed only exasperation. "I'd heard you could be like this, Master Fireforge," she commented.

Flint swiftly crossed before her and opened the hutch to display the dozens of toys he had brought with him from a winter's worth of carving in Solace. Some had not survived being jounced on the back of a tylor-panicked mule, but most were in fine condition. He gazed at the contents of the hutch, selected a whistle that was too big for the toddler to swallow, and handed it to the little boy, who blew such a ferocious blast on it that the dwarf immediately wished he'd chosen something else. Flint's thick hands continued to move over the toys, plucking out one here, one there, until more than a dozen rested in the front pockets of his loose leather tunic.

Minutes later, the toddler was seated happily on the end of Flint's cot, arranging lines of carved animals on the dwarf's clothes chest and intermittently tooting the whistle. Flint waited for an iron kettle of water to come to a boil on a hook over the forge's fire, and Eld Ailea measured into a tea strainer a tantalizing mixture of dried orange peel, cinnamon pieces, and black tea. She paused to sniff the potpourri. "Wonderful," she said in a low voice, and sighed. "It reminds me of a drink my family used to make when I was a child."

"Where did you grow up?" Flint asked automatically. The spiced tea he carried with him from Solace every trip was more a human specialty than an elven one.

"In Caergoth," she said. When Flint raised an eyebrow at her, she continued, "My father was banished by the Qualinesti."

"For what?" Flint demanded without thinking. The elves almost never banished anybody; the crime must have been deemed one of the most menacing possible under Qualinesti law.

"He led a movement to open Qualinesti to outsiders," she

explained. "He was banished. The family, of course, went with him. Eventually, we settled in Caergoth, where the family had distant relations." Human ones, Flint guessed; that's where the link came in. "I trained as a midwife with a group of clerics, and when I grew old enough, I returned here."

"Why?" The water was boiling, and Flint swung the kettle away from the fire. Catching up a thick woolen sock—practically clean, he figured, having been worn only one day—to use as a potholder, he hauled the water over to the table and poured it over the tea leaves in a heavy ceramic pot.

An expression of sadness slipped across Eld Ailea's face but was gone so quickly that Flint couldn't be sure it had ever been there. "I had no friends but humans, and by the time I'd finally grown up, they'd all died of old age. I know something of weak forms of magic—potions to ease the pain of labor, illusions to amuse children, and the like—but I could do nothing to halt the aging and the death of my child-hood friends."

Flint wondered whether among those long-dead friends was a special man, a human lover, whose passing occa-sioned the sadness that pooled in the old elf's eyes. Sitting at the table and mindlessly moving the strainer through the tea, she looked away and said matter-of-factly, "My parents had died. There were few other elves in Caergoth. I was lonely, so I came back here."

A mist of orange and cinnamon scent wafted from the thick teapot. Over on Flint's cot, the toddler slept sprawled on his back, a wooden cow in one fist and a toy sheep in the other. Eld Ailea spoke again, suddenly cheerful. "I fit in bet-ter here than I did there."

She looked up and must have seen the sympathy in Flint's eyes, because she bristled, her greenish brown eyes growing hard within the corona of silvery braid. "Don't you feel sorry for me, Master Flint Fireforge," she said. "I chose the path I walked."

He cast around for something to say.

"You're sure I can't interest you in some ale?" Flint said.

Eld Ailea leveled a severe look at him. "I'm babysitting," was all she said.

They sat and sipped their drinks for a short time, then Flint reflected that, after all, it was nearly lunchtime. So he got out some *quith-pa* and sliced off a few chunks of cheese, and Eld Ailea retrieved plates from the cupboard. Flint had been to Caergoth on one of his travels, so they talked about the city. It seemed Eld Ailea had left it before Flint had been born. Then Flint demonstrated how he'd made the toddler's bobbing bird toy, and he made her a present of one just like it. And Eld Ailea told him about some of the babies she'd delivered during several centuries—"I delivered the Speaker of the Sun and both his brothers," she said proudly—and how she had retired as a midwife but continued to care for people's infants and small children. "I love babies," she explained, showing animation for the first time. "That's why I came for the toys."

All in all, it was a comfortable way to spend a spring day.

Eventually they finished the last of the cheese and bread. Eld Ailea rinsed their plates and put them away, and Flint went back to work on Tanis's sword—after moving the sleeping elf child from the cot, too near the forge, to a spot on Eld Ailea's lap. The tap of the hammer, while it initially roused the child, ultimately served to lull him more deeply into slumber. The old woman sat quietly, humming to the youngster, sipping one last cup of tea and watching the progress on the sword. An hour passed, and Flint looked up to see Eld Ailea asleep, too, one green-sleeved arm leaning against the table and her cheek resting on the little boy's head. The dwarf smiled and continued working.

The tin chimes on the oaken door of the shop sounded again, and Flint hastily looked up, preparing to hurtle himself at the door and shove Tanis back outside. The sword was beginning to take shape, the blade smooth and tapered, the handguard a fantasy of curving, shimmering steel. Flint heaved a sigh of relief as a robed figure stepped into the shop.

"I didn't interrupt something, did I, Master Fireforge?" Miral asked, a quizzical smile on his thin mouth. His voice, normally raspy, had hoarsened to a whisper. After a sharp glance, he nodded at Eld Ailea, who was slowly awakening. On her lap, her babysitting charge shifted and opened blue eyes.

"Not really," Flint said, "I thought you were someone else . . ." He stepped away from the glow of the forge and swabbed the sweat from his forehead and beard with a handkerchief.

"Tanthalas?" Miral asked, his smile broadening. The old woman sat up purposefully and whispered to the toddler; the child slipped from her lap and ran to collect the carved animals he'd left strewn on the cot. "As a matter of fact," the mage continued, "I came here seeking Tanis. It seemed a safe guess that if he weren't practicing archery in the courtyard, he was probably here with you. Still, if there is some reason you wish to avoid him . . ."

"I just don't want him to spoil the surprise."

The expression on Miral's drawn face asked the unspoken question.

Flint grinned and rubbed his hands together. "It's a gift," he said, gesturing to the half-finished sword, which lay cooling by the forge.

Miral stepped closer to examine the weapon, the orange light of the coals glowing in his pale hair and reflecting off the black leather trim of his long-sleeved, blood-red robe. He reached out a gloved hand and touched the warm metal gently, almost reverently.

"And a wondrous gift it will be," he said, turning to regard Flint. His thoughts appeared far away for a moment. "It's beautiful."

"Bah, it's not even finished yet," Flint said gruffly, but his chest puffed out just the same. He pulled out a grubby length of cloth and tossed it over the weapon. Eld Ailea stood by the door, making preparations to leave. "I made some arrowheads for him, as well, last winter in Solace," Flint added. "I thought I would present Tanis with one grand gift."

"Hmm?" Miral said. Suddenly he shook his head, as if coming back to himself after being lost in reverie. "I'm sorry,

Master Fireforge. I fear I slept little last night. The Speaker plans to make an important announcement tomorrow afternoon—though what it is, only he and Lord Xenoth seem to know—and preparations have kept everyone busy. Even a minor mage has duties. And so does Tanis, if ever I find him."

Saying that he would look for the half-elf in the Grand Market, Miral took his leave of Flint and Eld Ailea, pausing to pat the toddler on the head. The youngster took a swing at the mage with a wooden horse; Miral deftly sidestepped the blow and headed out the door.

"Minor mage," Eld Ailea whispered, her brows knit. She appeared deep in thought. Even after the mage was out of earshot, Eld Ailea continued to hover in the doorway. Twice, she appeared to be on the verge of saying something, then she stopped herself. Meanwhile, the child busied himself with denuding the climbing rose of its lower leaves and strewing them over the doorstep. "I have a confession, Master Fireforge," the alto voice finally confided. "I too came here hoping to find Tanthalas. I . . . I am not welcomed by some at the Palace anymore. Thus I hoped to find him here."

"Oh?" Flint questioned, still watching the receding mage's red robe. "Why?"

"I knew his mother."

She refused to say more, then left immediately.

Chapter 12

The Sword

Qualinost was silent. The night lay over the city like a dark mantle. Although it was closer to dawn than midnight, an orange light still flickered behind the windows of Flint's small shop. Inside, the dwarf sank wearily to a wooden chair, regarding his handiwork before him. The sword was done.

It glimmered flawlessly in the ruddy glow of the forge, the light dancing on its razor-sharp edge and playing along the grooves of the dwarven runes of power that Flint had carved into the flat of the blade. The handguard was fashioned of smooth curves and graceful arcs of steel, so fluid it seemed as if it had grown about the hilt of the sword like the tendrils of some entwining vine. Even Flint—modest as the dwarf was wont to be—sensed there was something special about this sword. He could only hope Tanis would like it.

He enjoyed pleasing the half-elf. Perhaps someday he could show Tanis around Solace and let him see that elves weren't the only folk on Krynn. That would please Tanis even more than the sword would, he thought.

Flint sighed and then stood. He banked the coals beneath the ashes in the furnace and blew out the one tallow candle shining in the dimness. By silver moonlight, he found his way to his bed in the small room behind the shop and, kicking off his boots, he tumbled down into exhausted slumber. Soon the dwarf's snores rumbled upon the air, as rhythmic as the plying of his hammer only moments before.

* * * * *

It was the darkest part of the night. The door to the shop swung slowly open, smoothly, so that the chimes made no noise. A figure stepped through, carefully shutting the door behind itself. It paused, cocking its head, and then, as if satisfied, drifted soundlessly toward the workbench.

The sword shone faintly in the cool light of Solinari, spilling in through the window. The dark, cloaked figure lifted a gloved hand and ran a finger down the length of the blade, as if testing its edge, and then it held both hands above the weapon. Murmured words spilled forth on the air, spoken in an ancient tongue of a people turned to dust age upon age ago, the name of their people long forgotten. Few spoke the tongue now, save sorcerers and mages, for it was the language of magic.

The mumbling ended, the last syllables drifting on the air like motes of dust. The sword began to glow, not with moonlight, but with a light from within. It was a crimson brightness, growing hotter and hotter, until the sword gave off an angry illumination, the color of fire. Nearby, a small mound of iron arrowheads also took on the glow. Suddenly a shadow seemed to separate from the darkness beyond the ring of illumination and drifted toward the sword, as if beckoned by the stranger's hand. The shadow defied the crimson light until suddenly it flowed down, coursing into the blade as if it had been sucked in. The weapon gave a small jerk, then the illumination faded.

The door to the shop swung in the gentle night breeze. The snores continued, uninterrupted. The stranger was gone.

Chapter 13

The Announcement

Flint encountered Tanis the next morning in the Grand Market; the half-elf stood before a tent with a sign that read, "Lady Kyanna: Seeress of All Planes." Underneath, a smaller sign read, "Special Rates Available." The midnight-blue tent was decorated with silver silhouettes of moons and constellations. Several young elves, only a few years out of childhood, and giggling as they fingered their coins, slipped around Tanis and Flint and entered the tent. The scent of incense drifted from the tent as they moved the flap back, and a low voice intoned, "Welcome to a view of your futures, fair elves."

"Seers," Flint snorted. "Crooks and charlatans, all of them. Why, did I ever tell you the time I was at the Autumn Festival in Solace? Let's see, . . ." the dwarf mused. "It must have been not long after that day I bested those ten highwaymen in the Inn of the Last Home."

Tanis resisted Flint's efforts to draw him away from the seer's tent. "I wouldn't mind a look into my future," he said. The dwarf snorted and dragged him down the tiled pathway left open between the tents and stalls. The half-elf seemed suddenly to come to himself. With one last longing gaze at Lady Kyanna's tent, he looked at Flint with a quirk of his features and prompted, "You were saying?"

"A Solace street wizard tried to sell me an elixir he claimed would make me invisible," Flint said, allowing the half-elf to draw to a stop before the stall of an elf who sold, of all things, swords. "It looked suspiciously like clear water to my eye, but he said to me, 'Of course it's clear. Otherwise, it wouldn't make you invisible, now would it?' Well, when I got home with the elixir—"

Tanis turned from stroking the hilt of a sword. "You mean you bought it?" he asked in disbelief.

"Not because I believed a word of the street wizard's sly talk, mind you," Flint said testily, his eyes flashing, trying once again to hustle the half-elf away from the sword display. "I knew all along it was a hoax. I just wanted to have some evidence so I could turn him in to the authorities for the charlatan he was."

"So what happened when you used the elixir?" Tanis asked smoothly, his attention still engaged by the weaponry display. "Those are beautiful swords. I could use—"

"Shoddy workmanship," Flint interjected, hauling on the half-elf's arm, ignoring the furious glance of the weapon seller. "You don't need a sword. Who is there to fight in Qualinost? Anyway, I drank the potion down and thought I could get away with pinching a tankard or two off this snub-nosed innkeeper who had cheated me a few days back, giving me a mug of watered-down ale instead of the good stuff," Flint said, a wickedly gleeful grin on his face. But then he frowned. "Except that somehow the bouncer—who was sure to be half hobgoblin if he was anything at all— managed to see me and . . . Hey!" Flint said indignantly, realizing he had told a bit more of the tale than he'd meant to.

He glared at Tanis, but the half-elf only regarded him with a serious expression.

"And . . .?" Tanis asked.

"And keep your nose in your own business!" Flint griped. "Don't you have other things to be worrying about?"

Slowly, deftly, Flint lured Tanis past the entrancing displays in the Grand Market and back to the dwarf's shop. They entered silently, Flint trying out various small speeches in his head, but ultimately, wordless, not knowing what to say, Flint stalked over to the table, where something long and slender lay concealed beneath a dark cloth.

"What is it?" Tanis asked, stepping nearer.

"Just something I finished last night," Flint said, and then he whisked the cloth away.

The sword lay beneath, bright as a bolt of lightning frozen still and solid. Several dozen arrowheads, dull black and wickedly sharp, lay next to the sword.

Tanis's eyes, of course, went straight to the sword. "Flint, it's a wonder," Tanis said softly, reaching out a hand to brush the cool metal.

"Do you like it?" Flint asked, raising his bushy eyebrows. "It's a gift, you know."

"For . . ." The half-elf trailed off, and his face went stony. For a shocked half-moment, the dwarf feared that Tanis didn't like the sword; then he saw Tanis's hands clench, and he realized his friend was fighting back some strong emotion. "Oh, I couldn't take it," the half-elf said softly at last, gazing at the weapon with covetous eyes.

"Sure you can," Flint said testily. "You'd better, lad."

Tanis hesitated a few heartbeats longer, then reached for the sword with a tentative hand. Finally, he grasped the hilt. It was cool and smooth, and somehow it felt right. A shiver ran up his spine. The sword was more than a weapon. It was a thing of cool beauty.

"Thank you, Flint," he said softly.

The dwarf waved away the half-elf's words. "Just find a use for the thing, and I'll be happy," he said.

"Oh," said Tanis fervently, "I will."

*　*　*　*　*

Even after all his years amid the elves, Flint still felt awed every time he set foot within the Tower of the Sun, and he never failed to pause for a moment just outside the central chamber's gilded doors and shut his eyes, paying silent respect to the dwarven craftsmen who had built it so long ago.

The great doors swung open before him this afternoon, their bas-relief cherubs grinning wickedly for a second as they angled away, looking at the dwarf out of the corners of their eyes. Flint shook the notion from his head and stepped inside, being careful not to look all the way up at the six-hundred-foot ceiling.

It's not that it makes my stomach a bit flopsy to gaze all the way up there, mind you, Flint told himself. I just don't want to spoil it all by going and looking at it every single time I walk into the room.

Most of the courtiers had arrived, Flint saw, but the Speaker himself was absent, as was Tanis. "Sure as a hammer is heavy, he'll be late," Flint grumbled, shaking his head so that his beard wagged back and forth. Figuring he was on his own for a while, he moved away from the gathered elves, leaned against one of the pillars that lined the chamber, and waited for court to begin.

Courtiers, opulently attired in long tunics of green, brown, and russet silk embroidered with silver and gold thread, stood in groups around the hall, their quiet voices echoing in the upper reaches of the Tower. Much of the conversation, Flint realized as he stood by the pillar, centered on the Tower guards' inability to catch the tylor.

"How difficult can it be to locate one twenty- or thirty-foot monster?" one old elf complained. "In my day, the beast would have been slain days ago."

The elf's companion sought to mitigate the elder one's ire. "The forest is large and magical. The Speaker should form a special troop, with a wizard and the best-trained men, to track, corner, and slay the beast." The old elf nodded his agreement.

"Everyone's an expert," Flint muttered.

Porthios's friends Ulthen and Selena, the woman's slender arm entwined around the elven lord's waist, glided by and took up a position on the other side of the pillar. Selena's eyes, the dwarf saw, were constantly on, not her companion Ulthen, but Litanas, Lord Xenoth's new assistant, who stood with the adviser at the foot of the rostrum. Flint moved over a foot or so, hoping they wouldn't see him. He knew Selena, Litanas, and Ulthen were part of the group of elves that didn't want outsiders in court, even though the blond Selena rarely failed to gush over Flint's "wonderful dwarven artistry" when she saw him.

Selena's cutting voice came clearly to his ears.

"Well, Litanas told *me* that Tyresian threatened Xenoth if the adviser didn't stop throwing impediments in his way. But Litanas didn't know exactly what the argument was about. I think Xenoth hides things from Litanas, which just isn't fair because Lord Litanas is one of the most intelli—"

Ulthen tried to quiet her. "Selena, your voice . . ." he said.

"Oh, Ulthen, leave me be. Anyway, Litanas said . . ."

Ulthen grimaced, and Flint realized that the young lord probably heard "Litanas said" a lot.

"Well, *I* heard that the Speaker is going to cancel the *Kentommen* until the tylor is captured."

Ulthen's voice was growing impatient. "Oh, Selena, don't be ridiculous."

Her voice rocketed to a screech. "Ridiculous! How safe do you think it is, to have people coming in from all over, on the same trails that the tylor has made so dangerous?"

Ulthen—and Flint, on the other side of the pillar—had to admit that Selena had a point. Perhaps that's what this announcement was all about. It would almost certainly be the first time a *Kentommen* was canceled; tradition dictated that the ceremony be held on the lord's ninety-ninth birthday, and quite a crisis would be required to delay one.

Just then the gilded doors swung open, and the Speaker stepped through, followed by Laurana. The reflected sunlight that filled the Tower shimmered off his green-gold robes, and Solostaran walked with regal grace into the chamber. Flint made his way toward his friend.

The Speaker was greeting various courtiers, exchanging pleasantries, but Flint noticed immediately that there was something odd about the Speaker today. If the Speaker of the Sun had changed at all in the twenty years that Flint had known him, then the dwarf was unaware of the differences; the Speaker stood as straight as the Tower itself, his face still as timeless as the marble of the Tower's inner walls. But today, though his eyes were normally as clear and warm as a midsummer's day, there was a troubled look in them.

"Master Fireforge," the Speaker said as he turned to see the dwarf standing patiently beside him, not wishing to interrupt the Speaker's conversation with the courtiers. "I am glad you could be here."

"I'll always come, should you ask it," Flint said. For the first time, he noticed a faint wrinkle in the Speaker's smooth brow, beneath his gold circlet of state.

The Speaker smiled at the dwarf, but the expression seemed wan. "Thank you, Flint," he said, and Flint was slightly surprised. It was the first time he could remember the Speaker calling him by his first name in a formal setting. "I fear I'm going to need a friend such as you today."

"I don't understand," Flint said.

"The bonds of friendship are strong, Flint, but sometimes they can bind too tightly." The Speaker's gaze flicked over the crowd, came to rest on Lord Xenoth and Litanas, then moved away.

"Oh, I see," Flint said gruffly. "I'll just leave you alone, then."

"No, Master Fireforge," the Speaker said then, placing his hands on Flint's shoulders before the dwarf could walk away. A hint of a smile played across his lips before drifting away again. "I am speaking of a different sort of friendship, that between two houses. While such ties have helped me— and my father before me—in the past, I regret the price I must pay for that friendship now."

"But what is it?" Flint asked. What could one do for a friend that would be so distasteful?

The Speaker softly shook his head. "I'm afraid you will hear soon enough. But tell me, Flint, that later you'll have the time to drink a cup of wine with an old elf."

The Speaker smiled once more as Flint assented, then walked toward the rostrum in the center of the chamber. The Speaker ascended the podium, and the courtiers ended their conversations to turn their attention toward him. Where was Tanis? Flint wondered.

Porthios stood to his father's left, near Lord Xenoth and Litanas, seemingly trying to appear as regal as the Speaker, but looking to Flint more like a puffed-up young rooster. Porthios's younger brother, Gilthanas, stood to the right of the rostrum with the rest of the ceremonial guards. The guards wore black leather jerkins, glinting with silver filigree entwined in the symbol of the Sun and the Tree. It was the same symbol that had adorned the flag that Kith-Kanan had borne with him when he had first set foot within the forest of Qualinesti.

Gilthanas had joined the guard not half a year ago. He was still little more than a boy, only slightly older than Laurana, but Flint knew that Porthios had argued long and hard with the captain of the guard to gain the position for Gilthanas. Although Gilthanas did his best to imitate the rigid stance of the other guards, holding his sword before him in the traditional salute, the weapon seemed too heavy for his slight frame. Flint shook his head. He had to give the boy credit for trying so hard to be strong, but Flint wasn't exactly sure what Gilthanas seemed to be trying to prove.

Just as the Speaker raised his hands in greeting to the entire court, signaling the beginning of the proceedings, Flint was jostled from behind. He spun around, eyes flashing, to give a piece of his mind to the clumsy idiot who hadn't the sense to watch where he was going.

"Tanis!" he whispered, relieved that his friend was finally here. Tanis was breathing hard, and a sheen of sweat slicked his skin. "What in Reorx's name are you doing traipsing in here so late?" he whispered hotly.

"Hush, Flint," Tanis said softly, gesturing toward the rostrum where the Speaker was beginning his address.

"I thank you all for coming here today," the Speaker was saying to the nobles gathered about the rostrum. "I have great news to share with you, news which I hope will give you all cause for joy.

"First, however, I must confess to an ulterior motive in inviting you all here." The Speaker smiled. "You know, of course, that a rapacious beast has been ravaging the countryside around Qualinost. Several people have been lost to the creature, and farmers on the outskirts of the area have reported that increasing numbers of livestock have been missing. My advisers tell me this beast, a tylor, no doubt has built a lair somewhere near one of the trails from Solace. Troops who have been sent out to hunt for the monster have been unable to locate it, but they have seen signs of the beast and believe they have pinned down the general area where the creature . . ."—he paused— "feeds."

The Speaker's features softened as he looked out over the group of courtiers.

"Thus, I am asking for volunteers to join together and seek out the tylor. Because the creature has some magical abilities, Mage Miral has graciously agreed to go along." Miral, standing by a pillar across from Flint, inclined his head, crossed his arms, and slid them far into his sleeves. "And Lord Tyresian has accepted the position as leader of the hunt." Tyresian's tight smile looked more like a grimace than a grin.

"I am hoping that the most skilled of you will consent to accompany this volunteer troop to the area where we believe the tylor's lair is located. Are there volunteers?"

Porthios was the first to speak. "I will go, of course."

The Speaker hesitated as he beheld his elder son. Lord Xenoth, silver robe swishing in his agitation, interjected, "Are you sure it is wise for the heir apparent to be exposed to such danger, Speaker?" Porthios tensed and flushed deeply, and sympathy shone on the Speaker's face.

"My son is about to go through his *Kentommen*, Lord Xenoth. I believe it would be the gravest of mistakes to refuse him the right to participate with the other men."

Porthios eased his stance and flashed a look of barely disguised thankfulness at his father and an equally strong glare at the adviser.

"Then I will go, too. To protect him," Xenoth rejoined, pulling his frail body into a vengeful stance. Tyresian laughed, joined by several courtiers, and turned away.

Now it was Miral's turn to interrupt. "With all respect, Speaker," the mage said, unfolding his arms from his sleeves, "I think the hunt should be restricted to the young and the strong, not the elderly and infirm."

Flint felt a wave of irritation. As much as he could live without the crotchety, stranger-hating Lord Xenoth, it was unlike the mage to be so cruel in public—especially toward a long-time member of court. Xenoth opened his mouth to protest, but the Speaker silenced his adviser with an imperious look and a quietly spoken, "I will not turn down volunteers, Miral."

Xenoth stared daggers at the mage, who looked impassively back.

Selena poked Ulthen in the side, and that lord volunteered nervously. That prompted Litanas to speak up as well. Soon a half-dozen other courtiers added their names to the list. Suddenly, Flint felt Tanis stir at his side. "And I, Speaker," he called.

"Tanis!" protested Laurana.

"Tanis?" echoed Flint, more quietly.

"What better way to try out my new sword and arrowheads?" Tanis whispered to his friend.

Lord Tyresian, coldness emanating from him like a chill from the marble walls, glowered at the half-elf. "It's bad enough that I must have a useless old man in my troop, but a half-elf?"

That was enough. "And a dwarf, as well, Lord Tyresian," Flint chimed in.

What happened then might have been funny under other circumstances. The elves between Flint and Tyresian parted and drew back, leaving an unbroken stripe of unoccupied floor between them. Elf lord and dwarf engaged in a brief stare-down, until Solostaran's resonant voice drew all eyes back to him. "I accept your offers, Master Fireforge, Tanis." When Tyresian opened his mouth to argue, the Speaker said simply, "I am Speaker still, Lord Tyresian."

"What do you suppose *that* meant?" Selena asked Ulthen in a stage whisper.

Tyresian was quick to back down. "Very well, Speaker. You know best, of course."

When no other voices were forthcoming, Tyresian told the volunteers to meet at the palace stable one hour after dawn the next day. Then he turned and faced the Speaker, and the rest of the courtiers followed his lead.

It appeared that the moment had arrived for the major announcement.

"All of you know, of course, my daughter, Lauralanthalasa Kanan," Solostaran said. "And you know, as well, that the time when she will no longer be a child is not so far off. It is right then, that her future should be made clear, to her and to all of us, and so I've chosen this day to make that so."

He held out his hand, and Laurana stepped to his side, her green dress whispering as she drifted across the floor, her hair shimmering like molten gold in the sunlight as she came to a halt before the rostrum. She curtsied gracefully to her father, and then to the courtiers. Laurana gazed out over the crowd and located the half-elf, a questioning look in her green eyes. Flint felt Tanis shrug beside him, and he wondered what was afoot.

Turning slightly so he could see Tanis's face, Flint noticed Tanis watching Laurana intently. He looked troubled and fidgeted with some small object in one of his hands, but Flint couldn't see exactly what it was. Laurana appeared as much in the dark about what exactly was going on as the rest of the courtiers did. Tyresian alone seemed confident; Xenoth's wrinkled features looked unrelievedly disgruntled.

The Speaker smiled at his daughter, but it seemed a sorrowful expression, then he turned his gaze back toward the courtiers. "It has been the longstanding honor and joy of my family to count among its closest friends the Third House of Qualinost. Indeed, it was the Lord of the Third House who lent me the strength of his hand in the dark years following the upheaval of the Cataclysm, and so helped me assure the continuance of the peace we cherish here in our homeland." The courtiers nodded; they knew that.

"At that time, the Lord of the Third House—whose name I may hold only in memory, now that he has stepped beyond the edges of this world—had a young son, and in my gratitude to him, I promised a great gift for that son. The son of the Lord of the Third House stands among us today, and you know him now as the lord of that honored house himself: Lord Tyresian."

The tall, handsome elf lord, resplendent in a tunic the color of dark red wine, bowed deeply to the Speaker. Too deeply, Flint thought to himself, if there could be such a thing. It was only that the gesture had seemed more of a show, rather than an act of sincerity.

"Speaker, I thank you for calling me forward on this joyous day," Tyresian said. He cast a sideways look at Laurana, but the elf woman seemed hardly to have noticed him. Her eyes were on Tanis.

The Speaker nodded at Tyresian and then lifted his arms, as if he were encompassing both the elf lord and his daughter. "I give to you, then, an occasion for celebration," he said in a voice as clear as a trumpet's call. "For on this day, it is my duty and pleasure to announce the great gift that was granted Lord Tyresian long ago. Let all the people of Qualinost know that, from this day forward, the hand of my beloved daughter, Lauralanthalasa, is betrothed to Lord Tyresian of the Third House, until such day as the two be joined as husband and wife."

A whispered gasp ran about the chamber, followed by scattered applause that gained rapidly in strength and volume. Tyresian seemed to glow before the courtiers, but Flint saw that the Speaker seemed exhausted. Miral had stepped onto the podium—an action against protocol—and he appeared to be surreptitiously supporting the Speaker, preventing him from stumbling. The mage cast a dark glance at Tyresian.

Flint cast a hurried look at Tanis, but the half-elf seemed hardly to be marking the furor around him. He only stared glassily forward, clutching the small object, the one he had been fidgeting with, tightly in one of his fists.

"But . . ." Laurana said, and stopped. Her need to express

herself clearly battled with her deference to court decorum and her love for her father. "Why didn't you tell . . . ?" She faltered and grew silent. The applause ended abruptly, and a tenseness descended over the Tower.

"I thought . . ." Laurana tried again and looked desperately toward Tanis. "But we made a promise long ago . . ."

The courtiers, some looking shocked, others pleased, still others merely fascinated by the turn of events, began to swivel to gaze at the uneasy half-elf.

Tyresian looked annoyed but unworried. Porthios narrowed his eyes and glared at the half-elf. The Speaker's face held a worried expression; little is as important to an elf as honor. Laurana continued to watch Tanis beseechingly.

Tanis suddenly blinked, as if startled. "Oh, no," he said, so softly that only Flint could hear.

"Is this so, Tanis?" the Speaker asked. "Are the two of you promised, without my knowledge or approval?"

The half-elf looked around wildly. Only Flint's eyes held any sympathy. "I . . ." he said. "Yes, but . . . It was long ago . . ."

Flint edged closer and caught his friend's elbow with one strong hand. "Gather your thoughts, lad," he hissed. "Or be silent."

But Tanis stammered, "We were children . . . not serious. I thought so, anyway."

Laurana gasped, then slipped quickly from the chamber, not meeting anyone's eyes, her slippers tapping against the floor. Tyresian followed.

Court, needless to say, quickly came to an end.

Chapter 14

The Aftermath

"I trust you'll be able to take care of this little ... problem, Speaker," Tyresian said smoothly. He calmly refilled his wine glass from a crystal decanter and smiled absently. He swirled the ruby-clear liquid around so that it glowed like a dark gem in the light of the sunset that spilled through the glass walls of the Speaker's private office.

The Speaker nodded wearily. "Of course, Tyresian. Indeed, there is no problem." The Speaker's own glass stood untouched on the table before him, but though his face seemed haggard, his green eyes were as clear as ever, his shoulders as straight and square.

Tanis watched anxiously from a position as near the door as he could get without looking as if he were about to flee. After the chaos following Laurana's outburst had subsided—due largely to Xenoth's good sense in herding the agitated courtiers from the Tower—the Speaker had bid a private meeting be held in the palace. Only a scant few had been called to attend: Tyresian, of course, since the matter directly concerned him; Miral and Porthios, standing beside the Speaker; and, lastly, Tanis. Solostaran had ordered a servant to fetch Laurana, but the Speaker's daughter was nowhere to be found, the servant reported.

Laurana's actions left Tanis as confused as anybody—probably more so. He sighed and tried not to fidget with the ring concealed in his pocket. It felt as if it were glowing white-hot, about to burn a hole in the cloth of his breeches and fall shimmering to the floor, betraying its presence to everyone.

He desperately wished Flint were here. Flint would have had some gruff words that would make things all right, but the dwarf had not been invited.

"Remember, she is little more than a child, Tyresian," the Speaker went on.

"True. But sometimes childish infatuations are those that linger most strongly, especially when they are denied." Tyresian cast a glance back at Tanis. The half-elf expected a look of malice in the elf lord's eyes, but there was no such darkness in Tyresian's expression, only a look of mild curiosity. That was all, as if somehow he found it puzzling and almost amusing to find Tanis playing the part of a rival—unwilling or no—in all of this.

"Tyresian," the Speaker said then, standing up. "Long ago an agreement was made between our two houses." He moved to the windows and gazed for a moment out into the myriad colors of the dwindling sunset before turning his attention back to the elf lord. The Speaker seemed very much in control now, despite his weariness.

"The word of my house is held important above all else, for without honesty, there is nothing. And in honesty, I must tell you that I would rather my daughter did not have to think of her future while still so young. I would rather she might know the joy of wedding one who has courted her and won her heart rather than one who was chosen for her by two old men before she was born, her betrothed little more than a child himself. Now, I do not mean to belittle what your father did for me—the Lord of the Third House was too great a friend for that—but still, I wish one thing to be clear: There is little in this world that means more to me than my daughter. And while her hand will be yours, her blood will always be mine. Do not forget this. And treat her accordingly."

Tyresian stared for a long moment at the Speaker. A bit of the overbearing pride seemed to have been washed out of him. "Of course, Speaker," he said finally, his voice subdued. "I should not have doubted, but I thank you for your assurances all the same." With a stiff half-bow, the elf lord stepped away from the Speaker, then brushed past Tanis and left the chamber.

"Was that the right thing to do?" the Speaker asked after Tyresian had gone. He seemed to be addressing no one in particular, but Porthios stepped to his side.

"Of course it was, Father," he said earnestly. "You have kept your word. Beyond that, what else is of importance?"

"Yes," the Speaker said, though it was apparent this was not what he had implied.

"You've assured Tyresian of what he wants, if that's what you mean," Miral said. There was a hardness to his voice that Tanis had never heard before. "He stands closer on the line of ascendancy now."

The Speaker waved his hand, dismissing the statement. "Only through marriage. That matters little. There are those who stand before him." He glanced at Porthios.

"Of course," Miral said, but the Speaker's words hardly seemed to have assuaged his troubles.

"I think I would like to be alone for a time," the Speaker said, and Tanis breathed a quiet sigh of relief. Miral nodded, then he and Porthios joined Tanis at the door, leaving the Speaker to gaze out the windows and into the twilight.

"Tanthalas," the Speaker said softly then, halting Tanis in his tracks. "I'll wish to speak to you before the hunt tomorrow morning." Tanis waited a long heartbeat, but no more words came, and he followed Miral and Porthios, shutting the door behind him.

Miral was already disappearing down the corridor, his stride quick and purposeful, but Porthios was waiting outside the door for Tanis.

"This is all your fault, you know," Porthios said. Shadows darkened his deep-set eyes, and the muscles about his jaw were clenched.

"I didn't know, Porthios," Tanis managed to say, though his tongue felt as stiff as dried leather. "How could I know what Laurana would do?"

Porthios seemed hardly to have heard him. "The Speaker's pain is on your hands, Tanis. Don't forget that. *I* certainly won't." He spoke the words so sharply they might have been knives cast, one by one, into Tanis's heart. "I will not allow you to hurt him with your childish games with Laurana." With that, he turned on a heel and walked swiftly down the corridor.

Tanis shook his head. Why was everyone blaming him for something Laurana had done? He didn't want this to happen any more than anyone else did. He sighed, clutching the smooth, delicate ring in his pocket. For a moment, he had the impulse to throw it as hard as he could down the marble corridor, but then the feeling faded, and he shoved it deeper in his pocket as he started down the lonely hallway, wondering where Flint was.

* * * * *

Working at the forge that evening did little to lift the worry that nibbled at Flint's thoughts.

He kept his hands busy, as if he could beat the memories of the day's troubling events from his mind with the ring of his hammer. It was to no avail, however, and he found himself wondering where Tanis was, and how the half-elf was faring.

Ah, things'll settle down soon enough, you worry-wart, Flint told himself. They'll all forget Laurana's outburst, and then folks'll leave Tanis alone. But deep down, he sensed the untruth of those words. Something was changing here in the peaceful elven city where nothing had changed in years and years. Briefly he wondered if the Speaker *had* erred in allowing trade with outsiders—including Flint himself. Already the dwarf had affected the practices of the elven smiths, who were adopting some of the techniques that Flint had learned from his father. Perhaps there were other, more important, changes that could be traced to his presence.

He hoped Tanis would stop by.

* * * * *

The central wing of the palace was the largest of the three wings. The wings focused around the courtyard in the back, with the gardens behind that. In the middle of the central wing, the corridor widened into the palace's Great Hall, and here the ceiling was vaulted in a series of arches. The hall's periphery was lined with smooth stone columns, skillfully carved to resemble trunks of trees, and leaves of silver and gold shimmered in the dimness on the ends of their marble branches. The tree-columns supported a promenade that encircled the Great Hall, and it was here that the nobles of the court stood to watch elaborate ceremonies take place below them: funerals, coronations, or weddings.

In the center of the ceiling was a great stained-glass skylight. It glowed, its colored patterns mysterious. Solinari must be rising, Tanis realized as he stopped to gaze at the skylight for a time. The moon's beams filtered through the sunburst-shaped skylight. He found himself wondering how Laurana was. An image of the bright-haired elf flickered through his mind. Tanis shook his head. This was something that was going to take him a long time to figure out—if he ever would at all. Perhaps the fresh air of the garden would clear his thoughts.

Although it was spring, there was a coolness to the air that reminded Tanis more of the dark months of deep winter, and he wrapped his gray cloak tightly about his shoulders as he walked to the garden.

The twilight sky was clear, but on the western horizon, just above the tops of the trees, he thought he saw the first iron-gray wisps of clouds gathering. But if it was a storm brewing there, far to the west, over the jagged peaks of the Kharolis Mountains, it would be a long while before it reached Qualinesti.

He wandered along the stone pathways through the great courtyard nestled between the palace's wings. The crocus and jonquils had already faded, and now the lilies were beginning to bloom, their pale, slender flowers swaying with the breeze, seeming to nod like faces as Tanis passed by.

He made his way past the gate that marked the entrance to a twisting topiary maze and rounded a corner, coming into a small grotto. Suddenly he stopped.

He heard a gasp, and a fair head turned as his moccasins crunched on the gravel. It was Laurana. She stood, a lily clutched in one of her small hands. When he drew near he could see, by the puffiness of her smooth face in Solinari's reflected light, that she had been weeping.

But she had her emotions under control now, and in her self-possession, Tanis could see that Laurana truly was the daughter of the Speaker of the Sun. Even in sorrow and anger, she had grace.

"Hello," she said, her light voice low.

He surveyed her quietly for a short time. Off in the distance, as if in a dream, he could hear the roar of the water in the ravines that protected Qualinost. Nearby, the leaves rustled in the evening breeze.

If anything, her exotic elven features were more arresting in the half-light. "I am sorry about today," Laurana said, twisting the lily. "I spoke without thinking, and now you're in trouble. But I *cannot* marry Lord Tyresian. He's . . ." She trailed off. "I'll just have to explain that to my father."

"It's all right," Tanis said, for want of anything else to say to ease her troubles, but this seemed enough, for she smiled at him then and took his hand.

"Laurana, I—" Tanis began, but his words faltered. He wanted to tell her that she was wrong, that the Speaker would never go back on his word, that it was best for her to stop playing these silly games with him. Their vows to marry had been children's promises, and they weren't children anymore. At any rate, if the Speaker of the Sun ordered her to marry Tyresian to uphold the honor of the house, she was going to have to wed the elven lord, unless she were willing to destroy her father politically.

Laurana continued relentlessly, "My father *has* to listen to me." And Tanis realized that at this moment, despite her exterior calm, she was very close to panic.

He should give her the ring back, he thought. But somehow, in the state she was in, he knew that would break her heart, and so all he said was, "I'm sure you're right. The Speaker has to listen."

He winced at the lie, but there was nothing else he could say. It seemed to ease Laurana's torment at any rate, for her coral lips curved and she began to talk of other matters as they walked through the garden. The paths were silvery in the growing moonlight, and even though little detail could be seen in the gardens, the two could inhale the heady scent of roses.

They reached the end of the path closest to the palace. Laurana hesitated. "We should go in separately," she said.

Tanis agreed. It wasn't a time to be spotted sneaking into the palace together.

"I'll see you soon, love," she whispered to him, and, standing on tiptoe, kissed his cheek. She slipped away then, through the garden, leaving Tanis, slightly dazed, to continue alone.

"It didn't take you long, did it?" a voice said sharply, and Tanis spun around. He sucked in a sharp breath of air. Porthios stood near one of the pear trees, so straight as to appear one himself. "She's been betrothed for mere hours, and already you're sneaking around in the dark with her."

The young elf lord watched him warily as Tanis stared in shock. How much had Porthios seen?

"It's not what you think," Tanis began hurriedly, but Porthios only scowled at him.

"It never is, is it, Tanis?" he said. He moved, as if to turn away, but then he stopped, regarding the half-elf intently. "Why are you doing this, Tanis? Just once, couldn't you try to behave like a true elf? Must you always be different?"

When Tanis failed to answer, Porthios stalked away through the twilight.

* * * * *

Miral knew the upheaval of the day would give him nightmares. He struggled to stave off the demons of his dreams. Sitting at the desk in his dim room, surrounded by spellcasting materials, he forced his weak eyes to gaze into the flame of a candle until the tears streamed.

Yet in the end, his efforts proved futile. He finally had to wrench his pained gaze from the candle fire and close his eyes, and in the moment it took his lids to touch, sleep claimed him. His head fell forward on his crossed arms.

He was in the cavern again. As always in his dreams, he was a child again. Light, with the power of ten thousand torches, drilled into his young eyes and he cried until he was hoarse. The light pulsed, pounding into him until he shook in its grip. He feared the light.

Yet he feared the dark as well. For at the fringes of the light waited the evil creatures of every child's dreams—dragons and ogres and trolls, all hungry and mean and willing to wait forever to get at him. The child Miral gazed from light to dark and tried to choose, but he was little and afraid.

Then warmth suffused him like a pleasant bath. He heard a simple childhood tune, played on a lute. The scent of his mama's perfume—crushed rose petals—filled his nostrils, and he knew she'd be there soon to save him from the light, give him dinner, and put him to bed with a story. That's what mamas were for, after all. He waited eagerly.

But she didn't come, and he grew impatient, then afraid that this meant she never would come.

He heard the sound of footsteps. And he knew instinctively that, not only were the steps not from his mama, but that they were made by someone his mama would want him to stay away from.

He began to cry and clenched his tiny hands into fists.

The hands of the sleeping mage also clenched and relaxed, clenched and relaxed, in growing fear.

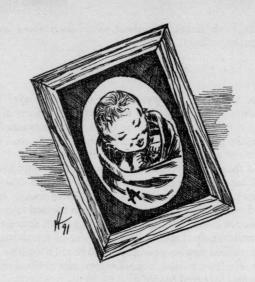

Chapter 15

Late-Night Visits

Tanis, looking as somber as the deepening night, had no sooner arrived at Flint's shop than the dwarf hustled him back out the door and slammed it behind them.

"Where—?" Tanis protested, tripping on the fieldstone path that connected shop and street. His sword, which he had refused to be without ever since Flint had presented it to him, slapped in its sheath at his side.

"Never mind," the dwarf snapped, hurtling along ahead of him. "Come on."

The spring night was chilly, and few elves were out, but the two or three who were on the streets stared as the dwarf towed the half-elf down the lane before Flint's shop, then across the mosaic of the Hall of the Sky and into a tree-lined path beyond. The scents of spring—earth, vegetation, and blossoms—filled Tanis's nostrils, but he paid little attention to anything other than the dwarf's head bobbing before him.

Finally, Tanis set his moccasined feet, grabbed a branch with his free hand, and refused to move until Flint told him their destination.

"We're going to visit a lady," the dwarf explained testily.

Tanis grimaced. "A lady got me into this mess, Flint. Are you sure this is such a good idea?"

Flint crossed his arms before his chest and looked as stubborn as his friend. "This lady knew your mother. I want you to meet her."

Tanis, mouth agape, beheld the dwarf in confusion. "A lot of people at the palace knew my mother. What's so special about this one?" he demanded, beginning to grow angry. "Is she a wizard? Can she bring my mother back from the dead? What's the point, Flint?"

"Oh, leave that," the dwarf replied irritably. "Would you rather sit in your quarters and mope? Or in my shop and mope?" Flint tugged at his arm. "Just come on, son."

"No."

Tanis's voice was mulish, and the dwarf knew there would be no strong-arming him now. "All right," Flint said. "The lady was with your mother when she died."

Tanis felt a quiver go through him. "She told you that?"

"No," Flint replied. "I put two and two together. Now come on."

Tanis reluctantly let the dwarf lead him again, albeit at a slower pace and without the arm-tugging that had accompanied the first leg of their journey. "Who is she?"

"A midwife. Retired, anyway."

"Where does she live?"

"I don't know."

Tanis dug in his feet again. "Then how will we know when we get there?"

"Trust me." The dwarf's voice was curt. Flint resumed walking, and Tanis had to keep going or be left behind.

Minutes later, they emerged from the trees into the western portion of Qualinost, overlooking the site of the Grand

Market. At this time of night, the open space was nearly deserted, of course. But on the other side of the park more rose quartz homes had sprouted, gleaming with a purplish hue in the blue evening light.

Flint accosted a middle-aged elf. "Can you tell me where I can find the midwife Ailea?" he asked, panting from the effort he'd expended so far.

"Eld Ailea?" the man repeated, looking from Flint to Tanis with a befuddled look. "Down that way." He pointed. "Don't waste your time. Hurry!"

"Come on, Tanis!" Flint said, thanking the man and trotting in the direction the man had indicated. "That one looked confused."

Tanis smiled and jogged loosely to keep up with the short-legged dwarf. "I think he was wondering which of us was the father-to-be."

Flint's pace slackened. "Now that's an interesting thought," the dwarf said, grinning wickedly. "I wouldn't mind dandling your and Laurana's kiddies on my knee. 'Uncle Flint,' I'd tell them to call me . . ." He stopped teasing Tanis when he caught the glower on the half-elf's face.

Soon they came to a crossroads. "Which way now?" Flint mused. He asked directions of an elven woman, strolling along the street with a basket of yarn. Wordlessly, she gestured with the basket at a tall, narrow house built of quartz, with a gray granite doorstep and matching window frames. The downstairs was dark, but a warm light glowed through the shutters of the second-level window.

Tanis hung back. "Flint, I don't think . . ."

"Sure you do," the dwarf said, and pounded on the door of the abode. He shoved Tanis in front of him and stepped back into the shadows.

They waited in the dark, the chill air making them shiver as they watched a lamp flare within the home and heard footsteps descending stairs and approaching the door. "Coming, coming, coming," an alto voice sang.

Soon the door swung open, and Eld Ailea poked her cat-like face out, gazing up at Tanis.

"How far apart are the contractions?" she demanded.

"What?" Tanis asked.

Her voice picked up an impatient tone. "How long has she been in labor?"

Tanis gaped. "Who?"

"Your wife."

"I'm not married," he said. "That's part of the problem, you see. Laurana wants to . . ."

But Eld Ailea had spotted Flint. She looked from the dwarf to Tanis, and understanding dawned in her face. She swung the door open wider. "You are Tanthalas," she whispered.

"I am."

"Come in, lad. Come in, Flint."

Moments later, half-elf and dwarf were standing in one of the most crowded homes Flint had ever seen. Tiny paintings in frames of wood, stone, and silver cluttered every horizontal surface, hung from every inch of wall space. The midwife had even fastened the miniatures on the back of the door to the street. Nearly all the paintings, of course, were of babies—newborns, toddlers, and young children. Some, for variety, were of mothers with babies.

Eld Ailea pushed her guests into cushioned chairs before the fireplace, the half-elf doffing his scabbard with Flint's sword and leaning the weapon against the stone wall that encapsuled the fireplace. Then the elderly elf, waving aside their offers of help, made a new fire and bustled off to the kitchen to collect items for a late-night tea.

Flint picked up one painted miniature from a low, square table; it showed a newborn elf, ear tips drooping, almond-shaped eyes closed in sleep, tiny hands bunched, squirrel-like, under its chin. In the lower left was the scrawled initial "A."

Ailea returned with a plate of dark brown biscuits with currant-and-sugar glazing. Flint closed his eyes and breathed; he smelled cloves and ginger. These delicacies would make up for the lack of ale, he decided. He replaced the painting on the table and noticed a few of the wooden toys he'd given the midwife scattered nearby.

"Ah, you found Clairek," the midwife exclaimed. "The

daughter of a friend, born just last month. And there"—she pointed at the other miniatures on the table—"are Terjow, Renate, and Marstev. All born in the last year."

"I thought you were retired," Flint commented.

She shrugged, and a lock of hair escaped from the silver bun at the back of her head. "Babies are always being born. And when someone needs me, I'll not say, 'Sorry, I'm retired.' "

Finally, after each guest had munched one of her feathery biscuits and drained a cup of black tea, Eld Ailea prepared to place the tea items on the small table, but it was too cluttered with portraits and toys. She spoke a few sharp words in another tongue and—Flint blinked—suddenly an open space just the right size was available among the miniatures. She placed teapot and biscuit plate in the spot, within easy reach of her guests, and sat on a low footstool. Both Flint and Tanis jumped up to give her their cushioned chairs, but she declined.

"This is better for an old lady's back," she said with a wink.

She gazed at Tanis as though she had been waiting for this moment for years, drinking in his features with her eyes, seemingly oblivious to the half-elf's squirm. She murmured, "His mother's eyes. That same lilt. Have they told you, son, that you have Elansa's eyes?"

Tanis looked away. "My eyes are hazel. They tell me I have the eyes of a human."

"As do I, Tanthalas," Eld Ailea commented softly. The firelight flickered across her triangular face, and her eyes crinkled in gentle humor. "I also have the shortness of my human forebear. In a forest of elves that grow tall like aspens, I am . . . a shrub. But the world needs shrubs, too, I guess."

She laughed gaily, but the half-elf looked unconvinced. She continued.

"I am part human, but I am also part elf, Tanthalas. I may be short, but I am slender—and that's an elven trait. My eyes are round and hazel, but my face is pointy and elven. Look at my ears, Tanthalas—elven, yet I wear my hair like a human, to the consternation, I might add, of some of my elven patients."

She laughed, and her warm eyes were liquid in the firelight. "Like humans, I am open to changes. Like elves, however, I have some habits that I will *never* modify—even if someone has the unmitigated gall to suggest a way that probably is better."

Tanis's gaze reflected wonder and, Flint thought, loneliness. But when the half-elf spoke, his voice was bitter. "But *your* human traits are not those of a rapist, I'll warrant."

Eld Ailea winced, and Tanis had the grace to look embarrassed. The midwife excused herself to refill the biscuit plate, and when she returned, her eyelids were red.

"I am sorry, Eld Ailea," Tanis said.

"I loved Elansa," she replied simply. "Even half a century later, it pains me to think about what happened to her."

She passed him the plate, which he handed to Flint without looking at. Then she resumed her seat and clasped her arms around her knees. Suddenly, Flint saw how she must have looked as a young elf in Caergoth—lithe and lively and wonderful. He hoped she could look back on a happy life.

"Tanthalas," she said, "I had hoped someday to meet you again—to compare the man with the baby. I must say you are much, much quieter as a man"—and she laughed silently to herself—"but you also are less trusting, which is, I suppose, to be expected in any adult. But I can see that your life at the palace has not been easy. I hoped to learn something of you by talking to your friend here. I'm glad he brought you to me now."

"Why didn't you contact me before?" Tanis asked. His eyes were dark.

Eld Ailea sighed, reached for a spiced biscuit, and set small white teeth into the treat. She chewed and wiped her mouth with a napkin before answering. "I decided long ago that I would not seek you out while you were but a child, that because the Speaker of the Sun was set on raising you as an elf, seeing me could only be a constant reminder of your 'other' half.

"But I realize now that my absence was a mistake. And I

apologize."

Tanis, without taking his gaze from her worn face, groped for his tea mug and took a sip. Eld Ailea warmed the drink with a refill, and Tanis sipped again.

"I gave you your name, you know," Ailea said. "It means 'ever strong.' I did that because I knew you would need great strength to live in an elven world. You may find, as I did, that you will have to live away from Qualinesti for some time before you can appreciate both parts of yourself."

Tanis's voice dripped contempt. "Appreciate the part of me that's like an animal?"

She smiled. "I like to think that I have the *best* traits of both races. Remember, Tanthalas. You have a father who, yes, certainly, was a brutal, terrible human being. But through him, you are related to many other humans who, most likely, were much better than he."

Tanis blinked. Flint could see that the old midwife had shed a new light on his viewpoint.

"I . . ." he stammered, then gulped down his tea in one swallow. "I'll have to think about this."

Eld Ailea nodded, and the conversation veered to other topics, especially the news announced at the palace that afternoon. As it turned out, Ailea had already heard.

"Lord Tyresian . . ." she mused. "I have heard that he is very . . . traditional."

Flint queried, "Did you deliver him, too?"

Ailea shook her head. "Ah, no. Well, not exactly, young dwarf."

Young? Flint shook his head, then thought that he probably was, in comparison to her.

"Why 'not exactly'?" Tanis pressed.

Ailea hesitated. Tanis pounced. "It was because of your human blood, wasn't it?"

Eld Ailea hesitated again, then nodded. "I'd have put it another way, but it comes to that, yes. I attended Tyresian's mother early in her confinement; things seemed to be going well, and I had high hopes of her delivering a healthy infant."

She trailed off. "And?" Tanis asked.

Ailea looked into the fire, her words lifeless. "Tyresian's father came into the room and discovered who was attending his wife. He ordered me out, but I remained outside, near the home, in case I was needed after all. He sent for a full elf to stay with Estimia, but none was available."

"When he learned that, he ordered the children's governess to deliver the baby," the midwife continued. "The poor lass had never attended a birth, much less actually delivered a baby. But Tyresian's father—I could hear him shouting even through the rock walls of the mansion—said that any full elf woman would be better than a part-human."

Tanis opened his mouth to say something, but Eld Ailea continued on. "Then I heard Tyresian's mother screaming." Ailea's face contorted as though she were still at the scene. "I pounded at the door. I begged them to let me come in and help Estimia, but Tyresian's father came outside himself and forced me away. He said he would have me arrested if I did not go away."

"Interesting, considering Qualinost has no jail," Flint noted drily.

Eld Ailea rose and selected a miniature of a pretty elven woman from the mantle. She brushed slender fingers over the uneven paint. "Tyresian lived, but Estimia died."

She wandered around the room, Flint and Tanis following her progress in the firelight as she touched a frame here, a cheek there. When she arrived at the door, she swung around and said simply, "Tyresian's father said the death was my fault."

Tanis gasped. "How?"

She looked down and, suddenly officious, smoothed her loose gray skirt. "He said I must have done something wrong before he had a chance to order me away."

"That's absurd," Flint snapped. Tanis nodded, his face angry.

Ailea nodded. "Yes, it is," she said calmly. "I have my weaknesses, but incompetence is not one of them." She returned to the kitchen with the mugs, teapot, and plate, and Flint followed her to help, leaving Tanis browsing through the baby portraits in the entry room.

"When you were at my shop," Flint said, hoping to prolong the conversation even though it was nearly midnight, "you told me that you'd delivered the Speaker."

"And his brothers," Ailea added, handing Flint a dish to dry with a towel that apparently used to be a woven shirt of the sort she'd worn to Flint's shop. "Why?"

"I'm curious about the third brother."

"Arelas? Why?"

"The Speaker said Arelas was sent away from court because he was ill, but he didn't say what illness his brother had. Do you know?"

Ailea rinsed the teapot in a bucket of clear water brought in from a well behind the house. "I'm not sure anyone knows. He was fine until he was a toddler, but about the time he learned to walk, well, he changed."

Flint looked up from under one salt-and-pepper eyebrow. "Changed? How?"

Eld Ailea's voice took on the tone of someone used to telling stories to babysitting charges. "One day," she said, "he, his brother Kethrenan, his mother, and I went for a picnic in the Grove," naming the tree-shrouded area between the Tower of the Sun and the Hall of the Sky. "Arelas wandered away and got lost."

"Did you find him?"

"Not at first. We combed the area, but it was as though the earth had swallowed him. We saw no sign." She handed the teapot to the dwarf. "Someone must have found him, but we never discovered who. After three days of fruitless searching—Solostaran's father must have called out nearly every soldier in Qualinesti—little Arelas was found sleeping on the moss in the courtyard of the palace one morning. He must have wandered in—or someone brought him in, past the guards—through the opening to the gardens. He had been covered with a cloth, to keep him warm."

Flint gave the burnished copper teapot one last polish with a rag and placed it in the middle of the kitchen table. "He became ill?"

"Very. He had a fever when we found him. He hovered near death for days. I administered what nostrums I had. I used what magic I could, but I cannot cure. I can only ease symptoms. No one was able to help. Finally, the Speaker at that time ordered Arelas sent to an elven cleric outside Qualinesti."

Flint leaned against a countertop as Eld Ailea sloshed clear water around the ceramic container she'd used to wash the dishes in. The conversation seemed to have reminded her of other things, for she continued to speak after she'd laid the container, upside-down, on the counter near Flint's elbow. "Solostaran and Kethrenan were relatively easy deliveries—as easy as childbirth ever is, of course. But Arelas . . . even before he was born, he was not . . . right. He simply wasn't positioned correctly within his mother. The birth took more than a day, and I finally had to use forceps to deliver him, something I try never to do.

"That time, however, it worked out fine," she said cheerfully. "Nothing but a little cut on his arm, and it healed quickly, left only a scar. Just a little mark shaped like a star. It reminded me of the mark that I've heard some of the Plainsmen place on young men when they reach manhood."

"Now, come, Master Fireforge," she said briskly, placing strong arms on the dwarf's shoulders and turning him around, "let's see what young Tanthalas has been up to."

They returned to the main room. Tanis stood next to an open cupboard near the front door. "You painted all these portraits," he said, his reddish brown hair swishing against his leather jerkin as he turned.

"From memory, yes," Ailea said, smoothing the braid that encircled her head and ended in the bun at the back of her head.

"Is there one of me?" His voice was gruff from his attempt to be offhand. Flint found himself hoping the midwife wouldn't disappoint him.

"Not down here, no." Tanis's shoulders sagged at the reply.

"I keep *your* painting in my room," she added, and stepped efficiently to a stone stairway that led up from the entry room, left of the door to the kitchen.

Flint found himself exchanging a wordless glance with the

half-elf as they marked the elderly midwife's steps above them. It was well past midnight now, and the two had to rise in mere hours for the tylor hunt, but Flint would have died rather than hurry Tanis away now.

Suddenly Eld Ailea was standing on the bottom step, and Flint found himself wondering whether her magical skills included teleportation. She was remarkably quick-footed for someone several centuries old.

"Here," she said, and handed Tanis a portrait encased in an ornate frame of silver and gold filigree, and a steel pendant on a silver chain. "The pendant belonged to Elansa. She gave it to me before she died."

Almost reverently, Tanis took the painting with one hand and the pendant with the other, seeming not to know which to examine first. The half-elf's greenish brown eyes looked wet, but it may have been the effect of the light. "So this is the face she saw," the half-elf whispered, and Flint found himself turning away to stare into the fire. The smoke was to blame for his own misty vision, certainly.

Eld Ailea looked over his shoulder. "You were a robust infant, Tanthalas—remarkably healthy for one whose mother was so frail by the time he was born."

Tanis swallowed, and Ailea continued, her voice barely audible to Flint, only several feet away. He wondered if that was the voice the old midwife used to sooth laboring mothers, to bring calm to colicky infants. "Elansa loved Kethrenan dearly, Tanthalas. She decided, early in the pregnancy, I think, that she didn't want to live without her husband, but she stayed alive, hoping the baby was his."

Tanis's face grew hard. "Then when she saw me," he said, "she knew the truth." He tried to give the portrait back to the midwife, but she wouldn't take it.

"No, Tanthalas." Eld Ailea's voice was gentle, but her hand was strong on his shoulder. "When she saw you, when she saw *that face* that you look at now, she seemed, I think, to change her mind. She roused enough to nurse her baby, but it was too much for her. She was simply too weak from all she had been through from Kethrenan's death onward." The midwife's voice faltered. "She held you until she died."

Silence hung in the room like a darkness, broken only by someone's heavy breathing—Flint's own, the dwarf realized. He cleared his throat and coughed.

After a pause, during which none of the three met the others' eyes, Tanis asked, "What about the pendant?"

Eld Ailea took it from him. "It's steel, very valuable. Kethrenan gave it to her when they were married. She wore it always. I've considered it a blessing that the brigands didn't take that from her. She seemed to draw from it what little strength she had during those last months." She walked over to Flint and showed him the amulet. Ivy and aspen leaves encircled the intertwined initials "E" and "K." Scalloping decorated the edges of the circular disk.

There didn't seem to be anything more to say. Flint and Tanis were drooping with fatigue, and even the ostensibly tireless midwife looked weary. As if by unspoken agreement, the men gathered by the door to leave; Eld Ailea moved to retrieve Tanis's sword from where he'd left it by the fireplace. She hoisted it in its scabbard, then hesitated, an odd look on her face.

"This sword . . ."

Tanis spoke proudly. "Flint made it."

"Yes, I know," she said, stammering slightly. "It's beautiful. Yet . . ."

The dwarf and half-elf waited while the midwife collected her thoughts. She inhaled, and seemed suddenly decisive. "Flint." Her voice was sharp. "Come here."

Flint moved to her side, gazing worriedly into her hazel eyes. "Could you fasten this pendant to this sword?" she asked. "Would it ruin the weapon?"

"Well, certainly it can be done, and no, it wouldn't hurt it, but . . ."

"Permanently? That can be done?"

He nodded. Her expression caught him; it was an unsettling mixture of urgency and fear. He pointed to an open swirl in the hilt of the weapon. "I could attach it there."

Her hand closed over his on the sword's hilt. "Then do it," she urged. "Tonight."

"It's so late . . ." Flint hedged.

Eld Ailea grasped his arm. "It *must* be done tonight. Will you? Without fail?" So close to the midwife, Flint suddenly saw the exhaustion, the years, that her sprightly character normally overshadowed. He promised, and she relaxed her grip.

Flint parted from Tanis at the Hall of the Sky. The half-elf continued north to the Speaker's palace, and Flint went on home, carrying his friend's sword.

The dwarf spent the next two hours doing as the midwife had asked.

* * * * *

Miral made almost no sound as he passed the pair of black-jerkined guards posted outside the Speaker's private quarters at the palace; the guards hailed him and waved him on. At ease in the darkness, with only occasional torches to pain his eyes, he made his way quickly down one corridor to the stairwell. But instead of going down to the courtyard, he climbed the steps to the building's second level.

He paused at Xenoth's quarters, hearing the adviser's roisterous snoring even through the door, then slipped by Tanis's door, which stood slightly ajar, revealing a dark and empty interior. Miral imagined the half-elf was out walking the tiled streets of Qualinost, agonizing over the day's developments.

In succession, the mage passed Porthios's and Gilthanas's rooms, until he arrived at Laurana's. A light shone beneath her door, and he heard pacing within.

He knocked softly. The footsteps stopped, then approached the door. Laurana's voice was low. "Who is it?"

"It is Miral, Lady Laurana. I apologize for bothering you at such an unconscionable time, but I need to speak with you."

She opened the door. Miral caught his breath, as he did almost every time he saw the young princess. She was resplendent in a robe of watered silk. The aqua color brought out the glitter in her ashy hair and the coral tones of her curved lips. Momentarily, he fell speechless; then he chided himself for his lack of control.

"May I talk with you in private, Laurana? It's about the Speaker's announcement of your betrothal."

Laurana's exotic green eyes widened, and color rose in her cheeks. "Certainly . . . but not here."

"No, of course not," Miral said smoothly. "In the courtyard, then? I would not want to disturb anyone. This will not take long."

She thought, tilting her head to one side. "Give me time to dress. I will meet you there in ten minutes." Then she closed the door.

* * * * *

Well within the appointed time, Laurana, now more suitably garbed in a cloak and gown of dove-gray satin, was seated on a stone bench in the courtyard—the same bench that had witnessed the archery contest between Porthios and Tanis so many years before. But now the pear and peach trees stood bathed in silver light from Solinari, and the scent of blossoms was almost cloying. The steel door in the two-story marble edifice gleamed in the moonlight. She pulled the cloak tight around her.

Miral paced along the tiled path before her, his red robe appearing nearly black in the deep of the night. He seemed agitated. His hood had fallen back slightly, revealing pale features and the elf's almost colorless eyes.

"What is it, Miral?" Laurana prompted gently. "You said it had something to do with Father's announcement."

"I . . . I wanted to offer my condolences." The mage dipped his head. "I know that you prefer Tanthalas to Tyresian—which, I might add, shows considerable taste on your part." He smiled engagingly, and she followed suit. "Tanthalas is by far the more suitable for one such as you, regardless of his . . . violent . . . heritage. I am certain that you could keep his uncontrolled tendencies under rein, my lady. After all, not all humans are savages, and I have long been impressed by Tanthalas."

He dipped his head slightly, and the hood fell forward

over his features again.

Laurana felt flustered, unsure how to sort the mage's combination of praise and condemnation of Tanis. "Thank you, but I don't see—"

"There is one even more suitable for you."

Laurana felt a look of amazement cross her features before years of court training took over and she forced her face to go blank. When she spoke, her tone was carefully neutral. "And who is that, Miral?"

"Me."

Laurana was on her feet before the word had stopped echoing in the night air between them. "You!" she said weakly. "Oh, I don't—"

Miral's tones were urgent. "Please hear me out, Laurana. If you reject me, I will never mention it again. I swear."

Laurana thought wildly, trying to figure out how her father would handle such a delicate situation. Miral had been a faithful member of court for years, and he had won her father's favor long ago for his service to her Uncle Arelas. In a similar situation, Solostaran, she knew, would give the mage time to speak.

"Please sit down, Laurana. This won't take long."

She sat. She had thought Tyresian too old for her, and Tyresian was only the same age as her brother Porthios. The mage, on the other hand, was decades older than that. "I am too young to marry, Miral."

"But not to be promised. Isn't that what you are with Tanis? Promised? Betrothed?"

Unbidden, Miral sank to the bench next to Laurana.

"I first saw you, years ago, when I came here at Arelas's urging. You know my story?" Laurana nodded, not trusting her voice. She was suddenly aware of how quiet and deserted the courtyard was at night. She tried to remember whether the guards patrolled the courtyard as well as the interior of the palace.

"You were just a tiny girl—but what a girl! I've never seen such perfection. A bit spoiled, it's true, and a bit more of a tomboy than I found attractive in an elf girl of noble blood, but perhaps, I thought, such vigor came from being born of the bloodline of Kith-Kanan."

Laurana edged away from the mage, but his hand shot out and caught hers. He was stronger than she'd ever imagined. And his eyes . . . Oddly, she could see them quite well in the dark, even within the gloom of his hood. Fear cast a cold grasp around her spine. The mage's voice continued, cutting through the silence of the Qualinost night.

"I loved watching you, Laurana. I volunteered to tutor you, even though it meant taking on that dolt of a brother of yours, Gilthanas. And Tanis. I loved and trusted Tanis, you know. For after all, weren't you two being raised as brother and sister? What threat could he be to my suit, when it came? Then I found out yesterday how wrong I was about Tanis." Miral's grip tightened, and Laurana made a sound of protest. The sound broke her fear, and she rose to her feet, the mage seeking to drag her back.

"Wait!" the mage hissed. "Laurana, choose me. I may not be all powerful, but I am a stronger wizard than people think. Ultimately, I can offer you more power, more riches, than Tyresian and Tanis put together, if only you will be patient."

Laurana, heart pounding in fear, broke away and retreated several steps. Miral rose slowly to his feet. "What is your answer?" he asked eagerly.

All thought of court decorum flew from Laurana's mind. All she could think of was escape. Alienating the mage was of no concern now. Flight was. The Speaker would never keep Miral at court after he heard of tonight's events.

"Leave me alone," she demanded, drawing all her strength together, investing her voice with as much power as she could. "Leave this court. If you are gone in the morning, I promise I will not tell my father what has transpired. You will escape the humiliation of being removed from court."

The mage stood, and she turned and strode through the moonlight toward the door. Behind her, she heard the mage mumble a few words, and she broke into a run. Mere feet from the steel doors, however, the spell burst within her brain, and she stumbled and fell in a faint.

She awakened in the corridor outside her room. Two palace guards, one carrying a lamp, gazed down on her with worried expressions; her head and shoulders rested on Miral's lap. She looked up, confused. "Miral?" Laurana looked around. "How did I get out here?"

"I was passing along in the corridor when I heard your door open," Miral said silkily. "I knew the day had been a grueling one for you, and I hastened to you to see if you were ill or needed help. You fainted as I approached. Don't you remember?"

Laurana lay back weakly. "I . . . don't remember anything. I recall walking around in my room, and then, suddenly, I was here." Yet, she thought, it seemed as though she were forgetting something important. She shook her head, unable to think.

The mage's clear eyes were fathomless. One hand dipped into the pocket of his robe and emerged with a small packet of dried leaves. "Pour this into a cup of hot water, my lady. It will ease your mind and help you sleep. I will send a servant to you with the water."

She waited, still trying to collect her thoughts, then nodded. Miral and one of the guards helped her to her feet. Then the mage disappeared down the hallway. She stood in her doorway, with the guards looking anxiously on. Down the hallway, Lord Xenoth's door suddenly opened and the adviser—curiously enough, fully clothed—peered out. Laurana ignored him, still annoyed by his unceasingly closed-minded treatment of Tanis and Flint.

Her irritation with the adviser vanished as she tried to clear her thoughts. Something, some memory, seemed to be niggling just out of her reach. What was it?

Well, whatever it was, if it were important, she'd remember it later. She bade the guards good night and shut herself in her room again.

Chapter 16

The Interview

ONE OF THE Speaker's servants intercepted Tanis shortly before dawn the next morning as the half-elf strode from the palace to the stables to check on Belthar, his horse. The servant informed Tanis that Solostaran wanted to see him in the Speaker's anteroom immediately.

But when Tanis arrived at Solostaran's chambers at the Tower, the guards standing outside the door told Tanis that the Speaker was with someone and that he would be ready for his conversation with Tanis shortly. Tanis thanked them, then slinked down the hall to wait, finding a seat in an alcove.

The door to the Speaker's office opened, and Porthios stepped out. He nodded to the guard and walked purposefully in the direction opposite Tanis, apparently not seeing the half-elf in the alcove. Tanis let out a tight breath of relief, and when Porthios had gone, he made his way to the door. The guard showed him in immediately, shutting the door behind him, and Tanis swallowed hard, wondering what the Speaker had to say to him.

The Speaker sat at his desk, looking over a sheaf of parchments, an oil lamp casting a pool of light on the papers. The golden trim on the Speaker's green robes glittered in the lamplight. When the door clicked shut, he immediately set the parchments down and looked up, as if he hadn't really been reading them. The room, with its glass walls, was beginning to glow pinkish gray in the dim light just before dawn.

"Tanthalas," the Speaker said, his voice neutral. He didn't offer a chair, so Tanis remained standing.

"You wished to see me, Speaker," Tanis said. He couldn't remember ever feeling like this before in the presence of the Speaker, but somehow, this day, Tanis found himself afraid.

The Speaker nodded. "Yesterday was a trying day, Tanthalas," he said softly. He stood and paced about the room, his hands clasped behind his back. "I knew it would be difficult to promise the hand of Lauralanthalasa to another, but I had little choice. The promise had been sworn between two houses long ago. Countless agreements, numerous treaties, depend on the elves' faith that the Speaker of the Sun *will always keep his word*. What could I do?"

He seemed to be arguing with himself, rather than speaking to Tanis. "Should I have stepped down from the rostrum, been Speaker no longer, to save my daughter?"

Tanis nearly gasped. Abdicate?

But the Speaker shook his head. "And what would that accomplish? Porthios would take my place, and then the promise would fall to his shoulders and little would have changed. So you see, Tanis, I kept the promise. The honor of our house demanded it." He looked piercingly at Tanis then, and the half-elf involuntarily winced.

"Nor is Tyresian a poor choice for Laurana," the Speaker went on, and Tanis felt his heart thudding. "So, though I knew it would be a difficult task, I resolved myself to do it, to announce the betrothal.

"Tell me, Tanis, why have things gone this way?" the Speaker asked. "I do not understand, nor has anyone been able to explain to me, how my daughter could somehow have promised herself to the boy I brought into my home and raised as her brother. And for the first time ever, I find Laurana unwilling . . ." The Speaker paused for a moment, a hand passing before his eyes. But then the moment was gone, and his regal bearing returned. "I find her unwilling to speak with me. Tell me, Tanis. Why does my own daughter defy me?"

Tanis shook his head. "I don't know," he said truthfully.

"But you, of all people, must know, Tanis," the Speaker said, his voice taking on an edge. "You have always been closest to her of my children. And now I find that perhaps you are closer than I thought." His eyes flashed green.

"No, it's not that at all," Tanis said, his heart galloping in his chest. "It was just a game we played, a long time ago, that's all."

"A game?" the Speaker said. His voice was soft, but there was a sharpness that left Tanis chilled. "This is a serious matter, Tanthalas," he said, advancing toward the half-elf, his robes rippling around him. "The integrity of our house, the harmony of the court, the very peace this city is founded upon, are at stake here. This is not a time for games!"

Tanis shook his head, his face hot. He tried to say something, anything, but no words came.

"First Laurana all but defies me before the entire court," Solostaran continued. "And I hoped that you would have learned from that, that you would have seen the effects of what you'd wrought, for you have always been dear to me, and I'd thought that you respected me. But then I learned that only hours later you were with her again in the courtyard, that she flung her arms about you and kissed you like . . . like . . ." The Speaker's words faltered, but then he gathered himself. His eyes glinted, and his voice was rough. "This is a dark game you are playing with her, Tanis. You are a member of this court and should respect its decrees. You are my ward. You are her brother and she, your sister."

The Speaker's eyes went wide, the rage draining from them, leaving his face gaunt. His shoulders sagged, and he grasped the edge of his desk as if to steady himself.

"Excuse me, Tanis," he whispered.

Tanis helped the Speaker into his chair.

"It's just that things have been so hard, leading up to this past day," the Speaker said. He gestured to a decanter of wine, and Tanis poured a cup for the Speaker to sip. "And since yesterday, courtiers have been at me like hounds nipping at the flanks of a stag. And what was I to tell them? That my ward was going to marry the woman whom all considered his sister—in name, if not in actuality? That I would break my word?" He shook his head. "But try to understand. It is not you I'm angry with. It's the court and its narrow-mindedness, about you, about your heritage."

Tanis sighed. He desperately wanted to believe the Speaker, and true enough, that old warmth radiated from his surrogate father now.

"I've told you the truth," Tanis said. "I love Laurana, of course, but as my sister. I'm not sure what to do now." Almost as an afterthought, he added, "Laurana can be pretty stubborn."

The Speaker almost laughed then. At least, a smile flickered across his lips. "Ah, I should have expected it, really. Her childhood playmate has become a handsome young elf lord. What wonder is it that she fancies him? For while he has been raised as her brother, she knows this is not truly so."

Tanis waited, unsure what to say, but the interview appeared to be over. Moments later, he was back in the corridor, alone.

Chapter 17

The Hunt

Tanis watched the sunrise from the vantage of the Hall of the Sky. The pale beams glinted like copper on the Tower of the Sun and sparked like fire off the city's crystal and marble buildings. As the sun rose above the horizon, it intercepted a far-off bank of dark clouds that hung low in the sky. The sun set the clouds ablaze, turning them from dull gray to blazing crimson in minutes. The clouds seemed thicker than they had the previous evening. Tanis made his way back to the palace, heading for the stable, where Belthar, his three-year-old chestnut stallion, was quartered.

Outside the gray granite stable, the nobles of Qualinost were already gathered. Tyresian, wearing black leather breeches and steel breastplate, shouted orders to Ulthen from the top of his bay stallion, Primordan. Miral lounged against one wall of the stable, cloth bags of spell-casting items dangling from the belt of the hooded red tunic he had exchanged for his customary robe. The knee-length tunic was split down the middle, allowing the mage to ride a horse comfortably. Several other nobles, whose names Tanis couldn't remember, chatted in a group to the left of the stable door. Nearby, Litanas saddled the mage's gelding. Porthios stood off to one side, watching but saying little; his brother, Gilthanas, wearing his black guard's uniform, mimicked his stance, to Porthios's apparent discomfiture. Tanis nodded to his cousins as he entered the livery stable to retrieve Belthar. Later, as he led the stallion forth onto the cobblestones of the stable yard, he saw Xenoth approaching from the palace and Flint, on Fleetfoot, riding in from the south, Tanis's sword flapping at his side. On the other side of the pack animal rested the dwarf's battle-axe.

"Now there's a memorable pair—a dwarf on a mule and an elf so old he probably knew Kith-Kanan," Ulthen shouted to Gilthanas, who glanced at his brother and quickly masked a smile. Porthios looked annoyed. Tanis paused by the Speaker's heir, holding Belthar by the reins and waiting for Flint to bring him his sword.

Lord Xenoth reached the stable yard first, his ankle-length robes, the color of the storm clouds gathering overhead, fluttering around his legs. He asked Tyresian where he could borrow a horse; apparently the adviser didn't own one.

"By the gods, Xenoth is going to have to ride sidesaddle in that outfit!" Porthios muttered to Gilthanas and the half-elf. "Even Laurana rides astride. Go give him a hand, Tanis. He can ride the mare Image."

Tanis handed his reins to Gilthanas and strode off to help Lord Xenoth. Despite the upheaval of the last few days, even though he knew the group of volunteers would seek a deadly beast that already had slain several elves, he was happy to be a part of the hunt. The half-elf felt a twinge of excitement shiver through him. He had never been invited to ride with Tyresian or Porthios on one of the elf lords' stag hunts—they were reserved for the highest of elven nobility—but this time Tyresian could not stop him. Tanis closed his eyes, imagining the branches whipping green and blurred past him as he galloped with his mount through the forest trails. It was going to be glorious.

In the dim light of the stable, Xenoth peered into stall after stall, apparently seeking a mount that was suitable for him—or, perhaps, suitable for the rider he had been decades earlier. Tanis went over to Image's stall and called her name, and the mottled head of the elderly mare appeared over the top of the half-door. A gentle creature, she whickered softly in response; Tanis and she had been friends for years, and she pricked her ears now, eyeing his pockets for apples or other delectables. He pulled a carrot out of his tunic, cracked it in half, and offered it on a flattened palm. He watched as her rubbery lips sought out the trifle, fed it into her crunching maw, and snuffled around for the other half.

"Sorry, that half's for Belthar," he said, then raised his voice. "Lord Xenoth. I have your horse for you."

At the other end of the stable, Xenoth paused by the stall of Alliance, a huge warhorse that even Tyresian could barely control. The adviser shook his head, silver hair gleaming in the gray light, and pointed at the beast. "I will ride this one," Xenoth said. "Get him ready for me."

Alliance lunged over the partition, teeth narrowly missing the wizened elf's hand. Xenoth leaped back with a cry. Tanis, shaking his head, led Image out of the stall, and a stableboy leaped to prepare the horse for riding.

"Ride Image," Tanis said. "She's a fine, gentle horse."

Xenoth's face went ruddy with anger. "Are you saying I can't handle this horse?" he demanded. He gestured again, and Alliance went crazy trying to snap the morsel that the adviser kept waving in front of his face.

Tanis sighed and stepped closer. "I'm saying that Kith-Kanan himself couldn't handle that horse." He heard footsteps behind him and guessed that Xenoth's screechy voice had attracted the attention of the other volunteers.

Xenoth's blue eyes protruded slightly; his voice trembled. "I was quite the horseman in my prime, half-elf."

"I'm sure you were, Lord Xenoth." Tanis tried to keep his

tones low and even, on the theory that what would quiet a panicky horse also would work with a hysterical elf. "But you don't even own a horse now. It's been awhile since you rode. Why not start out with a slightly . . . easier . . . mount?" He heard a muffled snort from behind him; his neck prickled with the realization that quite an audience had gathered. Seeking to end the brouhaha quickly, Tanis reached forward and laid a hand on the adviser's silken sleeve.

"Leave me be!" Xenoth cried. "I will not be manhandled by a . . . by a *bastard half-elf!*"

Several of the elves behind Tanis gasped and others burst into laughter. Tanis felt his chest contract and his hands clench. He took one step toward the adviser, whose eyes widened in fear. Behind Xenoth, Alliance bared his teeth again.

"Tanis. Lord Xenoth." The words were spoken in a baritone that brooked no disobedience. Tanis turned.

It was Porthios. "Tanis, go out to your horse. Xenoth, you will ride Image or you will not attend this hunt."

Porthios stood like an avenging god, his golden green hunting garb glittering like the Speaker's ceremonial robe. His eyes flashed in anger. The other courtiers fell back, looking slightly ashamed. Porthios waited until Xenoth moved from Alliance to Image, now ready for the hunt. Tanis pushed between Ulthen and Miral and stalked toward the stable's double doors. Porthios's voice halted him, however.

"Tanis," the Speaker's heir said. "I am sorry."

The half-elf waited, not sure if Porthios intended to say more. Then he shrugged and went out to Belthar.

* * * * *

Half an hour later, the volunteers were ready. Xenoth sat astride Image, the adviser's robes bulked up around his thighs, revealing long, skinny legs in black leggings. Xenoth, who actually appeared to be a passable horseman, stayed near the back of the group. Tyresian, Porthios, and

Gilthanas stood at the front.

Tanis's stallion pawed at the dewy cobblestones, and it snorted, breath fogging on the cool, damp air. "Are you sure you wouldn't prefer to ride a horse, Flint?" the half-elf asked.

"You know very well I can't," the dwarf said grumpily, his face pale and weary after only three hours of sleep. "I'm deathly afr—er, allergic to horses."

The dwarf gave a loud sneeze just for emphasis and then blew his nose like a trumpet in his handkerchief. Tanis's mount nickered, apparently in reply.

"Well, who asked *you*?" Flint said hotly, glaring at Belthar. The stallion rolled its eyes, showing the whites, and its ears went back as it chomped its bit.

"All right, you two," Tanis said, giving the reins a tug. "That's enough."

The horse snorted again, as if to say he didn't pretend to understand the peculiarities of dwarves. Nor did Tanis, always.

Tanis glanced at the other courtiers and young nobles who were mounting their steeds in the steadily brightening light, but few paid him much attention. Most likely they had taken his argument with Xenoth as just another sample of his human temper, though for the life of him he couldn't see that Xenoth had behaved with elven coolness, either.

Still, he felt a pang of excitement. Whatever the events of the last few days, to be finally given the chance to ride alongside the others . . .

He searched the gathering of elves. Tyresian sat straight and proud upon his mount, clasping the reins in black-gloved hands. Porthios was astride his gray steed next to the elf lord, and Gilthanas waited just behind them on a roan mare, a pretty creature with delicate legs and a finely drawn head.

A trumpet call rang out then, high and sweet on the clear air, and Tanis mounted his horse, reining Belthar in to stand near the others. Tyresian's gaze flickered in his direction for a moment, but it seemed an uninterested look, and then the elf lord turned his attention back toward his companions.

Tanis checked the arrows in the quiver at his knee; after leaving Flint last night, he'd spent an hour attaching to shafts the steel arrowheads the dwarf had made for him. The hard metal might be just what was needed against the scaly hide of a tylor. Then Tanis adjusted Flint's sword in its scabbard at his side. It was awkward—a short sword or even a long dagger was a more common blooding knife, used to dispatch, say, a stag that had been brought down with an arrow. But they were after a bloodthirsty lizard as long as several elves. Who knew what weapon would serve the hunters best?

Besides, Tanis was too proud of the sword to have left it behind. Its handguard glimmered coolly in the dawn light, like tendrils of silvery smoke that had somehow been frozen in place. In the middle of the handguard. . .

"Flint!"

The dwarf looked up from his seat on the gray mule's back.

"You fastened my mother's amulet to the handguard," Tanis said. Tyresian and Miral looked aside at the half-elf.

The dwarf sounded petulant. "Well, I *told* Ailea I would, didn't I? Spent two hours in the middle of the night on it, too. Poked holes in the handguard—nearly broke my heart to do that, I might add—and the pendant and then ran a chain link through 'em both." He huffed. "Amazing, the things I'll do for a damsel in distress."

Tanis smiled and shrugged. The midwife hadn't qualified as a "damsel" for some time, but he suspected that the dwarf was just a bit sweet on Eld Ailea, despite the several hundred years that separated them.

Tyresian's voice broke through the chatter. "Is everyone ready?" he asked quietly. Tanis had to hand it to the elf lord; he had the presence to command.

Tanis patted his sword. In addition to the sword and the quiver of arrows ready by his right knee, he wore his short bow on his back and carried a leather flask of wine, in case the creature injured anyone. Tanis checked everything and then nodded. He was ready.

An elf lord, one of those whose names Tanis didn't recall,

moved his mount forward to face the gathered group, to speak a ceremonial benediction for the start of the hunt. He was a thin, sharp-faced elf with hard gray eyes.

"We pray to Kiri-Jolith today, war god of good," the gray-eyed elf lord said, as the volunteers bent their heads. "We ask him to stand with us as we search out and face this terrible creature that has plundered our land and killed so many of our kindred elves."

Tanis heard Flint snort beside him. "Beast almost killed one of their 'kindred dwarves,' too, only four days ago," he muttered. Tanis hushed the dwarf.

"We also ask the intercession of Habbakuk, god of animal life. May your skills of the wild and your knowledge of the harmony within nature be with us today.

"And if one of us fails to return, may you, Habbakuk, receive his soul."

"So be it."

"So be it," the others echoed.

Then the trumpet-bearer gave another call, and the hunters spurred their mounts, guiding them through the streets of Qualinost to the western edge of the city. They clattered past the guard tower at the southwestern corner of the city, where two of Qualinost's encircling bridges arched toward land, then the horsemen continued past the overhead structure to the foot of the long bridge that crossed the ravine carrying the *Ithal-inen*, the River of Hope. There they halted at the very edge of the ravine. Out of sight, way off to the right, Tanis knew, was the landing, the *Kentommenai-kath*, where he and Flint had picnicked not long before. Tanis saw Flint take one look at the five-hundred-foot drop right before him and pull Fleetfoot back to the rear of the crowd. The dwarf's face carried a sheen of perspiration.

Tyresian nodded to the captain of the palace guard, who nudged his horse forward a pace and called out to the assembled volunteers. His voice echoed in the ravine as the aspens swayed around the hunters. The morning breeze was chilly, but Tanis's excitement kept the half-elf warm.

"The tylor was last spotted far to the south on the west

side of the ravine," the guard captain said. He pointed, and a dozen pairs of eyes gazed off to the left as though they expected the creature to burst from the shrubs at any second.

The captain continued, and the gazes of the hunters returned to him. "Remember several things: One, tylors' flesh changes color to match the land on which they travel. It is extremely effective camouflage."

Tanis, guiding Belthar back toward Flint, noticed the dwarf glance half fearfully at a nearby oak tree, almost as if he thought a tylor could masquerade as a tree.

"These creatures are intelligent," the captain called. "They can speak Common. Therefore, be careful what you say. Do not, for example, call out strategies to your comrades. The creature will hear and understand you.

Gilthanas pulled his roan to the other side of Flint. The Speaker's younger son was dressed in the black leather jerkin of the ceremonial guards. The early morning breeze blew his gold hair back from his brow. He looked a great deal like Laurana, Tanis thought, certainly much more so than Porthios did. Gilthanas had changed a good deal himself these past years, though nothing to keep pace with the changes Tanis himself had experienced. Still, Gilthanas was more an elf lord than a child now, and while he looked small, almost lost, within his guard's uniform, he sat straight upon his roan, his green eyes proud.

"In addition," the guard captain said, bringing Tanis's attention back to the fore, "while tylors prefer to kill by biting or by lashing their victims with their tails, they also can use magic. If they are losing a battle, they often will move out of range and use spells. Be aware of that. I am told we have the mage Miral with us today as a protection against the tylor's magic."

"Oh, terrific," Gilthanas muttered. "Miral. We're doomed."

Despite himself, Tanis looked across Flint and grinned at Gilthanas, who, obviously surprised, smiled back. Tanis realized that he hardly knew Gilthanas anymore. The two had been so close as children, but they had grown up and grown apart. Gilthanas had spurned Tanis to cast his lot with the court, seeking his friendship and recognition there. And, with Porthios's help, he had gained both.

"Tylors," the captain announced, "move very slowly in cold weather. That is why we are leaving so early today. We hope to corner the creature before it warms itself in the sun. And it appears, from the look of the clouds"—and several elves murmured at the gathering of thunderheads to the west—"that we may have the weather on our side."

The captain saluted to Lord Tyresian, who returned the gesture. Then the elven lord raised one arm to the volunteers, and silence reigned as the hunters waited expectantly.

Faint yellow light suffused the eastern horizon, but to the west, the sky was dark, as if night still reigned there. The storm had been hovering above the distant mountains for several days now, gathering strength, its clouds building higher, growing darker. During the night, it had begun to move eastward, like a great dark wall across the sky, threatening the land. Flashes flickered within the swirling clouds, and already Tanis could feel the faint rumble of thunder, charging the air.

The trumpet called out on the air then, and Lord Tyresian raised a black-sleeved arm to motion the hunters onward across the bridge. With a glorious cry, the elves spurred their mounts, triple-file, onto the bridge, and Tanis felt himself shouting with them, the sound bursting from his lungs onto the morning air. It was a cry as old as the world itself, as old as life and death.

"Reorx save me," Flint muttered to himself as Fleetfoot, Belthar, and Gilthanas's mount approached the bridge. "At least I'm in the middle. Lad"—and he turned suddenly to the half-elf— "you will tell me if I'm about to dive over the edge, now, won't you?" When Tanis agreed, the dwarf tilted his face downward and Tanis saw Flint's eyes clench shut, just before his hair swung forward to hide his features.

"What's wrong with him?" Gilthanas asked sharply. "Is he ill?"

Tanis shook his head. "A moment of prayer. It's a dwarven religious tradition." He saw a smile flit across Flint's knobby features. The smile was followed in time by an audible sigh of relief as their mounts' hooves sounded on wood no longer, but on the beaten rock of the western side of the ravine.

In the green wood, the air was fresh with the fragrances of pine sap and mushrooms, an almost medicinal scent that left his head clear and heightened his senses. He heard every rustle made by the small forest animals in the underbrush, saw the outline of every leaf, sharp against the sky above. The trees moved past him as the elves pressed their mounts along the twisting game trails, deeper and deeper into the forest.

The morning continued chilly, with occasional drizzle as the storm clouds marched in from the west. Trackers from the palace guard moved ahead of the main group of volunteers, but with no success. The only animals the hunters saw were squirrels, chipmunks, and one groundhog, slender from a winter's hibernation. The squirrels and chipmunks darted away immediately. The groundhog peered over a log atop a hillock and watched until the hunters had passed.

The trail was wide enough to permit only double-file riding. In some stretches, underbrush grew thick, nearly up to the path. "I don't like this," Tanis told Flint, who nodded. Time and again, the half-elf found his hand returning to the hilt of his sword, and he caressed the intertwined "E" and "K" on the handguard.

Conversation had long since waned among the hunters. The only sounds were the occasional chatter of birds, the creak of saddle leather, and the sniffling of one allergic dwarf. Once Flint sneezed, and Xenoth turned in his saddle and hissed, "Hush!"

"I can help it?" Flint retorted, too softly to be heard by anyone but Tanis.

Suddenly, Tanis saw Tyresian shoot up one arm, and the line halted. One of the trackers, on foot, was standing next to the elf lord, one hand resting on the glossy neck of Tyresian's stallion and the other hand gesturing up ahead. Word filtered back through the column.

"They've found the first spoor!" Gilthanas whispered back to Tanis and Flint. The dwarf clenched the reins so tightly that his knuckles whitened.

"What was it?" Tanis asked.

The answer came filtering down the line like the children's game Gossip: Five-toed tracks, four toes pointed forward, one back, pressed into the damp ground, and only a few hours old. The creature, no doubt, was out looking for food.

"And here we are," Flint said grimly, looking to each side and clasping his battle-axe like a talisman. "Lunch."

"Won't we hear the tylor coming?" Tanis asked.

"Not necessarily," Flint answered. "It may be lying in wait."

The volunteers, faces set, moved into single-file; if the monster crashed out of the underbrush, it would carry away fewer hunters. They pressed on, but every man carried a weapon at the ready. Most of the elves carried short swords.

Midday came and passed unnoticed by the hunters. There was no time for thoughts of food and rest. For a long while they lost the trail, but after an hour of searching, they picked it up again, fresher than before. The hunters cantered their mounts down a narrow, muddy trail, following the tracks. Tanis was forced to duck every few seconds to avoid low-hanging branches.

Suddenly, the horses at the front of the party reared as their riders pulled hard on their reins.

"What is it?" Flint hissed from behind Tanis.

The half-elf rose in his stirrups. The trail widened into an opening. Xenoth was waving his arms as the adviser spoke vehemently to Porthios and Lord Tyresian, who looked impassively ahead as though Xenoth weren't there.

Gilthanas swiveled in his saddle and answered Flint's question. "There's a ravine ahead. Xenoth wants to go around. Tyresian thinks we can jump it."

"*Jump it?*" Flint demanded. "On a mule?" He looked aghast.

Tanis edged Belthar around Gilthanas, trotted the animal to the front of the line, ignoring the irritable glances of the other hunters, and hailed Tyresian and Porthios. The three studied the ravine—as deep as two elves were tall, its banks too steep to be negotiated by horse or elf. The remains of a bridge lay in splinters at the bottom of the crevasse.

"It's not that wide," Tyresian said.

"We could jump it," Porthios agreed.

"Most of the horses could jump it, certainly," Tanis said, "but what's Flint supposed to do?"

Tyresian looked back down the line, past the elven hunters arrayed in leather and silver, their weapons gleaming in the noon light. At the end of the line, Flint and Fleetfoot looked like the runts of an unusually large litter.

"Leave him," Tyresian stated, his blue eyes hard. "He'll find a way around." Porthios shifted uneasily, started to speak, then fell silent.

"Find a way around?" Tanis snapped. "That ravine stretches out of sight in both directions!"

"No one asked the dwarf to come along," Tyresian answered. "Let him go back."

"Alone? With a tylor loose in the forest?"

The elf lord's handsome features tightened. "You're under my command on this operation," Tyresian whispered. "You're also outclassed as a swordsman and as an archer, half-elf."

"Lord Tyresian," Porthios said warningly, and the commander turned and faced the nobles.

"It appears we have come to an impasse," Tyresian called. "We can cross this ravine and seek out the tylor that has been slaying elves and livestock across this section of Qualinesti. Or we can go back in disgrace." He took his time surveying the elves, looking each noble full in the face and studying him for a few heartbeats. "Who is willing to continue?"

The group was quiet for a time. Then Gilthanas spurred his roan forward, pounding past Tyresian and Porthios without a look to either side. With a running start, horse and rider jumped gracefully over the ravine, tracing a smooth arc in the air, and then landed with a spray of mud and gravel. Gilthanas wheeled and saluted.

Ulthen, Litanas, Miral, Porthios, and most of the other nobles quickly followed Gilthanas's lead and waited, milling, on the other side of the ravine. Soon only Tyresian,

Tanis, Flint, and Xenoth were left. Tyresian reigned his nervous mount and cast the three an arrogant smile. "Well?"

Xenoth spluttered. "Lord Tyresian, you can't honestly be thinking of leaving us . . ."

"Then follow along." The elf lord's voice was implacable. "You were the one who wanted to ride Alliance, Xenoth. Certainly you are horseman enough to jump the ravine."

"But this nag can't—"

"Try it!" Tyresian slapped Image's back with the flat of his sword. The horse leaped, Xenoth dropping the reins and clinging to its mane, then balked just feet short of the edge, dumping the Speaker's elderly adviser unceremoniously on the rocky ground. His silver robes in violent disarray, Xenoth struggled to his feet as Tyresian thundered by on Primordan and almost effortlessly took the ravine, scattering the riders on the other side. Then the elf lord led all but one of the riders on down the trail.

Only Porthios lingered at the ravine. Finally, he cupped his hands to his mouth and shouted, "It's all right! Go back to the palace!" and followed the other volunteers.

"Tanis," Flint said, "Go with them. Lord Xenoth and I will go back, as he says."

"What?" squawked the adviser, who had remounted. "And leave me with a dwarf for a protector?"

Flint snorted. "Protector, what?" the dwarf retorted. "I'd sooner protect Fleetfoot here than you." He patted the gray mule's neck. "Tanis, Belthar can easily leap that gap. Go on."

Tanis narrowed his eyes at the dwarf. "We will *not* separate. Even Xenoth here could be of some use if we meet the tylor."

The dwarf didn't meet Xenoth's eyes. "Don't count on it," Flint said. "Unless you're thinking about using him as bait." Flint examined the scrawny adviser. "Even then . . ."

Xenoth wheeled and kicked Image into a canter down the rocky trail toward Qualinost. Flint and Tanis watched, wordlessly. Finally, as Xenoth was vanishing around a bend, Flint shouted, "Don't get too far ahead! The tylor may cut you off!"

The adviser paused, his mottled brown mount tossing its

head and dancing sideways in agitation. Tanis frowned. "Something's wrong," he said. "Look at the horse. Image isn't normally nervous."

The day had begun to turn dark, and an eerie, premature twilight was descending upon the forest. The surrounding woods were nearly impenetrable to the eye. No breeze moved the leaves in the aspens. The squirrels, the chipmunks had vanished; only moments before, they had been skittering through the underbrush and darting playfully along the trails that bordered the ravine.

"Flint . . ."

The dwarf already had his battle-axe at the ready. "I know, lad. No birds. No animal noises. As though . . ." He scanned their surroundings and waved at Xenoth to return.

Tanis finished the sentence for him. "As though the animals had all gone aground."

A low booming echoed upon the air. Flint and Tanis exchanged glances. "Thunder?" Tanis asked.

"I hope so," Flint replied.

The storm hit when Xenoth was halfway back, with thirty or forty paces separating them.

But the storm took the form of a tylor.

"Reorx!" thundered the dwarf. The bushes to the left of Xenoth shuddered, and then, with a force that sent stray leaves and twigs fluttering upon the air, a gray-green blur burst from the undergrowth. The adviser shrieked, and Image crumpled beneath the ferocious beast, the mount's neck broken with one snap of the gaping maw. The adviser, thrown clear, landed hard on his back. He rolled over slowly, pain on his face, as the monster busied itself by tearing at the dead horse. A look of horror froze on Xenoth's face when he saw what the tylor was doing to the animal. He lunged to his feet and ran frantically to one side, away from Flint and Tanis, and into the underbrush.

"Xenoth!" Tanis cried. He jumped off Belthar's back, and Flint slid off Fleetfoot. The two mounts pounded down one of the paths, the mule leading the way by several lengths.

"Xenoth is safer there, lad," Flint hollered, pulling Tanis behind the moldering trunk of a fallen oak. There was a scant six feet between the tree and the edge of the ravine.

The tylor dragged its horned body fully into the clearing, lifted its plated, pointed head, and roared a challenge. The animal then took a stance on the rocky earth, opened its mouth, and began to chant words of magic. Chief among the words was the name "Xenoth."

"By the gods!" The half-elf fell back against Flint. "What is it doing?"

Flint didn't answer the question, but merely muttered, "It's an intelligent creature."

"Can we . . . Can we reason with it?"

Flint grabbed his arm. "I wouldn't recommend that just now, lad."

The creature roared again and continued chanting. "*Xenothi tibi, Xenothi duodonem, Xenothi viviarandi, toth,*" it called, again and again.

"Flint, we've got to alert the others," the half-elf said.

"I think the beast's already done that for us," the dwarf commented, and he pointed back toward the other side of the ravine. Tyresian, Miral, and Litanas were clustered at the edge, seemingly at a loss about what to do. Jumping a horses across the gap would land mount and rider only ten feet from the monster, well within the range of its whipping, deadly tail. Already, the creature's nervous twitching had shredded the underbrush in a crescent behind the animal.

The three-foot horns on the creature's head were sharp and wicked-looking. Its eyes, half-shut, showed yellow as it chanted, "*Xenothi morandibi, Xenothi darme a te vide, toth.*" Its clawed front legs stamped on the rocky ground, sending sprays of pebbles flying into the underbrush.

"Reorx!" the dwarf exclaimed again.

Xenoth, his gray eyes terrified and glassy, stepped out of the underbrush into the clearing. He approached the monster, seemingly unable to resist the creature's call. The chanting intensified. One of the nobles on the far side of the ravine cried out with the horror. Tanis stood. "Xenoth!"

Tyresian shouted from across the ravine, "Half-elf! Stay where you are!" But Tanis leaped over the log and nocked an arrow as he ran. Flint followed, swinging his battle-axe.

The creature, from its tail to its beaklike snout, was nearly sixty feet long, with scaly armor. Tanis kneeled within the huge curve of the beast's body, aiming for the tylor's head, off to the half-elf's right. He released the arrow just as the creature's thirty-foot tail whistled through the air, to Tanis's far left. The razor-sharp appendage slashed through an aspen sapling, then slammed into the adviser. Xenoth's scream died in a gurgle.

The words "Tanis, don't move!" came crying from the opposite side of the ravine. The half-elf remained where he was but sent another arrow arcing toward the tylor.

Suddenly, hoofbeats crashed on the mud-splattered rocks near Tanis. Miral, crimson tunic vivid against his white and gray mare, hurtled toward the tylor, chanting as he rode. Lightning burst from his fingers and rocketed toward the animal even as the tylor began a new chant.

The ensuing explosion rocked the clearing, knocking Tanis and Flint into a heap. Dazed, they watched the rest of the hunters pour over the ravine and into the clearing.

The tylor's screams rent the clearing as its claws dug gashes in the rock-hard earth. It struggled to crawl into the underbrush, away from the arrows that now poured toward it from the phalanx of elven nobles. Tanis and Flint could only sit and watch.

Finally, the tylor was dead, scorch marks visible all along one side, arrows cutting into its hide and another arrow protruding from an eye. It lay on its side. Just ten feet away, Miral was raising himself on bent elbows, his face blackened with ash. One hand was bleeding.

Xenoth lay dead, face down on the muddy, rocky ground of the clearing, a crimson stain soaking his silver robe and seeping into the earth. The tylor's thrashing tail had crushed his chest. Litanas, Xenoth's assistant, kneeled beside him, shouting something incoherent.

Then suddenly it seemed as though all the elves were staring at Tanis. Even Flint was looking at him with a disbelieving expression. "What is it?" the half-elf asked.

Litanas moved aside, and Tanis saw.

Protruding from Xenoth's heart was the half-elf's arrow.

Chapter 18

The Arrow

Tanis looked from face to face, each showing the same accusing stare. Only Flint looked anything but convinced that the half-elf had slain the adviser.

"You saw!" Tanis cried. "You all saw! I shot to the right, toward the body of the beast. Xenoth was to my left when the creature's tail hit him. How could my arrow have struck him?"

"Yet it did strike him, Tanis," Porthios said quietly.

Tyresian gestured, and several of the elves moved forward as if to restrain the half-elf. With a bound, Flint, still clutching his battle-axe, thrust himself between Tanis and the approaching captors. He raised the weapon, glared fiercely at the advancing elves, and shouted, "Stop!" Obviously taken aback by the sight of a dwarf outfitted for battle and ready to fight, the nobles stopped.

"We volunteered for this expedition knowing that it could bring our death," Flint said angrily. "Isn't that true?"

Ulthen, who with Litanas had been kneeling by Xenoth, stood, his cape splashed with blood. "But we expected the death to come at the jaws of the tylor, Master Fireforge, not by one of our fellow hunters."

The elves muttered and growled. The adviser had been disliked by many of the courtiers, so there seemed to be little real sadness at his demise, merely shock that it appeared to have come at the hand of another elf.

"Who says Tanis killed him?" the dwarf demanded.

Tyresian sighed loudly. "It was Tanis's arrow, Master Fireforge. Now, let's get on . . ."

But Flint pressed ahead. "Lord Xenoth was dead when the arrow hit him."

"How do you know?" Tyresian demanded with a sneer. Behind Tyresian, Litanas had withdrawn the yellow and scarlet arrow from Xenoth's chest and was laying his travel cloak across the body of his former superior. Several other nobles stood apart, poking the tylor's body, glancing at Tanis and Tyresian, and talking in low voices.

Flint folded his arms across his chest, the axe still clenched in one thick hand. "I saw it."

"Don't be ridicu—"

Flint interrupted, raising his voice until it boomed across the clearing. "I was there, Lord Tyresian. You and the others were on the far side of the ravine. I had a clear view. You did not."

"They argued," Tyresian said doggedly. "Tanis all but threatened Xenoth at the stables. Who's to say the half-elf's human blood didn't prompt him to avenge himself? And who will trust the word of a dwarf who also happens to be the half-elf's closest friend?" He turned to Litanas and Ulthen. "Bind his hands. We will return to Qualinost and set the case before the Speaker of the Sun."

But Miral, supported by Porthios and Gilthanas, had finally risen to his feet. He staggered forward, holding his bleeding right hand inside his cloak. His eyes were glazed with pain and fury. "You are wrong, Tyresian."

Tyresian bristled. "Mage, you forget who is in command here."

"Being in command does not imbue you with wisdom, Lord Tyresian," the mage replied.

Flint interjected. "Let's examine Lord Xenoth's body. Perhaps that will tell us something."

After a long pause, during which several elves began to drift over the rocky clearing toward the adviser's corpse, Tyresian nodded and pushed his way through the crowd around the body. Flint followed. Kneeling, the elf lord gently withdrew the cloak from Xenoth's face. The adviser's visage was blank with death and surprisingly free of wounds. His white hair moved with the breeze. He looked as though shortly he would open his blue eyes and speak.

"Farther, Lord Tyresian," Flint prodded. "Look at his chest."

The elf lord drew in a deep breath and pulled back the cloak. The tylor's knifelike tail had caved in and lacerated Xenoth's chest. Gilthanas gasped and looked ill. Porthios laid a steadying hand on his brother's arm.

"Where is the arrow?" Flint said.

"Here." The new voice belonged to Litanas, who sidestepped through the other elves and placed the arrow into Tyresian's black-gloved palm. Fully one-third of the shaft was stained with blood. Litanas, brown eyes angry, pointed at the shaft. "Lord Xenoth's blood," he said.

The dwarf stayed calm. "I'm not disputing that it is Xenoth's blood," Flint said.

"Well, it's definitely Tanis's arrow," Tyresian said stubbornly.

"Certainly," Flint conceded. "I'm not arguing that, either. In fact, I made the arrowhead."

Tyresian laid the cloak back over Xenoth's torso and head, and rose. "Then what, dwarf?" he snapped, towering over Flint.

"By Reorx, use your brain, elf! Don't you notice anything unusual about the arrow?" Flint put all his scorn into the statement.

Porthios joined Tyresian and studied the weapon. Finally, the Speaker's heir spoke carefully. "It is a perfectly formed arrow, stained with blood but with no other marks."

"Correct," Flint said, nodding.

"So?" Tyresian's voice throbbed with contempt. "You've admitted it's the half-elf's arrow. So what?"

Porthios made a small noise, and Flint's blue-gray gaze shifted back to the Speaker's son, whose eyes were suddenly wise. "You understand, don't you?" Flint asked.

Porthios nodded and explained. "If Tanis's arrow had struck Lord Xenoth before the tylor's long tail did, the arrow would have been crushed by the beast. As you can see, the arrow is undamaged."

The commander's sharp blue eyes widened. Then he swept one arm aside, all but knocking Gilthanas into Miral. "His arrow still found its way into Xenoth. So what if the half-elf didn't *kill* him. Tanis is still guilty of a gross error of judgment."

Flint and Tyresian stood frozen, gazes locked, for a long moment. Miral's voice finally broke the spell that held them. "All this talk is not getting our comrade's body back to Qualinost," he stated wearily. "I suggest we return immediately and discuss this matter with the Speaker."

Tyresian balked. "I have one more question," he said. "Who killed the tylor? Tanis?"

"Did the mage kill the beast, perhaps?" Litanas murmured. Several other elves nodded agreement. "Look at his hand, after all. Even from across the ravine, we saw the lightning burst from his fingers and hit the lizard."

Porthios turned his gaze to Miral, still supported by Porthios's younger brother. "Show us your hand, mage," Porthios ordered.

Miral's hood had fallen back from his pallid face, and the mage's eyes squinted against the light. He gingerly drew his right hand from beneath his cloak. The sleeve was in tatters. Nails were missing from his first two fingers, and all five digits were blackened from the tips to the palm. Angry red streaks extended from the mage's wrist to a scar near his elbow.

This time it was Flint's voice that rose above the rest. "I didn't know you were capable of such magic, Miral."

The mage looked confused. "Nor did I." He appeared to be on the verge of collapse.

"What happened?" Porthios asked gently.

The mage stammered as he spoke, and a blotch of red appeared high on each blanched cheekbone. "I saw the beast threaten Flint and Tanis," Miral said. "I am but a weak magic-user. Under normal conditions, I would have had no power against a beast such as this. I came along merely to tend some of you, should you get hurt.

"When I saw the monster looming over Tanis, I could not stand the thought of losing yet another beloved friend to a violent end. I . . . I thought of Arelas, if you must know, and suddenly I and my horse were in the clearing with Tanis and Flint, and . . . I felt power like I'd never known course through me." The mage's breath was shallow, his voice nearly a whisper. "I felt a jolt, as though I'd fallen from a great height, and my hand . . . pained me. Then I awakened on the ground, with all this around me."

A gesture of his left hand encompassed the adviser, the dead tylor, and the bloodstained clearing strewn with shredded leaves and bark. Then Miral slumped to the ground in a dead faint.

*　*　*　*　*

The hunting party rode slowly from the forest. The rain continued to hold off, the threatening clouds sparking tempers already stretched thin by the events in the clearing. Xenoth's body had been lain across the back of Litanas's horse, and—at Tyresian's order—Litanas rode with Ulthen. The mount was skittish, rolling its eyes, the scent of blood in its nostrils.

Porthios and Gilthanas kept their horses close to Tanis and Flint. Although the elven brothers said nothing, their actions spoke clearly enough. They were guarding him until the case could be laid before the Speaker.

Miral had awakened from his faint and was sharing a

mount with one of the nobles, who supported the weakened mage, his horse tethered behind.

The journey back to Qualinost stretched endlessly. The thunder drummed overhead, and the wind rose, with no rain to ease the tension of the charged air.

When they neared the city's boundaries, Gilthanas pushed his roan ahead, to go inform the guards of their coming. The Tower of the Sun loomed like a specter in the leaden sky. When they reached the city's south archway, a quartet of guards was waiting for them.

"These guards will escort Tanis to his quarters, where he will remain under guard until we have met with the Speaker," Gilthanas said.

Flint protested. "You mean this one"—and he gestured at Tyresian—"will get a chance to tell his story to the Speaker without Tanis being there to defend himself? Is this elven justice?"

Porthios spoke. "Lord Tyresian, as commander of the expedition, has the right to report to the Speaker of the Sun."

"Will you be there?" Flint demanded of Porthios.

"Certainly. As will Gilthanas. And Miral, if he is strong enough."

"Then I'm going, too," the dwarf rejoined. "I'll tell the Speaker Tanis's side of all this." Flint set his jaw; it was obvious there would be no dissuading him.

Two guards, dressed in their glossy black livery, accompanied Tanis, still mounted on Belthar, through the streets of Qualinost to the palace. The somber trio drew some glances from passers-by, but all in all, the city's residents appeared to find nothing odd in the Speaker's ward traveling with two palace guards.

* * * * *

"Out of my way!" Tanis heard a deep voice growl outside the door to his palace chambers several hours later. The half-elf turned from where he'd been gazing out of his second-floor window, which overlooked the courtyard. He faced the source of the noise.

"Who goes there?" came the voice of one of the guards, but Tanis shook his head. He recognized the voice.

"You know darn well who it is," Flint roared. "Now stop this nonsense, and let me pass. I intend to speak to Tanis, and I warn you, don't you cross me."

"But Master Fireforge, Tanis is a prisoner," one of the guards protested. "He cannot—"

"Prisoner schmisoner!" the dwarf spat. "I come by order of the Speaker of the Sun. Now let me pass, or by Reorx I'll . . ."

Tanis could only imagine the look in the dwarf's steely eyes at that moment, but suddenly there was a jingling of keys. The heavy door swung inward, and the dwarf stepped through.

To Tanis's surprise, Miral had come with the dwarf. The mage's right hand was heavily bandaged, and his face was as colorless as his eyes, but he appeared pleased.

The guard shut the door, obviously glad to have the dwarf on the other side of it.

The glower on Flint's face couldn't disguise the fact that he was as pleased as Miral. "We explained everything to the Speaker," the dwarf said, refusing a seat. He remained standing on the thick, hand-knotted rug, which depicted a stag hunt in swirls of green, brown, and orange.

Miral made his way to a canvas-and-aspen chair next to a spare-looking table that served Tanis as a desk. The mage eased his body into the chair. Tanis offered him water from a porcelain pitcher, but the mage shook his head wearily.

"Your friend here," Miral said with a nod at Flint, "told the Speaker everything that happened in the clearing—how Xenoth was yards away from the path of both arrows, how you shot to protect the adviser as the creature attacked . . ."

". . . and how Miral came thundering through the clearing to release his magic against the tylor," Flint added. "There was some debate over who killed the beast. The mage contended it was your arrow that slew the tylor. Others said it was the mage fire that killed it."

Tanis could well guess who those "others" were. He leaned against the windowsill and crossed his arms over his chest. He'd exchanged his hunting garb for a soft leather shirt and buckskin leggings.

Miral interjected. "Tanis's arrow was in the creature's eye. I but raised a little smoke and fire."

Flint raised an eyebrow. "Your 'little smoke and fire' was far more than a mere distraction." He looked at the half-elf. "More important, the mage here also proposed an explanation for the strange deflection of your arrow."

Tanis, wordless, looked at Miral. The mage smiled. "Tylors are creatures capable of strong magic. I, as you know, am not. Yet somehow, back in the clearing, I was able to send a blast of lightning so strong that it knocked me out of my saddle and, quite possibly, killed the creature."

"Yes?" Tanis asked, not sure where the mage was leading.

Miral sat up a little straighter in the canvas chair and gestured with his left hand. His bandaged one remained motionless on the arm of the chair. "I merely conjectured whether, in the heat of the emotions of that moment, the creature released its magic and I somehow unwittingly deflected it, turning it back upon the tylor."

"Is that possible?" Tanis's face looked dubious.

The mage shrugged, and slumped again. "I don't know. It's only a guess. But if that did happen—and it's a big 'if,' I know—could that same burst of powerful magic also have deflected an arrow from its path?"

Tanis looked wonderingly at the mage. "You are saying . . ."

Miral drew a deep breath. "That what happened to Lord Xenoth was an accident, that you were in no way to blame." He paused to gather his thoughts. "And that, in fact, you behaved honorably and bravely in the face of near-certain death, seeking to save Lord Xenoth."

Flint stomped over to Tanis's desk and helped himself to a handful of sugared almonds from a covered wooden bowl. "The Speaker said he will check with experts in magic to see if that is a plausible explanation," he added. "And thus, it appears, you are cleared. The guards have been dismissed from your door."

With the tension finally eased, Tanis realized he'd gotten

four hours of sleep in the past forty-eight. He yawned expansively, and the dwarf and mage grinned.

"Lad, you look as though you've lived through ten years in two days," Flint said, clearly unaware of the pouches under his own bloodshot eyes.

"I have."

With no more words, the dwarf and the elven mage left then, one to his shop and the other to his rooms at the palace. Tanis moved to his wardrobe to prepare to retire. He had just shrugged out of the leather shirt when he heard a knock at his door. Thinking it was Flint, he strode to the door and threw it open, not bothering to throw anything over his torso.

A light voice greeted him, and Laurana stepped out of the shadows of the corridor into his room. She appeared hesitant, which was unusual for her but probably not surprising considering Tanis's level of undress. The only light in the room came from a lamp on Tanis's desk and the moonlight streaming through the window behind him. The lamplight glinted against the metallic strands in her long silver gown. "Tanis."

He said nothing. Tanis hoped this interview wouldn't last long. He was suddenly so tired that he could barely focus on the elven princess.

"I . . ." She faltered and tried again. "Father talked to me about the discussion you and he had this morning." She passed him and stepped onto the thick rug that Flint had occupied only moments before.

Tanis, shaking his head, remained in the doorway. Was it only that morning that he had met with Solostaran in the Speaker's private chambers at the Tower? How badly the half-elf needed sleep. He reeled and caught the stone door frame.

"He said you don't love me," Laurana continued. "Not the way I hoped you did." She kept her chin high, but her agitation showed in the way she kept smoothing the lace at the wrists of the gown.

What it must be costing her emotionally to force this conversation, Tanis suddenly thought. He hoped to make the discussion as short and honest as possible. "You are my sister," he said gently.

"That's not true!" Laurana protested. "Just because we were raised in the same house doesn't make that so. I can love you, and I do." She moved toward him and grabbed for his hand with her slender fingers.

Tanis groaned inwardly, yet he knew deep down that Laurana was right. She was his cousin only by marriage—and even that link was tenuous. She certainly was not his true sister. But did he even wish her to be so? He shook his head, thinking of the golden ring that lay hidden still in the bottom of his leather purse.

"Laurana, please understand," Tanis said, his voice weary. "I do love you. But I love you as a—"

"—as a sister?" she finished acidly, and suddenly pulled away from him. "That's what you told father this morning, wasn't it? 'I love her only as a sister.' "

Only the ragged sound of her breathing broke the silence in the room. When she spoke again, her voice was bitter.

"I've been a fool, haven't I? I won't trouble you any longer, Tanthalas, my *brother*. I should thank you, really, for opening my eyes to the truth."

Her face was as cold as the quartz walls of the room, but Tanis saw Solinari's light reflected in the tears in her eyes.

"I could learn to hate you, Tanis!" she cried, and then shoved past him to the corridor, leaving Tanis to stare after her. Just before she disappeared down the hallway, she stopped and turned. Her voice was nearly calm again. "Throw away the ring, Tanthalas." Then she vanished.

Tanis mentally kicked himself. There must have been a better way to have handled that. He shook his head and sighed, then closed the door.

Chapter 19

The Medallion

A.C. 308, Early Summer

Weeks went by without any further word on the controversy over Lord Xenoth's death. A quiet funeral was held for the longtime adviser two days after his death. Truth to tell, few people in the court missed the irascible adviser, and more than one elf silently breathed a sigh of relief at not having to cross verbal swords with him anymore.

Xenoth's funeral did not prevent the general population from conducting spontaneous festivals to celebrate the slaying of the tylor. The beast had done much to inhibit the trade that increasingly formed a basis of the Qualinesti economy. The beast's horned head was displayed for a time at the southwestern guard tower, and long lines of elves, many with excited children in tow, formed to view the trophy.

Tanis found himself the focus of admiring glances by the common elves in the Grand Market, and suspicious ones by the courtiers in the Tower and palace. Both situations made him uncomfortable. In addition, Laurana was avoiding him and treating him with elaborate coolness on those instances when they could not evade each other. As a result, he spent more time than ever in Flint's shop, watching the dwarf prepare sketches for Porthios's *Kentommen* medallion.

"The Speaker filled Lord Xenoth's position yesterday," Tanis observed one morning as he watched the dwarf's hands fly over the parchment with a piece of charcoal.

"With . . . ?" prompted the dwarf.

"Litanas, of course."

"I imagine that has sealed Litanas's suit with Lady Selena," Flint remarked.

Tanis nodded. "Ulthen is walking around like a lost soul, sighing and gazing at Selena like . . ." He cast about for an appropriate simile. Suddenly, a clatter of mule hooves interrupted his reverie, and Fleetfoot appeared in the open doorway to the shop, limpid brown eyes alight with affection. ". . . like a lovelorn mule."

Flinging down his charcoal with a soft curse, Flint intercepted the creature just as she placed a hoof inside the sill. Berating the animal, he led her back to the shed.

When Flint's grumbling had receded, Tanis rose and moved to the table. More than a dozen sketches, showing different views of the medal, lay on the wooden surface. Flint was working with various combinations of elven symbols—aspen leaves, of course, and other woodland elements. He'd even roughed in a caricature of Porthios that suggested both stubbornness and strength but emphasized too much the permanent glower on the elf lord's face; Flint had drawn a big "X" through the sketch. Tanis decided that a medallion showing intertwined aspen, oak, and ivy leaves was his favorite.

Flint stomped back into the shop and slammed the door, inadvertently cutting off the welcome breeze that had eased the midsummer heat. He'd doffed his usual tunic in the heat, and wore only a lightweight pair of parchment-colored breeches and a loose shirt, the color of a robin's egg, gathered in the front and back and left untucked.

"That blankety mule," the dwarf groused. "I've made four different latches for her stall, and she's outsmarted every one."

"She adores you, Flint. Love conquers all, you know," Tanis commented, hiding a smile.

"My mother used to say, 'Love and a penny will get you a crusty bun with cheese at the Saturday market,' " Flint remarked, his concentration back on the drawing.

Tanis was opening his mouth to comment on Flint's sketches when he snapped it shut again. He gazed at the dwarf in befuddlement. "So?" he finally asked.

"So?" the dwarf echoed, raising one bushy brow.

"So what does that mean?" the half-elf demanded.

"Reorx only knows," Flint said, seating himself at the table and taking up the charcoal again. "It was just something my mother said."

"Ah."

Flint twirled the drawings around so Tanis could see them. "Which do you prefer?"

Tanis pointed to the intertwined leaves. "That one, but it's too plain."

The dwarf pondered the sketch. "That's what I thought. The problem is, I can't figure whether to do the medallion in metal or wood."

Tanis looked questioningly at the dwarf.

"It seems," Flint explained, "as though wood would be a good medium—to show the elves' connection to nature. But a carved wooden medal will look like one of those birch disks the children use for play coins." Flint turned the sketches back toward himself. "Not exactly an image to celebrate the coming of age of the Speaker's heir."

"How about steel?" Tanis asked.

Flint thought, his voice far away, musing. "There's that. It's a precious metal, but everything comes across cold and heartless in steel. Take your mother's pendant." Tanis touched the hilt of the sword he still insisted on carrying everywhere with him. "It's beautiful, but it's . . . distant somehow. Beautiful—and full of meaning for you, her son—but it's not warm."

As the half-elf watched, the dwarf rested his forehead on his hands. "I don't have that much time left," he complained. "The *Kentommen* is coming up in two weeks, and I've yet to take my sketches to the Speaker for approval."

When Tanis didn't say anything, the dwarf rubbed his eyes one last time, rose, and crossed the dwelling to an oak sideboard that held a huge trencher of raspberries. There he used a wooden scoop to fill two pottery bowls with berries.

"Another gift from Eld Ailea?" Tanis asked ingenuously. "Like that shirt you're decked out in today?"

Flint glanced suspiciously at Tanis. "Exactly what is that supposed to mean?"

"Oh, nothing." Tanis held up his hands in mock-surrender.

The dwarf pointed the scoop at the half-elf. "Ailea has become a good friend. And I might add that you yourself have spent a fair amount of time with her in the past few weeks, lad."

Tanis plucked a berry from one bowl and ate it. "Do you want me to get some cream to pour over these?" Flint cooled his provisions, including milk and cream, by sealing them in ceramic jugs and lowering the containers into a spring in his back yard.

The dwarf spooned a generous portion of raspberries into his mouth, closed his eyes, and chewed slowly, murmuring, "Wonderful, just the way they are." Then his blue-gray eyes flew open, and he glared at the half-elf. "And anyway, I pay Ailea with toys. These are not gifts." He lifted the bowl and took it back to the table to examine his drawings.

Tanis decided it was time for a change of subject. "If you can't decide between wood and steel, why not mix them?" His voice was muffled with berries.

Flint nodded, not paying much attention. Then he turned to Tanis. "What was that you said?" he demanded.

"Why not mix . . ."

But Flint had already pulled out another sheet of parchment and was sketching away furiously. He mumbled to himself, but Tanis couldn't catch the words. The half-elf sighed. It was just as well; with the day's stultifying heat, Tanis was ready for a nap anyway. Five minutes later, the half-elf was curled up on Flint's cot, sound asleep.

The dwarf worked on.

*   *   *   *   *

It was early afternoon when Flint finally raised his head from the page. "Look at these, lad. I need your opinion." He looked over at Tanis, but the half-elf barely stirred. "Well!" Flint gazed again at his design, then rolled the sheet into a cylinder, leaving the others on the table, and departed, closing the door quietly.

Thirty minutes later, Flint had unrolled the paper on the Speaker's marble-topped table in the Tower. Solostaran leaned over to examine the dwarf's suggestion.

"I've decided to mix gold, silver, steel, antler, red coral, and malachite," the dwarf said excitedly. "And aspen wood."

The sketch showed a medallion about the size of a child's fist. The medal depicted a woodland scene, with an aspen in the foreground and a path leading back through spruce trees to a hill. Above the hill were two moons. "I'll make the medal by sandwiching a back plate of steel with a fore plate of gold. Into the gold fore plate I'll cut out the figures—the trees, the moons, the path."

Solostaran nodded. It was a clever plan. "What of the coral and malachite?" he asked. "Where do they fit in?"

"I'll inlay the piece," Flint explained. "Once I've sandwiched the two plates together, I'll fill in the outline of the trees—green malachite for the leaves and branches and brown antler for the trunk. The path will be of antler and steel. One moon, Lunitari, will be of red coral. The other, Solinari, will be formed of silver."

But the Speaker looked dubious. "It's beautiful, but it's so elaborate. Are you sure you can fashion this in two weeks?"

Flint winked, and dipped a handful of dried figs and

glazed almonds from the silver bowl on the desk. The bowl always seemed to be full whenever the dwarf arrived, but Flint never paused to consider the significance of that; he merely congratulated himself on his good fortune in having a friend whose taste in snacks mirrored his own. "The hard part is the thinking," the dwarf said. "The rest comes easily.

"Is the design all right?" Flint waited confidently, knowing the Speaker would be pleased but wanting to hear him say it.

"It's perfect," Solostaran said.

A smile split the dwarf's face. "Good. Then I'll get working right away." He reached for his drawing.

Solostaran's voice stopped him. "Master Fireforge. Flint."

The dwarf looked at his friend.

"What are people saying in the aftermath of Lord Xenoth's death?" the Speaker asked quietly.

Flint's hand remained suspended above the parchment. Then he slowly rolled up the sketch. "Well, you know I don't have much business with many of the courtiers now." Especially since he'd taken Tanis's side after the tylor hunt, he might have added.

"What are the common folk saying, then?"

Flint tied a string around the rolled paper and exhaled slowly. "Lord Xenoth wasn't much liked by many people, especially those he considered . . . lower-class," he said carefully. "But many elves also approved of his views about keeping Qualinesti apart from the rest of Krynn." He decided to plunge on ahead. "Those same elves don't approve of my being here, and they're not overly fond of allowing half-elves to live in the city, either."

"There are fanatics on every issue," Solostaran murmured. "The question is, how prevalent are they?"

"That I don't know, sir."

Solostaran smiled wanly. "Call me 'Speaker,' " he said. "Remember when I told you that, the day you arrived in Qualinost?"

"Remember?" The dwarf hooted. "How could I forget? How many folks get lessons in court decorum from the Speaker of the Sun himself?"

Solostaran didn't speak, and eventually his smile and Flint's grin faded. "Many of the courtiers are not pleased, Flint. They say . . . they say I am protecting Tanthalas because he is my ward. They say I should banish him."

Banish Tanis? "That's absurd," Flint said. "He didn't kill Xenoth. Didn't Miral explain how the burst of magic might have diverted the second arrow?"

"Flint," Solostaran said, "I have talked to a number of magic-users in the past weeks, and they all agree. Circumstances such as those Miral painted are extremely unlikely. His explanation would call for the tylor's powerful magic to 'ricochet' off a weak mage like Miral and somehow force one small arrow off course to land in an elf's chest. They say it's not impossible, but not probable, either. For one thing, such an occurrence most likely would have killed any but a powerful mage.

"For the past weeks, I've been going from expert to expert, hoping to find one who will say, 'Yes, that's probably what happened.' "

Solostaran pushed his leather chair away from the massive table and turned to face the huge windows. "It can't be done, Flint. No one who understands magic will say that." Despite the blazing heat outside, the marble and quartz building stayed cool inside. Flint shivered.

"What will you do, Speaker?"

"What can I do?" Solostaran demanded, his angry movements rustling his robe of state. "I am left with a situation in which the closest eyewitness—and someone I trust absolutely—says that the most obvious explanation—that Tanis aimed badly—simply is not true. The other explanations that would exonerate my ward are deemed virtually impossible by elves who should know.

"That leaves me with one conclusion. *What happened to Xenoth could not have happened.* Yet it obviously did." The Speaker paced before the window wall. "My courtiers feel I should 'do something,' but the result they want appears morally indefensible to me. I cannot banish Tanthalas solely because some hidebound members of court resent his presence and have found a way to get rid of him. And yet . . ."

He returned to his chair, where he slumped backward. "Somehow I always get back to 'and yet . . .' "

Flint cast about for a reply, but none was forthcoming. All he could promise to do was to think on the subject, and to keep his ears open to gauge elven opinion on the matter.

When Flint emerged from the Tower of the Sun moments later, prepared to walk slowly down the blue and white tiled streets to his shop, a familiar figure was waiting on the steps of the Tower. A small crowd of admiring children had gathered around Fleetfoot, who lifted her graying muzzle and brayed enthusiastically as Flint drew near. A ragged length of rope hung from the collar that Flint had fashioned for her—his latest attempt to clip her wings.

"You doorknob of a mule!" the dwarf huffed. "Only a kender could be a bigger pest." He grabbed the chewed length of rope and hauled the infatuated animal along the street.

Chapter 20

A Summer's Dream

The scorching weather, so unusual for Qualinost, forced even calm sleepers into nightmares. And Miral was no exception.

He was back in the cavern. Stalactites, glowing with some inner light—the only illumination in the cave—dripped from the ceiling. Stalagmites had grown up from the damp floor. He could barely keep his balance on the slippery surface.

He looked down then and saw that he was wearing the type of thin leather sandals that elven children wore. His playsuit was torn and filthy from all the falls he'd taken.

Miral didn't know how long he'd been in the cavern. It seemed like days, but time was fluid for young children. He was not hungry. As he'd clambered about the caverns, moving through tunnel after tunnel, always seeking the Presence that called him, he'd fortuitously found food whenever hunger pangs gripped him. Like a child, he did not question these finds; he merely ate his fill and moved on.

He was not really frightened. When he'd longed for a nap, he had found a warm pallet by one of the walls, with a down pillow and a flannel comforter turned back as if to beckon to him. And when he'd awakened, a plate of toasted *quithpa* with cinnamon and sugar had been waiting.

Little Miral had accepted these gifts, and never questioned where they came from. If he'd been asked, he'd have said that his mama probably sent them, though he hadn't seen her in what seemed like ages—ever since she'd called to him to "Come back here immediately, young elf," so long ago at the mouth of the cave.

He had no idea where the cave mouth was anymore. He had no idea where Qualinost was, or Mama.

The Presence called from deep in the cavern. With the calling, however, came a buzzing, a roaring that confused young Miral. He was alternately frightened and consoled by the sound.

The Presence wanted him. It would comfort him.

Suddenly, the calling became more urgent, as though the Presence were fearful and angry at once. *Come this way, little elf. Come this way. I will protect you. I will provide everything you want, if you only set me free. Come this way.*

At that moment, Miral knew where to go. The Presence told him. He set his pudgy toddler's legs moving and began to run down one stone corridor after another. He spurted around one last corner, knowing that the Presence was nearby, and . . .

Sudden light flared through the new chamber that Miral found himself in. For minutes afterward, he could not see. The sense of great good was gone from the Presence. In its place was overweening evil.

He grew hoarse from screaming, shrieking for his mama, running in circles from the buzzing that reverberated through the cavern, which suddenly lacked entrances and exits. In the middle of the cavern—the source of the noise, the light, the terror, he understood even in his young innocence—stood a pulsating gem larger than his head. Its faceted sides sent beams of gray and red darting into every depression in the rock. His eyes ached, yet closing them did not keep the rays out. He renewed his sobbing.

The gray gem wanted him. Its words pounded inside his tiny head. *Release me. Let me go and I will give you everything you want.* Pictures of toys, Mama, Eld Ailea, delectable foods, appeared in succession before his eyes. Miral felt feverish. His voice was raspy; he wanted a drink.

Suddenly, a cup of sweetened water appeared before him, suspended in midair. When he lunged for it, it vanished. The combination of the familiar and the impossible set the little boy wailing. He spotted a crevice along one wall and ran to squeeze himself into it. He pressed back, far back, while every monster he feared as a child threatened him from the cavern.

Then came the part he knew was coming—the strong hand yanking him farther back into the crevice.

Miral awakened, bathed in perspiration.

Chapter 21

Attempted Murder

A.C. 308, Midsummer

MORE than a week later, Flint was working on
Porthios's *Kentommen* medallion when Lord Tyresian
walked through the doorway of the dwarf's stone
dwelling—without knocking, of course, Flint noticed. Only
Tanis was welcome entering the shop without giving a
warning. Even Fleetfoot knocked, in a way, her hooves'
noise usually giving the dwarf enough warning to leap for
the door.

The weather had cooled since the blazing heat of a week
earlier. It was the kind of day that made most folks want to
pack *quith-pa*, cheese, and pickled vegetables in a picnic
basket and head for one of the ravine overlooks. But the

dwarf had no thought for relaxation. He was running apace with a deadline; the *Kentommen* was only a week away.

With the holiday impending, of course, numerous Qualinost nobles had discovered metalwork that they simply *had* to have completed before Porthios's coming-of-age ceremony. Flint took their work but gave them all the same answer: He was working on an assignment for the Speaker of the Sun and, alas, might very well get to the supplicants' projects after the *Kentommen*. They weren't happy, of course, but the elves of Qualinost had long ago learned that Flint Fireforge, while he was undeniably the most gifted metal-artisan around, also could be as unyielding as a minotaur.

The two disks that would go into the medal lay before him; he was painstakingly cutting into the gold fore plate with a thin-bladed chisel and a small hammer. He surveyed the effect critically; the chisel gave the openings a rough-edged look that he rather liked. It worked especially well in fashioning the trees. "That's a good thing, too, seeing as I've got no time to do it over," he muttered.

That was when the door swung open, the chime sounded, and the arrogant elf lord with the short blond hair appeared in the portal.

"Dwarf, I require your services," Tyresian announced.

Taking his time, Flint covered the components of the medallion with his sketch, looked up from his chair next to the table, and flashed the elf lord a smile that looked more like a dog baring its teeth. "Come in, Lord Tyresian." He pointed his chisel at his stone bench. "Have a seat."

Under elven protocol, Flint should have risen to his feet when the elven noble entered the room, though he and Solostaran had long since dispensed with that formality on occasions when the Speaker visited the dwarf alone. Tyresian, however, flushed with annoyance. The fact that the elf lord did not complain of the slight was proof to the dwarf that Tyresian wanted the dwarf's services badly. That brought another smile to Flint's face.

"What service is it that you 'require'?" Flint asked expressionlessly, leaning back in his chair. He again pointed to the bench with the chisel. "Have a seat."

Tyresian appeared uncertain whether to sit where the dwarf told him—and thus appear to be following an underling's orders—or to remain standing, which might imply that he, not Flint, was the underling. He compromised by moving restlessly through the room, never stopping long enough to sit anywhere. After wandering insolently around the room, surveying the hutch, Flint's cot, his carved chest, and the forge, Tyresian drew his short sword and presented it, hilt forward, to the dwarf.

Wordlessly, Flint accepted the weapon and examined it. It was a ceremonial weapon, carried on formal occasions, encrusted with emeralds and moonstones and inlaid with steel. The weapon, if sold, could feed a Qualinesti family for eight months.

"Not very practical in battle," Flint commented.

"It's for state occasions," Tyresian said loftily.

"Such as the *Kentommen* of Porthios Kanan," the dwarf finished. The elf lord nodded.

Flint resumed his examination of the weapon. The wood of the hilt had split badly; some of the steel inlay had dropped out, and one gem—an emerald, he judged, from looking at the pattern— had fallen out. It was not a simple repair job; a skilled craftsman would have to rebuild the implement, abandoning all other work during that time.

"It would take a week," Flint finally said. "I don't have time."

The elf lord's temper flared and his eyes snapped blue fire, but he kept his voice as bland as the dwarf's. "The *Kentommen* is still a week away, Master Fireforge."

"I have other work."

Tyresian straightened. "Then put it aside. Do this assignment."

Flint handed the short sword back to the elf lord. "Perhaps you can find another metalsmith to fix this."

"But . . ."

The arrival of Eld Ailea and Tanis interrupted Lord Tyresian's remark. The old midwife was dressed in exuberant colors, as usual—striped yellow and blue overblouse, red gathered skirt, and red slippers, all embroidered with pale yellow daisies. Next to her, Tanis looked practically colorless in tan shirt and leggings. Between them—a situation made lopsided by the great height disparity between the midwife and the half-elf—they lugged a huge woven basket filled to the top with ears of corn. In his spare hand Tanis carried a small plate with an overturned bowl on top. They paused on the doorstep and, squinting in the bright midday light, peered into the gloom of the dwarf's shop.

"Lunch, Flint!" Ailea sang, her round eyes large in her triangular face. "Just-picked sweet corn!"

"With fresh butter," Tanis added, holding out the crockery.

Then Lord Tyresian moved into the rectangle of light near the door, and their faces fell.

"Well, look at this," the elf lord said laconically, crossing his arms over his chest and looking down at both of them. "Two murderers keeping time together. Comparing notes, perhaps? The virtues of shooting an arrow into Lord Xenoth's chest versus, say, letting my mother die in childbirth? Oh, but I forgot, Tanis. Ailea allowed your mother to die as well, didn't she?"

Eld Ailea went white under her tan; her hand went to her mouth, stifling a small cry. Moving menacingly toward Tyresian, Tanis dropped his hold on the basket, and two ears rolled off the pile and bounced into the flowers outside Flint's door.

Then suddenly, Flint was between them, his back against Tanis, shoving him back out into the sunshine, and one hand against Tyresian's chest. The dwarf's voice was frightening in its quietness.

"Leave, elf," he said to Lord Tyresian, spitting out each word, "or I will show you what an experienced fighter can do."

"You . . . !" blustered Tyresian.

"I have fought in battle against ogres. You, despite your airs, have no military experience. It is easy to threaten an elderly woman and an elven youth who doesn't dare rock the boat in Qualinost right now by challenging you. Would you care, instead, to take *me* on?"

Tyresian glared down at the dwarf and seemed to notice, for the first time, the worn battle-axe that had materialized in Flint's right hand. The handle was scarred and dented, but the runes of power on the flat of the blade glinted in the sunlight and the blade edge gleamed sharp enough to cleave the hardest armor.

The elf lord relaxed his stance.

Flint, however, continued speaking. "Never forget, *Lord* Tyresian, that you were the one who suggested that the hunters cross the ravine and leave Xenoth—and me, as I recall—on the other side."

Tyresian started to object, but Flint tightened his hold on the elf lord's arm. "You were the one who left three people alone against a monster powerful enough to destroy them in short shrift," he said, his voice barely above a whisper but commanding in its intensity. "As far as I'm concerned, you are more responsible than anyone for the death of the Speaker's adviser." In an aside, he added, "Certainly more to blame than the half-elf who acted to save his life—all our lives."

As if the small shop weren't crowded enough, Miral chose that moment to appear on the path to the dwarf's dwelling. But the four involved in the drama on the doorstep didn't see the heavily hooded mage immediately. He drew to one side of the tiled path and waited.

"Now, leave, Lord Tyresian," Flint ordered. "And don't forget: Although I've never told the Speaker my own theory of who is really responsible for Xenoth's death, there's nothing stopping me from enlightening him. I've always suspected that you glossed over that part in your 'report' to him after Tanis killed the tylor."

With an effort, Tyresian shoved Tanis aside and then brushed past Miral, leaving the trio staring after the blond elf lord. Finally, as a group, the three friends became aware of Miral and ushered him inside the dwelling.

Knowing how weak Miral's eyes were, Flint closed the door behind the mage and set about fastening the shutters in the window at the front of the shop. Meanwhile, Eld Ailea built a fire and set a cauldron of water over it while Tanis stripped husks and silk from the corn. Although none of the three felt particularly hungry anymore, they went through the motions of preparing a meal, obviously hoping to recapture their previous happiness.

Miral took little time explaining his errand: One of the plates on a metal box that held some of his spellcasting ingredients had worked loose, scattering powder throughout the corridor before his palace chambers. "I know you are busy, Master Fireforge, but I'd hoped you could fix it," Miral said, holding the fist-size box in an outstretched hand.

Flint took the silver box. It appeared to be an easy repair; a rivet punched through one plate into the corner piece would hold the piece easily. The box was decorative enough—etched with dragons, minotaurs, and jewel shapes—to hide the tiny rivet. Flint set about the task, temporarily putting aside the Speaker's medallion, while Tanis and Ailea prepared the sweet corn.

The mage said little throughout the process, a fact that Flint laid down to weariness from lack of sleep. Everyone at the palace was busy from the hour before dawn until late in the night, preparing for the *Kentommen*.

"Do the hill dwarves have *Kentommens*?" Tanis asked Flint, who nodded.

"We call them Fullbeard Days, but they're nowhere near as elaborate as this," the dwarf said. "What are your duties in Porthios's ceremony, Miral?" Flint bore down on a slender punch as he worked it through the soft metal.

Miral blinked and looked up from his seat on Flint's clothes chest. "In the actual ceremony, none. But I've been put in charge of coordinating the staff that's preparing for the *Kentommen* and arranging for entertainment on all three days of the event."

"What does that include?" Tanis asked from his position next to the boiling corn.

Miral looked over and smiled wanly. The whites of his eyes were bloodshot, in odd contrast with the near-colorless hue of his irises. "Five dozen seamstresses are sewing banners"—which, indeed, had begun to appear on poles along Qualinost's main thoroughfares—"and three dozen swordsmen are preparing a demonstration of weaponry skills that frightens me to watch. I am amazed none of them has been sliced in half, and I will be stunned if the Kith-Kanan mosaic at the Grand Market amphitheater is bloodless when they are through."

Flint cast the mage a sympathetic look as Miral continued his recitation. "Ten jugglers and twenty jesters have overrun the palace," he complained. "Can you imagine the noise? There are also fourteen acrobats, one of which wanted to hold her high-wire act four hundred feet up in the Tower of the Sun!"

"You're allowing that, of course," Ailea said as she dipped a perfectly cooked ear from the boiling water.

"Of course not," Miral rejoined, then did a double take as he realized that the midwife had been joking. "But it's never sufficient just to say no. Each elf has two hundred reasons why his case is different, why I should allow him to do what no one else can." The mage slumped against the wall. "I haven't slept more than three hours in a row in two weeks."

"Care to join us for lunch, and then nap here?" Flint asked, gesturing toward his cot with the spell-box. "We can be a pretty quiet lot, if we have to be."

Miral shook his head. "I have to meet with a troupe of singers. They want to know why they can't sing bawdy ballads in the rotunda of the Tower right before the *Kentommen*—to 'warm up the audience,' as they put it." He rose to his feet. "I can pick up the box later."

"It's repaired now—on the house," Flint said, and passed the silver container to the mage. The dwarf opened the shutters and then yanked open the door for Miral, who pulled his hood far forward over his face, gave his thanks to Flint, nodded to Tanis and Ailea, and trudged down the path toward the Tower, which shone over the tops of Flint's fruit trees.

"Get some sleep!" Flint shouted. The mage waved without turning back. Then he moved on as the dwarf shut the door.

Miral's visit, however brief, helped lift the pall that had

descended on the trio when Tyresian had left. The dwarf moved his medallion-making tools off the table, and instead of moping, Flint, Tanis, and Eld Ailea found themselves waxing almost gay as they nibbled ears of buttered corn. Finally, they passed around a kitchen rag to clean themselves up, and leaned back, satisfied.

"Ah," Flint said, "as my mother would say, 'The way to a dwarf's soul is through his dinner plate.' "

"Oh?" Tanis asked, elbowing the dwarf. "And what else does your mother say?"

Flint laughed. "She has an adage for every occasion. 'Too many cooks make light work,' she'd say, and order my thirteen brothers and sisters and me to clean up the barn. It took me years to find out what the saying really was. It sounded like a dwarven law to me."

Ailea laughed and wiped her long fingers, one by one, on the rag. "What else does she say?"

Flint settled back in his chair. "I remember once I complained because one of the children in the town school was bullying me. She patted me on the head and said, 'Don't worry, Flintie. One rotten apple won't spoil the whole kettle of fish.' "

Flint raised his voice into a falsetto as he quoted his mother, and Tanis smiled. But the half-elf's look was wistful. "What does she look like?" he asked. "Is she pretty?" Eld Ailea cast a wise glance at the half-elf, then at the dwarf, who didn't seem to notice.

"Oh," Flint said, "I suppose she wouldn't seem pretty to your tall, slender elven friends, but we fourteen frawls and harrns think she's just fine. Sure, she carries some extra weight . . ."

"Try bearing fourteen children and see what it does to your figure," Ailea interjected.

". . . but she has a sweet face, and she cooks like one of the gods. Nice big portions, too." Flint patted his protruding gut, then blushed, straightened, and attempted to pull in his belly. Ailea's smile grew wider.

"What's your father like?" Tanis asked.

"Ah, lad, my father died when I was just a youth. Bad

heart. Runs in the Fireforge line, among the men, at least."

"Your poor mother," Ailea said softly.

Flint nodded. "She held the family together in those years after Papa died. Set my elder brother Aylmar to work at Papa's forge—and occasionally took a turn herself, on lighter tasks."

Ailea rose quietly and dropped the lunch dishes in the boiling water that had cooked the corn. When Tanis raised his eyebrows, she smiled and said, "No point wasting water. This will clean those plates just fine." Then she resumed her seat and motioned for Flint to go on.

"I was the second-born," the dwarf said dreamily. "After Papa was gone, Mama put me in charge of the barn. I remember one early spring morning in Hillhome. I came out of the barn, trying to get away from the damnable smell of cheesemaking, and I gazed around me at the hills and the conifers." He sighed. "Qualinost is beautiful, lad, but so is Hillhome. Still, it was a small, small village and ultimately I had to leave it to see the world."

"I'd like to see it someday," Tanis said, then prompted, "Your mother . . . ?"

Flint frowned, thinking. "Oh. I was standing there in the open barn door, enjoying the sun and the weather and the trees and the green hills, and Mama came out on the porch and hollered"—and he switched into the falsetto again—"'Flint Fireforge, don't you close the barn door after the early bird catches the worm!' " He jiggled with silent laughter. "I figured that meant she wanted me to go back to work."

He stood and stretched, then stepped over to the boiling water to fish out the plates with his forge tongs. "Once," he said, turning back toward his guests, "when my younger sister Fidelia was complaining about how poor we were, and how much the mayor's children had, my mother looked at us all and said, 'Oh, the grass is always greener on the other side of the fence.' "

Eld Ailea and Tanis waited for the punch line, but Flint shook his tongs and said, "We were stunned. For a moment, we didn't say a word. She'd gotten it right!"

He paused, still holding the tongs. "Then, I recall, the

fourteen of us started to laugh, and we couldn't stop. I still remember Aylmar, sprawled on his back on the stone floor, holding his sides and giggling until he couldn't breathe. Even my brother Ruberik, who normally has the sense of humor of an anvil, found himself gasping for air, he was laughing so hard. When we came to ourselves, we realized that Mama was out in the kitchen, muttering and banging the kettles together in a rage.

"She didn't speak to any of us for days. And, what's worse, she refused to cook!" He looked aghast.

"What did you do?" Ailea asked.

"Aylmar and I went to work at the forge. We fashioned a sign for her, bending slender bars of iron into words and fastening them to a piece of barn wood. We put it up over the fireplace for her. It said . . ." He suddenly erupted in a chortle. "It said . . ." Flint coughed, and wiped his streaming eyes.

"It said . . . ?" Tanis prodded.

" 'Waste makes haste!' "

"But that's not right." Tanis caught himself. "Oh, of course."

"She loved it," Flint said. "Oh my, she just loved it."

* * * * *

The three decided that, notwithstanding Flint's impending deadline, it was too lovely a day to spend indoors. So they gathered up the most portable of Flint's metalworking tools and headed toward the mountains just south of Qualinost. While the two rivers guarded the city on three sides, to the south was a forested slope rising to a ridge of mauve granite. On the opposite side, the top of the ridge formed a sheer cliff a thousand feet high. Tanis persuaded Flint to make the trek, which was not all that steep anyway, by pointing out that the ridge offered a marvelous view of the mountains of Thorbardin, the ancient homeland of Flint's people.

"A little exercise never hurt a dwarf," Flint replied then, and led the way. And thus he was the first to view, beyond an undulating sea of green forest, the sharp-toothed mountains of Thorbardin, looking almost like dark ships sailing on the southern horizon.

He found a comfortable spot at the foot of a tree and spent several hours inlaying the medallion, nearly completing the work, while Tanis and Eld Ailea walked, talked, and gathered herbs for the midwife's potpourris and potions.

Hours later, dusk was beginning to creep through the city as Flint made his way alone to his shop in its grove of aspen and fruit trees; Tanis was off escorting the midwife home. Flint's dwelling, of course, was dark; he'd not fired the forge for several days because of the summer heat and because this portion of the medallion-crafting process involved working only cold medal.

The blooms of the morning glories that were entwined about the door were twisted tightly shut against the descending twilight, but one of the new rosebushes Flint had planted next to the stoop was just beginning to bloom. Flint plucked one of the pale yellow blossoms and inhaled its perfume. He sighed. It didn't do to forget life's small pleasures. Notwithstanding the dispute with Lord Tyresian, the day had been a good one.

Perhaps a mug of ale—Flint's favorite of those small pleasures—would be in order this evening, he mused as he opened the door of his shop and started to step through, twirling the rose in his fingers.

"Ow!" Flint said suddenly, dropping the rose. He had pricked himself on a thorn, and he stuck his finger in his mouth, sucking on it to ease the sting. "So much for simple pleasures," he grumbled around his wounded finger, and then bent down to retrieve the rose, mindful of its thorns this time.

Just as he was about to stand back up and step into the shop, something caught Flint's eye. It was a thin black thread, lying before the doorway, about a pace into the room. Usually a keeper of a clean—if cluttered—shop, Flint reached for the thread, intending to pick it up and throw it away.

The thread seemed strangely stuck to something.

"Confound it!" he groused, and he tugged harder.

Suddenly there was a faint snick, and, acting on some survival instinct, Flint threw himself face down on the floor. Just as he collided with the stones, he caught a glint of light flashing from across the room. Something whooshed over his head and landed with a thunk in the wood of the door above and behind him.

Swallowing hard, he forced himself to roll over and, still on the floor, examine the door rising above him. Sunk deep into the hard oak, directly at chest level to a standing dwarf, was a leather-hilted dagger.

"Reorx!" Flint whispered. He moved cautiously to his feet, alert for any sudden noise that might signal another attack. He felt his knees trembling despite his firm orders for them not do to so. Slowly, he gripped the dagger and pulled it out of the door. Its tip glinted wickedly in the waning light of day. Had he stepped into the shop and snagged the thread with his boot, that dagger wouldn't have sunk into the door, but into Flint's heart.

Why would someone want to kill him?

Flint began to turn around, to step over the thread and into the shop, but just then there was a faint clunk, reminding the dwarf of the sound a stuck mechanism might make when it suddenly falls into place.

Before he could so much as cry out, there was another flash as a second dagger glittered through the air directly at the dwarf.

"Flint, you old knob-head," he said hoarsely, and stumbled backward against the door, clutching at the knife that had pierced the shoulder of his pale blue shirt. Blood seeped between his fingers and stained the fabric. "You should have guessed . . ."

He sagged against the door and then slid down to the ground with a groan. "You old knob-head . . ." he whispered once more, and then his eyes fluttered shut. Flint lay still as night cast its cloak over the city.

Chapter 22

Help Arrives

_____

"*Flint! Can you hear me?*"

Tanis shook the dwarf gently, and then more insistently, but Flint remained motionless, his hand still gripping the dagger. His fingers were dark with dried blood.

"Flint!"

Tanis gave the dwarf one more shake, and suddenly Flint let out a low groan. Tanis breathed a sigh of relief.

"In the name of Reorx," Flint groaned hoarsely, "can't you leave a poor dead dwarf alone?"

Tanis put his arm around Flint's neck to help the dwarf sit up straight to ease his breathing. "Flint," the half-elf said softly, "you're not dead."

"Who asked you?" Flint said testily, if weakly. "Now just leave me here to be dead in peace, will you? All this shaking is making my head ache." The dwarf groaned again, slumping back against Tanis's arm. A relieved grin flickered across the half-elf's face.

"You must not be seriously hurt," the half-elf whispered. "You're still complaining."

Moving gingerly to avoid starting the wound bleeding again, Tanis lifted Flint and placed the dwarf as gently as he could on Flint's cot. He checked the wound, decided against removing the dagger until he had assistance, and ran for help.

Outside the shop, he debated whom to fetch—Miral or Eld Ailea. Miral was overwhelmed with the *Kentommen* preparations, but the Tower was closer than the midwife's west-side home. That decided the half-elf.

Ten minutes later, Tanis returned, still at a dead run, with the mage panting behind him. Soon Tanis and Miral had propped the dwarf against some pillows and removed the knife. The dwarf's breathing eased.

"No physicians," he murmured. "Too late." His voice took on a dreamy tone. "I can already see Reorx's forge . . ."

"That's *your* forge, Flint," Tanis said.

"You *are* a pest," the dwarf griped.

"Here," Miral said from behind Tanis, and handed the half-elf a mug with steam rising from it. Chopped leaves floated on the water. "Make him drink this."

Tanis held the mug beneath Flint's bulbous nose, and the dwarf sniffed the drink. It smelled of bitter almonds. "That's not ale," he said accusingly.

"True," Miral said. "But it's better for you."

"Impossible," the dwarf groused. He took a deep breath and drained the mug nonetheless.

Eld Ailea—summoned by one of the *Kentommen* acrobats, whom Tanis had bribed with one steel coin—arrived just as Miral was binding and cleaning the wound. The slash from the dagger proved relatively easy to cleanse and bandage, though Flint made it more difficult by fussing and grouching through the entire process. Surprisingly, the treatment seemed to pain him less than it annoyed him. Miral rolled his sleeves up to his elbows, scrubbed his forearms with soap, and closed the wound with seven stitches—accompanied by seven dwarven oaths, and seven dwarven apologies to Eld Ailea. Then Miral daubed on a bubble of salve the size of a walnut and bound the dwarf's hairy chest with a bandage made of soft linen.

"I'm all right!" Flint finally shouted. "Leave me be!"

At that, Miral pronounced the dwarf fairly fit and prepared to head back to the Tower. The mage rolled his sleeves down again; his right hand was nearly healed, but the fingers that had lost their nails still looked ugly.

"I have to oversee a troupe of actors who want to entertain the crowd by declaiming the dying speech of Kith-Kanan," he said, and grimaced.

"Why is that bad?" Tanis asked.

"I'm not sure he made one," the mage said, and grimaced. Miral handed Tanis a folded paper filled with herbs, and told him to make a cup of tea from them every hour and administer it to the dwarf, "even if you have to tie him down to do it."

"If he's too difficult, mix it with ale," Miral told Tanis quietly at the door.

"I promise I'll be difficult!" Flint shouted from his cot, where Eld Ailea was unsuccessfully trying to lull him into sleeping. At that, the mage took his leave.

Eld Ailea attempted to soothe Flint with a lullaby that, she said, usually worked wonders with toddlers. He didn't seem sure how to take that, but he listened to her warm alto as she intoned the ancient melody. "Lullay, lullay, little elf," she sang, "sleep in the stars 'til the morrow, little elf. Search all the forests, ride 'mong the trees, then home with a smile on the morn, little one.

"That's an old, old song. My mother sang that to me," she said, then looked over at Tanis, who was examining the trap that had thrown the daggers. "And I sang that to you and Elansa when you were just minutes old, Tanthalas."

Tanis smiled. "I'll bet I liked it then just as much as I do now," he said.

"Flatterer," Ailea said. "You'll find yourself an elven woman to marry with no problem, with that silver tongue."

A blushing Tanis suddenly redoubled his efforts with the trap. He disarmed it carefully and began to dismantle it for inspection. "Whoever set this trap knew what he was doing, Flint. It's a sophisticated design, and the aim was perfect. What luck that the mechanism jammed on the second dagger; that's why it tossed only one of them at you at first. Then the tension released the second mechanism after a few moments."

Tanis had avoided looking at the old midwife as he spoke. "And what if I find a human woman, Eld Ailea?" he added at last, his voice carefully matter-of-fact.

A shadow passed over Ailea's catlike face as she drew the covers around Flint's bearded chin one more time. "It will bring you little but pain, in the end, Tanthalas," she said. "Humans are frail, and even if you find one to love, it's terrible watching them grow old while you remain young. It takes a strong love to survive that." She sounded weary.

He looked up from the trap. Round hazel eyes met almond-shaped hazel eyes, and a spark passed between the two part-elves.

"Try to remember that, Tanthalas," Ailea said sadly.

Tanis swallowed. "I'll try."

"Hey!" Flint crabbed from the cot. "Isn't it time for my ale?"

Eld Ailea threw off her gloom and laughed then, and patted the dwarf on his hale shoulder. "You're good for me, Master Fireforge." With renewed energy, she moved briskly to the table, where Tanis had deposited the paper of herbs.

"There's a bucket of ale in the spring," Flint suggested helpfully.

After some thought, Eld Ailea announced that ale might help the dwarf sleep—and, especially, keep him quiet. So she retrieved the near-empty container from the spring and poured the last splash into a mug. When she opened the packet of herbs, a look of consternation crossed her sharp features, then disappeared under her usual pleasant expression. "Flint, did Miral make you a drink of these leaves?" she asked casually.

"Yes," Flint said. "With water. It tasted awful. I'm sure the potion will be much better with ale." He grinned engagingly over his white bandage. "Lots of ale."

Eld Ailea stood for a moment, perusing the packet, then refolded it and slipped it into a pocket of the gray cloak she'd thrown over the bench when she arrived. From another pocket, unnoticed by Flint and Tanis, she drew out a small cloth bag, gathered with a leather thong, and measured a teaspoonful of the powder within. Then, while Tanis searched the rest of the shop for more traps, Ailea added the powder to the ale and gave the beverage to the dwarf. He drained it in a gulp.

Whatever it was, it didn't agree with him. Flint fell into a deep sleep, but awoke a short time later to vomit into the empty ale bucket, which Ailea had left by the bed. Then the dwarf's head fell back, and he slept again, his black and gray beard rising and falling with his deep breaths.

Tanis joined Ailea at Flint's bedside. The tiny elf was looking down at the dwarf with a half-smile that did little to mask her exhaustion.

"Is he going to be all right?" Tanis whispered.

"He'll be fine," she said. "My herbs will put him right again. At least, they work for nursing mothers . . ." She caught Tanis's startled look and patted his arm. "I'm just jesting, Tanthalas. Flint will be fine."

"Do you want me to walk you home?" Tanis asked. "I'll spend the night with him. I can give him Miral's tea, if you leave it here."

Eld Ailea's head came up then, and her eyes probed Tanis's. "It's best not to leave him alone at all right now," she said. "I'll stay here. We can take turns watching him."

Chapter 23

The Rescue

He was back in the dream. The rough hands clenched Miral and, just as the tylor's armored jaws jabbed into the crevice, powerful arms hauled him through the back of the crack in the stone.

"Truly thou hast gotten thyself in a royal fix, little elf," a deep voice said above the toddler's head.

Miral, eyes wet with tears, lifted his head and peered up through the gloom of the cave; this portion seemed to be lit less well than the tunnels he'd come through. He gulped back a sob and tried to focus on his rescuer.

It was a man, the youngster saw, but what a man! Bands of muscle rippled across a corded, barrel-shaped chest. The man's shoulders were huge, brushed with white hair that curled from his head and chin. When the man looked down at him, Miral looked deep into violet eyes that shone with kindness.

"Methinks thou art too young to be wandering about without thy dam, youngling," the man said.

At that moment, Miral became aware of hoofbeats clopping against the damp stone of the tunnels. The man came to a fork in the tunnel and turned to the right without stopping. But how had he signaled his intention to his horse? the little boy wondered. Miral looked down.

The man was a horse! Or the horse was a man; Miral couldn't decide. He looked up again, a delighted smile lighting his face.

"You're a centaur!" Miral cried.

"Of course," the creature replied, cradling the youngster in strong arms.

The centaur must have been seven feet tall from hooves to the top of his aristocratic head. He moved gracefully on the wet rocks, long tail flowing behind. Around the shoulders of the horse portion of the centaur, the creature wore a leather purse. Miral slipped little hands down to investigate the purse, but the creature held him higher, out of reach.

"Thou art a curious one," the centaur murmured in a bass voice. "No doubt 'tis why thou art so deep in the caverns."

"Someone called me," Miral explained, wanting this creature, above all, to like him. "From the tunnel."

The centaur's pale purple eyes widened and his gait slowed somewhat, then speeded again. "Thou heard the Voice? Truly thou hast magic in thy soul, young elf. 'Tis not all who hear the Graygem call." He took another turn, and another. Soon the toddler had no idea where he'd been or where he was now.

The creature continued to speak soothingly to the child. "Thou art warm, child. Thy dam should give thee a posset for thy fever. I will take thee home directly."

Miral, rocked by the steady pace of the gentle centaur, was growing sleepy. "Why are you here?" he asked drowsily.

"Ah, the Graygem hath great treasure indeed," the centaur said. "And, in truth, the beastly rock hath done me grave ill in the past and I'm sworn to vengeance. And that, little elf, be all thou need know."

The centaur picked up his gait, and soon the toddler dozed in the creature's arms. He awakened periodically, once when fresh air fanned through his hair and he realized he was moving through the moonless night, somewhere outside the caverns, and once while the centaur moved nearly silently through the tiled Qualinost streets.

Finally, they arrived at the palace. Miral roused enough to note their passage around the back of the structure, through the gates into the garden—Why didn't the guards look up? he wondered—and from there into the courtyard. Large hands laid him down on soft moss and covered him with a cloth.

"Go to sleep, little elf," the centaur murmured. "Thou wilt not remember this experience in the morn."

With a last pat on the toddler's shoulder, the centaur wheeled in the courtyard and, silently, was gone.

Chapter 24

Another Death

The next few days, Tanis and Eld Ailea took turns staying with the dwarf in the shop. Flint told them a score of times not to bother with him.

"You've got too much to be worrying about to be concerning yourself with a lame dwarf!" Flint would grumble, but the effect of the words seemed lost upon his caretakers. Solostaran visited once and seemed reassured by Flint's cantankerousness. Miral stopped by twice to check on the dwarf.

By noon of the second day, it was apparent that Flint was regaining his strength, and, judging from the reduction in the number of oaths when he moved about, the pain was lessening. Still, Eld Ailea was adamant that the dwarf not be left alone, and she remained with Flint while Tanis went back to the palace to pick up some clean clothes.

She did, however, allow Flint to work on Porthios's *Kentommen* medallion from his nest on the cot.

"After all, the ceremony starts tomorrow," she said nonchalantly, spreading a bandage on the table and folding it so it would best fit the stocky dwarf.

"Tomorrow?" boomed Flint, rocketing out of bed, then grasping his shoulder with a groan. "I thought I had three more days!"

Ailea intercepted the dwarf on his way to the door—though what he hoped to accomplish running shirtless through the streets of Qualinost was unclear—and shooed him back to bed, her greenish brown eyes merry. "Relax," she said. "You do have three days."

She explained the intricacies of the ceremony while she removed the old bandage from the dwarf's chest.

"The word '*Kentommen*,' or 'coming of age,' actually refers to the final portion of the four-part ceremony," she said as she eased the linen away from the wound. "That's the showiest part of the ceremony, the part most folks would like to witness. Most elves use '*Kentommen*' to refer to the whole three-day extravaganza, however.

"The first part is the *Kaltatha*, or 'The Graying,' " the midwife explained, fingers gentle as she cleansed the healing wound. "That part starts tomorrow morning. In the *Kaltatha*, the youth—who can be male or female, as long as he or she is a member of the nobility—is led by his or her parents to the Grove," referring to the ancient forested area in the center of the elven capital.

Ailea rinsed the cleansing cotton in a basin of clear water. "When the youth undergoing the *Kaltatha* is of as high a rank as Porthios, most of the common elves use the occasion as an excuse to parade through the streets, wearing their most colorful finery or even costumes. They dance and sing songs as ancient as the ceremony itself," she said. "That's why the palace is overseeing the making of brightly colored banners—to mark the route from the palace to the Grove."

"I'd like to see that," Flint said.

Eld Ailea scrutinized the spot where the dagger entered Flint's shoulder. "You should be well enough to walk to the procession route tomorrow morning, I'd think."

She rinsed the wound one more time, then emptied the basin out the shop's back door.

"What will happen to Porthios in the Grove?" the dwarf asked.

"The Speaker will take Porthios to the center of the Grove, then ceremonially turn his back on him," the midwife said. "Porthios will remain in the Grove for three days, alone, eating nothing and drinking only from the spring in the Grove's center. No one can enter the Grove to disturb him, nor is he to attempt to leave."

"Sounds like they should post guards," the dwarf commented gruffly, trying not to appear as though he were enjoying the midwife's ministering touch.

"Oh, they do," Eld Ailea assured him. "Elven nobles take turns standing guard, carrying their ceremonial swords—like the one Tyresian brought here for repairs."

"Are those guards really necessary?" Flint asked.

"Probably not," the slender elf admitted. "To fail in the *Kaltatha*—or in any portion of the *Kentommen*— means that the elf will forever be regarded as a child, no matter how old he grows to be."

Flint looked impressed.

Ailea continued. "In the Grove, Porthios will purify himself, cast off all the layers of childhood life. On the last morning, he will bathe in the spring, emerging cleansed in body and soul.

"That third morning, a gray robe—symbolizing his unformed potential—will be brought to him, and he will be led from the Grove," she concluded. "This time, there will be no merrymaking in the streets. In fact, the common elves are always careful not to look at the *Kentommen* youth at all as he is led through the streets in his gray robe."

"Why not?" demanded the dwarf.

"Because the youth is neither child nor adult. Technically, he does not exist. The elves would be ridiculed for looking at someone who is not there."

Flint snorted, but it was not a contemptuous sound. "It's not at all like my Fullbeard Day celebration. That consisted mostly of giving me lots of gifts and large tankards of ale." He looked thoughtful. "Come to think of it, I'd prefer that to spending three days without food or ale."

With a light laugh, Ailea fastened the clean bandage in place. Then she brought him his supplies for completing the medallion.

Tanis returned from the palace early that evening, prepared to spend the night. He fixed a simple supper for himself, the midwife, and the dwarf: a loaf of brown bread, half a cheese, the last of the sweet apples that had been stored away last fall, and a pitcher of ale. Finally, the sun dipped behind the tops of the aspen trees, the last rays of light glimmered through the translucent green of the feathery leaves, and the shadows crept from the darkened groves to steal along the streets of the elven city. The half-elf persuaded Eld Ailea that it was safe for her to leave Flint for a while, and she conceded that she had plenty of tasks of her own to complete.

"But don't let anyone in but me or the Speaker," she warned Tanis.

"Why?"

Eld Ailea seemed to be on the verge of confiding something, but at the last minute she caught herself. "It's best to keep Flint quiet for a while. You know how visitors excite him." Then, telling Tanis she'd be back in the morning, she stepped quickly down the path, slipped between two treelike houses across the way, and disappeared.

"Flint? Excited by visitors?" the half-elf asked himself softly, then shook his head.

* * * * *

Flint opened his eyes the next morning to a cacophony. "Reorx at the forge! What's that racket?" he demanded. The sun was barely over the horizon, from the soft look of the shadows in the shop.

Tanis stirred from the pallet he'd fashioned on a thick rug next to Flint's table, and rose to unfasten the shutters. Flint raised himself on one elbow and looked out into a blur of colors. Dozens of elves streamed past his shop, their voices raised in a boisterous song in a different tongue; he recognized only a few elven words, and even those were pronounced oddly.

"The old language," Tanis explained, "from the time of Kith-Kanan, though some of the songs themselves are more recent. They celebrate elven victories since the Kinslayer Wars, and praise the different ages of life, from babyhood to old age. They also celebrate folk who have achieved great things in life." He stopped and listened, a faraway look on his face. Suddenly, an elf dressed in a dark pink robe paused before the shop and opened his mouth in a new song. "Why, Flint!" Tanis exclaimed, not meeting the dwarf's eye. "It's about you! Written in old elven, too."

"You don't say," Flint said. He struggled out of bed and gingerly slipped his arms into the sleeves of a pale green shirt, the latest product of Eld Ailea's needle. He straightened the shirt's front over his bandage. "Well, lad, what's he saying?"

"He says"—Tanis concentrated—"he says you are a prince of a dwarf." The half-elf concentrated more, keeping his face carefully averted.

"Go on, lad," Flint urged. "Tell me." He mistakenly put both feet in one leg of his breeches in his haste to get dressed, and had to wiggle to straighten things out.

Tanis squinted. "He says you are an inspired worker—no, a 'true artist'—of metal."

Flint looked impressed, and peered out the window. "And I don't believe I even know the gentleman . . ." He pushed one foot into a boot without looking at it, hopping about the floor on his other foot. Outside, the elf continued to sing, head thrown back, hands clenched before his robe. Other elves gathered to listen.

"He also says," Tanis recounted, "that you are a valorous fighter and a loyal comrade of the first order."

"Well, that's certainly true," Flint said, the other boot dangling from one hand. "What a lovely song!"

Tanis fought to hide his smile. "And he says you should finish dressing and follow Tanthalas Half-Elven to the

Kaltatha procession before the two of you are late."

"He . . ." Flint paused. "What?" He stood motionless, an eyebrow cocked, his foot poised above his boot, until Tanis could no longer hide his mirth. "You . . . you doorknob!" The dwarf flung the boot at the snickering half-elf, who ducked just in time.

Ten minutes later, the two emerged from the shop into a maelstrom of colors, scents, and sounds. After some sulking, the dwarf had decided to speak to Tanis again. "Where do we go, lad?" he demanded, looking remarkably healthy for a dwarf who'd been knifed only a few days before.

Tanis pointed between two dwellings, rose quartz like the rest, glowing pink in the early morning light. "The procession will pass down that street over there. But first I think we should buy breakfast from one of these street vendors."

The idea sounded good to the dwarf, so the two descended on a young elf seated before a stand, selling frybread dusted with crushed sugar. Munching, they skirted a table manned by an elf selling fanciful masks of some of Krynn's creatures: minotaurs, woodland creatures, and gully dwarves, though those last didn't seem to be selling well; the Qualinesti weren't much interested in dressing like short, smelly creatures and carrying a simulated version of the dead rat that spelled the ultimate in gully dwarf accessories. Another vendor sold Flint and Tanis tiny venison sausages on hot, crusty buns, and, finally, they purchased mugs of hot spiced tea—which the dwarf pronounced nearly as good as ale. Tanis's purse was lighter when they emerged on the processional street, but his and the dwarf's bellies were much fuller.

"Now, that's a breakfast to restore a dwarf's health," Flint said, wiping his greasy fingers carefully on his dark brown breeches. "Will they still be around for lunch, do you think?" he added hopefully.

"Most likely," Tanis said, and was opening his mouth to say more when a new commotion off to the north caught his attention. The crowd appeared to thicken, to converge, around the disturbance, and Tanis spied the black and silver plumes of the ceremonial uniforms of the palace guard. He pointed.

"Here come Porthios and the Speaker," he shouted through the increasing din to Flint, who nodded.

The attendants around Porthios and Solostaran marched at the four corners of a huge square, with the Speaker and his elder son keeping regal pace in the center of the entourage. The crowd parted as the troupe stepped wordlessly through, looking neither right nor left.

Flint was jumping up and down, clutching his right shoulder with his left hand. "I can't see!" he complained. The crowd thickened around him and Tanis even as he groused, and the jostling soon forced the two apart.

"Flint!" Tanis called. "I'll meet you back at the shop when it's over!"

But the dwarf had been swept away in the crowd.

Despite the noise as the entourage approached, the crowd grew silent as Porthios and his attendants marched by. "That's something to remember all your life!" Tanis heard one elven father tell a young daughter, who appeared more interested in the chunk of sugared frybread she was devouring than in the history taking place before her.

Tanis caught his breath at the poise and presence that the Speaker possessed, his face commanding, his shoulders erect in the golden robe that flashed like the gold circlet on his forehead. Next to him, Porthios, dressed in a plain dark green robe, walked nearly as proudly, matching Solostaran step for step.

The half-elf stood stock still as the Speaker and Porthios strode by; pride for them and envy of them battled within him. He wondered who would stand as his parents when the time came for his own *Kentommen*, or whether his human blood would deny him that right.

The crowd surged off after the Speaker, but Tanis stayed where he was. Then he walked off in the opposite direction.

* * * * *

Shouting oaths, holding his shoulder, and wishing that that doorknob of a half-elf would find him, Flint bumped against several elves. But he was nearly half their height, and he was carried along with them like a leaf in a swollen stream.

Finally, through the moving bodies, he spotted a figure he knew, standing in a doorway about thirty feet away. Flint braced his feet and shouted, "Miral!" The mage swung toward him, a look of surprise on his face, and gestured the dwarf over, but Flint only shrugged helplessly. If he could have fought his way through a crowd like this, he would have been able to remain back with Tanis.

The tall mage had better luck than he in parting the sea of elves, and Miral's hooded figure soon reached the dwarf and pulled him into another doorway. "It's easier to attach yourself to something permanent and let the crowd flow around you," the mage commented with a wry smile. They watched in silence as the elves swirled by in a singing tide of reds, greens, yellows, and blues.

"What happens now?" Flint demanded.

The mage looked startled. "To whom?" he asked.

"Porthios." Flint pointed at the departing procession, only the plumes of the guards visible above the throng. "After he completes his vigil in the Grove."

"Have you visited Qualinesti for two decades and not learned the ways of the *Kentommen*?" Miral asked in surprise.

The dwarf grew huffy. "I've seen small celebrations, but nothing to pay particular attention to."

"Ah." The mage nodded sagely and moved out of the doorway, pacing toward Flint's shop. "Well, after the *Kaltatha*—that's the three-day vigil that starts today—Porthios will be led from the Grove by three nobles, their identities concealed by black robes, gloves, and masks. The Speaker will not be present. He will have gone into seclusion for meditation and prayer the day before.

"Porthios will be in a gray robe, as will Gilthanas, who will be returning from his one-night vigil in the *Kentommenai-kath*, overlooking the River of Hope." Miral broke off his recitation. "Have you been there?"

Flint nodded.

"The townspeople will pay no attention to either brother," Miral said. "It's part of the strictures of the *Kentommen*.

"I know that," Flint said. "Ailea told me. Where does Porthios go?"

The mage resumed, stepping around a child waving a teal and silver banner. "The three nobles will lead him to a stone chamber hewn deep beneath the palace. It's a shadowed room, and he will be made to sit in a small circle of light in the center." Miral and Flint skirted a glittering quartz home shaped like an oak; they turned a corner.

"The masked nobles will stand in a triangle around the youth," Miral said. "They are the *Ulathi*, the Gazers, and each is called by a ceremonial name: *Tolethra*, Ambition; *Sestari*, Envy; and *Kethyar*, Pride. Each questions the youth relentlessly, accusing him of self-serving ambition, of coveting the greatness of others, and of foolish pridefulness. With their wrath, goading, mockery, and criticisms, they test the strength of will and the purity of soul that the youth gained in the Grove."

Flint imagined the scene and shivered. He still preferred his Fullbeard Day party. "What's the point of the questioning . . . What's it called?"

"That portion of the *Kentommen* is called the *Melethkanara*, or 'The Heart's Shadow.' " Miral said. "The point, as the name implies, is to see if any shadow remains on the youth's heart. If so, he will become frightened, angered, or despairing at their words. To shout, cry, or even flinch means failure in this test. However, if at the end of the trial the youth is still calm and at peace with himself, the *Ulathi* will simply nod and then depart from the room, leaving the doorway open."

The dwarf had a sudden sense of where the Speaker had developed the impenetrable mask that fell over his features in times of turmoil. He wondered how Porthios—and, for that matter, Tyresian—would be changed by their own *Kentommen*s.

They had arrived at Flint's shop; there was no sign of Tanis. Flint, grateful—though he'd never admit it—to be able to rest for a few moments on his favorite stone bench, invited Miral in for a visit. Miral agreed, and soon the two were sharing a bag of toasted, salted *quith-pa* that the dwarf had purchased on the way back from the procession. The dwarf held a tankard of ale in one hand; the mage drank water.

"And how have you been feeling, my friend?" Miral asked. "Have you learned anything about the ones who set this foul trap?"

Flint shook his head in response to the second question but answered the first by proclaiming himself fit as a dwarf half his age. "Tanis and Eld Ailea took fine care of me. They fed me nothing but healthy food and drink. It was terrible," he added glumly.

"And did the potion I left have any effect?" Miral queried. "I wondered how you would be faring, downing a cup of the tea every hour."

"Potion?" The dwarf looked bewildered. "No. Ailea forced enough cold water and milk down me to leave me practically floating—she claimed it would prevent a fever from the wound— but I drank no potions. Unless, of course, she slipped it into the water. I wouldn't put it past her."

"No, this tea would have been taken warm," the mage said. "Ah, well. Perhaps I forgot to leave the herbs. I've been so busy lately that I'm never quite sure whether I've actually done something, or only thought about doing something."

Suddenly, Flint heard light footsteps on his front walk. "This must be Tanis," he said.

But it was a young elf just Flint's height, with hair the color of wheat and eyes like the sea. She said nothing, merely blurted, "This is from Eld Ailea. For Flint Fireforge or Tanthalas Half-Elven," and thrust a folded parchment at Flint.

The child continued to stand before Flint, shifting from foot to foot, as the dwarf unfolded the paper and squinted at the note. "'Flint, Tanthalas,'" the dwarf read aloud. "'Come immediately. I understand about Xenoth. Ailea.'"

He looked up. "What on Krynn . . . ?" Flint stared, unseeing, at the elf child for a long moment, then suddenly seemed to focus on the youngster. "What do you want, girl?" he growled.

"Eld Ailea said you would give me a toy for delivering the message if I ran all the way." The child was still breathing hard. "It was hard work. The parade's coming back. It's crowded out there!" She sounded petulant.

Flint gestured at the hutch. "In there. Take your pick. How did Ailea appear when you left her, lass?"

The child already had the cupboard open and was rummaging through its contents with a greedy hand. Her reply floated back to the dwarf. "Excited. She kept saying, 'Now it all makes sense. The scar. The "T." The air. Now I understand.' And she practically pushed me out her door." The childlike tones were injured.

Flint looked bewildered as he gazed from Miral to the back of the child's head as she poked through the toys.

"The scar. The 'T.'" Flint mused. "The air?"

"I know of no elves with a T-shaped scar," the mage said, pushing aside the bag of salted *quith-pa.* "Except perhaps Tyresian."

Flint sat up excitedly. "That's it! Tyresian's arms are scarred from years of weaponry practice. Ailea must have found a way to link him with Lord Xenoth's slaying." He pushed himself off the bench and made for the door. "Come on, we have to hurry," he shouted to Miral, adding to the little girl, "Take what you want!"

The mage was behind him as he dashed to the street, pushing through the celebrants as they once more jammed the streets, having left Porthios at the Grove.

The child stayed happily behind in Flint's shop, up to her elbows in toys.

*　*　*　*　*

Ailea paced her house impatiently, occasionally pausing to pound one small fist into the palm of her other hand—a masculine movement somewhat unusual in an elven woman, but she was rocking with excitement.

"That's got to be it!" she whispered to herself. "Of

course!" She wheeled at the fireplace and turned back toward the front door. Once more, she crossed to the door and peered out into the street. "Where are they?" she grumbled. "Has Fionia found them yet? I hope that child didn't get lost . . ."

She heard a click at the back of the dwelling and closed the front door. "Flint? Tanthalas?" she called, her face almost feline in expression. She hurried back through the entry room, past the fireplace, and paused in the doorway to the kitchen. "Who . . . ?"

The figure turned, and Eld Ailea froze. In all her centuries, she had never known more terror. Her hands sweaty, her breath short, she stepped back blindly, knocking over a square table. Three baby portraits and one of Flint's rocking-bird toys crashed to the floor.

The figure followed her into the entry room, and she opened her mouth to scream.

But the sound never emerged. She crumpled to the floor in silence.

And then the figure was gone.

* * * * *

When Tanis walked away from the procession, he picked the most deserted lanes he could find—which wasn't difficult because most of Qualinost's residents were following Porthios and the Speaker to the Grove. He stalked for half an hour, until the call of a vendor reminded him that he'd promised to meet Flint back at the shop.

He arrived at the dwelling shortly, and found only one occupant—a blond elf child, playing happily with several dozen wooden toys on the floor of the shop. She introduced herself as Fionia, pointed out Eld Ailea's message, which had fallen to the bench, and announced that the dwarf had given her all these toys.

Tanis read the note and was out the door, running, before the girl had finished speaking.

Later, he would remember little of the dash from Flint's shop to Eld Ailea's house; it was a blur of singing, dancing, and chattering Qualinesti. Once he spotted Flint Fireforge standing alone on a street corner, looking around as if he'd lost someone, but when the next opening in the throng occurred, the dwarf had vanished. The half-elf pressed on.

The front door of the midwife's rose and gray dwelling was unlocked, but that was not unusual. Few Qualinesti locked their doors; there was too little crime in Qualinost for an elf to become fearful. Tanis knocked, tentatively at first, then harder as he failed to hear the midwife's usual reply of "Coming, coming, coming." He called up to the second-level window, but there was no answer.

A neighbor poked her head out of her front door and gave the half-elf an odd look as he pounded at the door. "Ailea must be home," the elven woman called. "I saw her at the window not five minutes ago."

Finally Tanis pulled the door open and stepped inside. Even before his eyes adjusted to the dim lighting, he knew something was wrong. He'd expected an excited midwife bustling out of a back room to tell him she'd solved Xenoth's slaying.

Instead, he smelled death. The door banged shut behind him.

The elderly midwife lay on her back before the fireplace, in a pool of her own blood. Her round eyes—those human eyes she had never been ashamed of—stared sightlessly at the beamed ceiling. Dozens of miniature paintings lay scattered around the room. Tanis could see that she had been able to move after the fatal blow was struck; a wide stain of blood stretched from the front door to the rug before the fireplace. One sleeve was pushed up past her elbow, and her lilac-colored skirt had been lifted slightly, revealing a slender calf and knee. Ailea's other hand held a portrait of two elven children.

Tanis didn't even have the breath to cry out. He found himself on his knees beside the elf's tiny body, mindless of the crimson liquid that soaked his leggings, his moccasins. Ailea's purple skirt was streaked with blood. He found himself fruitlessly trying to wipe it off, succeeding only in smearing it even more. He touched her face, hoping to feel her breath on his hand. But the elf's flesh, while still warm, had taken on the heaviness of death.

His fingers were covered with red. He rocked back to his heels, heart contracting in sorrow and rage.

Suddenly, he realized that someone had been pounding on the front door for some time. And at that moment, the door crashed open behind him. Tanis swiveled to face the newcomer.

"Great Reorx!" Flint cried out, then, "Ailea!"

* * * * *

Halfway to Ailea's house, Flint had stepped into the sea of elves and lost sight of Miral. But figuring that a mage who was eye-level with other elves had a better chance of penetrating the throng than a four-foot hill dwarf did, Flint had plunged on without looking for him.

Miral caught up with the dwarf on the doorstep of Ailea's house, as Flint knocked for the first time. The mage looked winded.

Flint ignored him. Instead, he began pounding at the door. Finally, he swung it open, saw Tanis's tear-streaked face look up at him, and cried out at the sight behind the half-elf.

. . . Then Flint had looked up to see the words scrawled in blood on the mantlepiece, words already turning brown as the fluid dried.

"Ailea," the message read, "I'm sorry."

* * * * *

"Understand the judgment that I must make," the Speaker said later from the rostrum in the Tower of the Sun. Hundreds of elves, attracted by the upcoming *Kentommen*, packed the entryway, though only nobles were allowed within the central chamber itself when the Speaker was holding court. There was a constant murmur of conversation in the background.

"Not since the Kinslayer Wars, Tanthalas, has the blood

of an elf been spilled by an elf," Solostaran said, "and not only will we grieve the passing of a long-time faithful servant of this court, we will mourn the loss of the peace that this city has cherished for so long.

"But before we can mourn, he who has wrought this shadow must abide by its darkness. Thus you stand before me, Tanthalas Half-Elven. You have been accused of the murder of Eld Ailea, midwife."

Litanas muttered from his new position to the right of the rostrum, "He probably killed Lord Xenoth as well."

"In this deed, and in my wisdom," Solostaran intoned, "I have found you guilty."

Still garbed in the bloodstained garments he'd been wearing when the palace guards took him away from Ailea's house, Tanis winced but stood his ground. He heard a low growl behind him, and he knew it was Flint.

"Thus I proclaim that you, Tanthalas Half-Elven, shall be banished from all the lands of Qualinesti, and that the people of the land shall shun you as if you were one who had never been, lest they suffer a like punishment themselves."

Tanis's head reeled. Death would have been easier, he thought. The thought of leaving Qualinost made Tanis's heart ache as surely as if a dagger had been driven through it. For all his yearning to travel through Krynn, he had always assumed he would have Qualinost to return to.

Tyresian looked grimly triumphant as the Speaker spoke.

"Tanthalas, do you accept this judgment?" Solostaran asked.

Tanis opened his mouth to answer, unsure just what words were going to come out, but suddenly one of the guards next to him stumbled, and Tanis blinked in surprise as Flint clomped angrily forward to stand before the podium. "I don't know whether he accepts it or not," Flint growled, his hands on his hips but his eyes sorrowful. "But by Reorx, I know that I won't stand for it!"

Those gathered about the rostrum stared at the dwarf, stunned.

Flint was acutely aware of all the pairs of almond-shaped eyes gazing down on him, especially the Speaker's. They'll be tossing me out of the city any minute now, Flint thought, and then I won't be able to do the half-elf one bit of good. He thought suddenly of Ailea and realized that with Tanis banished and the midwife dead, he had little reason to remain in Qualinost.

He shook his head and assembled his thoughts. Surely Ailea would understand if he gathered his strength now to defend Tanthalas, her favorite. Flint would mourn the old midwife later, privately.

But Tanis needed him now. "Look here, Speaker," Flint started in a rumbling voice before the Speaker had a chance to say anything. "You've apparently listened to everything these elf lords have said about what happened—about what they believe happened, at least. There are no eyewitnesses—*no* witnesses, remember.

"Yet they've been quick to point the finger for this dark deed at Tanis," Flint continued. "I can think of others who are equally—no, more—suspect than the half-elf who had grown to love Ailea in the past weeks."

"Love!" snorted Tyresian. "An act!"

"And you, Lord Tyresian, are chief among my suspects!" Flint bellowed, pointing at the elf lord.

"Impossible," Tyresian rejoined. "I was helping to guard Porthios at the Grove when the old lady was killed."

Flint was momentarily nonplussed. Then he continued, "There is the question of the note. Presumably, the death of Eld Ailea is related to the slaying of Lord Xenoth. The midwife figured out the solution to that death, and as a result, someone killed her. Why, then, would she address the note to me *and Tanthalas* if she had evidence linking Tanis to Xenoth's death?"

The Speaker seemed inclined to allow the dwarf to continue, despite the affront to court decorum. "Yet the note is missing, Master Fireforge," Solostaran said. "No one but you saw it. Mage Miral only heard you read it, the child Fionia is too young to read, and Tanis, who also claims to have seen it, is the chief suspect. Further, no one but Tanis was seen entering or leaving the home before you and Miral arrived. And finally, why would Ailea's murderer apologize to her in a message on the mantlepiece if the murderer were not someone close to her?"

"I . . ." Flint faltered. "I confess that I don't know, Speaker. All I know is that the tale the evidence seems to spin cannot be the true one."

A wrinkle crossed the Speaker's brow; a look of puzzlement touched his face—and perhaps a flicker of hope.

"With all respect, Speaker, this is ludicrous," Tyresian objected, his voice low but his eyes flashing. "Since when does a common smith, and a dwarf at that, question the wisdom of the court?"

The Speaker held up a hand. "Master Fireforge has ever been able to speak freely to me," he said softly. In that moment, Flint saw how tired, how old, Solostaran seemed. "Please," the Speaker said, gesturing for Flint to continue.

"All I'm saying, Speaker," the dwarf said gruffly, "is that maybe you should let Tanis tell his side of the story."

"We've heard his story," Tyresian protested. "And a ridiculous one it is. 'I arrived, and she was dead.' Why, then, was her blood fresh on his hands? Why, then, did no neighbor see anyone enter or leave the house but Tanis? There is a space of only five minutes in which, logically, the midwife could have died, and Tanis was the only one to enter the house during that time. Does he expect us to believe—"

"Hold!" the Speaker ordered, and there was metal in his voice again. Tyresian's words ended abruptly. "I'm afraid there is some truth to Lord Tyresian's words, Flint," Solostaran said regretfully, turning back to the dwarf. "We have heard Tanis's story, and there is little in it to exonerate him."

But Flint wasn't finished yet. "Sure as my beard is long, there are some queer things at work here, Speaker, and I don't think you can argue with me on that. It may be that, given time, Tanis might be able to make sense of them and prove his innocence. Now, it looks like everyone's minds are made up. But I think he deserves a chance."

Flint could be as immovable as a mountain when the mood struck him. The Speaker considered the dwarf for a time, and then a smile flickered across his lips. "As usual, Master Fireforge, the wisdom of the court pales before your inimitable common sense. I will heed your advice."

Tyresian looked furious, but the Speaker ignored him.

"Tanthalas," he said, his voice taking on the ring of authority again, though this time the coldness was missing. "You will be granted three days to find proof that it was not your hand that committed this dark deed, the slaying of our Eld Ailea. If by sundown on the third day, you have not convinced the court of your innocence, then the punishment I have decreed will be placed in effect, and you will be banished from the Realm of Qualinesti forever."

Tyresian protested. "The half-elf is dangerous! The city is filling with travelers for the *Kentommen*. The ceremony will be held in three days. What if another slaying occurs? How many elves must die before the Speaker faces facts?"

Solostaran looked gravely around the chamber. Gilthanas, Litanas, and Ulthen had the same uneasy expressions. "Has anyone else something to say?" the Speaker asked.

Litanas suddenly seemed to remember that he was the Speaker's adviser now. He stepped forward. "I agree that Tanis should be given the opportunity to prove his innocence, but there seems to be some concern among the nobles about the advisability of allowing an accused murderer to continue to walk the streets of Qualinost."

Tyresian snorted. " 'Some concern'? That's an understatement."

"My adviser has the floor, Lord Tyresian," the Speaker said. "Continue, Lord Litanas."

Litanas straightened, and his brown eyes looked directly at the elven lord. "Perhaps a suggestion would be this: Confine Tanthalas to his quarters, with a guard at the door, for the three days. Allow his friend Flint Fireforge to amass any evidence pointing toward his innocence. At the end of the three days—immediately after the *Kentommen*—meet with Flint and the rest of us to discuss the situation."

The Speaker nodded gravely, but his green eyes appeared pleased. "Are there other ideas?" No one spoke. "Then it shall be as my adviser Lord Litanas has suggested.

"This is the wisdom I have spoken!" he concluded. With

those ancient words, the council was adjourned. After one last look at Tanis and Flint, the Speaker left the chamber, his robes ballooning behind him.

As Flint approached Tanis, he saw that Miral was speaking with the half-elf. "I hope you can make good of the time the dwarf has gained for you, Tanis, but I fear the task will be difficult," the mage said, a sad expression on his face.

"So you think I did it, then?" Tanis asked him.

"No, I believe you didn't, Tanis. But the evidence against you is strong." Miral shook his head. "Let me know if you need help, Tanis. I will aid you however I can." The mage turned on a soft heel and walked briskly from the chamber.

Gilthanas and another guard stepped forward to escort Tanis to his chambers.

Flint glowered at them both, but he was surprised to see only a look of sorrow on the young elf lord's face.

"The old midwife did not deserve to die," Gilthanas said softly.

"I know," Tanis said. "I did not kill her."

"She delivered me and Laurana and Porthios, too," Gilthanas said, then took a deep breath. "Tanis, reason tells me that you are the only one who could have killed Eld Ailea. My soul, on the other hand, hopes that you are exonerated, to save my father's heart.

"I would be glad if you proved your innocence," he added simply. Gilthanas brushed his golden hair away from his green eyes. He seemed small in his black uniform. "But don't expect any aid from me. I cannot help you. And if you try any further ill . . ." He touched the silver emblem of the Tree and the Sun on his black jerkin, the symbol of the city and its guards. "I will be forced to stop you."

Flint snorted. A lot of good that did. But Tanis seemed to understand, for he nodded, and then the other guard stepped into position on Tanis's other side. Tanis removed his sword and scabbard and handed it to Flint.

Gilthanas and the other guard led the dwarf's friend away.

Chapter 25

Looking For Clues

Early in the afternoon two days later, Flint wandered through Qualinost, despairing his lack of evidence and wondering how in the world he was supposed to gather clues into Eld Ailea's death when he had no idea why she was killed. He'd spoken to everyone who might have known something, from Ailea's neighbors to women she'd recently helped give birth. He had stopped at the Tower to deliver Porthios's medallion and had interviewed a few of the elves whose opinions he didn't already know.

"The note said Ailea understood about Xenoth's death," he mused, pausing to sit at the edge of the Grand Market.

The market, always a melange of colors and sounds, was even more exuberant today. He'd never seen elves as gaily attired as they were for Porthios's ceremony. They normally dressed in quiet earth tones; this afternoon, pinks, teals, and purples swirled past his eyes, and more than one elf wore a mask carved in the face of an animal or bird. To the celebrants' amusement, one elf was even dancing about dressed as a tree—garbed all in dark brown leather, his head covered with a brown cloth sack with two eye holes cut into it, his outstretched arms holding aspen branches. Another elf had fastened white feathers to her head and arms, and was wearing a white mask fashioned to resemble an owl. A third elf darted over the Kith-Kanan mosaic wearing a dark green dragon suit—an object of great mirth to her companions because dragons hadn't been seen on Krynn for millennia, if, in fact, they'd ever existed.

The passage of Porthios from youth to adult seemed to have given the Qualinesti cause to behave like children, and they were making the most of it.

For once, the Qualinesti had dropped some of their characteristic reserve, and while they'd never match the fervor of a dwarven Fullbeard Day, they were coming close.

How Ailea would have enjoyed this celebration, Flint thought sadly. Then he pulled his thoughts back to the question at hand. "Who would Ailea have told about her discovery?" he mumbled, reflecting on his searches of the morning. "Her neighbor said she was home all that morning, and the woman saw no one enter but me and Tanis."

"Yet Ailea must have talked to someone," he added.

The scent of sausage and hot *quith-pa* met his nostrils, and he stepped into line with four elves at a luncheon vendor's stand. The dwarf continued to mutter, which, given the carnival atmosphere, didn't seem to faze the elves.

What if she had discovered something about Tyresian—something that Xenoth also knew? The aged elf lord had been in court for hundreds of years; certainly he was privy to vast amounts of information, some of which could have been intended to be kept secret. "Tyresian would have the same reason to kill Ailea that he had to slay Lord Xenoth," he murmured. He wished he had Tanis to talk to, but the half-elf was barred in his chambers at the palace.

He reached the front of the line and paid the vendor, then

walked away, tearing off a juicy mouthful of sausage and bread. But the lunch went tasteless in his mouth as he realized he would have to do what he wanted least to do: go back to Eld Ailea's house and search it for clues.

Minutes later, he was standing before the midwife's dwelling, mindless of the singing, costumed elves who eddied around him. A black-uniformed palace guard, who looked as though he'd caught the carnival atmosphere despite the gravity of his task, leaned against the front door frame. He looked sharply at Flint as the dwarf stepped off the path and picked his way to the edge of the white petunia bed that the midwife had planted before the shuttered front window. None of the plants were damaged, and, brushing the white trumpet-shaped blooms aside, Flint saw no footprints in the rich dirt. The other window in front led to the second level. An elf would have to stand on another's shoulders to reach it.

The absurdity of his search suddenly struck Flint. "As if someone would have gone in through the window in broad daylight when there was an unlocked door an arm's length away," he said sotto voce. "Flint, you doorknob!"

He rose and brushed blades of crushed grass from his knees. The guard, a sharp-featured youth slightly older than Gilthanas, still watched. It occurred to Flint that the blond guard had not challenged him. "Has anyone been in the house since the death?" Flint demanded.

The guard shook his head. "The Speaker said no one was to be allowed in or near except you, Master Fireforge."

Flint felt a glow of warmth for the elven lord. "Are there other guards?" he asked from next to the petunias.

"One at the back door. No one inside."

The dwarf moved around the side of the house and peeked toward the back. The guard was sitting on the back stoop, eating a tomato—from Ailea's garden, no doubt. He leaped to his feet when he saw Flint. The dwarf said nothing, however; the youth could watch the door just as well sitting down as standing up, Flint figured, and Ailea would have welcomed someone enjoying the produce of her garden if she could not have used it herself.

Flint stepped back a few paces. The dwelling was only one room wide. The downstairs had held only the entry room and, behind that, the kitchen, which had no windows, only a small door to Ailea's backyard herb garden. The fireplace stood between the downstairs rooms, serving both the kitchen and the entry. Flint assumed Ailea's private room was upstairs, though he'd never seen it.

The guard didn't challenge Flint as the dwarf came around the curved side of the house and stepped up to the back door. That, too, would have been unlocked, knowing Ailea. The dwarf took a deep breath and moved through the door into the kitchen.

Ailea's presence was still strong in the kitchen. Crocks of preserved vegetables and dried fruits lined a hutch along one wall of the low-slung room. Flint remembered how Tanis had had to duck when he entered the kitchen, moving carefully to avoid the bunches of chives, sage, and basil that hung from the low rafters. The scent reminded the dwarf overpoweringly of Ailea, and anger swept through him.

His chin set, he moved through the kitchen, which still carried the memories of cheerful lunches with Tanis and the midwife, and resolutely set a foot into the entry room.

The room had not been cleaned after the midwife's body was removed. The smear of blood still stretched from door to fireplace. Baby pictures lay scattered. The square table, however, had been set upright, and on it was the painting that Eld Ailea was holding when Tanis found her.

Flint stepped over the brownish stain and reached for the painting. Done in Ailea's deft hand, it showed two youngsters, an infant and an older child, both blond with green eyes. The older child's eyes were deepset and serious, however, while the infant's were open and ingenuous.

"I wonder who they are," Flint murmured. Ailea had never labeled her portraits; she'd known from memory whom each one was, even though hundreds crowded the cramped room. He set the painting back on the table.

Flint suspected he wouldn't know a clue if it leaped out and challenged him with a long sword. His gaze moved from painting to painting around the room, remembering how the abode had looked when Ailea lived there and seeking any element that no longer fit the room's coziness. Finally, shaking his head wearily, he trudged up the stone steps to the second level.

As with most folks, Ailea's bedroom showed more of her personality than did those rooms that the public might visit. The upstairs room smelled of lavender; bunches of the fragrant herb, tied with gray ribbons, had been laid on the midwife's dressing table, next to her tortoise-shell brush and the silver-inlaid combs that had held her braid tight on fancy occasions. Blackened iron hooks, a gift from Flint, held the gathered skirts she sewed in profusion: purple, red, green, and bright yellow. On a nearby table was a new beige shirt, brother to the green one and the blue one she'd made for Flint earlier. A skein of brown embroidery thread and a needle waited by the new garment.

A large feather bed, laid with a purple and green coverlet, stood in the center of the room, while a smaller pallet had been erected in an alcove near the fireplace. Before the hearth sat an ancient wooden rocking chair, scuffed and scarred but polished to a sheen. The dwarf stepped into the alcove and saw the lamps at the head and foot of the pallet, a cauldron on the hearth, and thick piles of sheets, towels, and swaddling rags on a night table nearby. A basket cradle swung from a long iron hook set deep into the ceiling. This was, Flint realized, the alcove to which so many elven women had come to give birth.

Several hours later, as shadows began to lengthen into late afternoon, Flint finished going through Ailea's private records, searching for clues but feeling like a thief. Most of her pieces of parchment referred to births or to herbal remedies that had been effective in treating particular ailments. A search of the eight-drawer chiffonnier next to the feather bed yielded no information that, as far as he could see, had any link to the crime.

Then Flint saw the painting, in a delicate silver and gold frame, that sat atop the chiffonnier. The sidepieces of the frame had been rubbed shiny, as though the owner had often stood here, beholding the painting. He touched a thick finger to it; the paint was faded and old—older, he knew, than he was. It showed a young elf, slight of build, with round, greenish brown eyes and a face like a cat's, standing next to an elderly human man with a square jaw and clothes that proclaimed him to be a farmer. A tidy but small house, with white petunias framing the front path, stood in the background. The two figures were holding hands, and the expression on the faces managed to reflect both great content and overbearing sadness at the same time.

Feeling suddenly as though he were peering through a window into a private scene, Flint returned the painting to the chiffonnier and stepped briskly around the bed and back to the stairway. There was nothing here that contained the slightest clue pertaining to Lord Xenoth.

Downstairs, as twilight grew in the street outside, Flint found himself once more picking up the painting that Ailea had been holding when she died. It wasn't Tanis's portrait; the dwarf had found that one upstairs on the table next to the feather bed. Holding the framed likeness of the two elven youngsters and reflecting that he was still just a bit weak—only a little, though—from the attempt on his life, Flint eased himself into the overstuffed chair that waited at one side of the fireplace. Propping his legs on a footstool and gazing alternately at the portrait and the toy robin he'd given Ailea, he let his thoughts wander.

He'd arrived back home two nights ago to find his toy hutch cleared of everything but the soldiers. In the center of the table, however, Fionia had left him a chunk of rose quartz, fuzzy with lint and smudged with something that smelled suspiciously like grape jam.

What had the child said? "Ailea was excited. She kept saying, 'Now it all makes sense. The scar. The "T." The air. Now I understand.' "

"The scar. The 'T.' The air." Flint settled deeper into the chair and gazed at the painting. "The scar. The 'T.' The air," he murmured. "The air."

Suddenly, with a shout of "Reorx!" that brought the guards crashing through the front and back doors, Flint leaped to his feet. What met the guards' eyes was the sight of a dwarf hugging a portrait and chanting, "The air, the air, the air!"

* * * * *

But the guard outside Tanis's palace chambers was adamant. No one was to be allowed in to visit the half-elf. Even the guard saw Tanis only when he allowed a kitchen elf to set a tray of food just inside the door and collect the old tray—and even then the half-elf often stayed out of sight at the back of the room.

"How am I supposed to gather evidence if I can't talk to Tanis about it?" the dwarf demanded, waving the painting in front of the guard's face. "Well?"

The guard, nearly as old as Porthios, was unshakable. "The Speaker left orders for no visitors," he repeated.

"He didn't mean to shut *me* out, you doorknob!"

The guard's face grew even more stubborn. "Go talk to the Speaker, then."

"I will!" Flint promised. "And I'll be back!"

But the dwarf had no better luck outside the Speaker's anteroom at the Tower.

"He's in seclusion," one guard explained, "meditating and praying, as part of the *Kentommen*. Absolutely no visitors unless a crisis of state develops. Interrupting him now could mean canceling the *Kentommen*."

The dwarf practically threw the portrait on the floor in his ire. "This *is* a crisis of state! I'm in a state of crisis, by Reorx! Now open that door." He advanced threateningly toward the guards . . .

And suddenly found himself facing twin short swords held by a pair of grim-faced palace guards. "Sorry, Master Fireforge," one said.

Flint threw up his hands in despair. "Now what?" He stalked away down the corridor. "You elves and your traditions!" he shouted back.

He returned to the palace. There he found a spot on the steps and sat down to do some meditating of his own. Solostaran, now in seclusion, was the only one who could order the palace guards to admit him to Tanis's room. But the Speaker was in seclusion—unless, Flint assumed, Qualinesti was attacked by minotaurs or some such thing.

Porthios, who probably would not have aided the dwarf anyway, was under guard in the Grove, not to be disturbed for anything less than another Cataclysm. Gilthanas had pledged not to help Tanis in any way, and Laurana hadn't spoken a friendly word to the half-elf in more than a month.

Flint sighed. What a prime selection of helpers. Not for the first time, he wondered if it was time to move on to another spot in Ansalon, someplace with ale that didn't taste like rainwater and wine that didn't leave a dwarf reeking of blossoms.

Someplace like Solace, perhaps.

The dwarf threw that thought off, however, and reviewed the candidates. If Gilthanas even bothered to listen to the dwarf's entire idea, the neophyte guard almost certainly would raise an alarm that would scare off the murderer until another time—most likely until after Tanis had been banished. Which would not help the half-elf at all.

That left . . .

* * * * *

"Laurana, I have to talk to you," Flint said through the closed door.

"Go away, Master Fireforge," came the peevish reply.

"It's about Tanis."

A pause. Then the same voice, a bit less ill-humored, was heard. "I don't want to hear about Tanis.

"Fine," Flint groused. "I'll just let him die without speaking to you one last time. I'll let you know when the funeral is. In case you're interested in attending." He stomped on the marble floor, loudly at first, then gradually more softly.

The door swung open. "Flint, wait!" Laurana called, dashing into the corridor, past the dwarf.

"I figured that might work," Flint said smugly from next to her doorway. He traipsed into Laurana's chambers.

The elf swung around and faced the dwarf, then stalked

back into the small sitting room, a common feature in the palace's private chambers; it was outfitted with fireplace, small table, and two straight chairs before the fire, one of which already held Flint comfortably ensconced. She slammed the door upon entering.

Her scowl gradually turned to a look of confusion as Flint sketched in the background that he'd sorted out. He concluded, "Then I realized 'the heir'!"

But the princess still looked mystified. "The air?"

"The heir," Flint corrected her. "That's what Ailea was saying. The portrait she held was of Gilthanas and Porthios. The murderer, the one I now believe slew Lord Xenoth and Eld Ailea, intends to kill the Speaker's heir, Porthios."

If he'd been hoping for a big response, Flint was to be disappointed. Laurana just sat there, stroking the edges of the pale yellow cloak she'd thrown over her gown.

"But we're all his heirs," she objected. "Me, Gilthanas, and Porthios. Which one?"

Flint sat back. He'd been thinking in terms of Porthios all along. Why not Gilthanas and Laurana as well? Someone seeking to move up the ascendancy to become Speaker would have to eliminate them, too. Pieces of the puzzle were missing, but Flint still had a day to reveal the slayer before the Speaker would renew his vow to banish Tanis.

The seeds of another idea sprouted in his brain. "What better time to kill Porthios than at his own *Kentommen*?" the dwarf asked.

"What better time to kill all of us?" Laurana asked reasonably. "We'll all be together in the Tower at the same time. But why, Flint? And anyway, the suspect can't be an elf. We don't do things like this." She turned away from him and faced the fire.

Flint sat a few moments, gazing at the princess's silhouette. "Ah, lass, you've seen so little of the world."

She still objected, rising and pacing on the hearth rug in her agitation. "You want me to get you past the guard to see my father. But you don't have enough evidence to warrant my interrupting the Speaker and canceling the *Kentommen*," she said heatedly. "Your only evidence is your guess about what Eld Ailea was thinking right before she died."

"But don't you see?" he boomed. " 'The heir'! And she was holding the heirs' portrait!"

"If I order the guards to let you in and it turns out that this is all nothing but an elderly midwife's fantasy, my father . . ." Her voice faltered, and she grew pale. "But if I don't, and something bad really does happen . . ." She sagged into the chair. "I'm too young to be making these kinds of decisions!" she complained.

Flint watched her, realizing that he was viewing the beginning of the metamorphosis of a spoiled little girl into an elf woman with great strength—if she'd only let herself show it. She jumped to her feet and resumed pacing.

"Why, Flint?" she asked. "Why would someone want to kill the Speaker's heirs? Not that I believe you for a moment," she hastily added.

"Greed," Flint suggested. "Vengeance. Insanity. Unrequited love. This isn't the kind of scheme someone comes up with overnight, you know. I'd guess the murderer has been working on this for years."

"Well, then . . ." Laurana faltered again. "Then he's probably someone we know."

"Well, certainly," Flint snapped. "What did you think?"

They glared at each other for a long moment, then Laurana looked away and softly said, "It won't help Tanis if we argue, you know."

Flint grunted. Then, more quietly, he asked, "How close is Tyresian in ascendancy?"

"To the Speakership?" Laurana looked surprised. "He's of the Third House. We are of the First."

"That leaves the members of the Second House?"

Laurana nodded absently. Flint pressed on. "How close is Tyresian in ascendancy, if he doesn't marry you?"

"Oh, about twelfth or thirteenth in line," she replied, then narrowed her eyes. "You don't honestly think it's Tyresian . . . Why, he's a member of the nobility!"

Deciding that Laurana still had a lot to learn about life, Flint abandoned the tack he'd been taking.

"How safe is Porthios?" he asked.

Laurana faced him again. "There are more than a dozen guards around the Grove. They can't see Porthios, but they could hear him if he called. I don't think anyone could sneak in, with them there."

Flint rose and strolled around the anteroom. Across the mantlepiece, Laurana kept a collection of whimsical dragon figurines. He picked up a golden one and examined it. "And Gilthanas will be with his regiment tonight? He'll be safe there, at least."

"Oh no, Flint," Laurana objected. "Gilthanas will be keeping a vigil at the *Kentommenai-kath* all night."

The phrase sounded familiar, but Flint had been exposed to a plethora of new elven terms in the past few days. "The *Kentommenai-kath*?"

"It's the spot overlooking the River of Hope, west of Qualinost," she explained.

Flint remembered; that was where he'd picnicked with Tanis and almost fallen to his death. "Gilthanas will have a guard with him, certainly," he said, bending one of the legs of the figurine. The softness of the metal proclaimed it to be pure gold. Laurana gently took the little dragon from him, straightened the leg, and returned the piece to the mantle.

"Gilthanas will have an escort from Qualinost to the *Kentommenai-kath*," she explained, seating herself again. "The guards will leave him, and he'll remain alone at the spot until sunrise. Then he will return to Qualinost alone, arriving for the final portion of the *Kentommen*."

Flint felt a hand of ice snake around his spine. "He'll be alone?"

Laurana's already pallid face became whiter. Her reply, when it came at last, was not a question. "He'll be in danger, won't he."

He waved her to silence and leaned both arms against the fireplace, staring into the flames. Finally, he turned and leaned over the chair where Laurana waited.

"Laurana," Flint said, "do you trust me?"

After a pause, she nodded. Her hair glittered in the firelight.

"Then listen," he said. "I have a plan."

Chapter 26

The Ruse

Two hours before midnight a golden-haired figure
in an aqua gown shot with silver threads appeared in the
corridor outside Tanis's door and flashed a dazzling smile at
the guard.

"Hello," she said, then hesitated prettily, a movement
she'd been practicing in the mirror in her room for the past
hour.

The guard blushed. Lauralanthalasa knew he'd seen her
from afar before, of course, but he'd never been this close to
the Speaker's daughter.

"Uh," he said. "Hello."

She smiled again. "Aren't you supposed to say 'Who goes
there?' " she asked lightly.

The honey-blond elf, about Gilthanas's age, swallowed

and grinned lopsidedly. "But . . . I know who you are," he whispered. "Um, so why ask?"

"Oh." Laurana let her eyelids droop, then gave him a sidelong glance. "That's very wise."

Her voice oozed admiration—just the amount that Flint had declared necessary. "The guard will never buy it," she'd argued, only the hour before in her quarters. "How stupid do you think the palace guards are?"

But the dwarf had insisted, saying only, "Trust me. I've seen the way the elven lads watch you." She'd blushed. Flint had continued, "You'll knock the guard out of his ceremonial boots."

"Oh, Flint, don't be ridiculous," she'd snapped.

But now she wasn't so sure. The guard looked positively weak in the knees. Ascribing his reaction to a mild case of indigestion from a rich *Kentommen* feast, she said sweetly, "I need to see Tanthalas, please." She looked demurely away. ("Flint, he will *never* swallow this!" she'd protested. "Trust me," the dwarf had repeated.)

The guard looked suddenly miserable. "I can't let anyone in."

Laurana let her features fall into disappointment. "Not even me?" she whispered. "It's so very, very important." She hoped her eyes were filling with the tears that Flint had declared crucial. But even more, she hoped she wouldn't giggle.

Now came the dangerous move. She reached forward quickly and plucked the large key-ring out of the guard's front pocket and smoothly slipped the key in the lock. "Oh, I'm sure it's all right," she said, letting a note of supplication enter her voice. "Here . . ."

But the guard reverted to training, grabbing her gently but firmly by her wrists and backing her away from the door. "I'm sorry, Princess, but I have my orders." He sounded sincerely regretful, to Laurana's surprise.

She took several tentative steps backward, drawing him farther from Tanis's door. "Oh, I just hoped . . ." She let her voice trail off and thought very hard about the pet kitten who had died when she was a little girl. Thankfully, she felt tears finally rise in her green eyes, and she blinked, causing one huge drop to slip down her cheek.

The guard, obviously feeling like a heel, released her wrists and watched as she stepped femininely away, dabbing her already dry eyes with a linen kerchief. Just as he turned to resume his post at the door, she stumbled and cried out. ("Not loud enough to bring anyone else into the corridor!" Flint had demanded. "Just enough to convince the guard and cover a bit of noise.")

The young guard was at her side in seconds, supporting her with an arm slipped quickly around her waist. "What's wrong?" he asked.

"Oh, my ankle," she whimpered, feeling like an idiot. "It's these shoes." ("Flint!" she'd protested. "I haven't worn these shoes in years!" "All the better to fall off of," he'd replied.) She whimpered again.

Behind the guard, a short figure with a rope ladder and a leather sack slung over one shoulder whisked around the corner, twisted the key to unlock Tanis's door, and slipped inside, leaving the key in the lock. The door would be unlocked now, Laurana realized, hoping the guard wouldn't try it when he returned the key ring to his pocket.

Laurana assured the guard that she would be able to make it back to her room. She thanked him profusely for his help. Then she walked slowly down the corridor and back to her room, trying to remember to limp.

Chapter 27

Escape Into Danger

Tanis obviously had overheard Laurana's conversation with the guard. He was standing expectantly off to
one side when Flint slipped into the room.

The dwarf handed the half-elf the sword and scabbard
that he'd surrendered when the palace guards took him
away. Then, wordless, a finger to his lips, Flint crossed to
the window and peered over the edge. The outside wall was
a seamless sheet to the courtyard twenty feet below.

"What are you doing?" Tanis demanded in a whisper.

Motioning the half-elf quiet again, Flint unwrapped the
iron claws at the end of the rope ladder and slipped them
over the windowsill. He checked the courtyard again. It was
still deserted; most of the palace occupants were celebrating
in the streets of Qualinost. Sounds of revelry drifted in.

The dwarf looked satisfied and flung the ladder over. Then, checking to make sure the bulky sack he carried was secure on his shoulder, he swung his stocky body through the window and stepped onto the ladder, pausing to motion to Tanis to follow him. He closed his eyes, awaiting the passing of a mild case of vertigo.

But the half-elf balked. "Do you know the penalty for disobeying an imprisonment order?" he asked.

The dwarf's eyes opened again, and his bushy eyebrows rose on his forehead.

"Banishment!" Tanis whispered.

Flint leaned back through the window, his mouth near Tanis's ear. "Then what do you have to lose?" the dwarf said sotto voce. "Anyway, you'll be coming back."

Moments later, Tanis stepped from the ladder to the courtyard surface, and the half-elf watched as Flint tugged on a side rope that released the ladder from the iron claws that still gripped the windowsill. "My own design," the dwarf commented quietly as he pulled the half-elf behind a pear tree. Flint rummaged within the leather sack and drew out a mask fashioned to look like the head of a gully dwarf. He motioned for the half-elf to put it over his head.

Tanis's hazel eyes widened. "You want me to dress like a gully dwarf?"

"It's a costume," the dwarf whispered. "It will get you from the palace to the western bridge."

"A six-foot gully dwarf?" Tanis hissed.

Flint hushed his friend. "It was the only one the vendor had left. You should feel fortunate that I threw away the fake rat corpse that came with it."

"But . . ."

Flint plunged ahead. "Laurana tells me the elves will dress in costumes until midnight, when the celebrating will end and they'll observe a somber period until the *Kentommen* is over. That gives us an hour to escape from Qualinost."

Tanis still held the gully dwarf mask, surveying its olive skin, scruffy beard, and stupid expression. Anger rose on his own face. "If you believed I would flee, you don't know me well," he said, making no attempt to lower his voice. He turned, as if to toss the mask aside.

Flint caught his arm. "Trust me!" he snapped—for about the thousandth time, he thought. Anger turned to indecision in the half-elf's eyes. "Trust me," Flint whispered again.

Finally, Tanis donned the mask. "I feel ridiculous," came the muffled words from within the wooden cylinder.

"You look lovely," Flint said. "Come on."

They made their way through the courtyard and gardens, then around the front of the palace to the street, where they plunged into the crowd of celebrating elves. "Don't they ever sleep?" Flint asked irritably as the third elf in a row bumped against him.

"Very little, until the *Kentommen* is over." Tanis's voice sounded hollow through the mask.

Flint kept to the edge of the street, creeping along the edges of buildings to avoid being jostled by revelers.

Half an hour later, they passed beneath the graceful arch that spanned the western edge of the city, and turned south toward the bridge that crossed the River of Hope. The tiled avenue narrowed, and trees leaned in from either side. The revelers dwindled until Flint and Tanis were nearly alone, moving through the night. Tanis began to remove the mask.

"Best wait until we're across the bridge, lad," Flint said, and the thought of crossing the bridge in the dark, the River of Hope crashing hundreds of feet below him, made him queasy. He fought off the feeling as he quickly filled Tanis in on what the dwarf had learned—or rather, surmised—in the past two days.

"So you think someone may attack Gilthanas during his vigil at the *Kentommenai-kath*?" Tanis asked.

"It's a possibility," Flint said. "And right now possibilities are all we have to go on."

After two days of *Kentommen* revelry, the guards at the bridge were obviously used to revelers in costumes and masks. They merely watched as the dwarf and an overgrown gully dwarf headed out on the structure. Flint clutched Tanis's arm—to keep the half-elf steady, of course.

Then suddenly they heard the clatter of hooves behind them, and a familiar bray blared through the night. Flint whirled. "Fleetfoot!"

Back in the dimness that shrouded the entrance to the bridge, one of the guards held the animal by her bridle. "Flint," the guard called, his voice echoing in the ravine, "your friend wants you."

Flint was unsure what to do. If he took the animal home, he'd be leaving Tanis to face the murderer alone. If he took her along, she'd betray them with her infernal braying. Finally, he gestured, and the guard released the mule, who rocketed out to the dwarf.

Dodging Fleetfoot's nuzzling muzzle, Flint pulled out the ladder, which he still carried, and removed the rope that had released the ladder from the base, back at the palace. He knotted the rope to Fleetfoot's collar and tied the other end to an aspen tree at the western edge of the bridge. Tanis hid the mask in the underbrush. Fleetfoot's brays reverberated off the rocks as he and Tanis climbed along the path.

The night was black; no moons lit the sky. He could smell the musty odor of moss and hear Tanis breathing heavily behind him. The day they'd rested at the *Kentommenai-kath* seemed ages ago, back when Xenoth and Ailea still lived.

Fortunately, elves—even half-elves—could see fairly well in the dark, and dwarves had developed keen sight from generations of work in dim mines underground. Thus, the pair made relatively good time as they followed the path along the edge of the ravine.

"Unless Gilthanas and his guards are making the trip at a run, we should catch up with them soon," Tanis whispered once as they paused to rest in a grassy inlet. Flint averted his eyes from the steep drop, just off to his right, and nodded his agreement. They resumed hiking.

The pathway began to wind upward, and here and there Flint recognized gnarled trees and jumbles of granite. They came to a fork. The way became steeper, and soon Tanis and the dwarf were breathing hard.

At that moment, they heard footsteps ahead and leaped behind an outcropping of granite. Flint peered around as two figures passed by, heading back toward Qualinost. "Gilthanas's guards," Tanis whispered once they were out of earshot. The dwarf and half-elf redoubled their efforts, for Gilthanas was unguarded now.

Finally, the trees began to thin, and the ground was strewn with more granite boulders. Flint knew the rocky crest was near.

"Listen!" Tanis whispered.

A clear tenor voice soared in the distance, singing words nearly as old as the rocks that framed one side of the path.

"Gilthanas's vigil song," the half-elf explained. "It asks the spirits of the trees and the earth to protect Porthios and guide him throughout his days. That's why Gilthanas is unarmed for this vigil. It shows the woodland spirits that he trusts in them."

The song echoed in the ravine and made the dwarf shiver.

"My Fullbeard Day was nothing like this," he breathed. "And praise Reorx for that."

They kept walking, being more careful now that they drew close to the *Kentommenai-kath*. For if they didn't want Gilthanas to see them, they were even less interested in revealing themselves to the murderer, who might be hiding behind any boulder or tree. Flint felt the hair creep up at the back of his neck, and he placed a reassuring hand on the hammer he carried at his belt.

Finally, they reached the *Kentommenai-kath*. Flint placed a hand on the half-elf's shoulder, and the two paused, watching as Gilthanas stepped back and forth along the slabs of granite that capped the ridge. Tanis gestured that they should circle to the right, and Flint nodded. The two crept along, hugging the boulders for cover, making their way perhaps two hundred yards along the crest of the ridge from where Gilthanas stood, still singing. They passed the last of the trees and stepped briefly into the open, ducking quickly behind an upturned slab of granite.

Flint peered around the slab. Gilthanas, wearing a plain gray robe with the hood pulled up, stood at the edge of the cliff, gazing out into the black abyss and singing a lament that jumped through intervals unknown to human and dwarven music.

"What are we waiting for?" Flint whispered gruffly, and

Tanis shook his head.

"I'm not sure. Maybe we should try to get closer."

Flint nodded in agreement. Tanis loosened his dagger at his belt, and the dwarf did likewise as they began to pick their way through the jumble of boulders. All the while, Gilthanas's musical supplication formed a backdrop.

"I have a bad feeling about this, Tanis," Flint grumbled softly. "It's like we're just waiting for something to go—"

The earth dropped out from under the dwarf.

* * * * *

A scuffling sound, like something sliding against stone, and a muffled oath interrupted Flint's words. Tanis spun and twisted his head about.

"Flint!" Tanis whispered as loudly as he dared, crouching to be sure he was out of Gilthanas's line of sight. "Flint!"

There was no answer, only Gilthanas's tenor, unabated.

Tanis cursed himself. Why hadn't he been paying closer attention? He shook his head. But the dwarf had been right behind him. Where could he have gone?

A patch of shadow among the stones—or, rather, a patch of black deeper than the rest of the blackness—caught Tanis's eye, and he crawled closer to examine it. When he drew nearer, a puff of dank air wafted against his face and he saw that the dark patch wasn't a shadow at all. It was a crevasse, riven in the rock, just behind a lump of stone.

Tanis had stepped right over it without even noticing it. But Flint, with his stocky legs and his shorter stride . . .

Oh, gods, no, Tanis said to himself, and he threw himself down on his stomach, peering into the crevasse. "Flint!" Tanis whispered down into the deep darkness, but the shadows swallowed his voice. There was no answer.

The opening was large enough to admit the dwarf— though just barely. Frantically, Tanis tried to think. The dwarf could be hurt down there—or worse.

"Flint!" he tried one more time, but there was still no answer. Tanis was utterly alone.

At that moment, behind Tanis, Gilthanas's song broke off

with a cry, and the half-elf leaped to his feet.

"You should not be here!" Gilthanas cried. "The *Kentommen* forbids . . ."

Tanis looked back at the crevasse that had swallowed Flint. Then, moving as quickly as he could and drawing his sword, Tanis slipped from boulder to boulder.

A figure, barely discernible even to Tanis's sensitive sight, stood before Gilthanas. It advanced a step.

"Who are you?" cried Gilthanas, edging backward. The edge of the cliff loomed dangerously near his heels.

The figure, wordless, drew nearer. Gilthanas looked to the right and left, but the stranger was blocking the only escape. "Who are you?"

As Tanis watched, picking his way as close as possible while staying behind cover, he saw the figure move as if to gather its forces for a lunge. The half-elf dashed from behind a granite block, shouting, "Gilthanas!"

His cousin turned. In that same heartbeat, the robed figure feinted at Gilthanas. With a scream, the blond youth disappeared over the edge of the cliff. Another scream broke off abruptly.

The murderer dashed toward the forest, and Tanis hesitated, not sure whether to follow the figure or to go to the spot where Gilthanas had disappeared. But the ravine had swallowed his cousin, Tanis was sure. The half-elf darted into the trees after the evil one.

He had run only ten or twenty paces into the forest when the underbrush closed around him. There was no path; where, then, had the figure disappeared to? Tanis cursed the vines that clutched the sword blade, and squinted into the darkness. He held his breath and listened, but heard no muffled breathing from his quarry.

Tanis retraced his steps to the granite slab from which his cousin had disappeared. "Gilthanas!" he cried hopelessly into the gloom. Then, "Flint!" he cried, for good measure.

He got a response, but not the one he'd hoped for.

A figure loomed behind Tanis, placed strong hands on the small of his back, and pushed.

As the half-elf fell, he heard the words, "I'm sorry, Tanis."

Chapter 28

"In Shadow the Ancient Kingdom Fell"

Flint slid at breakneck speed down a narrow shaft of stone. Desperately he pawed at the rock with his hands and dug in with the heels of his boots, searching for some knob or crevice he could get a grip on, to stop—or at least to slow—his descent. But the cold stone of the chute was like glass, polished smooth by centuries of rainwater. Flint plunged down into the darkness. The chute bent to his right.

He was beginning to wonder when this dark ride would end— abruptly and messily, no doubt, when the chute stopped suddenly in a wall of solid stone—when he began to notice a lessening in the steepness of his descent. The shaft was leveling out.

By the time the end of the chute finally came, it had become nearly level, and Flint's momentum had slowed nearly to a creep. One moment, the stone of the chute was all around him, and the next, Flint was surrounded by nothing more than dark, musty air.

"Reorx!" Flint swore as he flailed in space, then he fell with a splash into frigid water. The rope ladder, which he had continued to clutch uselessly during the fall, landed next to him.

The dwarf thrashed and sputtered, choking on the metallic-tasting water—until he realized that, somehow, he wasn't sinking any farther into the bone-chilling wetness. It was then that Flint noticed he was on his hands and knees and that the water came halfway up his forearms. In fact, if he hadn't thrashed around so much, he would hardly have gotten wet at all.

All this—plus the fact that the fall had reopened his shoulder wound—did nothing to sweeten his temper.

"Reorx's forge!" he muttered, dragging himself out of the shallow pool. Instantly, however, he regretted the words. They echoed hollowly around him in the darkness, as if he were in a vast cavern. Flint had the disconcerting impression that the blackness swirled angrily, as if it resented having its stillness disturbed by his words. The dwarf felt a shiver dance across his skin—from the chilling water, no doubt, he assured himself, though for the time being he kept the rest of his grumbles to himself.

Flint sat on the cold ground for a moment, shivering in the darkness, trying to catch his breath. He looked about, but he couldn't see a trace of light from anywhere—not surprising in the dead of night and inside a cliff, he supposed. He might have fallen a short distance or halfway down to the ravine; he couldn't tell. His heart gave a lurch as he thought of Tanis up above. Flint shook his head. All he could do to help Tanis now was whisper a gruff prayer to Reorx and try to find his way out of wherever it was he'd landed.

Flint peered into the darkness around him. Dwarves possessed a curious sense of vision enabling them to see the heat that radiated from an object—which helped Flint not one iota in the cold blackness down here.

But suddenly he did see something—something that looked like two pale circles floating side by side where he knew the pool of water was. The circles were so faint he could hardly see them, their luminescence sickly green. Then he noticed another pair of the small circles, and another, drifting slowly before him.

Flint slapped at the pockets of his leather vest and breeches until he found what he was searching for—flint and steel, tinder, and a stump of a candle. Fortunately, the items had been wrapped in a piece of oiled leather and were still dry. In moments, Flint had struck a spark and a tiny flame flared.

In the flickering light, Flint saw the darkened pool of water stretching like polished onyx before him. The dwarf shuddered when he saw the source of the strange, pale lights: fish, swimming in the ice-cold pool of water. The fish were pale, flabby-looking things, about as long as his forearm, with bulbous eyes as big as saucers. It was their eyes that had radiated the sickly light. The glow of his candle seemed to disturb them, for they silently slipped away through the water, seeking the darkness they had dwelt in, undisturbed, for eons.

"Gods above, what is this place?" Flint mumbled under his breath. He lifted his candle and looked about. The floor was of gray stone—limestone, probably, he surmised, underlying the granite above—and the walls were the same. But the stone seemed too smooth, too even to be natural. Tall spires like stalagmites rose from the floor, but as Flint stepped near them, he saw that they were columns, fluted and intricately carved. These were not formed by the action of water, Flint knew, but by the hands of living beings. He walked slowly about the vast space he had landed in, wincing at the echo of his footfalls but continuing on just the same.

He saw that this was not a cavern at all, but a great hall of some sort. Columns lined the towering walls that rose into the shadows above, beyond the reach of Flint's faint candlelight. Rows of benches faced some sort of raised dais, and beyond that was a wide staircase, its steps leading up into shadow and places unknown.

The stonework was immensely skilled; Flint ran a hand over the carefully polished edges and convoluted designs of the pillars. Such craftsmanship as this the world no longer knew, but Flint was certain it was dwarven. It could be nothing else, not here, so far beneath the ground. But it was ancient as well. The ages rested as heavily here as the ponderous weight of the stone that stood between Flint and the outside world. But what place could this be, so close to the elven kingdom? It had to be very old, perhaps even older than Qualinesti itself.

A sudden realization struck Flint, and the candle's small flame quavered as his hand began to tremble. The words of an old poem he had learned as a child came unbidden to him. He remembered sitting in his father's lap when he was very small. It was one of the few memories of his father, who had died when Flint had been little more than a child. Flint had listened, spellbound, as his father chanted the words softly in the firelight, of a kingdom of long ago:

> *By the thane's dark word, the gates were shut*
> *With the toll of a cold death knell.*
> *Closed to the folk of the sunlit realms,*
> *In shadow the ancient kingdom fell.*

Flint shuddered at the thought of his grandfather dying in the Dwarfgate Wars, then he turned to considered where he might be.

"Thorbardin? Pax Tharkas?" Flint whispered to the shadows.

It was entirely possible, he told himself, that he'd fallen through another of the elves' infernal *sla-mori*—one that led to the ancient mountain dwarf capital or the elven-dwarven fortress. If that were so, he'd be wise to escape from the hated cousins of the hill dwarves as quickly as he could.

Tentatively, reluctant to discover the truth of where he was, Flint continued on.

* * * * *

Tanis landed hard on a narrow slab of granite that protruded from the cliff side, thirty feet down from the edge—and hundreds of feet above the valley floor.

As he landed, the stone slab shuddered, shifting beneath his weight. A handful of limestone pebbles skittered away from the slab to fall, spinning and silent, into space. The stone tipped slightly, toward the river far below. Tanis scrabbled for a handhold as a shower of dirt and pebbles cascaded over him, filling his eyes and mouth. His left hand caught a piece of solid rock, and he stopped sliding.

He blinked the dirt away, then shouted, "Gilthanas!"

His cousin was sliding down the stone, about to plummet into the canyon. Desperately, Tanis snaked out a hand and caught Gilthanas's wrist. At first, the half-elf feared the added weight would make him lose his own grip, sending them both into the void, but Tanis managed to dig the toes of his boots into a fissure in the cliff face. He lay with his stomach against the smooth stone, straining to keep his grip on Gilthanas. Tanis couldn't tell if the young guard was alive or dead.

The midnight blackness that pressed around them made it all the more terrifying.

Already Tanis could feel his palm growing slick with sweat. The stone slab shifted another inch. How long could he maintain his grip? Not that it might matter. The slab could go at any moment.

With a monumental effort, Tanis tightened his hold on Gilthanas's robe. The stone lurched again, and another spray of pebbles went tumbling into the blackness. Tanis squeezed his eyes shut, breathed a silent prayer that Gilthanas's tailor had used strong materials, and heaved on the ceremonial robe.

His cousin groaned, and Tanis's heart leaped. Gilthanas was alive! That gave him renewed strength and, for once blessing the human blood that gave him his strong build, the half-elf hauled Gilthanas away from the edge and back up to him. Clutching his cousin, he sat huddled on a narrow ledge of limestone and granite, three feet wide and twice as long.

Tanis shifted a bit, trying to find a position that felt less precarious, but it was no use. Moving cautiously, he nudged his cousin until he was propped against the cliff wall, a position that—Tanis hoped—would keep the youth from rolling off the ledge if Tanis fell asleep and lost his grip. Who would hold the half-elf himself back from certain death, he did not know.

Tanis looked back up the cliff; he could see nothing but the constellations. Moonlight might have showed toeholds and handholds that the two could use to climb back up, but the night was as black as the inside of a tomb. Far off to the east, Tanis could see torchlights ablaze in the Tower of the Sun; palace servants were still at work, he was sure, readying the Tower for tomorrow's *Kentommen* climax.

He looked over at Gilthanas. The youth was unconscious, but at least he breathed. But even if the morning showed that the cliff could be climbed, Tanis wondered how he would get Gilthanas up the sheer face.

At any rate, they weren't going anywhere until dawn. He settled back against the cliff wall, sending another wave of pebbles and dust skittering over the edge, and tried to divert his thoughts.

He wondered where Flint was—and who would mourn the dwarf's death if Tanis were gone as well.

Far more mourning could be in store before the robed figure was through, Tanis thought. He no longer had any doubt that the murderer also planned to kill Laurana and Porthios, and probably the Speaker as well. He looked again at the Tower, a finger of light in the darkness, where the Speaker was holding his own vigil for Porthios's *Kentommen*, then gazed at the palace, off to one side. He hoped Laurana was safe; at least the guard, who no doubt was still at Tanis's door, was not far from Laurana's quarters, though not in direct sight. And he knew Flint had told her to lock herself into the room until the morning.

Tanis looked off to the right of the Tower, at the darker patch he knew was the Grove, and he hoped the murderer was not, even now, moving toward the trees of that sacred place, seeking the defenseless heir.

Sure at last that the murderer's next victim would be

Porthios, Tanis wondered how he could warn the heir, assuming that the half-elf would be able to escape from his current predicament. There would be no way to interrupt the *Melethka-nara*; the three questioners would prevent that, even if he made it past the guards outside the chamber, deep under the palace.

Perhaps there would be a way to intercept Porthios as he made the walk from the chambers to the Tower; under tradition, the youth was alone during the walk, the third portion of the *Kentommen*, called the *Kentommen-tala*. There were two key problems: All the palace guards knew Tanis was under a confinement order, and it would not be easy to persuade Porthios that the Speaker's elder son was in danger. Maybe . . .

Suddenly, out of the darkness above him, a mule brayed.

Tanis nearly lost his grip on Gilthanas; as it was, the sound sent his pulse leaping. "Fleetfoot!" he called, and the stone slab moved slightly. The mule brayed again, closer.

Tanis's thoughts raced. What use could he make of the mule? Flint had tied her with the long length of rope from the ladder. Perhaps if she stood at the very edge, with the rope hanging down . . .

He called again, and Fleetfoot answered. A hoof clunked against a stone up above, sending the rock bouncing past Tanis. At Tanis's side, Gilthanas stirred, murmuring against the racket. For a moment, hope surged through the half-elf.

Then the mule stepped away from the cliff. "Fleetfoot!" he cried. Gilthanas groaned and tried to sit up, then slumped back. But the sound of Fleetfoot's hooves receded.

Of course, Tanis thought; she was looking for Flint. He slumped back against the cliff himself.

Chapter 29

Shedding Some Light

Regardless of where he was, Flint knew he was go- ing to have to go up if he was going to get out, and the stairs behind the dais seemed to be the only way.

His boots kicked up clouds of dust as he ascended the long staircase, but the dwarf pinched his nose shut to avoid sneezing. As far as he was concerned, the less he disturbed the oppressively silent darkness, the better. He already had the disconcerting notion that something watched him from the concealing shadows—and watched in disapproval.

Flint could feel—as well as he could feel the prickling of the hair on the back of his neck—that his intrusion was not welcome. But as long as it looked as if he was doing his best to make his way out of there, perhaps whatever—or whoever—it was that lurked in the inky shadows would leave him be.

Like walking through a dark dream, Flint wandered through the labyrinthine corridors and chambers, slowly making his ascent and trying to ignore the shivering that intermittently clutched him. His clothes clung damply to him.

The place must once have been a wonder of glory, with its cavernous halls and delicate, spiraling staircases. But the action of water had transformed once-proud statues into little more than grotesque forms. Rich tapestries that had adorned the walls hung in ghostly tatters, like the spinnings of some great, shadowy spider. Flint leaned close to one of the weavings, and the touch of his finger was enough to send the tapestry crumbling to dust. Chambers that once had been bright with the reflection of a thousand torches gleaming off their gilded walls were now murky dens, barely pierced by the feeble glow of Flint's candle, the air fetid with the smell of ancient but unforgotten death.

The atmosphere weighed heavily upon Flint and his dwarven heart. Tales of long-lost dwarven kingdoms echoed in his ears.

As he wandered through the darkened halls, Flint was sometimes forced to backtrack along his footprints in the dust when a corridor suddenly dead-ended or led back to a chamber he had passed through before. But generally his dwarven senses—registering the slightest changes in the movement of the air or sloping of the stone—led him on a course that wound its way steadily upward. Exactly how far he needed to go, however, Flint was unsure. He couldn't know how far he had fallen down the chute—or even if he were anywhere near Qualinost anymore.

Finally, however, his stump of candle burned low. Flint let out a yelp as the flame scorched his finger, and the last bit of the candle flew from his hand, sizzling as it landed in a puddle and went out. Darkness closed swiftly and silently over the dwarf, as if no light had ever been there.

"Damn!" Flint swore softly, sucking on his burned finger. He knew in his heart he had been getting close to the outside; just a minute ago he was sure he had caught a whiff of slightly fresher air. But there was little he could do. Realizing how exhausted he was then, he supposed it couldn't do him any harm to rest his eyes for a bit while he tried to think of some way out of this mess. And perhaps his clothes would dry out a bit.

The shadows were troubling, but Flint pushed thoughts of them from his mind. They had left him alone so far, so he hunkered down against a wall to rest. Meaning to shut his eyes for only a moment or two, the dwarf quickly fell into a deep sleep.

* * * * *

Imperceptibly at first, there was a faint lessening of the darkness along the horizon, the half-elf noticed. Soon the stars began to fade, and a faint light crept from the horizon into the sky.

With the raucous visit from Fleetfoot, Gilthanas had partially awakened, then slipped from unconsciousness into sleep. Tanis, too exhausted now to doze, could do nothing but watch as the light slowly grew, until eventually the sun rose above the wispy clouds of morning, staring like an unblinking crimson eye. Below, the ravine was shrouded in silken mist.

Off to the east, Tanis heard the drum that signaled that the three *Ulathi* had left the Tower to seek Porthios at the Grove. There, they would dress Porthios in a gray robe, the mate to the one that Gilthanas wore, and lead him to the palace for the *Melethka-nara*, the ordeal of questioning, criticism, and goading.

Tanis looked up at the thirty feet of cliff face. With the coming of the light, it looked as though an agile climber might be able to scale the rock, taking advantage of cracks and remnants of juniper stumps. He only hoped that his cousin would be able to follow.

* * * * *

The first thing Flint realized upon waking was that he could see. Barely, that was true, but a wan light hovered on the air, pale and gray, just enough so that he could make out the dim shapes cluttering the chamber he was in.

Flint groaned as he stood and stretched. He must have slept for several hours. The shadows seemed less menacing now; whatever the source of the grayish light, they appeared to be wary of it. Although the light was pale, it wasn't an eerie light, not like that of the fish he'd seen earlier. Rather, it lifted the dwarf's heart. Flint searched about the chamber, wondering where the light came from, then suddenly he saw.

In the wall, just above the place he had curled up to sleep, was the tiniest crack in the stone. The dwarf knew exactly what it meant. The light was daylight, and beyond the wall, somewhere, lay the outside.

Flint examined the crack and the area around it. The lines were almost imperceptible, but Flint grunted. He was certain this had been a window once. It probably had been sealed for some reason. Flint could see the barest outline where the opening had been secured.

He hefted the heavy hammer he kept faithfully at his belt and, with all his forge-hardened strength, struck the stone. It shuddered, and Flint grunted in satisfaction as he saw the crack lengthen. He swung again, then a third time. The crack widened, and another joined it, letting in a thin shaft of light. This heartened the dwarf, and he began to pound at the wall in earnest. Luckily, the stone was not thick, and the one crack had been a symptom of a general weakness that pervaded the rock. No doubt the hastiness with which this window had been sealed so long ago was working to Flint's advantage. Had the craftsmen used all their skill in the wall's construction, Flint's hammer would have been as useless as a willow switch against the stone.

Within a minute, chunks of stone began to fly from the wall. The crack grew into a hole, then suddenly the whole thing gave way, crumbling before Flint, the stones cascading away as light flooded the chamber, sending the shadows fleeing into the deeper recesses of the halls.

Feeling triumphant, Flint thrust his bearded head through the hole—but his triumph paled, for he was at the bottom of another stone chute.

Once again, there was no way out but up.

* * * * *

There was no way out but up, Tanis thought as he glared up the cliff face. Next to him, Gilthanas finally stirred and opened his eyes. Despite a bump the size of an egg and the color of rose quartz on the side of his head, Gilthanas appeared healthy.

"Tanis!" he exclaimed. A flicker of relief, then anger crossed his face. "You defied the Speaker's decree!"

"I came to rescue you," Tanis said as the *Melethka-nara* drums sounded again from Qualinost.

Gilthanas struggled to sit up, sending a shiver through the ledge. "The drums!" he said, green eyes panic-stricken. "I have to get back for the *Kentommen-tala*." His movements brought him perilously near the edge of the outcropping, and Tanis caught his cousin's arm to pull him back. Fear was added to the relief and anger battling for ascendancy on the blond guard's face.

"Do you think you can climb up?" Tanis indicated the thirty-foot rock face above them. "Or should I leave you and bring back help?"

"Leave me?" Gilthanas echoed, easing to his feet and reaching up for the first handhold. "I'd be remiss in my duties if I let you escape."

"Escape?" Tanis murmured. The stone ledge, loosened further by their movements, shuddered again.

But the call to duty seemed to have given the neophyte guard strength, for he was doing a passable job of clambering up the cliff, though the ankle-length robe hampered his efforts somewhat. Finally, Gilthanas tucked the hem of the robe into his belt, which made it easier for him to climb. It did, however, delay Tanis's departure from the slab, which showed more signs of weakness. Nervously, Tanis waited until Gilthanas had climbed above the half-elf's head, then he followed, using the same handholds and footholds that his elven cousin had.

The escape prospect that had seemed hopeless in the murk of night turned out to be arduous but possible in the daylight.

Half an hour later, Gilthanas helped Tanis over the edge of the precipice. The last scramble loosened a medium-size boulder, which slipped over the edge with a scraping noise and bounced off the slab where the two had spent the night. The slab creaked, then tipped further, then slowly came loose from the cliff and dropped, turning, through the clear air to the river below.

In the distance, the drums gave one last roll and ceased. "The *Melethka-nara* has begun," Gilthanas said. "Porthios is in the chamber far beneath the palace. Now the ordeal begins. I have three hours to get to the corridor between the underground chamber and the Tower." Still, Gilthanas stood quietly, gazing to the west, and Tanis knew he was in the chamber with his brother, in his mind's eye.

"Gilthanas," Tanis said. "Did you see your attacker's face?"

The elf wrenched his attention from Qualinost and looked at Tanis. He then shook his head and began moving toward the ravineside path. "It was dark. He was hooded. Did you see him?"

Tanis shook his head and explained what had happened between his escape from the palace and his dive off the cliff. He diverted Gilthanas from his trek toward the path, returning to the crevasse that Flint had disappeared into. Tanis shouted for the dwarf; he tossed pebbles down the slender opening to see if he could tell by sound how far his friend might have fallen. There was no reply, and Tanis was too large to fit into the hole.

"We have to hurry," Gilthanas urged.

Tanis, still not sure he should leave Flint, hesitated. Gilthanas swiftly reached over and drew Tanis's sword from his scabbard. It never occurred to the half-elf to stop the cousin he trusted—then suddenly Tanis was facing the point of his own blade. His mother's pendant formed a spot of silvery light on the hilt. Forest birds continued to chatter around the pair as though nothing were amiss.

"What are you doing?" Tanis whispered.

"You're my prisoner," Gilthanas said formally. "You've violated an order of the Speaker. It's my sworn duty as a ceremonial guard to arrest you and return you to Qualinost for judgment."

Tanis glanced again at the sword that Flint had made for him, then up at Gilthanas. The serious look on his cousin's face squelched any protest. Tanis pondered the situation. He was stronger and larger than his slight cousin, and he had a dagger. Tanis knew he could overpower Gilthanas, even if his cousin was armed with the half-elf's sword.

But then what would he do? Tie up Gilthanas and leave him here unguarded? Such a prospect might be acceptable nearer to Qualinost, with folk about, but the area around the *Kentommenai-kath* was deserted. Reluctantly, silently vowing to return, Tanis allowed Gilthanas to lead him away from the crevasse.

* * * * *

The chute was a ventilation shaft, Flint decided. He looked straight up, about twenty-five feet. Striving to avoid straining his tender shoulder, the dwarf angled his stocky body through the opening and crawled into the chute, which was about as wide as a barrel of ale—a wistful thought that Flint quickly squelched. He stood atop the litter of old pine cones and dirt; near the wall lay the desiccated skeleton of something about the size of a raccoon. He tried not to think of the animal dying down here, however many years ago.

The dwarf saw a circle of light at the top, with a few spruce branches waving far above that. He searched for handholds—no luck. The shaft may have been wide enough for him to inch his way up by bracing his shoulders on one side and his feet on the other, but his shoulder was too weak; his attempts only landed him with an "oof!" on the spongy bottom of the chute.

"Reorx!" he said softly. Then, louder, "Reorx's hammer!" He sat, disconsolate, at the shaft's bottom. His fingers traced the scars that stoneworkers had etched into the walls millennia ago—T-shaped chisel marks. The shaft's artisans were long dead now, probably plying their craft with Reorx in the afterlife. Flint examined one of the T-scars; he'd seen a mark just like it on Lord Tyresian's forearm. Unbidden, the sight of Eld Ailea lying dead before her fireplace came to Flint's mind again: The exposed calf, the purple skirt, the sleeve pushed up to her elbow. The "T," the scar, the heir, he recalled. . . .

The force of the realization brought Flint's nodding head up so fast that he cracked it on the stone behind him.

"The scar, the tea, the heir," he whispered. He'd made the same mistake with "T" that he'd made with "air." He remembered, now, after the attempt on his life, taking the cup of tea from Miral, and the way Ailea had later administered one of her own potions, causing him to vomit. Then, several days later, the mage had asked Flint whether his medicinal tea had had any effect—minutes before they'd received Ailea's message that she understood Lord Xenoth's death.

The mage had given him poisoned tea! And Ailea had realized it. Yet Ailea had taken the time to mull over the situation before making an accusation. Then, when she was sure, when some last bit of information had snapped into place, she had excitedly sent a message to Flint—who had immediately shared it with . . . the killer!

"Reorx, help me!" the dwarf prayed as he scrabbled through the debris at the bottom of the shaft, flinging pine cones aside in his search for anything that would help him.

If he was correct, Porthios, the Speaker, Gilthanas, and Laurana would not survive the day.

In the middle of his search, as though Reorx had heard his call and sent the most unlikely rescuer possible, Flint heard a mule bray. Suddenly the light dimmed, and Flint looked up. Something was blocking the chute's opening. Instead of out-of-focus pine boughs, the dwarf now saw a grotesque muzzle, two ears nearly as long as his leg, and a pair of brown eyes steaming with passion.

"Fleetfoot!" He stood. "You wonderful animal!" The creature blinked. "I'm still in Qualinesti!"

He never thought he'd see a day when the sight of his mule

would bring tears to his eyes. What particularly thrilled him, however, was the ten feet of chewed rope attached to her collar. The elves had laughed when he'd fashioned a collar for a mule; now he'd have the laugh on them. A bridle never would have held.

Except that he was still fifteen feet short of the rope that dangled in the shaft while Fleetfoot snorted above.

Flint took stock. He had flint and steel, hammer, dagger, and rope ladder. The ladder probably would reach from the top to the bottom of the shaft, but the mechanics of setting up a limp rope ladder from the bottom seemed hopeless.

Fleetfoot brayed again. The sound reverberated in the stone chute, nearly deafening Flint.

"Stop that noise!" Flint called. When the mule began to back away from the hole, pulling the lead rope with her, he shouted, "No! Wait! I didn't mean it!"

Tentatively, Fleetfoot peered over the edge again. Not very attractive at eye level, she looked absolutely absurd from below. She also looked irked. Flint had a sudden horrible vision of the mule stomping off in a huff. And indeed, she began to pull away from the edge again, and the end of the rope rose higher in the chute.

"Fleetfoot, you"—He thought quickly and changed to a wheedling tone—"entrancing creature, please come back."

The rope stopped, trembled, and dropped down a few inches. Wet brown eyes searched his. One ear flopped.

Flint unwrapped the rope ladder from his middle. If he could just get the thing up to the mule . . . He gauged the distance and tossed the ladder overhand.

The thing dropped back down on him like a pile of snakes, and Fleetfoot brayed.

"Sure, you beast," Flint muttered. "Laugh."

He untangled himself and tried again, with the same result. Finally, on the third try, his shoulder aching from the effort, he tried an underhand toss and a foot of the ladder looped over the edge of the chute, where it snagged for the barest second on a rock. Fleetfoot lowered her wet muzzle and snuffled at the ladder, dislodging it and sending it spinning back down on Flint.

"Fleetfoot!" Flint chided. He affected a falsetto that reminded him of an elf girl addressing her dolls. "Do you want me to die down here, my dear?"

A hee-haw boomed down the shaft like thunder.

He threw the ladder again. This time, two feet of ladder flipped over the edge, lying on the ground right next to the mule, who gazed at it with stupid eyes. The bottom edge of the ladder dangled before Flint's face, but the dwarf didn't dare touch it lest he jiggle it loose. The ropes began to slide back into the chute, and Flint cursed softly.

Then Fleetfoot lifted one dinner-plate-size hoof and held it above the inching ladder. The dwarf held his breath.

Just as the last rung was going by, the mule delicately, deliberately, placed her foot on it. The ladder stopped with a jerk.

With a delighted cry, Flint placed one hand on the bottom rung and tugged. The mule snorted and appeared disconcerted at this sudden pressure on her hoof, but she maintained her stance.

Favoring his shoulder as much as he could, Flint clambered halfway up the ladder. Soon the end of the rope that he'd attached to the mule's collar swung at his side. He had another ten feet to climb.

The mule shifted restlessly.

"Fleetfoot, no!" the dwarf shouted.

She lifted her foot.

Flint lunged for the dangling rope, and the mule's neck bobbed a foot because of his sudden added weight. The ladder hurtled by him to the chute floor below. "You mule-brained idiot!" he hollered, dangling from the rope.

With a jerk, the mule reared back from the shaft and galloped several paces. With a strangled cry that exploded as he emerged, the dwarf came shooting up out of the hole like a trout hooked by an angler.

* * * * *

"I'm sorry, Tanis," Gilthanas said as they trotted along the path above the ravine.

For a moment, the words sent a shock of recognition through Tanis. The murderer had said that.

"You know I have to do this," Gilthanas said. "I'm pledged, as a ceremonial guard, to uphold the Speaker's edicts." He'd long since sheathed the sword in the scabbard, which he'd also taken from Tanis. He seemed to assume Tanis would make no move to escape.

The half-elf nodded. He was too busy pondering his situation to engage in chitchat. Yet . . .

He might learn something that he could use later.

"I understand," the half-elf said. He looked over at the elf. Gilthanas's face was ruddy from the pace they'd maintained for nearly an hour. His cousin looked back, and for the first time in years, Tanis saw the friend he'd had when they were little. "What part do you have in the ceremony?"

Gilthanas, panting, drew to a stop in a clearing. He waved Tanis to a seat on a nearby boulder and took one himself, not far away.

"When Porthios leaves the chamber beneath the palace, he will lift his hood—he's wearing a gray robe, like this one—to conceal his face. He will pass from the chamber to a spiral staircase—ninety-nine steps, one for each year of his life so far. The steps are called *Liassem-eltor*, the Stairway of the Years. Porthios must climb the stairs in complete darkness. At the top, he'll find an alcove with a single candle, plus flint and steel to light it."

"And you . . . ?" Tanis prompted, wondering briefly why he himself had not been taught the specifics of the ceremony.

Gilthanas continued. "Beyond the alcove will be a long hallway, which appears on no maps of Qualinost because it is used only by elves who are neither child nor adult—elves who, therefore, don't really exist. Thus, the corridor doesn't exist and appears on no maps."

Tanis tried again. "Your part . . ." But Gilthanas, entranced by the celebration that he too would undergo someday, appeared determined to tell the whole tale.

"The corridor is called *Yathen-ilara*, the Pathway to Illumination. It leads to the Tower of the Sun. The youth makes his way along the pathway in silence. At the end is a door, where he waits until the one who has conducted the vigil at the *Kentommenai-kath* opens the door, admitting him to the central hall of the Tower of the Sun.'"

So that was where Gilthanas came in. He sounded as though he had learned his role by rote—repeating it to Miral, no doubt. "I will wait outside the door until a gong sounds. Then I will open the door, slip inside, let the door close, take the candle from Porthios, and say—in the old tongue, of course—'I am your childhood. Leave me behind in the mists of the past. Pass ahead to your future.' Porthios will open the door and move into the Tower of the Sun."

A glimmer of an idea began to form in Tanis's mind.

"You will remain in the hallway?" the half-elf asked.

Gilthanas sounded a little peeved. "I'm supposed to represent Porthios's vanished childhood, so I really shouldn't be at the ceremony itself. But Miral says no one will notice if I crack the door just a bit to listen. After all, I'll be having my own *Kentommen* in only sixty years."

Tanis had his plan now to stop Porthios's murderer.

They resumed their run to Qualinost. Finally, the path sloped downward. Drums and trumpets sounded again from the direction of the palace and Tower, and Gilthanas cried, "We have to go faster! I'm late!"

Through the thinning aspens, Tanis could just barely see the western bridge arcing over the River of Hope. Without pausing to think, he misstepped and bumped into Gilthanas. When his cousin turned toward him, startled, the half-elf tackled him.

Five minutes later, a gray-robed figure emerged from a copse of trees. Behind him, the shrubbery jiggled and a muffled noise came forth, as if a large animal had been bound there. Someone who looked closely at the robed figure now trotting down the path would have seen the faint outline of a sword under the left side of the robe.

Tanis hoped no one would.

He pulled the hood over his face, broke into a run, and crossed the bridge.

Chapter 30

Converging on the
Tower

Flint released the rope when he bounced off a pair of aspens, then slid to a stop on mud and moss. Fleetfoot ran a few more steps, then stopped to glare back at him. Flint shook a fist. "You . . . you *mule!*" he cried.

He looked back at the crack in the rock, tempted to mark the place so that someday he could return to examine it more closely. He decided then that the secrets of the past—and the shadows that lurked there—were better left alone. Still, he wondered.

Far below him, in the cool depths of the earth, silence had cast its heavy mantle again over the empty halls and corridors. In the darkness, the shadows waited, as they had for centuries.

Flint heard the drums and trumpets blare in the distance.

Another memory popped to mind: the sight of the mage shoving a sleeve above his elbow as he showed the dwarf how to empty the wondrous bathtub at the palace. The dwarf had seen a small, star-shaped scar on Miral's forearm.

Finally, the dwarf remembered Ailea in her kitchen, the first time he'd taken Tanis to see her. She'd recounted tales of some of the births she'd attended, and she'd mentioned one that went awry, leaving the tiny infant with a star-shaped scar.

Soon, Flint knew, Miral would unleash the fury he had built in decades of resentment. The Speaker and his three children—assuming Gilthanas wasn't dead already—would die. Flint had no doubt that the portion of Miral that was still sane, the part that had lived on the surface for years, be-friending dwarf and half-elf alike, would call, "I'm sorry," as he slew them.

"Weak mage, indeed," he said, and grimaced. Deep lines of worry had etched themselves into his face.

Even on a mule, he'd never get to Qualinost in time. For that matter, he had no idea where in Qualinesti he had emerged—just that he was somewhere across the ravine, west of Qualinost. The area looked slightly familiar. He gazed around, trying to get his bearings. Fleetfoot edged closer to Flint, but the dwarf ignored her. He squinted and racked his brain. The Speaker's life hung in the balance.

There was no way he could get back in time—unless he found a shortcut.

Like the oak *sla-mori*!

He closed his eyes and tried to recall it all—the panic, the pursuit by the tylor, Fleetfoot's pounding hooves. He opened his eyes and examined the mule with more interest. She yanked a mouthful of grass and gazed back.

He turned. He was pretty sure the area where he met the lizard beast was southwest of here. If he just struck out that way, something might strike him—or the mule—as familiar. Mules were known for their sense of direction, if not for their intelligence, sweet breath, or tractable nature. He took a step and waved to Fleetfoot.

"Come on, sweetheart," he crooned.

The mule continued to chew, a suspicious look in her eyes.

He plucked a handful of grass and held it out. "Have a snack?" he asked.

A spark of interest stirred in the creature's face.

"Ah, well," he said with an elaborate sigh, and turned away, casually flopping the morsel of grass across his un-wounded shoulder. "I guess my poor old heart will break." He feigned a sob.

A slippery muzzle caught him at the back of the neck, wrenched the grass out of his hand. He turned and let an ex-pression of joy fill his face. "Fleetfoot!" He threw his arms around her neck, reasoning that he could always bathe later, and swung himself up on her back.

Seconds later, they were trotting off to the southwest.

* * * * *

The guards at the city edge of the western bridge waved as Tanis ran by in Gilthanas's gray robe. "You're late, Gil-thanas!" one shouted. Tanis kept a tight hand on his hood, fearing that his momentum would send the headpiece flying and reveal his identity.

If so, the guards certainly would arrest him.

Tanis ran on through the tiled streets.

* * * * *

Miral stood gravely at the edge of the central area of the Tower of the Sun. The double mosaics soared six hundred feet above him, marble walls gleaming in the light of four hundred torches and the sunlight reflected by countless mir-rors, fitted right into the wall. Already the hall was filling with nobles. Lord Litanas stood at the base of the rostrum. Lady Selena, whose hair looked distinctly blonder than the last time the mage had seen her, gazed at the new adviser with violet-eyed fondness from her position near the entry hall. She spared no glance for Ulthen, who sulked near the back.

Lord Tyresian obviously had found someone to repair the ceremonial sword he now wore at his side, as he stood next to Laurana, near the rostrum. Paying no attention to Tyresian, Laurana appeared nervous, continually looking around her.

As a coordinator of the *Kentommen*, Miral had been able to tell the nobles where to stand, implying that he was merely passing along the Speaker's will. Laurana's position would put her near Porthios and Solostaran when Miral released his magic, he mused.

It was a shame that Lauralanthalasa had refused his marriage offer. He would have changed so many of his plans for her. In fact, he'd delayed them for years, waiting for the day he could declare himself to her and receive her love. He would have given up the Speakership for Laurana; he wondered if he should have told her that. Women adored feeling that their suitors would give up the world for them. In Laurana's case, that was close to true; he might have.

"Weak mage," he said hoarsely to himself, and laughed. He had been strong since he was a child—since he'd met the Graystone of Gargath in the caverns.

Miral moved toward the right of the rostrum, edging toward the stairs that spiraled upward between the marble inner wall and the gold outer wall of the Tower. Anyone who saw him would assume that the elf who was helping to coordinate Porthios's *Kentommen* was trying to get a better view of the proceedings from the second balcony, one level above the musicians. The crowd, however, wouldn't be able to see him when he released the magic that would open the top of the Tower and rain fire from above. And if someone saw him, it wouldn't matter anyway.

No one would be left alive to tell.

He stepped slowly up the steps, pausing to catch his breath. He'd become weaker of late. Like it or not, Xenoth's death by magic had drained him. But the tylor hunt had been such a splendid opportunity, once the adviser threatened to reveal what he'd learned about Miral. It had been so easy to buy a few extra days of silence, promising many more riches to come. Nosy old coot, Miral thought; the midwife, too, though he'd genuinely regretted ending her life. The mage had hoped the nobles would blame Xenoth's death on the tylor's magic, but then Miral had seen Tanis aiming the second arrow—fitted with the arrowhead the mage had enchanted when he slipped into Flint's shop late one night. And the mage had seized his chance to confound them all. It had been a small matter to order the enchanted arrow to fly into the dead adviser's chest.

What a shame that the nobles gathering in the Tower would not live to know his brilliance, Miral thought.

* * * * *

Leaves and branches swatted Flint in the face as he urged Fleetfoot through the forest. They'd been traveling for half an hour, and while the dwarf had experienced fleeting moments of recognition—that particular juxtaposition of boulder and bur oak, for example—he still could not say for sure where he was.

Fleetfoot, though, appeared to have a goal, and while Flint wasn't too happy about trusting the situation to a bone-brained, lovesick mule, it was the best choice he had right now.

* * * * *

The killer must be Tyresian, Tanis thought as he ran. The half-elf no longer made any attempt to hide the slapping of his sword between his robe and his leggings. The elves in the street, acting in accordance with *Kentommen* strictures, carefully averted their eyes as he passed. Just in case, he continued to hold the hood before his face, however.

Perhaps it was Litanas, Tanis added to himself. The young elf lord, who had completed his own *Kentommen* only a year earlier, had gained considerably from Xenoth's death; Litanas had succeeded the old adviser and won the wealthy Lady Selena. And perhaps Ailea had found a way to link Litanas with Xenoth's death.

This was discouraging and frightening. Tanis didn't have

enough information to know who had masterminded Ailea's and Xenoth's deaths and attempted two more—Gilthanas's and Tanis's own. All he knew was that the attempt on Gilthanas had meant Flint was right: Porthios, the Speaker, and Laurana were in terrible danger.

Ignoring his aching lungs, he ran on.

* * * * *

It was the same clearing, Flint was sure. The same huge boulder, the same stand of spruce. Trees still lay in splinters on the ground, and a path had been crushed through the understory of trees. Trees and stone alike showed slash marks.

He had found the clearing where the tylor had first attacked him.

From here, he hoped, he could find the *sla-mori*.

If he could just get there in time.

If he could just remember everything he had done to open the *sla-mori* the first time.

* * * * *

Miral looked down at the assemblage from the deserted second balcony. His clear eyes glinted.

He saw Laurana's golden hair glittering in the torchlight, and for a moment, he felt sadness—over what he had to do, over what he'd done, over what the Graystone had ordered him to do. The killing had started with the death of Kethrenan Kanan, the Speaker's brother, fifty years earlier. Miral had commanded, through magic, the human brigands who had attacked Kethrenan and his wife, Elansa, and while Miral had not wielded the swords that had struck Kethrenan down, it was his deed, born of jealousy.

That had been the first time he had sought to influence humans. And the last. They'd been too unpredictable to suit him. Originally, he had told them to slay Elansa as well. Instead, he had arrived in time to see her lying unconscious in the road as the brigands argued over who would get to murder her. Caught by a sudden upsurge of feeling that had taken him by surprise, he had ordered them to return Elansa's steel pendant to her neck and to leave her.

He knew, of course, all about the Graystone, that it was capable of great good—and great evil. Since his childhood, he had felt the same pendulumlike swing within himself. Within one body was the person who could order the death of one elf, then befriend the child of that elf's ravaged wife. Then kill that child when he grew up.

Movement below caught his eye, and he leaned over the bannister. The drums roared and the trumpets sang; it was the time in the ceremony when Gilthanas, garbed in his traditional gray robe, should have stepped through the entry hall of the Tower of the Sun, circled around to a small door at the back of the Tower, and gone through the door to find Porthios waiting for him at the end of the *Yathen-ilara*, the Pathway to Illumination.

Ah, how tired Miral was of infernal elven tradition. They kept the most trivial traditions, while the important one, the one that made Qualinesti uniquely pure, they threatened to let go. He would . . . Miral shook away the thought and sought to return his focus to the *Yathen-ilara*.

Today's celebration would stop there, for Gilthanas was dead.

It would be his, Miral's, joke on the nobles, on Porthios, on Solostaran especially. One last jest before they died. The mage imagined them all standing there waiting in their gold-threaded finery, secure in their wealth, in their status, in their belief that somehow they *deserved* all this. They would wonder where Gilthanas was. Eventually, they would grow restless, begin to murmur, look around.

Had things gone as normal, Gilthanas would have waited by the small door. Thus would have begun the *Kentommen* proper, where Solostaran would address the onlookers in an ancient prescribed speech, explaining that he had lost a child in the Grove and that he now had no heir. The three *Ulathi* would have stepped forward, still masked, to proclaim their lines. The gong would have sent Gilthanas into the corridor, from which he would have sent Porthios forth into adulthood. Porthios would have received from the Speaker a goblet of deep red wine, symbolizing Solostaran's bloodline—and his formal selection as heir. And Porthios, from that moment, would forever be considered adult.

Miral laughed. Instead of all the folderol that the elves liked so well, Miral would stand forward, call Porthios forth from the sacred corridor to join the others, then utter the words that would seal all the doorways. The ceremony would be over.

As would their lives. And when the dying ceased, he would be Speaker.

The drums boomed again. Miral leaned forward to chant. Then he stopped, speechless.

Gilthanas had entered the Tower.

ChapteR 31

The MuRDeReR
ConfRonTeD

Miral stood stock-still as the gRay-Robed figuRe en-
tered the Tower. The murmuring that had begun among the
onlookers quieted, and they watched expectantly as Gilthanas passed along the inner edge of the Tower.

But Gilthanas is dead! the mage screamed to himself.

There was something different about Gilthanas, though,
he thought. The youth appeared larger; the robe was
stretched taut across his shoulders. The figure in the robe
was more like Tanis than Gilthanas.

But Tanis was dead, too.

Miral's gaze followed the gray robe as it moved gracefully
to the appointed portal and waited.

Solostaran, dressed in his golden-green robes of state, entered from an anteroom and crossed to the rostrum. Sol-

emnly, he mounted the steps to the platform and turned to face the crowd with the small speech that every noble parent had delivered upon a child's *Kentommen* for two thousand years.

"This day is one of sorrow for me," he said simply in the old elven tongue. "I have lost a child."

In the balcony, Miral suddenly caught the humor of that statement. He rocked with silent laughter. Little did Solostaran know, he thought. The mage decided to allow the charade to continue a bit longer. Who knew what other tidbits of unwitting mirth the Speaker might come forth with?

His hawklike features somber, Solostaran continued, "I have lost a child to the Grove. Thus, I have no heir. Can anyone offer comfort?"

One drum roll boomed from the first balcony, below Miral. He heard a door open far below, and three elves, dressed in black silk leggings and capes, with masks and gloves of black leather, stepped into view. The *Ulathi*.

"We have found a child," said the first.

"He is pure of heart," added the second.

"This child is an empty vessel waiting to be filled," said the third.

They all intoned, "We have found a child who will be made your heir, your blood."

The gong sounded. Gilthanas swung the door open and passed within. The door closed.

* * * * *

Tanis, entering from the blazing light of the Tower, blinked at the sudden near-darkness. He could see the candle flame flickering, but the figure of Porthios was only a dim shape in the darkness. The medallion that Flint had made mirrored the candle's glow.

He had to draw Porthios nearer. What had Gilthanas said the words were? He dredged his memory.

"I am your childhood," he recited, trying to lighten his voice to sound more like Gilthanas. "Leave me behind. The mists are past—" That didn't sound right, but he was doing the best he could—"Go to your future."

"*Gilthanas!*" came Porthios's horrified whisper. "Say the right words—and in the old tongue!"

Tanis hesitated.

"Don't you remember them?" Porthios hissed. "Listen." The Speaker's son repeated the correct words in the ancient tongue. "Say them."

Still Tanis hesitated. Porthios stepped closer, as Tanis had wished.

For a heartbeat, Tanis considered merely using his superior strength to overpower his cousin. He had punched Porthios in the face once before, long ago in the courtyard of the palace. That had started the only physical altercation the two cousins had ever had. And it had earned him Porthios's enmity for years afterward.

"Porthios," he said in his own voice. "Listen to me. Don't go out that door."

"Tanthalas!" Porthios's face showed shock. "Where is Gilthanas? What have you—?"

"Listen!" Tanis hissed. "If you gained anything at all in your vigil in the Grove, listen to me now."

His cousin stepped back, seemed to force a calm mien to descend over his features. He inhaled deeply, then exhaled. "What, Tanis?" he asked in his normal tones.

"There is a conspiracy to kill you and the Speaker."

"The Speaker? Is he all right?"

"He's fine. I am here to stop the killer."

"You?" Porthios laughed shortly, but his face was surprisingly kind. "Tanis, you're only a child. . ."

Tanis spoke hastily, aware that the onlookers would be getting uneasy outside the door. The worst thing that could happen now would be for someone to open that door and look inside. "Porthios, the same one who killed Xenoth and Eld Ailea is after you and the Speaker, and Laurana. I know this."

"How do you know it?"

Tanis considered. He was running out of time for persuasion. He could resolve this situation by physical force, but his elven blood shuddered at the prospect of knocking out a youth during his own *Kentommen*, for whatever reason.

But he could lie.

"Porthios," Tanis said, "Gilthanas is dead."

There was a pause; Porthios's features never changed.

"The murderer slew him, too. Porthios, if you and Laurana and the Speaker are killed, it will throw the kingdom into chaos."

Porthios seemed to be struggling to digest all he'd heard. Tanis's heart ached for him, for the half-elf's part in causing that pain. "I have a plan, Porthios."

The answer came calmly. "What is it?"

"Listen," Tanis said. "I am expendable . . ."

* * * * *

Flint peered into the gap in the side of the oak tree that had saved his life months earlier. The tree had opened again in the interim, to the dwarf's relief. He entered the hollowness, Fleetfoot hard on his heels. Flint paid her no attention.

"How did I get through before? What did I do?" he muttered, ankle-deep in dry forest litter, holding a burning brand over his head. "The rune." He looked down. "The floor of the tree caught fire. Maybe that's it." He considered. "Well, if I'm wrong, I'll merely burn to death."

"Ah, well," he said, and touched torch to debris.

Flames roared.

* * * * *

Miral raced along the second balcony, his goal the spiral stairs to the main level. Gilthanas had spent far too much time in the corridor. Something was not going according to the mage's plan. He raged with the injustice.

As he reached the door to the stairwell, he heard expressions of horror ripple through the onlookers, and he turned back.

"Porthios enters armed!"

"What?"

"The *Kentommen* youth is never armed!"

"What does this portend?"

Solostaran was pallid as he gazed at the figure he believed was his son and heir, but his self-possession never faltered. "Porthios," he ordered. "Tell me what this means."

"There is a murderer in the Tower," Tanis cried, sweeping the hood back from his face.

More expressions of shock burst from the nobles as the crowd involuntarily parted and Tanis bounded through, his sword at the ready. With one leap, he was upon the rostrum, standing before Solostaran.

"Tanthalas!" Miral exclaimed from above. "But you're dead!"

The youth whirled to face the mage. Tanis's gaze caught Miral's, and the mage saw pain flare within the youth. "How do you know, mage?" he demanded.

"Guards!" Tyresian thundered.

Tanis held up his sword, Elansa's amulet glittering like a small sun. "The mage has twice killed, and he seeks to slay still more today." He pointed the sword at Miral.

Miral fought back a laugh at the chaos below him. What better time to unleash his final spell? He began to chant.

"By the gods," Tyresian barked. "The half-elf has lost his mind. And so has the mage. Guards!"

"Tanis, where is Porthios?" came Laurana's shrill cry. "And Gilthanas?"

Tanis had no time to reply. He was dashing through the nobles to the stairwell. Black-garbed ceremonial guards poured into the Tower but didn't immediately realize that the half-elf was the one Tyresian wanted them to capture. Tanis slipped through, threw open the door to the stairway, and took the steps three at a time.

As though the words pounded in his brain, Tanis could hear Miral continue his chanting. Above, the top of the Tower creaked.

Suddenly, Eld Ailea appeared before him on the stairs.

Tanis spun to a halt against the wall of the first landing. "Ailea!" he cried. "You're not dead." She looked down at him and smiled.

Then suddenly, she was not Ailea, but Xenoth, laughing

loudly and pointing derisively at the half-elf. Tanis held his sword before him and struggled to overcome the panic within him.

Xenoth turned into a middle-aged elf man with a slender face and eyes of purest blue. His arm supported a pallid woman with long, curly hair the color of wheat and eyes as brown as the earth. She looked at Tanis, raised one weak hand, and whispered, "Tanthalas, my son."

Tanis stood motionless, feeling his heart thunder. The agony of the moment tore into him. Then he wrenched away, shouted, "This is magic!" and the two figures vanished into shimmering air.

He pushed through the spot where they had stood; cold fingers of air brushed against his arm as he pounded past.

"Miral!" he cried, bursting onto the second balcony.

Three chunks of tile burst from the mosaic and plummeted into the teeming mass of elves. A thin crack rent the top of the Tower.

At that moment, with a crash of thunder, Flint and Fleetfoot appeared on the rostrum.

"Arelas!" the dwarf called. His voice reverberated. "Arelas Kanan!" He pointed his hammer at the mage.

Miral's chant slowed and stopped. Hands above his head, sweat starting from his palms, he held the spell and looked down at Flint. Suddenly, there was no noise in the Tower but tiny "pings" as bits of tile showered down from the double mosaic. The smell of rock and plaster was in the air.

"Arelas?" Solostaran said tentatively. "My brother?"

"Your brother never died, Speaker," Flint said. "Not Arelas. He came to you as Miral."

The mule brayed, breaking Flint's spell, and Miral resumed his chant. A groan sounding like agony came from the division between the mosaic of day and the mosaic of night, at the top of the Tower.

"He slew Lord Xenoth for discovering who he really was," Flint cried, his voice trembling with anger. "He killed Eld Ailea for the same reason. And now he wants to slay you and your children!"

Astoundingly calm, Solostaran simply turned to Miral—

to Arelas—and said, "Why?"

Looking down at them, Miral felt the rage he'd been carrying for nearly two hundred years. He lowered his arms and ceased his chant. "They sent me away, Solostaran!" he shouted. "They sent me from Qualinost!"

"You were dying, Arelas," Solostaran replied. "Or so we thought."

"I was ever the more talented, Solostaran," Arelas shouted. "I should have been Speaker. I *will* be Speaker! And I will keep Qualinesti for the pure elves. Now that I have the power of the Gray—"

A portion of a marble column that supported the first balcony burst, weakened by Arelas's magic, and sent shards of rock spewing into the chamber. The nobles scattered. Arelas grimaced and threw his hands out, sending a burst of lightning toward the rostrum. Flint hurtled toward Solostaran, knocking the Speaker off the platform. Tyresian threw himself at Laurana, sending her spinning toward the relative safety of the balcony overhang. A block of marble crashed down upon the elf lord, and Laurana screamed.

Porthios burst from the *Yathen-ilara*.

"Arelas!" Tanis shouted again, and raised his sword.

But the mage laughed. "It won't work, Tanthalas! The sword will not work against me." He threw his arms wide and danced a few steps of glee. "I enchanted it, you see, at the same time I enchanted those arrowheads that you used so well against the tylor and Lord Xenoth." The laughter turned into a coughing spell, and Tanis saw his chance. He sprang at Arelas, slashing with his sword.

But the sword clanged off something in the air and passed harmlessly over the mage's head. Arelas raised his arms, pointedly turned his back on the half-elf, and continued chanting. Another patch of mosaic tile came down.

Arelas leaned over the balcony, one arm drawn back as if to throw another bolt of mage fire at the onlookers.

Tanis tried again. "Miral! Arelas! Gilthanas lives."

Below, off to Tanis's left, he could see Porthios's head snap around, his face ablaze with hope as he learned that his younger brother had not died. Arelas turned, his face terrible, all color gone from his irises.

"He lives?" the mage demanded.

Even though the sword appeared useless against Arelas, Tanis kept it poised before him. "Gilthanas is above you in ascendancy, Arelas," the half-elf shouted. "You will not be Speaker no matter what you do here today."

Arelas quivered, as if he teetered at the edge of the Abyss. Then one arm shot forward, and lightning hurtled toward the half-elf.

Acting purely on instinct, Tanis raised his sword. The mage's bolt struck Elansa's pendant, melting it into drops of steel; a new burst of lightning arced from the sword back to the mage, who screamed with the blow and hurtled from the balcony.

His body burst into flame before it struck the floor of the Tower.

Epilogue

A.C. 308, Late Summer

"But where did he get the power?" Tanis asked
again.

Flint shook his head. There were rumors, of course, legends of a source of great chaotic power hidden in caverns
deep below Qualinost, but the dwarf was not of a mood to
recite legends.

He ordered ale for the both of them. The innkeeper at the
Inn of the Last Home brought the beverage to their table in
overflowing mugs, and Flint sighed. "Ah, lad, I have longed
for this. A comfortable table in the corner of a cozy inn.
Real ale, with a kick like Fleetfoot's."

But Tanis wouldn't abandon the subject. They'd been

over it ad nauseam during the past three weeks, and they had yet to come to a proper understanding of what had happened.

"Miral—Arelas—killed so many people because he'd been sent from Qualinesti as a child? Flint, that's not reason enough." The half-elf toyed with his mug, twirling it in a wet circle on the wooden table.

The dwarf nodded. "I know, lad. There's some power behind all this, something we don't know about. But there are tales that would explain it."

"The Graystone? That's a myth, Flint." The half-elf's tone was flat. There would be no convincing him.

Flint shook his head and hoisted his tankard, then he smacked his lips. Five days in Solace, and still the taste of a mug of good ale was a fresh treat.

"Flint."

"Now what?" the dwarf grumbled.

Tanis's tone was urgent. "The amulet saved my life. Why didn't it save my mother's? It belonged to her."

They'd been over this, too, during the weeks they'd spent on the trail, Flint rocking along on Fleetfoot and Tanis posting smoothly on Belthar. "I don't believe it was enchanted when Elansa had it, Tanis. I think Ailea had something to do with that."

The mention of Ailea cast a shadow over the friends.

"But I thought she could perform only magical illusions, tricks to amuse children," Tanis disagreed. "And minor magic to use in childbirth. Nothing major."

"We thought Miral was a minor mage, too."

Tanis nodded and was still for a bit. Then a new thought occurred to him. "The mage killed all of them—Kethrenan, Elansa, Xenoth, Ailea. Even Tyresian, when he saved Laurana from the falling marble. And why? So Arelas could eliminate all the heirs between himself and the Speakership. Did he think he could walk out of the rubble of the Tower and announce that he was really Arelas and that they should make him Speaker?"

Flint glowered at Tanis. "I expect he would have found a way." Or perhaps the Graystone would have, he added to himself.

"But . . ."

Flint nudged the half-elf's ale a bit closer to him. "Give it up, lad. Some things you have to take on faith. It made sense to Arelas." When Tanis opened his mouth, Flint held up a hand. "Enough."

They sat silently for a time. Then Flint lifted his mug again. "A toast," he said.

To turn down a toast was an insult. Tanis curled his hand around the handle of the tankard. "A toast," he echoed.

"To Ailea." They exchanged glances and clinked their mugs. "And to future fellowship," Flint added.

Tanis smiled.

"To fellowship," the half-elf agreed.

DragonLance™ Saga

Elven Nations Trilogy

Firstborn
Paul B. Thompson and Tonya R. Carter

Sithel, the leader of the Silvanesti elves, struggles to maintain a united elven nation, while his twin sons' ambitions threaten to tear it apart. Kith-Kanan leads the Wildrunners, a group of elves that stirs tension by forging contacts and trade with the humans of Ergoth; Sithas strongly allies himself with the elven court. When their father mysteriously dies, Kith-Kanan is implicated and Sithas, the firstborn twin, is enthroned.

The Kinslayer Wars
Douglas Niles

Kith-Kanan commits the ultimate heresy for an elven prince and falls in love with a human. Soon after, his twin brother, the firstborn ruler of all Silvanesti elves, Sithas, declares war on the humans of Ergoth, and Kith-Kanan finds himself caught between two mighty forces.

The Qualinesti
Paul B. Thompson and Tonya R. Carter

One of the most fabled of all of Krynn's legends—untold before now—is the founding of Qualinost and the creation of the magnificent society of the renegade elves, the Qualinesti. Kith-Kanan becomes the first Speaker of the Suns, but he is haunted by his failures: the unfaithfulness of his wife, and the mysterious behavior of his son and successor.

DragonLance® Saga

THE HISTORIC SAGA OF THE DWARVEN CLANS
Dwarven Nations Trilogy
Dan Parkinson

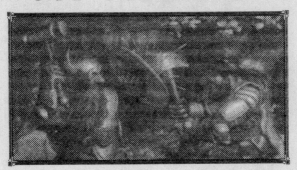

The Covenant of the Forge   **Volume One**
As the drums of Balladine thunder forth, calling humans to trade
with the dwarves of Thorin, Grayfen, a human struck by the magic of
the Graystone, infiltrates the dwarven stronghold, determined to
annihilate the dwarves and steal their treasure.   ISBN 1-56076-558-5

Hammer and Axe   **Volume Two**
The dwarven clans unite against the threat of encroaching humans
and create the fortress of Thorbardin. But old rivalries are not easily
forgotten, and the resulting political intrigue brings about
catastrophic change.   ISBN 1-56076-627-1

The Swordsheath Scroll   **Volume Three**
Despite the stubborn courage of the dwarves, the Wilderness War
ends as a no-win. The Swordsheath Scroll is signed, and the dwarves
join the elves of Qualinesti to build a symbol of peace among the
races: Pax Tharkas.   ISBN 1-56076-686-7

FANTASY ADVENTURE

The long-awaited
sequel to the
Moonshae Trilogy

The Druidhome Trilogy

Douglas
Niles

Prophet of Moonshae — Book One

Danger stalks the island of Moonshae, where the people have
forsaken their goddess, the Earthmother. Only the faith and
courage of the daughter of the High King brings hope to the
endangered land. ISBN 1-56076-319-1

The Coral Kingdom — Book Two

King Kendrick is held prisoner in the undersea city of the
sahuagin. His daughter must secure help from the elves of
Evermeet to save him during a confrontation in the dark
depths of the Sea of Moonshae. ISBN 1-56076-332-9

The Druid Queen — Book Three

Threatened by an evil he cannot see, Tristan Kendrick rules
the Four Kingdoms while a sinister presence lurks within his
own family. At stake is the fate of the Moonshae Islands and
the unity of the Ffolk. ISBN 1-56076-568-2